W9-CJM-015

WITHDRAWN

PRETTY DEAD QUEENS

ALSO BY ALEXA DONNE

The Ivies

PRETTY DEAD QUEENS

ALEXA DONNE

CROWN
NEW YORK

Text copyright © 2022 by Alexa Donne
Jacket photography copyright © 2022 by Maggie Holmgren
Girl and crown images on jacket used under license from Shutterstock.com

Visit us on the Web! GetUnderlined.com

Educators and librarians, for a variety of teaching tools, visit us at RHTeachersLibrarians.com

Library of Congress Cataloging-in-Publication Data
Names: Donne, Alexa, author.
Title: Pretty dead queens / Alexa Donne.
Description: First edition. | New York: Crown Books for Young Readers, [2022] | Audience: Ages 14+. | Audience: Grades 10–12. | Summary: Not long after seventeen-year-old Cecelia Ellis arrives to live with her estranged grandmother in a coastal California town, the high school homecoming queen is found dead and Cecelia, fearing a copycat killer is on the loose, throws herself into the investigation.
Identifiers: LCCN 2022009241 (print) | LCCN 2022009242 (ebook) | ISBN 978-0-593-47982-7 (hardcover) | ISBN 978-0-593-47984-1 (ebook)
Subjects: CYAC: Murder—Fiction. | Grandmothers—Fiction. | High schools—Fiction. | Schools—Fiction. | Mystery and detective stories. | LCGFT: Novels. | Detective and mystery fiction.
Classification: LCC PZ7.1.D648 Pr 2022 (print) | LCC PZ7.1.D648 (ebook) | DDC [Fic]—dc23

The text of this book is set in 12-point Arno.
Interior design by Ken Crossland

Printed in the United States of America
10 9 8 7 6 5 4 3 2 1
First Edition

For those who grieve,
however they grieve,
and come out the other side

CHAPTER ONE

Some people attract death.

When I was nine, my pet rabbit, Easter, flopped out of my arms while Mom was cleaning her cage, and my bunny's back snapped in two. The fall didn't kill Easter, but we had to take her to the vet to put her down. I didn't cry.

When I was six, Granddad went to the angels. That's how my grandmother put it. Mom had a more literal take. "He's dead!" she screamed at her mother. Wailed. It was the first time I ever saw my mom cry.

Then there was our dog, five years ago. My chemistry teacher, who was felled by an aneurysm when I was in ninth grade. The pretty junior girl my sophomore year, DOA in a horrific highway crash.

I am just shy of my eighteenth birthday and on my sixth funeral.

It's the worst kind of funeral that brings me to Seaview and my grandmother's creepy-as-hell Victorian mansion off Main Street. (Yeah, this place has a *Main Street*.) The peeling velvet wallpaper is straight from a Poe story.

"It's original hardwood!" my grandmother says. "People shit

themselves for floors like mine!" She sweeps across said floors, which surely hide long-desiccated corpses, without hesitation. I pause at the threshold, the porch creaking beneath my feet. If I step over, follow this strange yet eerily familiar woman inside, it will be real. I will live here now.

But I don't exactly have a choice. Everything I own has been packed up, sold off, or put in storage. It's this or foster care. Maura Weston is the only family I have left. Even if I barely know her, legally she's my guardian. This is my home.

My mom is dead, and I'm living with a stranger.

I step through the doorway. Look up the grand staircase to the landing, where Mrs. Danvers is surely waiting. But it's only Maura and me in this cavernous Victorian relic.

"Call me Grandma," she'd said on the drive from the airport. "My fans call me Maura. You're not a fan, are you, dear?"

It seemed like a trick question.

"I read the one set on the boat," I'd said, and it appeared to please her.

"That was a *New York Times* bestseller," she said, beaming.

A lot of them are *New York Times* bestsellers.

"You'll be on the fourth floor," she tells me now. "You have your own bathroom, so lots of privacy. Plus, you have those gloriously young knees, for all those stairs. Suzanne's in the carriage house out back. You'll meet her in the morning."

She mentioned in the car that her assistant, Suzanne, was supposed to pick me up but there was a last-minute change in plans. I can't tell whether Maura is annoyed by the inconvenience. It's late, eleven o'clock, because Seaview is on the ass end of nowhere. Northern California: where, with layovers, it can take you four hours to fly from one regional airport to another and then you still have to drive two hours to your destination. But her expression remained in a pleasant-grandma mask. A brave face for the orphaned grandchild. Warm hugs and sad smiles.

"You'll want to get to bed, since you have school in the morning. I'll take you to get registered. Eight o'clock sharpish. They're expecting you."

It's early October, so school has already started. I'll be the strange new kid with the dead mom, moving in with the town's most famous resident, and six weeks of work to catch up on, because death does not time itself conveniently to school schedules. Not to mention the lifetime of friendships I'll never edge in on. Kids in towns like these are born here, die here. Relationships go from womb to tomb. My mom hated it. People were always coming and going when we lived in LA. Easy to be anonymous.

I lug my suitcase behind me, the tired wheels scuffing against honeyed hardwood until I reach the foot of the grand staircase. I brace myself to heft my bag—my entire life somehow reduced to a single suitcase—all the way up.

"I think that will fit in the dumbwaiter," Maura says, backlit by the warm hallway light, haloed like an angel. Silver hair, peppered with the barest wisps of deep brown, cut short, ear-length, and flipping out at the edges. Big brown eyes with lids smudged smoky gray. Brows overplucked, the vestiges of a vintage trend. An old woman reflecting the heyday of her youth.

I search for my mother's face in hers. Try to imagine Mom if she'd been allowed to reach old age. Pointed chin, yes. Maybe the cheekbones. The turn of her mouth. Not the eyes, though. Mom's were deeper set. She'd have killed to pull off that eye shadow, or a delicate wing, like I can.

"You got that gorgeous wavy hair from me. You're welcome.

But those eyes . . . must be your father's," Maura says, apparently taking me in as well. "You're lucky. Such a pretty color."

Green, like the phantom man my mother wouldn't talk about. It was one of the few sore points between us. My father is a ghost. My mother, now ashes. My grandmother, a stranger. But she's agreed to take me in, and she's sweet enough. And very rich. This old mansion is nine times the size of the apartment Mom and I rented in Pasadena.

"It's this way." She tilts her head toward the kitchen, leads me back. It's an HGTV fantasy land. Old mixed with new. A show-stopping cast-iron stove alongside state-of-the-art appliances, an updated subway-tile backsplash and farmhouse sink, a sprawling kitchen island with barstools lined up like soldiers, and original wood cabinetry. And to the right as we come in, nestled at the very edge of a back stairwell, an unassuming cupboard door. Maura undoes the latch, swings the door wide. An extra-large dumbwaiter.

"We removed the shelves decades ago for this very purpose. Give it a try with your bag," she says.

It takes the both of us to haul it inside. The bag barely fits, and the bottom of the miniature elevator shudders under the weight. Maura seems nonplussed.

"My mother's tea service weighed more than this, surely. The bitch of it will be your having to haul it from the third to the fourth floor. I'm not cut out for that anymore. I'm a firm sixty-eight— but not that firm." She winks. It's strange hearing the word *bitch* out of someone so old, but she's already graced me with a creative array of curses in the car. It seems I have a cool grandma.

"Let's go," she says, halfway up the back stairs. The ser-

4

vants' stairs, they would have been, way back. I wonder when they stopped having live-in servants here, but then I remember Suzanne. Maura explained to me that she used to be her assistant when she lived in New York, and she couldn't function without her, so when she moved back to Seaview permanently, she set Suzanne up in the guesthouse in the backyard. Maura assured me she pays her a handsome salary to live in the middle of nowhere. I wonder if Suzanne has as rosy a view of the arrangement.

"This is where I leave you," Maura says on the first landing. I peer around the bend, spying a spacious bedroom at the end of the hall. "It's good to have you here, Cecelia, even if the circumstances are . . . well." She sighs. Sniffs. Dabs at her eyes, shiny with tears. "My poor baby girl, Vanessa. Parents shouldn't outlive their children," she says, more to herself than to me, I think.

"If only you'd called me," she continues. "I hate that you were alone at the end. That she didn't have her mother. And you cremated her? Honey, there's a family plot right here. Or if the problem was money, you know I have more than enough!"

"I'm sorry. I didn't know how to get in contact with you. I sent an email to your agent, but didn't hear back until it was too late." It comes out a jumble as panic slams through me. That I fucked up what I was apparently supposed to do.

Maura's mouth tightens into a white line. "Yes, well, he won't be getting his fifteen percent off me anymore, don't you worry. Anyway, you're here now. And don't worry about the burial thing. We'll scatter her ashes together when you're ready."

And now the grief chaser: that my mother's ashes are sitting in an ugly, overpriced urn at a family friend's house in LA because I was frozen by the thought of how the hell to get it all the way up here. Maura will kill me. But she's folding me into a hug before I can get the words out. I'm stiff, awkward, but she is warm. I relax into her, just so. Then it's over.

"See you in the morning. Holler if you need me, though you've got ten minutes before I'm out like a light. So make it quick if you do."

I continue up, up, huffing slightly as I reach the third floor. I'm going to need to develop better cardio and strength if I'm going to live here. I locate the dumbwaiter to my left. The door creaks open. It looks rarely used, but the inside has recently been retro-fitted. The rope is new, and all I have to do is push a button to the right of the door to activate the pulley system. Two minutes later and I'm hauling all my earthly possessions up the final, narrow staircase that leads to the fourth-floor attic space.

The landing is small; I'm in the eaves of the house. There are only two rooms on this floor. A door on either side of me. I try behind me and find a white-tiled private bath: nothing special, yet twice the size of my old one.

That makes the other door my new bedroom. Skylights have been cut into the slanted ceiling, bookshelves installed in the low-slung walls. The windows are open, but it's still a bit warm. This place must be murder in the summer. There's a window nook with a bench, framed with pretty purple curtains. A desk, by the look of it brand-new—some unpronounceable Ikea piece—against the left wall, and a double bed with an elaborate wooden headboard abutting the right.

Purple was my favorite color when I was six. I'm touched Maura remembered. Now, though, I love green. Like my back-pack, whose straps are digging hard into my shoulders. I'd nearly forgotten about it, a sea creature accustomed to its shell. I slide it off my back, sling it onto the bed. I leave my suitcase by the door. I can't unpack yet. My denial. Maybe this is a vacation and I'll fly back home in a few weeks to find my mom waiting for me.

She's here, though, I realize. This is her childhood home. She slept under this roof until she fled at eighteen to Southern California for college. It gets me thinking.

I poke my head out, listen on the landing. Maura's snoring rumbles in the distance like an idling car. A slow, moaning creak joins the chorus. The old house and the old woman settling in the night.

I creep down the narrow attic stairs to the third floor to find a sea of doors. Maura has so many rooms, so much space, and all closed doors. What's hiding behind them?

To my right, a bathroom, vintage with a pull-chain toilet and a charming claw-foot tub. Directly across from the stairwell, I find a hobby room, cluttered with boxes, an ancient sewing machine, shelves overflowing with scrapbooking supplies. I can't imagine Maura scrapbooking, and apparently neither can she—the first three albums I open are half-empty. And down the hall to my left, I flip on the light and find my mother.

Her room is frozen in midnineties glory, muted by the fine layer of dust covering everything, as though Maura shut it when Mom left for college and hasn't been inside since. Her desk is dominated by a boulder of a computer, flanked by built-in CD shelving filled with bubble-gum pop, boy bands, and feminist folk. Posters on the wall offer a snapshot of the teen girl my mom once was: *Romeo + Juliet, Jagged Little Pill, Titanic.* So she liked Leo DiCaprio and was . . . angry?

I do a turn of the room, drink in the details, expecting, *hoping,* to feel a connection. A sensation that she's watching over me, that she's here. Everyone always says that, that you feel your loved ones with you. But I don't. I feel suffocated. By this place that might as well be a mausoleum, by the gaping chasm of my own grief. These are only things, but they were hers. And they're falling away to dust, like she did.

I've held it together in the weeks since my mom took her final breath. I didn't even cry at the funeral.

But now, in my mom's old room, in my creepy new house, I fling myself onto her mothball-scented, dusty bedspread, desperately hoping to catch one last whiff of her. And I cry all the tears I've refused to shed when I realize she isn't there.

✦

I wake with a start, disoriented, sweaty, and still in my street clothes. For a moment, the anachronistic setting confuses me, until it all floods back. I'm in my mom's childhood bedroom. The nightmare is real.

The hall is blanketed with night. I should go back upstairs and go to bed, properly this time, but I'm parched. Careful as can be, I pad down the stairs on my way to the kitchen as moonlight streams through the warped windows. I find the glasses easily, fill one with water from a special tap attached to the farmhouse sink, and take a long draw.

The only sounds are the rhythmic croaking of crickets outside and the occasional snort from upstairs. There's something magnetic about the house. I can't resist the chance to explore unchaperoned. I take my water with me. The furniture is reduced to shades of gray in the night, but I pad around the first floor. I can make out a formal dining room, with an obscenely long table; a fussy sitting room, filled with knickknacks and china poised precariously in glassed-in cabinets. There's a proper living room, with a giant TV and a comfy-looking couch—I'm relieved to learn that my grandmother isn't the type of old person who refuses to own a television—and, tucked next to the stairs, a closed door. Quietly as I can, I slide the hulking wooden frame to the left and step into the most glorious space. I can make out wall-to-wall shelves of books. A desk in the center. A library? I should have brought my phone for light. Then I remember there are . . . you know, actual lights. I switch on a desk lamp.

Not a library. It's Maura's office. Every book on the wall bears her name. Hundreds of them—each title has at least a dozen copies, some in different languages, and they're arranged in chronological order. I know because *Killer Queen* is first on the left—Maura's bestselling debut—and *A Deadly Glen,* her latest, about a group stranded in the woods with a murderer, is to the far right. I search for the boat one, to jog my memory. I find it in the middle shelf behind her desk. *Out to Sea* is the title. The captain did it. I thought it was okay. A little soapy for my taste, with an annoyingly smug heroine.

Now that I live here, I probably have to read them all. A sort of macabre book club, to get to know my grandma through her work. I pull a copy of *Killer Queen* off the shelf and thumb through it. The back cover reminds me of the general plot. A homecoming queen is offed the night of the dance, drowned in her high school pool. I think they made a movie out of this one. My mom used to groan whenever she'd scroll past her mom's adaptations on streaming, steering us to dense foreign dramas and quirky indies instead. But I'm curious about Maura's breakout hit. I open to the first page and already see this one has a supremely

9

confident heroine as well. The opening paragraphs are a treatise on the haves and have-nots of high school, with an emphasis on the main character's beauty and popularity.

I shut the book, lost to anxieties about tomorrow, my first day at a new school. Is this the kind of place still deeply entrenched in the bullshit high school politics of old movies, which seemed quaint, retro cool at Pasadena Central High? According to my mom, the five-disparate-stereotypes teen stuff of John Hughes movies was legit back in the day, but at my school everyone was pretty friendly, and no one cared if you were into sports or academics or drama or whatever. There was definitely no nerds versus jocks dichotomy. I got decent grades and did theater and was on the swim team and fangirled hard for BTS. I contained multitudes, and no one ostracized or bullied me for anything. Wasn't particularly popular, either, but who cares? Seaview, however, is a small town. I'd heard things about faraway, less progressive places, lost to time.

Maura's book is certainly a time warp. She wrote it in the eighties but set it in the seventies. I return to the pages, picturing bell-bottom jeans and feathered hair as the pretty sixteen-year-old Melinda "Melly" Watts walks the halls of Seaside High (real life inspiring fiction, I guess), then discovers homecoming queen Cassidy's body in the pool at the dance. The writing is punchy, a bit melodramatic, but definitely engrossing. Maura paints her cast of characters with a vivid charm, but there's an ominous undertone. I'm already guessing at suspects. Melly's best friend screams frenemy, and her math teacher is on the wrong side of attentive.

A nearby desk clock tells me it's almost two a.m., and knowing I need to go to bed, or at least try to, I put *Killer Queen* back and return to my room.

Soon, in bed, I gaze up through the skylights to make out far-away pinpricks of stars through the closer and more menacing claws of swaying tree branches. I imagine myself in one of Maura's books, my sleep-adjacent brain chasing a series of morbid images: Trapped in my attic room with a killer. A hand shooting out from the dark maw of the dumbwaiter. An ax bursting around the corner of a locker-lined hallway. Pushed, bloody and flailing, into the deep blue of a pool.

Then, lost to sleep, I dream of beautiful sixteen-year-old girls, long dead and gone, and a vivacious, sharp forty-two-year-old mom, gone yesterday.

CHAPTER TWO

Though I am a born-and-bred Californian, it's like I have stepped onto another planet, rather than simply been transplanted five hundred miles up the coast. To me, California has always meant the urban sprawl of Los Angeles County or the sun-dappled beach communities of San Diego. Glass and steel and row houses crowding San Francisco. Silicon Valley mansions nestled in the mountains. Farmland, even, making us the nation's food basket.

But this? This is Americana with a coastal twist. Quaint Main Street cluttered with mom-and-pop businesses. Clapboard houses that could equally be a bar, a hotel, or a sea-glass museum. Or all three in one. It's small-town charm. *Friday Night Lights.* It could be Kentucky, if not for the ocean view. Not that you can see it from here.

"Don't you want to live at the beach?" I ask Maura on the drive to school—which is not even an eight-minute walk from home, but my grandmother insisted on a driving tour of Seaview before registering me.

I roll down my window, suck in salty air. We're still inland, but the cerulean line of the ocean winks in the distance. Refined California Cape Cods line the street, broken up by the very occasional sixties-style apartment complex or nineties duplex. We zoom around a bend, and a house on the horizon takes my breath away. Straight from the pages of an architecture magazine, it's all angles and modernity: Concrete and deep-red wood. Glass everywhere. As many windows as can fit into a contemporary piece of art.

"That's the mayor's place," Maura says, barely paying a glance. Her eyes remain on the road, which turns increasingly faded and cracked as we drive on. "He keeps a property in town, too. I do visit my beach cottage occasionally—we passed it back there— but I prefer the Victorian for every day."

Running at breakneck speed across the road to the warm sand. Building a lopsided sandcastle soon reclaimed by the sea. Maura ensconced in the front room, typing away.

"We used to spend summers there," I say. Ask, really. "Right?"

"You remember! Yes, you came up every July. Before—" She chokes on emotion, and I am shamed into silence. Before my mom cut us off. Refused to speak to her mother, effectively ending my relationship with her, too. One day I had a grandmother. The next I had a sore subject I quickly learned to never bring up with my mom. All she would say was my granny had done something she could not forgive, that we'd be fine on our own.

And we were, until the cancer.

A peculiar sight outside my window gives us something better to talk about. "What the hell happened there?" I point to the partial remains of a McMansion at the end of the road we're now on. Half of it is simply . . . gone. The edge of the building hangs over a cliff. The pavement around it is cracked and buckled.

"The sea came for it and half the block last year. Cliff face underneath simply slipped away," Maura replies matter-of-factly.

"God's way of scolding foolish mortals for building dream houses so close to the sea. Or that's what some in town say. The home-owners surely feel otherwise. There are more along the way here. No time for the complete tour, though."

A right turn takes us back toward downtown. We cruise past modest bungalows and apartment complexes, while Maura points out historic homes, churches, a corner store, the diner, "that Mexican place" that opened in 1986. That she remembers the precise year and makes a point to call it out tells me a lot about the homogeneity of this place. The faces I see outside the car do little to convince me otherwise.

We pull into the Seaview High parking lot, where Maura's late-model Mercedes finds good company in the front row. Pre-sumably all these luxury cars belong to the kids who live in those doomed beachside mansions. ESTABLISHED 1938 proclaims the stone sign at the parking lot entrance, but the main school build-ing must have been remodeled in the sixties, by the looks of the soaring stone archway at the entrance, and again in the nineties, judging from the new windows. Beyond the main building, I spot several squat classroom blocks through a grassy quad crisscrossed with covered walkways. And, much like the contrast between his-toric and salt-faded downtown Seaview and the mansions on the coast, there's a state-of-the-art addition on the far end of the park-ing lot that screams money. This entire town is a twisted juxtapo-sition between worn-down and ostentatiously new.

Maura powers up the staircase that leads to the front door of the main building. I follow, second-guessing my every choice. I run nervous fingers through my shoulder-length dark hair, which suddenly feels frizzy. I'm wearing jeans and a basic tee, which say nothing about me or my style. At home I wore cute-as-shit dresses in bright colors, patterned rompers, and heart-shaped sunglasses, shorts with off-the-shoulder ruffled tops. An Instagram cliché. But it's chilly up here, and all I had that felt warm enough was this, paired with a worn navy-blue hoodie. I realize I look like Bella fucking Swan. They're going to eat me alive.

I make it inside without hyperventilating, barely registering the wide hallway and blood-red lockers on either side before Maura hangs a sharp right, sweeping us into the front office.

"Grace, how are you? I love that sweater! This is my grand-daughter, Cecelia. We need to get her registered." My grand-mother is a tornado of purpose.

If Maura is a cool grandma, Grace is original flavor. Her kind eyes and her cardigan lead me to imagine she bakes a lot and would most certainly not say "fuck," though maybe that's more to do with her being a school secretary than anything. I find myself searching the front office for a plate of cookies.

"It's so lovely to meet you, Cecelia," Grace says. "Give me ten minutes, and I'll have you sorted. Thursday's an odd day to start, but I'm sure you'll get acclimated in no time. Maura! It's been too long. I should tell you how Joe's doing."

Grace starts to recap her latest visit to said Joe, and despite her smile, an annoyed boredom radiates off my grandmother. I wander into the hallway to wait, take in my new school.

Two stories. Scuffed marble floors. There's a trophy case with yellowing glass to the left of the front office; I lean close and do a double take. *Mom,* my brain screams, panic slicing through me. But the photo is too old—black-and-white—the dresses too retro, the hair too feathered. I realize it's Maura, not my mom, in an old homecoming-court photo. She and four other girls flank a blonde at the center, who beams, crown atop her head. Next to it is that same girl's yearbook photo and a plaque: IN LOVING MEMORY OF CAROLINE QUINN, 1953–1970.

It itches, familiar. But then Maura and Grace appear.

"Here is your schedule, dear." Grace hands me a class list printed on crisp paper. Maura gives me a kiss on the cheek and promptly departs.

"I'll walk you to your first class. Homeroom, actually. You are with Mr. Keating. They'll be nearly done, and then you'll be on your way. Don't worry—I'll make sure you have a buddy who can help you get where you need to go. Just show them your schedule."

She stops outside a gray door, with a bulletin board next to it displaying a giant paper Alexander Hamilton and cheesy wordplay. *Want to be in the room where it happens? Come on in!* I'm guessing Mr. Keating teaches History or AP Gov. Or both. Grace knocks twice in quick succession and opens the door. She marches over to Mr. Keating, a surprise in tweed. Not the tweed part, but that he's young—late twenties? Also handsome, in a goofy kind of way, and Black.

He offers Grace a nod, who gives my arm a reassuring squeeze as she passes.

"Miss Ellis, you can have a seat there." Mr. Keating points to an empty desk in the second row, and I follow directions, tucking my head down to avoid meeting anyone's eye. The morning announcements are being broadcast from a flat-screen TV affixed to the right of the board. Two fresh-faced and too-attractive teens flash blinding-white teeth while reading the news of the day stiffly from a teleprompter. The cafeteria lunch special is Swedish meatballs. French Club is canceled this afternoon. The homecoming-theme vote is tomorrow.

They start to wrap up, and I'm thinking I've gotten away scot-free without the teacher making me—

Mr. Keating locks eyes with me as the screen goes to black. "Miss Ellis, please introduce yourself! And Miss Morrow will help you navigate your classes. Wave, Amber?"

I catch the reluctant wave of a petite blonde shuffling intensely through pastel index cards. Now I have to perform for the crowd. I'm keenly aware everything I say will probably make it through the school grapevine by lunch. New-kid alert. Transferring in as a senior, no less.

"I'm Cecelia Ellis," I start, "I just moved here from Los Angeles." And I stop. The next part is tricky. Do I mention my famous grandmother? I probably can't not—they'll find out. And then they'll want to know why I live with her. There are only two real reasons someone like me would move in with their granny: unfit mom or dead mom. I've had to tell a few people that my mom died. No matter how you phrase it, it's an atomic bomb: The physical recoil. Eyes widening. Sympathy pouring from mouths, even though their bodies clearly display their revulsion. Talking about death reminds other people of their mortality.

Screw it.

"I'm living with my grandmother—Maura Weston—because my mom died." There are a few gasps behind me. I don't turn to look. I shrug and sigh. "Cancer sucks. . . . Anyway, at my old school, I was on yearbook, ASB, and, uh, in the Asian Pacific Islander Club, for some reason." I laugh at the nonjoke. It's a lie, anyway. I know the reason—my friend Claire Phan asked me to join with her. "It's Filipino American History Month, actually, and Diwali is in a few weeks, so, um, get ready," I add in a ramble.

A girl in the last row laughs. She's drop-dead gorgeous. And the only nonwhite face in the room, other than Mr. Keating. Oh God, I think she's Filipino, so she probably thinks I was singling her out. I finish up as a burn rises in my cheeks. "I also like video games, K-pop, bingeing murder shows, and karaoke." I sit back down and try to disappear into my hoodie. Then the bell rings. I turn to my escort, but she's a blur of blond and denim, whipping past me and out the door before I can utter a protest. Panic grips my chest. Where am I going now? I stare at my schedule, which tells me next I have AP Enviro in W-2. It's gobbledygook to me. Shit.

"What do you have next?"

My savior is the pretty Filipino girl. She gestures toward the printout in my hand. It's easier to give it to her.

"Oh, Environmental Science in Weston next. Better hurry. It's a hike." Upon seeing my horrified expression, she confirms, "Yes, it's named after your grandmother. I'm Bronte, by the way. Come on, I'll walk you. I'm in W-10."

I follow her like a lost but grateful duckling. Seaview High—the original building, at least—is basically a giant rectangle. When we exit Mr. Keating's classroom, there's a wide staircase leading up and down.

"Gym is there." Bronte points behind the main staircase. "Cafeteria is down the hall. And we're going here." She steers me down a long hallway with classrooms and lockers all along the sides. "This way leads to East Campus, which sounds fancy, but it's only a handful of extra classroom buildings, plus the performing arts center and the Weston Annex. It's simply in a slightly more easterly direction—hence the pretentious name."

We come to a set of double doors that spill out into the courtyard. A breezeway leads across a grassy space to the modernist structure I caught when I arrived. WESTON ANNEX reads a sign affixed beside the front doors. Inside is a sci-fi movie set, with soaring ceilings, floating walkways connecting the upper-floor classrooms, and white everything. This is a *high school*?

"It's excessive, I know," Bronte acknowledges. "More than this tiny town needs. But your grandmother donated the money, so they built the best it could buy. Most of our science classes are held here," Bronte explains as we cross the cavernous lobby. "You're down there." She points to a short hallway off the stairs. "I'm going up. Meet you back here after class to help you find the next one?"

"Thank you. Seriously. After Regina George left me in the dust, I thought I was screwed."

Bronte squints, turns her head. "Regina George?"

"Amber? The girl Mr. Keating told to take me around."

A laugh catches in Bronte's throat. "Well, I'm happy to help. I'm sure being new sucks."

"Do you get many new kids here?"

"Rarely," she affirms. "Every once in a while some new idiot buys a minimansion on the shore, so it happens more than you'd think. But I'm a lifer. Born and raised. See you later!"

I say much the same and stumble off to W-2. The next few hours will repeat on a loop: Find an empty desk. Make an awkward introduction. Frowning teacher tries to locate a stray textbook, murmuring about how much there is to catch up on. Sit through forty-five minutes of a torrent of information while furiously scribbling notes. Other students type away on laptops. I didn't know that was allowed here, and I make a mental note to bring mine tomorrow.

Bronte and I reunite before second period, where she draws me a rough map of the school and notes on it each of my classes, instantly making her my new favorite person. We end up on the same lunch, too. I skip the questionable-looking Swedish meatballs, opting instead for a veggie burger, potato wedges, and roasted squash. Bronte flags me over to her table. I hesitate on my approach. She is not the exception to the model-pretty rule; Bronte and her friends *are* the rule.

I see all the types: a classically handsome athlete, a preppy brunette, a hipster boho beauty, and a prototypical blond-cheerleader type I catch in profile. Probably all top of the class. My palms turn sweaty, and I double down on my grip so my tray doesn't slide to the floor.

"Hi," I say, addressing Bronte, who immediately slides over to make room.

"Yes! Hi! Everyone, this is Cecelia. She's new."

A girl to Bronte's left curses loudly. "I'm sorry," she says. "I totally left you, didn't I?"

It's Amber, from homeroom. "It's okay," I say as my cheeks go hot. I bad-mouthed Amber to Bronte, who is obviously good friends with her.

"I spaced, 'cause I had this test in AP Bio and I was running drills in my head, and when the bell rang, all I could think about was aerobic cellular respiration, and, well. Sorry." Amber is an energy force, chattering at full speed. She seems genuinely apologetic, too. So . . . not the bitchy type?

"How'd it go?" Bronte asks.

Amber wilts. "I probably failed."

Bronte rolls her eyes, but her tone remains warm. "You fucking didn't." She kisses her on the cheek and gives her hand a squeeze.

Fuck. I called Bronte's *girlfriend* Regina George. How am I sitting here? I wait for the other penny to drop, for the whole table to turn on me, dump their trays over my head for a laugh. It doesn't happen. We go around the table and everyone introduces themselves in a completely normal and friendly way.

The jock is Luke; the swim-and-dive team keeps him lean. Preppy Natalie, who either won the genetic lottery or got a blowout before school, is Associated Student Body president, regional mock-trial champion—and daughter of the mayor, to boot. She tosses her glossy dark curls over her shoulder and intros Morgan, on her left.

"We're in drama together, and she does swim team with Luke," Natalie says, as if the only relevant details about her friend are in relation to other, more important people. Morgan is a facsimile of Natalie but blond, though her curls are uneven and limp, her peasant top a cheap fast-fashion knockoff. Both sport glossy pink lips and a subtle winged eyeliner.

"I heard you're ARMY," Morgan says. "You should join the K-pop club. I started it sophomore year."

Natalie sneers, but she hides her expression behind a pleasant mask when she catches me looking. I guess I won't be discussing my K-pop biases with her. But Morgan seems cool.

Finally, Amber and Bronte round it out with their own laundry lists of extracurriculars and accomplishments. Amber is the master of wordage, spoken and written—she's captain of the debate team, a Scholastic Gold Key Award–winning poet who runs the lit mag, and editor of the yearbook. Bronte is a Renaissance woman straddling all groups. She does theater tech and Girls Who Code, runs cross-country, is the senior ASB treasurer, and works on the yearbook with Amber. And all the girls are cheerleaders, except for Amber. Guess I had her pegged all wrong in every way possible.

I marvel, sitting amid the social giants of Seaview High. They ask me questions about my former life with pointed interest. Where did I live in LA? What are my favorite video games? What did I do on yearbook? A huge weight lifts off my shoulders. I just might be all right here.

Morgan leans in, her wavy shoulder-length blond hair falling into her eyes. "I know this is, like, weird and kind of sad, but I have read every one of Maura Weston's books. I can't believe she's your grandmother."

"Oh, me neither," I say. "She and my mom weren't close, so it's all a bit overwhelming. I've only read one of her books, actually."

"Was it the one based on the murder that happened here?" Morgan drops her voice to a conspiratorial whisper. "It happened, like, right below where we are now. They say the janitor was obsessed with her, but she rejected him, so he drowned her in the pool during the homecoming dance. In the book, she made it a teacher, though. Creative license and all that."

This is all news to me. I knew Maura's first book made a huge splash in the early eighties, an instant *New York Times* bestseller, and, of course, there was the movie, but this true-crime angle is a surprise.

"I read the one that's like *Vertigo,* on a boat," I say. "I didn't know that her first book was inspired by real life."

Everyone at the table exchanges a look.

"It's notorious here," Natalie says, practically giddy about my ignorance. Like she's thrilled to impart her superior knowledge to me. "Every homecoming, there's a moment of silence for Caroline. She'd been crowned queen that night, and like an hour later, they found her dead."

"It was Cassidy in the book," Morgan adds.

Caroline in real life. I think about the homage in the trophy case, and it all comes together.

"Yeah, and Maura Weston superfans will show up this time of year," Luke joins in. "A few . . . enterprising business people host murder tours."

"He means him," Natalie quips. "Luke is the enterprising businessman."

"It's tradition! Passed down from Rinaldi to Rinaldi. My sister made enough extra cash to buy a new car. Besides, it's a great way to meet people. High school girls aren't my speed."

I wonder what girls *are* his speed. He's got the looks to be a player: He's tall, in a green polo shirt stretched tight across broad shoulders, with cheeks that dimple when he laughs—which is often, with confidence. His dark-brown hair is shaved into an undercut, the top gelled into a trendy wave. I would find him magnetic except jocks aren't my thing. I have a tragic history with hipster nerd boys.

"Caroline was my great-aunt," Morgan says. She pushes her dirty-blond beach waves off her face and, yes, I can see her as Caroline's relative. "It's so tragic. Cut down in her prime because some dude got his feelings hurt."

Luke shifts in his seat. "Not all men, Morgan."

I suck in a breath. Then everyone bursts out laughing, including Luke.

And then they're back on me, wanting to know all about my life in Pasadena. I can tell Morgan is dying to talk about Maura some more, but she refrains, thankfully.

Might as well call this place Forks, because I am definitely Bella fucking Swan today.

CHAPTER THREE

Maura doesn't even last one day with the nurturing, protective act, much to my relief. I'm left to find my own way home, and the barest slip of normalcy is a balm. Instead of the one-block trip direct to Maura's, I detour in the direction of downtown, savoring a canopy of deciduous trees that line the sidewalk, and the occasional towering palm on a street corner.

The houses are cookie-cutter California classics, a mix of dilapidated Craftsmans, compact ranches, and baby Victorians. No cars pass. The ones tucked neatly into each driveway are a blast from the past. Lots of boxy station wagons and sedans, like out of a nineties movie. I inhale sweet, crisp air. It *tastes* fresh.

I miss the sooty, sunny excess of Los Angeles, but I can't help thinking my mom walked these streets. I hop over a sidewalk tile cracked by the root of a towering tree and imagine her doing the same. Fresh-faced and seventeen, planning her great escape, dreaming about her future.

Judging by the look of things, the town hasn't changed much from when she was my age. The storefronts feature hand-lettered wooden signs, not a name-brand store or fast-food joint in sight. I've reached the main thoroughfare, the hum of cars on the PCH nearby. *No, it's the 1,* I correct myself. Calling it the PCH signals me as a Southern Californian, an outsider. But is there any point in talking like the locals if I don't plan on staying? My mom had the right idea: get through and get out. People here are nice enough, but I don't belong.

Amid mom-and-pop supply stores, grubby-looking bars, and the odd dispensary, I spot a diamond in the rough. A *bookstore*. GRABEL'S BOOKS says the marquee above the door, and to the right in a wide picture window: my grandmother's face. Her whole body, in fact. There's a life-sized cutout of her next to stacks upon stacks of her books. THE EXCLUSIVE HOME OF MAURA WESTON'S SIGNED COLLECTION boasts a sign. And a poster affixed to the window. And a nearby telephone pole.

WESTONCON! HOTEL SEAVIEW, OCTOBER 13–16. TICKETS AVAILABLE!

My grandmother is so ubiquitous there's a *fan convention* for her next weekend. Jesus. Suddenly, I've lost the urge to shop for reading material, so I test my sense of direction, guessing my way to Maura's monster Victorian.

As I near the house, tires crunch over gravel behind me; I wrench around and leap out of the way of a green Subaru station wagon in the nick of time. It pulls ahead of me, stopping before the carriage house that sits to the left of the main house, next to an ancient Toyota Corolla. A woman—midforties, average build, in a cream V-neck and cargo shorts—hops out of the driver's seat, exhaling a cloud of vape smoke in my direction. She offers no apologies, but grunts in my direction.

"You gonna help me?"

The trunk is packed with an assortment of cloth grocery bags. I hup to, grabbing several with each hand.

I follow Suzanne—because she has to be Suzanne—around the back of the house to a door that leads straight into the kitchen. We surprise a boy who is sitting at the marble island, playing on his phone. I peg him for sixteen or so. Blond, with not-quite curls, outfitted in a retro band tee, jeans, and chunky black-frame glasses. An unassuming kind of cute.

"Let me help you with that!" He jumps off a barstool, raking eyes over me before turning away with a shy grin.

Suzanne shakes her head, then hauls her bags up onto the counter. I follow suit. "We got it all. She need anything?"

For a second, I think she means me, but the boy shakes his head.

"She's DND for the next hour. Needs to finish this chapter."

Do not disturb, I assume, rather than a Dungeons & Dragons campaign. Maura must be on deadline. But who *is* this kid?

"I'm Cecelia. Maura's granddaughter," I say, offering my hand. He takes it, grip firm. Good. First test passed. But then he starts *singing.* I let him finish, polite expression plastered on, as always. Release a belabored sigh. "You're a bit young to be a Simon and Garfunkel fan. Usually it's boomers who pull that with me. And what's your name?"

"I'm Ben. No song for that, as far as I know." His blue eyes sparkle.

"Not a lot of slut-shaming songs written about dudes, I guess." I faux-shrug.

"Touché." Ben laughs.

Suzanne watches us shrewdly. Then she clears her throat. Ben and I get to work, helping to unload the groceries.

I put a carton of orange juice in the fridge, the one place I am sure of in this kitchen. There are a million cabinets, and I have no clue what goes where. Then I wager a guess: "Are you Suzanne's . . . son?"

"God, no," Suzanne barks at the same time Ben says, "Uh, no," like I've insulted him.

"I'm Maura's intern," he explains, like this is a normal thing.

"What does that mean?" I ask. I watch Suzanne put away a bag of chips, noting the location with interest.

"She's teaching me about the publishing industry. And writing."

"And the glorious world of being a PA," Suzanne cuts in. "Move to New York or LA, and that's what you'll be doing for ten years."

Suzanne is well past the ten-year expiration date. Being my grandmother's personal assistant is something she's chosen to do, well into her prime years. I had expected someone younger.

"So you're in college?" I must have been off by years with his age, for him to be interning, but then he shakes his head.

"I'm at Seaview, with you. We're in AP Enviro and AP Gov together, so I got to hear your intro speech twice. You don't pull punches."

"You're a senior?"

"Yep."

How could I have not seen him? "The Toyota yours?" I ask, and he nods. I hate that my cheeks burn when he looks at me. Like really *looks* at me.

"Well, uh, I'd better head upstairs. Homework. Lots to catch up on." I grab an apple from a fruit bowl and walk away. The last thing I need is any romantic entanglements. I'm getting in and out of this place. College next year, and my eighteenth birthday in the spring. Maura will be responsible for me until I'm twenty-four, for like college tuition and insurance and stuff, but in the meantime I can take care of myself.

✦

I fall into the black hole of schoolwork. What is it with teachers acting like theirs is the only class you're taking, loading you up with assignments? It's dark by the time Maura hollers up the back stairwell, her voice a faint echo.

"Celia! Dinner!"

It's horribly domestic, being called to dinner, and I trudge down the stairs with halting steps. My mom taught me to cook at a young age: pastas, salad, then chicken, fish. I was always home first from school, so it made sense for me to start dinner. My mom would collapse through the door around seven, and I'd have a simple but delicious meal ready. *Just don't burn the kitchen down and have social services on our ass,* Mom would say. I'm a pretty good cook.

Maura is not, it would seem. Suzanne made the spread—meatloaf with a side of mashed potatoes and green beans—and she eats with us, too. Suzanne's sautéed the beans in oil with salt and pepper, so they're delicious, rather than the gloopy mess I've had at school.

"Celia." Maura addresses me with that unasked for nickname again. I would correct her, but her tone brooks no argument. "Did you go into my office?"

"Uh." I hasten to chew a mouthful of meatloaf. Maura beats me to the punch.

28

"I found an abandoned water glass on my desk this morning. Sans coaster. And Suzanne affirms it wasn't hers."

"Oh, uh, yeah, that was me. Sorry. I was exploring the house and forgot about the glass."

"My office is private, Cecelia." *Now* she uses my full name. "It's not appropriate for you to go sneaking around my things."

Humiliation and adrenaline explode inside me like a nuclear bomb, spreading intense heat throughout my body. "I'm so sorry, Maura, truly. I didn't know it was off-limits. But I was so curious about your books. What you do."

"Of course you are, dear!" Maura seems to thaw instantly. "I saw a copy of *Killer Queen* out of sorts on the shelf. Were you reading it?"

"I was. It's . . . really good." I fumble my way through an apology by way of flattery. I'm surprised she noticed a single book askew, but I suppose she *is* a mystery writer, after all. "I was going to ask if I could borrow it."

"Absolutely! You're welcome to read all of my books. My earliest work is a tad bit embarrassing, but it's also considered a classic. Stop by my office after dinner, and I'll set you up with some trade paperbacks."

I have no idea what a trade paperback is, but I'm happy that Sassy Grandma is back. Disappointed Maura is terrifying.

"Do you think strangulation is overdone?" Maura asks, a chunk of meatloaf dangling off her fork on the way to her mouth. Before I can confirm whether I've had a heart attack, Suzanne replies.

"It's a classic for a reason. Efficient."

"Yeah, but nowadays they can do all sorts of forensics with that method, which kind of kills the suspense."

"Is that true?" Suzanne counters.

"I saw it on a *Dateline* special."

Suzanne simply shrugs. "Write what you want. You can always fix it later."

"I don't pay you to lie to me," Maura says.

"You also don't pay me to cook, but . . ." Suzanne lets it hang, like the green bean speared on fork tongs. Then they both burst out laughing.

"Sorry, dear," Maura says to me when she recovers. "Look at me, all up in my own head with this stupid book. How was school?"

"Good," I say. "I actually made friends. And I'm behind, but not as bad as I thought. I already read one of the assigned books for AP English sophomore year, and the AP Gov stuff is entry-level. Also, hey, you have a wing named after you. So that wasn't weird or anything."

Maura waves me off. "Technically, it's an annex. And that silly thing was your grandfather's idea. 'You should give back to the town, Maura. Children are the future.' He was a big ole softie, your granddad. But it did spruce up that dingy little school."

"All I remember is that he liked coffee ice cream. He didn't think I'd like it, but I insisted on trying it and then I did."

"You and your 'sophisticated palate,' as your mom put it." Maura clucks. "And, yes, I couldn't stand the stuff. Thought it was an awful waste of sugar and cream. In pure, liquid form, however . . . don't know how I'd write books without it!"

"Cocaine," Suzanne suggests dryly. They laugh again.

I like their banter, their in-jokes. I want to be in on this, learn the easy beats of their conversations.

"And who are these friends you've made, Celia?" There it is

again, but now I think I like the nickname. It's special, something just for me and her.

"Oh, I only know their first names," I say, just now realizing it for myself. You don't exactly do full introductions at school. "Except for Amber Morrow—I caught that. Oh, and Luke Rinaldi. The others are Bronte, Natalie, and Morgan. Natalie's dad is the mayor." I remember that.

"Morrow?" Maura narrows her eyes, thinking. "Mom works at Quinn's, father's the sheriff. And Rinaldi is ubiquitous. Mrs. Rinaldi is the president of the university, and her husband's family owns an award-winning vineyard. Only moved here a decade ago or so, but we like them, all the same." She looks to the sideboard and frowns. "Suzanne, can you get my phone? I want to text Grace about the others. Want to know who my granddaughter is spending time with."

I think she's joking until Suzanne indeed retrieves a cell phone and her fingers start flying over the screen. "Austen?" she asks. "Bronte," I correct before rattling off the rest of the names again.

I'm finishing up my meatloaf when Maura's phone buzzes on the edge of the table. She holds it up close to her face, squints. "Bronte Escano, Luke Rinaldi, Natalie Bergen, and Morgan Quinn. Oh." Her eyebrows rise. "Good job, girly. You're in with the titans of industry."

"What?"

She smirks. "Bronte Escano's mom runs the *Seaview Register*. Quinn, as I'm sure you can guess, owns the diner, plus the grocery store and two gas stations. It'll sound trivial to you, but it's the beating heart of a place like this. And Bradley Bergen, Natalie's father, is the mayor, as you know. Wife's a prominent therapist, too. That's a lot of power concentrated in one friend group. And my baby has a seat at the table."

Maura beams, and I realize with a twist in my stomach that she is legitimately proud. Social cachet has value to her, and I've lucked into a winning friend group, one worthy of Maura Weston. Though a part of me wonders if *that's* precisely why. Perhaps the only reason I was invited to that lunch table is because of who I'm related to. Even more reason to leave this town as quickly as possible.

As promised, after dinner Maura formally invites me into her office and gives me the grand bookshelf tour. She has an impressive collection of stand-alone commercial thrillers, but also several successful series. Much like the trade-paperback thing, she tosses out terms that go over my head, like *cozies* and *cooking mysteries*, but I gather she has multiple series set in the town of Alder Cove, a facsimile of our very own Seaview.

"My fans are my lifeblood," she says as she pulls books from the shelves, thrusting them at me one by one. "They started a fancon about fifteen years ago, which I keynote every year. It's next weekend at Hotel Seaview. You should come, see your ole grandma in action."

I've got a stack of eight books that threaten to topple onto the floor. I have to use both hands to keep them steady.

"That's so cool," I say. Then I clear my throat, asking the question that's been itching up my esophagus. "Do they do it that weekend because of the Caroline Quinn murder? It seems like a big deal in this town."

Maura snorts. "That's an understatement. Caroline's murder changed this town forever, in more ways than one. But really it's my books and their popularity in the nineties that put us on the map. That's when the tourist trade started, and once they made the *Killer Queen* movie and filmed it here . . . just you wait, girly. It's a wild week for you to arrive. Great timing."

I want to ask more, about the homecoming-court picture, since Maura clearly knew the murdered queen she based her book on, but I hold back. I hate when people ask me prying questions about my mom. They want every grim detail, and all I can manage are top-line platitudes. Anything deeper is too much, too soon.

Maura must see my face fall; her grandmotherly instincts kick in as she frowns with concern. "I'm glad you're here, sweetheart. Not under the circumstances, of course, but you're family. I've got you." She rubs my back, pulls me in for a tight hug. It's uncomfortable, and not only because it presses her paperbacks to my chest; I'm not accustomed to her smell, the feel of her. She's not my mom.

I swallow down a sob, focus on anything but my emotions. Maura's shelves are packed with her books, but at the bottom left corner of one of them, I spot an anachronistic set. An assortment of tall, alternately cream-colored, black, and red leather volumes, with embossed retro lettering on the spines: *Vikings 1967, 1968, 1969, 1970.* Yearbooks.

I pull out of the hug. "Thanks, Grandma." The name feels foreign in my mouth, but I try it on. Maura grimaces, and I correct myself. "I mean, Maura." No grandma-related monikers, then. All Maura, all the time.

"If it's okay, I'd like to stay here and read a bit," I add, praying Maura takes the bait. I free myself of my book bounty, unloading it onto a side table. "Your office is the perfect bookish space. Seriously."

Buttering her up works. "Of course. I'll check in on you later." She strokes my hair, then my cheek, finally booping me on the nose like I'm a cat. It's a learning curve.

Once I'm sure she's gone and out of hearing range, I plop myself down on the floor in the corner by the yearbooks, pull the 1970 edition out. The cover is simple, somber: black with a gold Viking stamped on the front. Can't go too peppy the year a student is murdered.

I flip it open, scanning pages packed with signatures. Maura was popular. Plenty of standard *Have a nice summers* and *URAQTs*, which I have to Google—"You are a cutie," apparently. A cheeky poem on the front right page, in pride of place by the yearbook title:

Roses are red,
Violets are blue,
You're a huge bitch,
But you know I love you.
Elaine 🖤

Not the only winkingly cruel poem I find, though the only one with a heart drawn next to the signature. Kids in the seventies were assholes.

The dedication to Caroline is right up front—*In loving memory*—and the same posed picture from the trophy case: a senior portrait for a girl who would never graduate. There's a footnote at the bottom right that says *Turn to page 128 for more.* I do, and I find an eight-page spread bursting with images, baby pics all the way up to that eerie one of the homecoming court, possibly moments before Caroline's death. I get a closer look now: everyone onstage, a glittering crown atop the queen's blond head. A chill runs through me.

My grandmother's legacy. This town's lifeblood. Dead things. Welcome home, I guess.

CHAPTER FOUR

When I walk into Seaview High Friday morning, things have erupted into chaos.

"Vote for Around the World!" someone screams down the hallway after the warning bell. I hurry up to homeroom, passing a sign that says BEACH PARTY, BITCHES! I imagine the administration will tear that down shortly. But by lunch, the frenzy has reached a fever pitch, the four corners of the cafeteria occupied by each faction, decked out in outrageous formal wear to fit each theme.

I do a turn of the room, tray in hand. A Malibu Barbie lookalike beckons from the Beach Party table, while a redhead in an ill-advised kimono shoots me desperate come-hithers. I note her table: anemically outfitted with a blow-up Eiffel Tower model and some paper printouts.

The real fight is between A Midsummer Night's Dream and Old Hollywood Glam, whose tables contain familiar faces.

I drift over to the Midsummer Night's Dream table, where Morgan is enthusiastically pitching a trio of younger girls who appear more interested in the half-naked boy beside her than how much money they'll save reusing sets from last year's production of *Into the Woods*. Judging from Morgan's glimmering green-and-gold eye makeup and the vines twisted in her hair and around the boy's bare torso, I'm guessing they're aping Titania and Puck.

"Caleb, why are you so obsessed with wood?" Natalie calls over from Old Hollywood Glam, her shoulders warmed by a faux-fur stole, her tone singsong but a barb apparent.

"I love wood. What can I say?" Puck—nay, Caleb—grins. Next to Natalie, Luke snorts a laugh, while Morgan's body tenses, her mouth going white, pressed into a firm line. I wonder if there's history there between her and Caleb. She proceeds to talk even louder about fitting the lights in the gym with green filters so the whole place will take on a dreamy, woodsy atmosphere.

Luke jumps in. "Hey, girls, come over here and I'll take my shirt off if you promise to vote for our theme." He shrugs off his smart suit jacket and starts to unbutton his crisp white shirt.

"Puck you!" Caleb shouts over, emphasizing the *p* sound so the teacher on cafeteria duty is unable to raise hell. Luke stops short of shirtlessness.

"And anyone who votes now gets an exclusive invite to my homecoming after-party," Natalie says. She preens as the girls flutter over to her table like moths to a flame, phones already in hand.

Having witnessed a battle I barely understand and have no wish to join, I find Amber and Bronte at what must be their regular table. I slide into a chair across from them. "Okay, what's with the battle of the hams back there?"

"Homecoming-theme vote is today. Have you registered your school email yet? You use that with the school app," Bronte explains.

Behind her, Amber frowns. "It might be too late, though. They announce the theme at the assembly this afternoon."

Bronte smiles encouragingly. "Even if you miss the vote, Spirit Week starts Monday. It's a lot of fun. You'll love it."

My school had a Spirit Week—that much is familiar to me—but our homecoming dances were not this well thought out. Unless Stringing Fairy Lights in the Gym is a theme. Our prom was when we'd go all out. Football wasn't the biggest deal for us, so homecoming was whatever.

Amber smirks. "So the choice is between casual racism, bikinis as dresses, wood sprite, and every girl dressing like Marilyn Monroe."

"Seems like a no-brainer," I say. "Any day I can dress up like Katharine Hepburn is a good day."

"I knew I liked you," Amber says.

"And who's that with Morgan?" I point over at Puck, who's flexing his muscles for the passersby now. "Also why the wood joke? Am I missing something?"

"Because his family owns the lumber mill and Natalie's not very original," rings a baritone over my head. The voice's owner pulls out the chair next to me, depositing a Gatorade and an apple onto the table as he sits.

"Ben," Bronte says, registering some surprise.

"His name is Caleb Hardy. The last name doesn't help," Amber supplies, then nods at Ben. "Benjamin. Fancy seeing you here."

He ignores her, laser-focused on me. I can't say I mind.

"I forgot to say yesterday . . . if you want help to catch up on AP Enviro or Government, I could share my notes."

"That would be great." Never mind I'm not worried about AP Gov, and the AP Enviro teacher already gave me detailed lecture notes. My stomach is tumbling like a washing machine, and I find I quite like it.

Ben sinks his teeth into the golden yellow of his apple, grins. "Awesome. I'll see you later?"

And then he's pushing back his chair and making a quick retreat.

Bronte and Amber blink at me, then at each other, then at me again.

Before I can ask why they're looking at me as if I've sprung a third head, the scent of citrus and spice descends, Natalie's perfume announcing her. She sits down in the very chair Ben recently vacated. She's left Luke behind to tend their table.

"So did everyone vote for Old Hollywood Glam?"

"You know it," Amber says with a little too much enthusiasm.

"Excellent." If Natalie knows she's being mocked, her tone doesn't betray it. "And do you all have your Spirit Week costumes set?" She helps herself to the oatmeal cookie on Amber's tray, takes a bite. Guess she figured it out. Amber glares.

I clear my throat, distracting Natalie. "Spirit Week?"

"Yeah, we all dress up before the big game," she explains breezily. "Monday is PJ Party, Tuesday is Superheroes. Wednesday is Decades Day. And thanks to yours truly, I ensured we got the seventies, and, yes, I will be dressing up as Cher, so dibs on that. Then Thursday is Twin Day." Natalie eyes me keenly. "You make an uneven number of girls, unless you want to twin with Ben. I saw you talking to him."

"Uh, I don't know him very well. We just met. Do I have to twin with someone?"

"No," Bronte reassures me. "Spirit Week isn't law. It's meant to be fun. Don't worry."

"Your hair is so pretty," Natalie says, twisting a strand between her fingers. Her eyes narrow. "Maybe you and I can pair up. Morgan refuses to dye her hair, so we can never complete the illusion."

I'm getting some serious *Single White Female* energy from her, so I inch away, my hair slipping from her grasp.

"I'd better get back to the table," she says. "Need to ensure those last-minute votes. I am not going to the dance dressed like a vine princess. Ugh."

Natalie leaves, and I'm left with my head spinning. "What was *that*?"

"We could ask you the same thing," Amber says wryly, arms crossed over her chest. "So you've met Benjamin."

"Yeah, he's my grandmother's intern. What am I missing?"

Another look exchanged.

"We used to be friends," says Bronte finally. Carefully. "Then some drama happened and things are weird now. He doesn't really hang out with Natalie—or us—anymore."

"I love how you sugarcoat things. Adorable." Amber pecks her on the cheek and then faces me with grim determination.

"Ben's mom died. He blames the city, ergo he blames the mayor, who is Natalie's dad, and he's suing. In a nutshell."

"Whoa." I take in the revelation.

"Technically, it's his grandfather suing." Now Bronte jumps in with details, though she's arguing with Amber, not me. "Ben's not a bad guy. And it's understandable he'd be hurting. You know I get it."

"Yeah, I know, but *you* didn't sue anyone. Not that it justifies Natalie being a bitch about it."

"I get her side, too," Bronte says. And then she turns her big brown sad eyes on me. "Sorry, I should have told you before. I lost my dad, too. A few years ago. So I understand losing a parent, and grief. Which is not the only reason I befriended you, for the record—though it did cross my mind we had that in common."

She's right; it is an anvil dropped that we're in the Dead Parents' Club together, yet all it does is endear Bronte to me more. It's oddly comforting knowing there's someone else at this school who gets what I'm going through, at least in some part.

Two someones. I see Ben with fresh eyes.

"How is it the city's fault?" I can't help asking. "What happened?"

"The full story is . . . messy," Amber says as Bronte grimaces. "Did you see that news story last year about the section of the 1 that fell into the ocean?"

"Uh, yeah." The images were mind-boggling, a whole stretch of the PCH simply . . . gone: the red clay cliff face interrupting the black line of highway, a sharp drop-off to the sea. "Maura took me on a driving tour, too. I saw those half-destroyed houses." Dread gnaws at my insides.

"Right," Amber says. "It's called coastal erosion, and it's a huge problem here. One of those buildings is—was—Ben's house."

I can put together the rest. "Oh God."

Bronte nods. "There's this whole thing going on in town called 'managed retreat,' where the city is supposed to buy back the houses in danger of falling. But it's taken forever to push through the city council, and that's after years of wasting millions on rock walls and trucking in sand. I wrote a paper on it last year for AP Enviro, if you want to read it. It's pretty complicated."

"But long story short," Amber cuts in, always the one to slash through the bullshit, "Ben's mom was behind on their mortgage, waiting on the payment from the city, and it's the reason they didn't move in time. My dad says the whole lawsuit is bullshit. It's really not the mayor's fault."

"Your dad's job is enforcing the status quo," Bronte scoffs. "And don't forget the smear campaign he ran to get Sheriff Vann out and him in. Aided by the mayor, his bestie since elementary school."

"You sound like your mother," Amber says, voice tight.

"No, I sound like *your* mother."

The air crackles, but then they break into laughter, shared references and miles of town history informing whatever I just witnessed. I clear my throat, steer us back.

"So Natalie's not a fan of Ben because his family is suing her dad."

"The city, technically, but yes." Amber nods. "The lawsuit could bankrupt us. No way the mayor stays the mayor if he can't tidy it up, and Natalie's pissed. We ended up in the middle, and it was easier to defer to Natalie."

"You make her sound awful." Bronte throws Amber a frown of disapproval. "They both have their reasons. Ben lost his mom. Nothing prepares you for losing a parent. And your only parent? In the most wrenching way possible?"

Oof, I feel that. Poor Ben. No wonder his family's grasping at this lawsuit. Money won't bring Ben's mom back, but a lawsuit could bring some justice. Maybe. If there were someone I could rage at, hit and hurt, for my mom's cancer, I would. But there's no one. It was shitty fate and bad luck.

"Ben is looking for someone to blame, and the mayor is an obvious target. And that sucks for Natalie," Bronte continues. "It's easier if everyone avoids each other until it's settled. He still hangs with Luke on the side, so it's not like he's completely cut off."

"Yes, how lovely for Ben to get shared custody of Luke in the divorce," Amber cracks. Then she returns her full attention to me. "Look, it's complicated, but if you like Ben, forget Natalie. You're never going to make everybody happy, so why not steal a little happy for yourself?"

I say nothing but feel warmed at Amber's words. After months of miserable, it would be nice to find a little happy.

✦

I find myself looking for Ben at the afternoon assembly. The gym echoes with friends yelling at one another from across the room and bodies climbing over each other on the bleachers to get better seats. I don't see him. Instead, I spot Luke and Amber across the gym, at the very far end of the front row; Amber signals me over and pats the bench space next to her.

The assembly is a production, to say the least. The gym lights wink out, dramatic music plays, we hear sneakers squeak on the slick floors, and then when the bass drops, brightness floods the room and the whole cheerleading squad materializes on a giant mat. Bronte, Natalie, and Morgan do backflips and basket tosses, intermixed with crisp dance moves. The principal welcomes us, brings out the football team, the school band plays, and there's even some poor kid in a foam Viking costume with a giant head that shakes his ass while the crowd whoops. It builds and builds to the big announcement: Old Hollywood Glam has won the homecoming-dance theme, and Natalie beams a thousand-watt smile. I can't help but wonder if she personally threatened the student body into voting her way.

The principal hisses into the mic for us all to quiet down, and calls Natalie to the podium. She smooths her long brown ponytail over her right shoulder and clears her throat.

The gym, which was previously chaos, falls into a hush, like everyone knows what is coming. The change of tone is so abrupt it unsettles me.

"Thank you, Principal Morris," Natalie says. "Please join me in a moment of silence and reflection for Caroline Quinn, taken too soon and robbed of so much. She is a reminder to us of all of life's preciousness. We honor her. Please close your eyes with me."

People cough. Shuffle their feet. I close my eyes. What is everyone else thinking about? Their plans for this weekend, probably. What do high school students know about death? Well, most of them, anyway. I think about Ben again. With my eyes closed, I almost feel his arm stroking my own. I lean into the intoxicating heat, seeking more, more, *more*. "Ow!"

I open my eyes to see a very real Luke grinning. The bastard pinched me!

"Come on," he says. "They're about to launch into eighteenth-century poetry about birds, and then the marching band'll blast our eardrums. We have something better in mind."

"We?" Amber hisses, but Luke waves her off, grabbing me by the hand and setting out in a half crouch. We slip through a side door and into a stairwell. When we're down one flight, he finally talks.

"You want to see the pool? Where it happened? It's right here." Luke points beyond the landing, to another set of double doors. Waggles his eyebrows.

Morbid curiosity tugs at me. *Yes*, something whispers. Then

I find myself saying it out loud, too. Luke grins, swings the door open with a flourish, like a demented emcee welcoming me to the cabaret.

I step inside, suck in a deep, chlorine-tinged breath. And . . . it's a pool. Like any other school pool. I've swum in enough of them. Metal bleachers to the left, locker rooms to the right, softly undulating blue waters, diving boards, body.

Body?

There's a body in the pool.

My heart leaps into my throat. And I sprint toward the pool.

CHAPTER FIVE

Instinct takes over: Throw off backpack. Sprint to the pool. Swallow down the burning, pulsating fear pushing up my throat. I dive in, fully clothed, the water shocking my system with cold. Still, I pump my arms and legs, hard, to reach the person. They need help. I *have* to help. I'm close—three feet, then half a foot away, close enough to touch. My fingers grasp at their arm; the skin is hard, plasticky. No, not plasticky. Literally plastic. What?

Laughter echoes around me, multiplies as it bounces off the walls.

"Luke, you asshole!" I hear someone say.

"I didn't know she'd jump in!"

Amber is scolding Luke.

"She's a goddamn hero!"

That's Natalie. I sputter, look closer at my victim. It's . . . a dummy. Like a CPR one. This is a fucking prank. And when I turn to see my "friends," Natalie's still in her cheer uniform, and she has her phone up, capturing the whole thing. Morgan hovers behind her. "You're going to be huge on TikTok, Cecelia. Love it!"

But they seem to be laughing *with* me, rather than at me, so I take it on the chin. Ha ha, great initiation ritual into the friend group. A good attitude doesn't make me dry, though. I pull myself from the pool, very, very wet. I drip onto the pool tiles and search in vain for a towel.

"Sorry, Cecelia," Morgan says, handing me my backpack, like that is remotely helpful. I look for Bronte but don't see her. Good. Pranks don't seem her speed, and Amber's scowling, still pissed.

Then Ben emerges from the locker room. He eyes me, soaking wet, dummy in the pool, Natalie and Luke tittering, and turns right around. Well, this is humiliating. But before I can despair, he's back, armed with towels, and the churn of embarrassment transforms into elation. A gentleman, he puts one towel around my shoulder and hands me the other so I can pat myself down. Then he rounds on Natalie, Luke, and Morgan.

"Not fucking cool."

Natalie rolls her eyes. "Oh, please, six months ago you'd have rigged the dummy yourself. You're just bitter because we don't like you anymore."

Luke coughs, and Amber gives Natalie the side-eye. It's not so much *we* as only Natalie. But no one calls her on it.

Ben doesn't take the bait, anyway. He zeroes in on Luke instead. "You owe her an apology."

Normally the chivalrous-hero routine would get on my nerves, but right in this moment, I'm grateful for Ben's defense. Charmed that he is protecting *me*.

Luke spreads his arms in a contrite gesture, and I signal an acceptance. *I'm fun! I can hang!*

"I'm sorry," Luke says with a boyish grin that makes it hard to hold anything against him for too long. "And, look, I'll make it up to you. Tomorrow. Seaview's premier murder tour, on me. By yours truly, and Ben here. Meet in Seaview Square at two p.m."

It's an unusual peace offering, but I am curious about Luke's enterprising business. And I have nothing else to do on a Saturday.

It's not because Ben will be there. I look at his eyes, bright with interest. Dimples threatening to appear on his cheeks.

Nope. Not because of Ben at all.

"Sounds good."

Ben and Luke launch into an elaborate fist bump/handshake thing, complete with a full-body spin and hip bump. The kind of thing prepubescent boys come up with and don't outgrow.

Natalie combines a cringe with an eye roll. "God, I can't stand you two." The delivery is pitch-perfect ice bitch, but my gut twinges at the note of sadness right under the surface. Then quick as I sense it, it's gone again. And Natalie's beckoning to me to follow her.

"Come on, Cecelia, I'll drive you home. Because I'm a *nice person,* and you can take a joke, unlike some people." She flips Ben off, then corrals me to the door, leaving me no choice. I will benefit from her hospitality, whether I like it or not. I remember what Amber said earlier. It's easier to defer to Natalie.

✦

"It takes three minutes to strangle a person."

So begins the murder tour of my new hometown, based on my grandmother's books. *I insist,* Luke had said. *Free for you,* he said. *Ben will be there,* he said.

Yeah, I knew he'd be here, but I thought as a ticket taker or something. Not as the maestro of murder facts. He's not done. And he's milking it.

"It's intimate. Brutal. This town lives with that legacy. One of our own, perverse enough to choke the life out of a beautiful homecoming queen."

Ben paces before a towering bronze statue at the center of the town green. We're about a ten-minute walk from the school, and his audience, a crowd of about a dozen, are rapt. Then there's me, horrified. Though on the plus side: free town walking tour.

Luke jumps in. "But from horrific beginnings can come beautiful things. Inspired by Caroline Quinn's 1970 murder, Seaview's beloved writer Maura Weston made sure her classmate's legacy did not go forgotten."

The crowd claps enthusiastically; a few people whoop. Then Luke zeroes in on me.

"And we have a very special guest with us on the tour today!"

Oh no. I shake my head vigorously, but Luke either doesn't notice or doesn't care.

"Maura Weston's very own granddaughter, Cecelia!"

There's a delighted gasp from a lanky midthirties East Asian man sporting a peach-colored sweater, part of a throng of Maura fans, occupying the front row. They all turn to stare, including a tall fortysomething woman in a stunning red vintage swing dress, whose assessing gaze lasers through me. I give a half-hearted wave and attempt to hide inside my jacket.

Ben mouths at me, *Sorry.* Then he gets back to work.

"So, first, you'll recognize this as the setting for the thriller chase scene in the *Killer Queen* movie, which they'll be screening right here on the green tomorrow night. A town tradition."

"Sponsored by Rinaldi Wines!" Luke pipes up, pointing across the street to a storefront bearing his family name. "At the end of the tour, you'll get a coupon for twenty percent off any bottle of

Rinaldi's signature red, redeemable at our tasting room or the winery itself."

We make our way through town. Luke's the showman, quick with dramatic stories and jokes, while Ben provides sobering context, with a funny Maura fact or two that delights the fans. Mostly it's fandom bullshit—scenes where they filmed the *Killer Queen* movie, Easter eggs from Maura's books, and schticks that cause such violent secondhand embarrassment I almost leave the tour more than once.

"She got one hell of a paper cut!" Luke quips of the college junior found with her throat slashed in the library stacks in the seventies. She's part of a trend: the dead and missing of Seaview. It's a longer list than I'd expected for such a small, remote town. The family annihilator in the nineties who stashed his wife's and kids' bodies in a freezer. The Coffee Clutch barista who simply . . . vanished a few years ago. ("Talk about a to-go order," Luke tastelessly joked at that one.) House fires and fatal flu strains, and weed grows turned deadly.

We come to a stop in front of an old-timey diner, and I can tell from the excited gasps around me I'm in for something ghastly.

"You may recognize this place behind me. Is it . . . Coulson's?" Luke dials the ham up to eleven. "Close! This is Quinn's diner, the inspiration for Coulson's, where Hazel works in the Hazel Minty Mysteries series! Wait, is that her?"

Luke points to a waitress inside, and I do a double take. Amber? No, too old. A relative though, for sure. The waitress catches wise to her audience and nails Amber's this-is-bullshit grimace-smile. Definitely related.

"Use our special code—'Bluke'—inside to get ten percent off

your meal," Ben adds, a blush on his cheeks. I can't help staring at the quirk of his mouth.

"Where's Cooper?" someone behind me shouts.

"Sadly, there are no sexy bakers in town. You'll have to settle for me." Luke winks lasciviously. "Or Ben, if you have lower standards."

They carry on with the comedy versus straight man act as we wend our way through downtown and over familiar terrain. I fear Maura's house is the final tour stop—bully for me, being dropped off at home, but then her superfans would know where I live. I swear one of them was trying to run their fingers through my hair at one point.

But as we strategically cross streets and take alleyway shortcuts to avoid haphazardly shingled houses with junker cars cluttering front yards and dilapidated ranches with foreclosure signs stabbed into yellowing lawns, in favor of the well-kept Craftsmans and Victorians, I realize we are leading up to the front steps of Seaview High.

"What are we doing here?" I whisper to Luke as Ben dutifully guides the group to the entrance.

"The grand finale," Luke says with a wink.

We file around the side of the main building, with brief stops at the Weston Annex before descending narrow, cracked concrete stairs to the lower level and a set of doors.

Ben and Luke face us. "Friends, what you are about to see is not for the faint of heart," Luke begins with a feigned somberness. "Behind me is the site where almost fifty-two years ago to the day, young Caroline Quinn took her last brea— Ah!" The doors slam open. A tall, muscular boy in a football uniform pushes past our guides, shouldering Luke a bit harder than necessary.

"Fuck off, Escano!" Luke explodes.

Ben grabs firm hold of Luke's arm before it can swing. Tension crackles between the boys, so much so that our entire tour group steps back to allow the football player clear passage.

Escano. The name rings in my head. Of course. This is Bronte's brother. Wow. Genetics have been kind to the Escano siblings. My eyes rake over his intense brown eyes and a chiseled jaw that flexes as he stares daggers at Luke.

"I can't believe you're still doing these tours. That the school lets you."

"I don't know, *Gabe*," Luke spits, his first name an upgrade, but only in derision. "The school allows a lot of people to get away with a lot of things. You 'forget' something in your locker? That why you're in here on a Saturday?"

Gabe bristles. "I'm here to practice. Not exploit a murder victim with disgusting pageantry." With that, he scans the crowd in judgment. His eyes catch on me, and I could swear he's disappointed. I flush in shame.

"Everyone, everyone!" Ben cuts in. "Just a bit of local color!"

"Hey, Gabe . . . Coach wants you. Hurry up!" Another football player appears at the top of the stairs. I recognize Puck-nay-Caleb from lunch yesterday, his jovial grin oblivious to the tension below.

"Thank you, Gabriel, for your help," Ben says. "We're good now. Right?" The air is thick with discomfort, but then an understanding passes between the boys, peace reached for now. Gabriel gives a tight nod before scaling the stairs after his teammate.

Ben and Luke have already recovered, back to their easy grins. "Shall we all go see what you paid for?" Luke dares us impishly. We sweep inside. We're at the pool, I realize. I came in through the gym the last time, so I didn't recognize the entrance from the lawn. Though it's hard to recognize as it is. The towering ceilings and LED lights render the lanes too bright. And there's a haze—is that a smoke machine? Then . . . Morgan screams.

"No, don't, please!" she cries, emerging from the locker room in a white linen tank dress. Luke wrenches her by the shoulders, forces her to the edge of the deck.

"If I can't have you, no one can!" Luke apes Marlon Brando, all but bellowing "Stella!" He gives her a shove into the glimmering blue of the pool, and she smashes the pristine surface.

Morgan jerks and flails, her body half submerged in the water as Luke restrains her. And that's when I realize what I am watching. They're staging Cassidy's murder.

Disgusting pageantry, Gabriel had said.

Holy fuck.

I peer around the fringes of the audience to see Morgan turn her head to the side on the water's surface, drawing a gulping breath. Then with one last jerk, she goes still. My breath hitches, my heart speeding to a gallop. *Dead body, dead body,* my mind screams as Luke pushes her prone form fully into the center of the pool. Gracefully, Morgan turns in the water onto her back, a bit of creative license, so she can, you know, breathe. And there she floats, limbs spread-eagled, her flaxen hair floating about her head like seaweed. I think of the line from *Killer Queen* that's stuck in my brain like chewing gum:

. . . the swirl of blond locks that fanned out from Cassidy's head like a halo.

And that's when I remember Cassidy was based on a real person. For ninety minutes, she and Maura's other characters have been a story for us to laugh at. A cautionary tale. But here, I can't deny that Caroline was an actual person with family. With friends. She had hobbies, and she loved and was loved. She was a living person who now isn't, like my mom.

Mom. With dull, yellowing skin and final breaths that scraped up her throat like radio static. Eyes I can never describe the horror of, the light gone. The person *gone*. The hollow nothingness that death leaves behind.

The clapping crowd titters with excitement. A superfan whispers behind me, "She's supposed to have a crown. They didn't even get the details right. I'm not tipping."

And I throw up.

CHAPTER SIX

The tour breaks up after I lose my lunch (or brunch, in this case), the splash of half-digested bagels and stomach acid on one's shoes a real mood killer. Guilt tugs at me when a few customers demand their money back. I've propped myself against the brick wall, waiting for Ben and Luke to finish so I can apologize, when someone approaches.

"Cecelia? Hi, hello." The lanky midthirties man from the tour goes so far as to grab me by the clammy hands and shake them.

"I'm Chris Wang. Huge fan of your grandmother's. It's such an honor to meet you."

"Thanks? She does all the hard work. I'm just, uh, related."

Chris hasn't let go of my hands. The vibration up my arms is uncomfortable. "I wanted to take this opportunity to introduce myself properly, to chat."

I inch back, not too much to let him know I think he's creepy, but enough that my hands slide from his warm, slick fingers. I hide my recoil behind a pasted-on smile. Maura will lose her shit if I'm rude to a fan.

"I'd love to buy you a coffee. Maybe at Quinn's? I'm staying at the hotel for the con, of course, and—"

"There you are, sweetheart. I was looking for you!" Cutting off my would-be stalker, Ben sidles up close, crowding Chris out.

Disappointed but undeterred, Chris hands me a business card. "Email or text me about that coffee."

He leaves without much more fuss, but the whole thing raises the hair on the back of my neck.

"Sweetheart?" I turn to Ben.

He shrugs. "Thought it would work best if I pretended to be your boyfriend. How are you doing? Better?"

My body flushes warm at the word *boyfriend*. I don't forget where I am, though. This is not the place for romance.

"I'll be fine," I say. "But this is a messed-up little business venture you have going."

Ben flushes, fusses his fingers over the pool divider rope hanging next to my head. "Luke offered me a cut, and I need the money. I know it's . . . I don't enjoy the end part, at least. It's Luke's thing. We can get out of here if you want."

I don't need to be asked twice. I follow Ben out, and we walk side by side toward the front of the school. The afternoon's blue sky is yielding to murky gray as we near dinnertime.

"You could have at least warned me about all the Maura content," I rib him. "It's a bit weird realizing my grandmother is on some kind of God level in this town. Like, I knew, but I didn't *know*."

"Wait until tomorrow night. The annual movie on the green is a real trip. The movie based on the bestseller your grandmother wrote, based on the real murder this town also celebrates, which was filmed in town."

"Like a murder turducken."

Ben guffaws—literally guffaws!—and there's that torrent of butterflies pulsing through my body again. He thinks I'm funny.

He stops at the front steps, threads nervous fingers through his unruly blond hair. "We could go . . . if you want. I mean, it doesn't have to be a date, it could be like a group thing."

"Is there a group?" I ask, teasing him a bit.

"No, um, it's just me. Unless you want to invite your grandmother."

"How positively Victorian. Or Edwardian."

"Where's Gabriel when you need him? He'd know."

"Oh?" I tilt my head in confusion. He's the last person I expected Ben to bring up.

"He's a local history buff. That's why he hates our tour so much. Thinks it cheapens the town history, going into all the murders and Maura Weston stuff."

"So he's a nerd and a jock, all in one? Seaview contains multitudes."

"Why, is that your type?" Ben plays at flexing an arm muscle.

"No, I'm more into blonds who awkwardly ask girls on dates after a murder tour to watch their grandmother's movie adaptation in the public square."

"Is that a yes, then?"

"Yes. Though we could make it a second date if you want. We could go grab dinner." Suddenly, I am as bold as I am starving.

"Uh, that's not going to work. If you blow off your welcome party, your grandmother will blow a gasket."

"My *what*?"

"You didn't know? Shit. It must be a surprise. Uh, act surprised, okay? Or Maura might kill me."

I oscillate between appreciation that my grandmother would throw me a welcome party and rage that she didn't tell me. I soften. How could she know I hate surprises? "Will I at least see *you* there?"

Ben stifles a laugh. "No, my grandfather and I are *not* invited."

"Why? Is there something I need to know?"

Any residual bitterness melts from his expression, giving way to a plain sadness. "No, it's nothing. I'm looking forward to tomorrow. I shine up real good, I promise. I'll pick you up at seven."

✦

Sure enough, when Ben drops me off at home, there is a florist's van in Maura's driveway, a catering truck parked by the carriage house, and then a small army of black-clad waitstaff flowing into the kitchen, carrying crates of wineglasses.

"Oh, you'll have to change! That won't do." My grandmother swans onto the porch, decked out in a magenta lace brocade dress and black kitten-toe heels.

"What's going on?" I leap out of the way of a petite blonde hauling a box of silverware.

"It's your welcoming party! Surely I said something earlier this week. No? . . . Sorry. Anyway, tonight worked best for everyone, and I do hope you didn't have other plans."

"And who is everyone? And, uh, no, I didn't."

"Oh, just some of my friends, the crème de la crème of Seaview. I wanted everyone to meet my stunning granddaughter." Maura ushers me inside and into the front room, where there's a dress hanging over the back of an armchair. "I had Suzanne pick this out for you in case you didn't have anything suitable." She dangles the dress on its hanger in front of me, checking how it looks. It's a navy-blue fit-and-flare with pleated ruffle sleeves: elegant and safe. So not my style. She thrusts the hanger into my hands. "Now hurry upstairs, shower, and change. Party starts in an hour. You may be fashionably late, but only for a stellar smoky eye. Make those eyes pop." Maura plants a kiss on my cheek and sends me off.

Annoyance blooms inside me anew. Nothing about this party is for me.

An hour later, I manage said smoky eye, and work magic with a curling iron, for good measure, before wandering downstairs like a shiny penny. The waiters are circulating through a moderate crowd with trays of champagne and finger foods. Some familiar faces mill about: Principal Morris, Grace the administrative assistant . . . And at that, my knowledge of the fifty-odd people who are crowding the ground floor is exhausted. I watch the back of a young waiter busing empty glasses from a table in foyer. I'm so desperate to talk to someone my age that I'm about to approach him when Maura appears and tugs on my elbow. Hard.

"There you are!" Her lips tighten and her eyes narrow as she notices my attire. I'm not in the safe navy blue with flutter sleeves, but my own bright-green sundress from Target. Mom and I picked it out on one of our last shopping trips before she got sick. It's like I'm carrying a piece of her with me, armor for the fray. "Not exactly seasonably or situationally appropriate," Maura says, "but the color looks gorgeous on you. Let me introduce you to the who's who of this town, senior edition."

And she does. Her good friend Elaine Harville, who owns Hotel Seaview. Councilperson Hardy, lumber mill owner and Caleb's mom. Grabel's Books owner Jane Aspen. And my friends' illustrious parents: newspaperwoman Laura Escano, Sheriff Kyle

Morrow, Alder University president Lucia Rinaldi, and her wine-baron husband Mark Rinaldi, Mayor Bergen and his wife, Dr. Shelby, and the notable grandparent of the bunch, grocery store and diner owner Frank Quinn. Amber's mom is absent, and I note there's no wedding ring on her dad's finger. Divorced?

I hover near a conversation cluster with the mayor and Maura at the center.

"We don't allow Natalie to work after school or on weekends," Mayor Bergen says, his wife nodding along. "Her academics come first. She's applying Stanford Early Action of course. Her old dad's alma mater."

There are murmurs of agreement. Then Bronte's mom pipes up.

"That's stunningly classist, Mayor Bergen. Many students don't have a choice in having to work on top of going to school. Their families either need that extra income to make ends meet, or an after-school job or two is the only way those students can afford extras that your child might take for granted. Yearbook fees, class trip expenses, football dues, or cheerleading boosters. Not to mention saving for college."

"Ah, yes," the mayor says. "That is your youngest over there refreshing wineglasses, isn't it?" I follow the mayor's head tip over to Gabriel. I realize he's the waiter I almost talked to moments ago. He hoists a tray of empties onto his shoulder, arm muscles rippling under the weight. I avert my eyes.

The mayor isn't done. "If some parents can't afford those necessities, then maybe they should have chosen more lucrative careers."

It's brave to insult the woman who runs the local paper. Either he has great faith in her journalistic ethics, or the relationship long ago soured and he doesn't care.

Maybe it's a good old-fashioned microaggression. It has not escaped my notice that Mrs. Escano is the only person of color in the room, aside from her son. But she's no pushover.

"Next thing, you'll tell me I should have asked my husband not to die, leaving me a single parent. What a failure of boot-strapping."

Maura clears her throat purposefully. "Come, now, we shouldn't look down on teenagers working if they want to. I loved working as a candy striper back in my day. Of course we didn't have all these extracurriculars required to get into a half-decent college, so we had more time." Maura plays perfect peacekeeper. Can't have her party—or my party, technically—devolve into a political debate.

The mayor and Mrs. Escano reach a détente, each grabbing a fresh champagne flute from a passing tray. I long to do the same, but the sheriff is ten feet away. Instead, I order a Diet Coke at the bar, where I get sucked into a boomer vortex of graying men and women who pepper me with intrusive questions—about my love life, political leanings, TikTok. Everyone's nice, but after the fourth time someone says I'm the spitting image of my mom, I can no longer pretend at niceties. Every moment, each well-intentioned compliment, reminds me of why I'm here. Without her. My face gets hot, and tears well up. Desperate to get away, I retreat to the kitchen at breakneck speed—and promptly collide with Gabriel and a tray of canapés.

"Shit!" I scramble to save the crostini that rain around us, managing to right but a single one. Gabriel, at least, rescues the tray before it can cause a large clang that would alert the party to our mishap.

"I'm so sorry," I say. "Are you okay?" I fish a bread square out of my hair.

Gabriel gives a confused head tilt. "Do I know you?"

"Sorry. I saw you on the murder tour earlier today. At the pool." I am immediately embarrassed after I say it, and ashamed I was there at all. "We didn't meet formally, but I'm friends with your sister," I add quickly, as though Bronte can save me again, even from far away.

"I wasn't *on* the murder tour."

"Right. Sorry. I know."

He bristles. "People deserve real history, not sensationalized soap. With all due respect to your grandmother, we're more than a murder, and then a series of books inspired by that murder."

"Aha, so you do know who I am, then!" I plop the toast slice, now free of my hair-sprayed curls, back onto the tray. Gabriel, unimpressed, slides everything into a giant trash bag by the door.

"Well, yes. It's Seaview. A pretty new girl is big news. And the granddaughter of our resident celebrity? Even more so."

I'm chewing on the fact that he called me pretty when Gabriel turns contrite.

"Shit, sorry, that was rude."

"It was?"

"Uh, yeah, reducing you to just a pretty girl? If either my sister or Amber were here, I'd get an earful about it."

"It's okay," I say, though his words reassure me if there's one friend I've chosen well thus far, it's Bronte. Amber, too. "Just don't whip out a fedora or start calling me 'milady' and we're good." Because I have a type.

That cracks his serious exterior, though his joy fades as he takes in his now-empty tray.

"We're going to run out of rolls now. I'll have to explain, and it'll come out of my wages. Fuck." He blanches. "Sorry. I mean, damn."

"I'm not some delicate maiden. You can say 'fuck' in front of me. And don't panic. I'll vouch for you. It's my fault, and I'll take the blame."

"You don't have to do that."

"No, I do. I will." I smooth down my hair and head for the door. But Gabriel grabs my arm—softly but firmly.

"I mean it. You can stay. They're so drunk they may not even notice. Nobody in there eats carbs anyway, and you don't want them to know you were crying. Right?"

I round on him. "How did you know I was crying?"

He takes a step back and pointedly assesses. "Red eyes, and I don't smell weed on you. As a member of the dead-parent squad, I made an assumption."

I remember how Bronte told me their dad died a few years ago. Of course he gets it.

"You know what helps with random bouts of crying?" Gabriel says. "Ice cream." Before I can protest, he's off to the freezer, where he retrieves a giant tub of French vanilla.

"You know this is my house, right?"

"Yes, which is why I'm not stress-sweating about getting fired over this." In a smooth dance-like move, he spins to the left, pulling open a drawer and plucking out the ice cream scoop. He knows my kitchen better than I do.

I forage for spoons while he grabs bowls, and then we sit side by side at the kitchen island and dig in. French vanilla melts on my tongue.

"It doesn't stop," he says, answering a question I never asked. "I'm nearly three years out, and a sappy commercial can get me. Dads helping sons, that sort of thing."

"Something to look forward to. A lifetime of spontaneous crying."

"And ice cream." He *cheers*es with his spoon. Licks the vanilla off, lets it melt in his mouth. "It does get better, though," he says after a minute. Then he seems to second-guess himself. "Kind of. You're a different person, after. Better is relative to who you are now, not who you were. It gets . . . different. More manageable."

I watch him take another bite. A lock of brown hair flops across his temple; he absentmindedly pushes it behind his ear, but it immediately springs loose. I wonder what it would be like to run my hand through it, then flush when he looks up to me staring.

"So, ice cream," I add quickly. "Any other pieces of sage wisdom for what helps?"

He licks the back of his spoon. "Friends. Ice cream, time, and friends." He responds seriously. "And if you're a friend of Bronte's, you're in with me. So call me if you need—especially if you've got mint chip." He pushes the offensively boring French vanilla away, and I laugh.

Then we hear the screaming.

CHAPTER SEVEN

"You son of a bitch!"

"Fuck you!"

Gabriel and I exchange a millisecond of a look before abandoning our bowls for the dining room, where we push through a semicircle of spectators. In the middle of the room: a graying old man in a checkered button-up shirt is half bent over and prepared to charge like a bull . . . into the mayor.

"Sheriff, arrest him. He's trespassing, and this is harassment!" Mayor Bergen shouts in no particular direction.

"I *am* the sheriff!" the old man growls back.

"Not anymore, Dick. Go home. You shouldn't be here." The mayor squares his shoulders. They inch closer to each other, an insult away from a full-on fistfight.

"Great party you have here, Maura. So flattered to not be invited!" the older man hollers.

Who is *this?*

Then Ben pushes into the circle. "Grandpa, come on!"

Ben, grandfather, the mayor . . . This is about the lawsuit.

The next seconds are chaos. Ben's grandfather rounds on the mayor, dropping language and an insinuation so filthy it draws gasps from the crowd, and the mayor finally snaps. He goes to throw a punch, but Ben steps in front of his grandfather, taking a blow to the face. There's a sickening crunch of bone, and glasses knocked askew. Before anyone can even blink, Ben swings back, landing a punch hard to the mayor's cheek.

Holy fucking shit. Ben punched *the mayor.*

"Hey, hey, stop it right now!" Sheriff Morrow appears, pulling Ben gruffly to the side.

"I want them arrested!" the mayor screams, hand pressed delicately to his face, like a big baby. Ben's ignoring his own rapidly purpling eye to look after his grandfather, who has retreated to the corner.

"Bradley, you punched a literal child," the sheriff responds, making no moves to apprehend anyone. "I could arrest *you.* But let's just call it done and everyone walk away."

Maura bustles in, all out of breath. "What on earth is going on here?" She takes in Ben and his grandfather, a tomato-faced mayor, practically apoplectic. "Dick, seriously, this is why you weren't invited. You're like children. Come here, Ben, let me get you an ice pack." Grandmother mode activated, she shoos Ben into the kitchen; the rest of his face goes red as he catches me in the throng. I offer a thin smile and, on humiliating instinct, a thumbs-up.

The party unravels spectacularly after that. The dining room empties, cater waiters begin to clear dishes and furniture. I manage to locate Ben's glasses in the corner, an earpiece bent but miraculously otherwise not broken.

On his way out, the mayor exchanges terse words with Laura Escano—surely, about keeping this affair out of the papers. His wife pauses at the door as her husband thunders down the porch steps. Her eyes are full of pity. "Your grandmother told me what happened to your mom," she says to me. "I'm here, if you ever want to talk. I work in family therapy, with plenty of experience in grief."

"I'm fine, thanks," I say, caught off guard.

"Well, think about it." She squeezes my forearm and trots after her husband, already waiting impatiently at the driver's-side door of a sleek black Mercedes.

Maura's no longer in the kitchen once I'm brave enough to check on Ben. He's a movie cliché, with a giant steak pressed to the left side of his face as he sits on a tall barstool, which an hour earlier Gabriel occupied.

"Here, I found your glasses." I hand them over. "Your black eye will be fun to explain at school on Monday," I say.

Ben groans. "Don't remind me. I'm already a pariah, and now you know I'm a mess. I'll understand if you want to cancel our date."

"Bronte told me about the lawsuit yesterday," I admit. "We all have things in our lives we wish we could change. I don't care."

"You don't?"

"Nope." I put an extra emphasis on the *p*.

Ben lowers the steak with a wince before managing a grimace. I whisper my fingers over his purpling cheek; he angles into my touch. It's intimate, and Ben seems to catch himself quickly. He flinches away.

Right. Way too soon.

But he's searching my face, seeing straight through me, as he does. He takes my hand in his. "I love how you don't care what other people think of you."

I focus on the thrum of Ben's pulse against my wrist, the way he smells mossy, with a hint of pine, like a sturdy, towering red-wood. I drift into his side, allow our thighs to kiss. Think maybe he could be an anchor in this place, even if it's only for this year. Entanglements aren't all bad.

Maybe it's the leftover adrenaline from the fight, or the ice cream sugar high reaching its apex, or just wanting to feel like this forever, but suddenly I'm brave. "Then why don't you take me to homecoming?"

"Seriously?" His good eye goes wide.

"That's what people do, right? Ask girls they like to go to homecoming?"

"Technically, you're asking me."

"Is that a yes?"

I wish I could bottle and get drunk off Ben's lopsided smile, even this half-grimace version of it. "Yeah," he says. "Let's do it."

"Let's. We can plan the details when I see you tomorrow," I say, hopping off my barstool and making for the back stairs. If I linger any longer, the spell might fade, and I want this night, this clusterfuck of a weird day, to end on a good note.

CHAPTER EIGHT

After my butterfly-inducing if surreal movie date with Ben—to watch a nineties cheese thriller, surrounded by my grandmother's fans, in costumes and novelty tees, screaming out lines at the screen—all I can think about is wanting *more*. More of this punch-drunk feel when I'm with Ben, more of being someone's girlfriend. More of being a perfectly normal student at a perfectly normal school and less of being a girl with a recently deceased mom.

One person won't let me forget, though. Monday morning over breakfast, Maura informs me she's scheduled an appointment for me Friday after school with Dr. Shelby. No negotiation. This is grandmother-mandated therapy. Natalie is thrilled; at least, she trills that her mom is the *best* and I'll love seeing her. It's weird that she cares, but maybe it's an act to distract from the news that Ben is taking me to homecoming, which she barely seems to register.

Perhaps to subconsciously make amends, I throw myself headlong into Spirit Week. Into being Natalie's new pet, much to the growing consternation of Morgan. The first few days blur by, with costumes, makeup, and more school spirit than Los Angeles could ever muster. Natalie ensures I'm dressed to the nines each day. I thought it was normal new-girl welcoming, but when we show up on Thursday as Audrey Hepburn clones—her doing *Breakfast at Tiffany's*, me *Funny Face*—the costumes begin to seem like a deliberate diss once Morgan arrives at lunch, her hair dyed brown, doing her best Sabrina. She sends me a look that could curdle milk when I ask her if it's permanent. I wonder if I've been a pawn in a game of chess I didn't know I was playing.

My grounding force and bright shining light all week is Ben. In class, we sneak texts like middle schoolers, developing in-jokes about US presidents and Mr. Keating's penchant for bow ties. He walks me home after school. "It means I get to talk to you longer than a car ride," he says, which makes me fucking melt.

I'm afraid to ruin our bubble, but the guilt of not telling him I'm at Natalie's on a routine basis is gnawing at me. Finally, on the walk home Thursday, my Audrey-esque kitten heels pinching my ankles and putting me in a bad mood, I mention the therapy appointment. Ben hisses air through his teeth, halts midstride, consternation deeply furrowing his brow.

"Why didn't you tell me you were seeing Dr. Shelby?"

"I didn't exactly have a choice. Maura set it up. Is it a problem?"

"...No," he says, but his tone says yes.

I'm suddenly irritated by his attitude. I knew he'd be upset, but this isn't my fault, and I have no patience for cryptic bullshit. "I was already nervous, and you're not making it better. I know you hate their family, but it's therapy, and Dr. Shelby is one of the only therapists in town. What's the big deal?"

Ben groans. "I used to see her. Before my mom died, actually. She was fine. I guess." He scuffs his sneaker on a cracked sidewalk tile, avoids eye contact. "But with a town this small, everyone already knows everyone's business anyway. Going to Dr. Shelby . . . Nothing good can come of it." His face darkens. "It's better not to touch anything having to do with that family."

"That's ridiculous. There's no shame in therapy. I'm sure Dr. Shelby is a professional, and Maura was only trying to help." Now I'm pissed he's making me defend Maura and therapy when thirty seconds ago I didn't want to particularly like either. I stop walking. It takes half a block before he notices.

"Cecelia." He turns back, but his voice is still laced with chill. "I'm only trying to help."

"No, you aren't. This is about you and *your* hang-ups, not me and mine. Some of us want to work through our shit instead of wallowing."

"I'm trying to *protect* you." The emphasis he puts on the word has me seeing red.

"I don't need your protection. It's therapy, not a torture chamber. In fact, I can walk myself home while we're at it. Maybe you haven't noticed, but I'm a big girl."

"Fine," he yells curtly.

"Fine!" I retort, like the petulant child I just insisted I wasn't. But despite my words, I'm surprised when he turns away, leaving me to walk the last half block on my own.

I can't help the frisson of annoyance buzzing in my brain. Not even a week into dating and we're having our first fight. Over something so stupid. The heels dig into my skin as I replay the argument in my head. Now I'm definitely going to therapy, and it is going to be amazing, thank you very much.

✦

I went to bed cursing *Good riddance,* but the morning brings waves of guilt. I'm not the only one with a dead mom, and I know I picked the fight. My queasiness only deepens as the lighthearted text I send about our AP Gov reading goes unanswered. Worry and longing tumble around my insides. I don't want this to be over before it's begun. We were just getting started. Homecoming is so close! The game is tonight, and the dance tomorrow. I want Ben to spin me around the dance floor and kiss me under the moonlight while I'm in a stupidly pretty dress. Maura's promised me something special, and this time I won't look that gift horse in the mouth.

I plan to apologize to him in AP Enviro, but Ben's chair is empty come bell ring and stays that way all period. And it's the same in AP Gov. My fingers hover over my phone. Is his absence because of me? Is it desperate or considerate to send a **you OK?** text?

In the end, with a bracing breath, I think, *Fuck it,* and send.

Ben's text comes back as the bell blares to end the school day.

> Granddad had a bad morning had to stay home to take him to doctor. All good.

Plain and perfunctory.

But then another text comes in.

> Missing you today. Will I see you tonight at the game?

I've barely stopped myself from squealing out loud when Natalie comes up behind me.

"Hey, gorgeous!" She greets me with an air-kiss on each side of my face. It's Spirit Day, not to be mistaken for Spirit Week, which means she's in her full-on cheerleading gear and I'm looking like Barney the dinosaur, in a purple sweater and jeans. "Ready to head to my mom's?" Natalie says.

Right, therapy. "You really don't have to drive me," I say for the eighth time this week. "It's like a five-minute walk, and I don't mind."

"Ten minutes, and I have to go there anyway. The stupid dress salon would only deliver to the town house and not the beach house."

I tilt my head. "You have . . . two houses?"

Here I was, assuming the address Maura gave me for Dr. Shelby was an office. Not Natalie's *town house*. I know she lives in the modernist dream by the beach, but jeez—how rich is she?

"Yeah, Daddy wouldn't give up the house in town because it would hurt his public image or something, and Mom says too many of her clients won't go all the way to the beach house for a session. We're at the beach house most weekends. Though I have the better bedroom there, plus my walk-in closet, so I'm there during the week a lot, too. You'll see!"

"I will?"

"Oh yeah, it's easiest if you come with me to the beach house after your session, and then I'll drive you back to school for the game. Unless you have a reason to go home first." She frowns. "I could take you there, but it'd be pretty tight."

I think about seeing Ben at the game tonight. What I'm wearing is so basic, if appropriately signaling school spirit. I push a greasy lock of hair behind my ear, flushing with shallow shame. I look *fine*.

Natalie takes my silence as assent, linking our arms together as she pulls me toward the parking lot. As we reach the front of the school, I see them. Maura's . . . *fans.*

"Oh my God, it's the granddaughter! Cecelia! Cecelia, over here!" Chris from the murder tour beckons me over to what, on first glance, looks like a picket line. But it's just the line at the curb, beyond which I'm guessing they cannot go during school hours. Luke mentioned something about how he can only run tours after school. There's maybe twelve people in the cluster.

"Don't bother her, Chris," someone pipes up. It's the vintage-glam chick, also from the murder tour. Today's outfit is a Peter Pan–collared salmon-pink sweater set paired with navy culottes.

"I'm Reama Ayad." She thrusts out her hand, and on instinct I shake it. Immediate regret spreads through me. I've opened the door now. They'll feel entitled. And, indeed, *entitled* is an apt word for Reama. "I run the biggest Maura fan blog on the internet." She tosses her silky dark hair over her shoulder, smug. "I get over one hundred and fifty thousand hits a year. I would love to interview you. You're a real surprise to the fandom. We had no clue Maura had a granddaughter."

"Don't lie, Reama." Another one of the fans, a petite white woman in a Michigan hoodie, offers a snort of derision. "You shouldn't trick the poor girl into being a source for one of your exposés."

Reama purses her lips into a hard line, her thick, natural eyebrows arching. "I mean, of course we were aware that your mother had a child. But to think that you're seventeen and could give even the best Melinda cosplayer a run for their money. The boards have so many questions about where your mother disappeared to all those years, the life you've had."

Chris chimes in, eyes shining wistfully. "And now you get to live here in Seaview with *her*. Any of us would kill to be adopted by the queen of mystery."

White heat flashes through me, rage racing up my esophagus like a herd of fire ants. I want to tell him exactly where to shove his envy of my situation, but Natalie proves a capable wingwoman, steering me away right on cue.

"Cecelia has better things to do than waste her time on pathetic cosplay. Go stalk some other Weston nostalgia site and stop creeping on kids." Natalie practically sneers at the crowd, as though daring them to follow. "And enjoy your *blog*," she tosses over her shoulder with a singsong derision.

Natalie may be harsh, but I find I don't mind when she is on my side.

✦

The Bergens' town house is a two-story cream Craftsman trimmed in sage green, with a gorgeous oak in the front yard that fills it with shade. Natalie breezes through the front door ahead of me, dropping her purse onto a waiting side table, and gestures to a receiving room to my left before heading toward the kitchen. "Hit the button on the door over there and wait until she calls you. Come up to my room when you're done."

I'm left to guess where said room is, but that's a later problem. For now, I do as instructed, pressing my finger to a doorbell to the right of a barn-style sliding door before stepping back to survey the sitting room. The house has been lovingly restored, dark walnut window frames and columns gleaming. There's a built-in window seat next to recessed bookshelf panels boasting beachy knickknacks amid a collection of dry clinical tomes mixed in with pop psychology books. The title *NurtureShock* catches my eye, and I pull it off the shelf and flip to the front flap.

There's a soft whir behind me, then a gently clearing throat; I whip around, fumbling the book in my hands, to find an older, somehow more attractive version of Natalie waiting. I didn't study her closely at the party Saturday. It's just unfair, that Natalie's destined to become more attractive as time goes on, if her mother is any indication. Some people are so pretty their beauty acts like a balm to set you at ease, and Dr. Shelby's is a soothing, perfectly symmetrical face I am fine to open up to.

I realize I'm still holding the book. "Sorry," I say, sliding it back into its place with some haste.

"Don't apologize. That's what the books are there for. I'm only sorry to not have given you proper time to browse. There's something lovely about the space in between things, when we can let our minds wander, take new ideas in."

How the hell did such a Zen creature birth the type-A Natalie? Guess she takes after her father, beyond her blue eyes and pointed chin.

Dr. Shelby steps backward into her office, exuding calm, as she directs me toward a brown leather two-seater couch that faces a matching armchair. Mild disappointment swoops through me.

"First time in therapy?" Dr. Shelby asks. "Everyone remarks on the pedestrian couch. Not what the TV shows promise, eh?"

"Sorry. Yeah. Though everything else is pretty much bang on." I gesture around the room. Wide windows throw sultry late-afternoon light onto built-in bookshelves along the inside wall, a sleek desk and iMac bookended by bougie filing cabinets behind Dr. Shelby's chair, and an ornate fireplace between the windows.

"Shall we get started?"

Her question is simple enough. It expands. Fills the room.

It's big, beginning.

Beginning means I have to acknowledge an end.

And then Dr. Shelby asks me to articulate my hesitation.

And like that, I am officially in therapy.

CHAPTER NINE

Natalie's room turns out to be easy to find. Simply follow the trail of photos of her up the stairs and down the hall to an airy pink-and-white room tucked under an eave that faces the spacious backyard. Hers is a pretty-princess bedroom with a horsey flair, and I think, *Of course she's a horsey girl.* Champion jumper, too, judging from the ribbons.

I find her typing away on her iMac keyboard; I'm mildly surprised to see it's an older model. But it fits in with the rest of the room. Pointedly dated.

Natalie reads my mind. "It's frozen in time, I know. I haven't bothered with redecorating since middle school. I only drop by here when Mom insists on dinner after a long day of sessions. Wait until you see my room at the beach house. Daddy gave me the upstairs master, since they have the master here."

"Are your parents separated?" I try to parse how having two houses works. Is this one just for shits and giggles? Or, I suppose, for therapy but not for living.

Natalie snorts, avoids the question, instead volleying with her own. "How was the session with Mommie Dearest?"

I can't tell if the moniker is ironic or if she's never seen the movie and doesn't know. "It was good," I say. "I'm new to, uh, talking about my emotions, but I don't think I completely fucked it up. Though I did feel silly some of the time."

"Everyone's kind of wary in the first session. You'll warm up. Spill all your juicy secrets. Anyway." She turns off her monitor and sprints over to me by the door. "The game starts in less than an hour, so shall we? I just have to grab my shoes and a purse from the beach house."

We cruise the two miles to the beach with the windows of Natalie's Audi rolled down, letting crisp ocean air tangle our hair and salt our lips while we belt Dua Lipa with abandon. If I thought Natalie's first house was impressive, it's got nothing on her beach house, the redwood-and-concrete modernist wet dream from Maura's driving tour of Seaview. And windows. So many fucking windows. Natalie lives in a magazine spread.

"You haven't even seen the inside," Natalie says off my slack-jawed expression. "Or the private beach."

"Not for long, though, right?" I think about the managed-retreat proposal. I looked it up on the city website. If I understood it right, they'll be repermitting everything so they can bulldoze and create safer, public beaches.

"We're fine. The Coastal Commission report says our beach should see slower erosion. Plus, there will be all sorts of preexisting-structure clauses built into that thing that protect houses like ours. Private will stay private for the most part. It's people who bought tacky McMansions next to public beaches who will get forced out."

"This isn't a McMansion?"

"Uh, this is a Bernardier house, not a cookie-cutter nouveau riche soulless stucco box. We only have to save enough of the beaches to make people happy. That's politics. Give a little, but never yours, and then take what you want."

I like Natalie, but the phrase *Eat the rich* rattles in my mind.

The inside is even more decadent. Vaulted cedar ceilings, herringbone hardwood floors, a sprawling open-plan layout, with living room, dining room, and great room cascading off each other back, back, back, in a straight shot to an ocean view. It's nauseatingly amazing.

Upstairs, Natalie has the master suite with no less an awe-inspiring ocean view. This is the polar opposite of her other bedroom. No trappings of juvenile memories affixed to corkboards or first-place trophies crowding bubble-gum-pink-painted book-shelves. No pink to be found at all. In fact, apart from a string of fairy lights interspersed with clothespinned photos, there's little personal clutter. This is a very grown-up bedroom.

I debate sitting on the expansive California king, but I worry my grubby jeans will dirty the blinding-white sheets. Instead, I follow Natalie to the walk-in closet. Which is like something out of a movie. Natalie is standing in front of a wall of rectangular cubbies, each containing a designer pair of shoes, until finally she selects a towering pair of silver-sequined stilettos.

"Sorry about the mess," she says, plucking a single black band tee from Urban off the floor and swishing it into the laundry basket.

"Uh, no, it's perfect."

She dangles the shoes off the end of her fingers, narrows her eyes at me. "You wanna come over tomorrow before the dance? We can pregame, and I can do your makeup. Lend you a pair of shoes, if you want. Do you have a dress?"

"My grandmother said she has something for me."

Natalie twists her nose in disapproval.

"You can borrow one of mine as backup, if it ends up being hideous. Want me to do your makeup now? We have a bit of time."

She doesn't even wait for my reply before snagging a hulking makeup case from the bathroom vanity and sweeping me over to the bed. I cringe, eyeing my jeans, but I dutifully sit.

There's that sense again, like I'm Natalie's latest pet. A Chihuahua tucked into her purse, until I fall out of fashion and she moves on. But the glow of her interest right now is intoxicating. That I could touch, even for one night, the things she has and takes for granted.

In a whir of brushes that dip into palettes, swirl, tap, and then swish over my skin, Natalie renders me her doll. As she's finishing off my lids with a finger glimmering with a rose-gold shimmer shade, she deploys the question, casual yet loaded.

"You really like Ben, then?"

"Uh, yeah, I guess. He's nice," I say.

"I don't know if he's nice." She practically snorts. "But he is fun. A good time."

I think for a moment she must be confused, describing Luke, not Ben. But she's not done.

"Look, elephant in the room—I know Bramber told you everything. Or maybe Ben himself."

Did she . . . just give Bronte and Amber a smushed-together couple name?

Natalie barrels on. "For my dad's sake, I can't be friendly with him. Not in public. That's exactly the kind of thing that could screw him over if there were a recall, or during his next election campaign. But Ben and I, we're cool. We don't hang anymore, but I know you'll have a good time."

Even when she's sincere, Natalie throws me off kilter. "Okay, go look at yourself," she instructs, effectively ending the conversation.

In the bathroom, I take in the final look. Natalie has transformed me into a bombshell: my green eyes sparkle; my mouth quirks into a sultry crimson pout. It's an out-of-body experience, the girl in the mirror someone I barely recognize. I finger my dark waves self-consciously.

Friendships like this feel like a test. Was her giving her blessing on Ben really a trap to ensnare me? Was I supposed to say *Oh, no, I couldn't possibly go out with him if it hurts our friendship!* or thank her profusely for her permission and forge on?

"Come on, let's go," Natalie says. "Coach will murder me if I'm late."

✦

We park in the satellite lot behind the school nearest the field. At the first sight of the squad, Natalie abandons me with a bright "See you later," her pom-poms sparkling in the setting sun. I wander past a brick shoebox of a building with a sign pronouncing it the athletic center, which I think is a fancy way of saying locker rooms.

I round the corner, stadium entry in sight, and there's Ben. Today's tee is Fleetwood Mac with an open flannel shirt layered on top. Boho lumberjack? I'm sure I light up like a Christmas tree.

"Hi," I say, lost for something more clever or winning to say. I've gone goofy, shy. Doubly abashed after our fight yesterday.

"Hi," he returns, pink in his cheeks. "You look . . . Wow."

I'd forgotten about the hot-girl makeover from Natalie. "Thanks."

"Shall we?" Ben's read my mind, it seems. He takes my hand in his and tugs me toward the field, where we stroll close past the band and cheerleaders warming up. I wave hello to Bronte.

"Is your grandfather okay?" I ask Ben.

"What? Oh, yeah, he's good. He must have caught a bug or something. I did still manage to make my shift with Maura. I was disappointed you weren't at home. Did you go straight to Natalie's?"

I'm not fooled by Ben's casual tone.

"Not exactly. I had that appointment with her mom, which is why Natalie gave me a ride over here."

I think about Natalie's house, protected on the beach, while Ben's home was swallowed by the sea. Guilt pangs me for even having brought it up. "Listen, about yesterd—"

"Stop," Ben says. "I was wrong. I know you are smart enough to make your own decisions. I didn't mean to impl—"

"I didn't mean to suggest—" I say at the same time.

We both grin, knowing all is forgiven.

I change the subject. "So are you going to sit with me during the game or what?"

He grins. "As much as I would love that, I actually can't. I have some game-day duties to attend to."

"What are you, the water boy or something? You're a bit too on the lean side to be a football player."

"You checking me out?" He waggles his brows suggestively, and I play coy.

"Maybe."

His laugh surprises me. It comes from his whole body. And his face is aglow, breaking the careful concentration he usually has. I quietly wish for the comedic powers to make him laugh all the time.

"I'll see you after the game. And then tomorrow. But now I do have to go." He's already backing away, clearly deflecting my questions.

"You're not gonna tell me what you have to do?"

Ben spins, his duffel slung over his shoulder, and smiles playfully before disappearing into the crowd.

CHAPTER TEN

The bleachers shake under my feet, vibrate my butt, which is freezing against the bare metal. The staccato drumbeats and the chatter of the growing crowd produce a swelling and ebbing cacophony. Game day. The whole school has turned out for the homecoming game, a showdown between the Seaview Vikings and Bay Town Tigers. Something about the crowd, the noise, the biting cold that forces my fingers into the middle pocket of my purple hoodie is contagious. Intoxicating. Cult leaders use this kind of energy to hook their followers. I half expect the cheerleaders to break for a faith healing at any moment. But, instead, they perform backflips and basket tosses while shrieking "GO VIKINGS!" They far eclipse the rival Tigers squad trying to rally the much smaller crowd from Bay Town in their green and yellow, which makes everyone look a bit jaundiced.

"FUCK YEAH, NATALIE!" Luke booms as she completes a killer-looking basket toss. He and Amber flank me, human space heaters at my side. As Luke rockets to his feet to further cheer our friends on, I gaze longingly at the cushion keeping him from freezing his butt off.

"We can steal it when he wanders off for his halftime hookup," Amber cuts in wryly. "If it goes well enough, he won't come back."

"Hey, first, I can hear you. Second, halftime hookups are a time-honored tradition. And third, I'm not a total asshole. You can have my cushion, Cecelia. Do you want it?"

Unsure if it's a trick question, I weigh my freezing behind against Luke's good favor. My chilled derriere wins.

"Thanks," I say, grabbing the foam. A three-hour home-coming game is not the time to play martyr. Once I'm situated more comfortably, I angle toward Amber. "Are halftime hookups really a thing?" I try to covertly scan the field for Ben. I don't see him. I do see Creepy Chris, however, whose eyes light up when he spots me. I pretend not to see his enthusiastic gesturing and focus my attention back on Amber.

"Uh, the cheerleaders use halftime to eat," she says, "not make out, so it's only a Luke thing, really. Why?"

"No reason," I answer absentmindedly. My eyes are glued to the field. No dice catching Ben, but number 19 is in fine form. Gabriel's hard to miss. My gaze keeps landing on him like a magnet. He's not just quick, darting across the field, but he watches the ball with careful precision. He seems to anticipate where the other team will go before the whistle blows. I may know jack shit about football, but one thing is clear: Gabriel plays with skill. And it doesn't hurt that his butt looks amazing in gold spandex pants.

"Suuuure," Amber teases, and for a second I'm mortified she's caught me ogling Bronte's younger brother, but her focus is somewhere else entirely.

She chuckles. "He's over there." I follow her finger to the left of the cheerleaders, where a giant blond foam Viking head with an equally ludicrous fake muscled body bores into my soul. I feel a sympathetic pang for the poor kid shamelessly gyrating at the crowd.

Amber looks at me expectantly, stifles a laugh. And it hits me.

"Oh no, you are not saying that—"

"Ben Vann is the school mascot?" Amber is outright cackling now. "Yep. Students get paid to do it, and it's good résumé fodder. I almost considered the job myself, but my dignity won out. Fortunately, or look at this *show* we would've missed!"

I do my very best to push down my horror. Caring about what's "cool" is so shallow, passé, but . . . Omg, did he just do a backflip? The crowd is going wild, and the foam Viking head is grinning at me vacantly, and the secondhand embarrassment is simply too much. I'm not sure I'm strong enough to be the school mascot's girlfriend. *At least he's a decent dancer,* I think, as he begins an overexuberant cha-cha slide.

"Here, I think you need this." Luke hands me a travel coffee mug. I slot open the top and get a whiff of spicy warmth. Mmm, hot apple cider. I take a sip and immediately cough through the burn.

"What the hell is in that?"

"Everclear and apple cider," he replies matter-of-factly. "Takes the edge off the cold, no? But go easy. A little goes a long way." He takes the mug back for his own, hypocritical long draw.

Amber nudges my arm, proffering a regular paper cup with slotted top. "Here. This one is just coffee. All the warmth, less of the idiocy." Grateful, I take it, cradling it in my hands and savoring the heat. We share it back and forth as the football team thunders onto the field and everyone—the crowd, the marching band, the cheerleaders—erupts into raucous celebration.

I barely follow along. First downs, yards run, breaks . . . or something? I don't know. Touchdowns are the only things that are obvious, and I shout with everyone else when our team gets one, and maybe a little louder when it's clear Gabriel's run a good stretch. Then the Bay Town Tigers score two. The mood on our side dampens, a tense thread of anxiety and frustration pulling everyone taut.

Two football minutes before the half—which, turns out, means at least ten normal-person minutes, apparently—Luke stands up.

"Okay, I have to go meet Nat on the field for the announcement of the court."

"We'll come with," Amber announces, beckoning me to follow. "I wanna say hi to Bronte."

"Oh, is she running?"

Amber smirks as she shimmies past knobby-kneed freshmen out into the aisle. Then she entwines her arm with mine, and we take the concrete steps two at a time.

"Bronte is too smart for that. This year is Natalie's, and we all know it. Could Bronte win? Yes, and that's the problem."

We come to a stop at the rail separating bleachers from field while Luke jogs ahead to get changed into his suit. My eyes catch on number 19, barreling down the field, closer and closer to the Tigers' end zone. My breath catches . . . and then Gabriel just misses his quarry; the player from the opposing team scores a touchdown that puts the Seaview Vikings behind by another point. We're losing.

But our favorite cheerleader is chipper as ever. Bronte spots us, body glitter gleaming in the stadium lights as she sprints over.

"Hey, babe. Hey, Cecelia! The game's a huge bummer, but did you see the pyramid?"

"You nailed it," Amber says. "That's why you're my favorite flier." And Amber tilts down over the rail, Bronte coming all the way up on tiptoes for a kiss. I step back, knowing when a third wheel should make way.

"Oh, I'm sorry, I—" I turn around to see the person whose knees I've stumbled over and find my therapist.

"Dr. Shelby, hi. Oh, and Mr. Mayor."

The mayor is overdressed for a high school football game—in a crisp white shirt and a blazer. He has the buoyant simper of a politician, but he squints at me with confusion.

"We met the other night at my grandmother's party. I'm Cecelia."

"Oh, right. Of course you are. Enjoy the game." And he goes back to scanning the track with hungry eyes. Probably waiting for Natalie to emerge.

"I cannot *believe* you!"

Our group turns in tandem. Morgan's voice is unmistakable, even over the band. It doesn't take long to spot the problem. Natalie and Morgan are making their way toward us in what appear to be *matching* seafoam-green dresses.

"Come on." Amber grabs me by the hand and tugs me toward the field. I get a closer look at the two competing queens as we thunder down the steep concrete stairs and onto the track. Natalie's hair is somehow perfectly curled, despite having been in a high pony not ten minutes ago, and she is resplendent. Morgan is less glowing. Brunette doesn't suit her. Guess it *was* permanent color.

With the hair and the dress, Morgan exudes a pathetic wannabe-doppelganger vibe. Her handmade dress is sweet, but it can't hold a candle to Natalie's designer tailored, sequined number. What must be real Swarovski crystals are carefully embroidered onto the bodice versus the cheap glittery fabric of Morgan's.

With Bronte in tow, we're careful to approach what is now a full-on fight, though Natalie and Morgan are smart enough to have lowered their voices so the whole crowd can't hear. They're like two cats circling each other before a brawl: Morgan's shoulders hunched up, Natalie's fingers tensed, as if exposing her claws.

"Why are you making such a big deal about this? It's just a dress."

"That's rich, coming from you. '*Don't you dare wear pink, Morgan. That's my color, Morgan.*'" Her Natalie impression is spot-on, if exaggerated. "You know seafoam green was *my* color for this dance."

"You can't own a color," Natalie snipes. "That's childish." She pivots with a perfect pout, addressing us. "I never said that. Can you believe her?"

"You know how little I have," Morgan says to Natalie, ignoring the way Nat is playing to the onlooking crowd. "How much this *means* to me. I had to work and save months for the fabric, spend days on it. You have . . . *everything,* and you had to go and buy the same color, same cut, only . . ."

"Better?" Natalie's voice is dripping with venom as she completes the thought. "Morgan, it's not like it even matters. I have a different dress for tomorrow night."

"So you get to have your procession pictures in that dress and then win in another?"

The quirk of Natalie's lips is smug, bordering on wicked. "You said it."

Morgan's eyes narrow, dagger-thin. "You know, maybe it's someone else's turn to win for once."

"Ladies, ladies!" Luke arrives, arms spread wide as he steps between the feuding friends. "The cars are waiting. Come on. Let's save this for later. We'll get shit-faced, and you can yell it out at my house. Without clothes."

Both girls round on Luke, united in scathing reproach.

"It's a joke," he says, trying to recover. "Let's get this bit over with. The sooner we take a spin and pose for the cameras, the sooner I get to my halftime honey."

"That's a great idea," Morgan says, squaring her shoulders, composing herself. "I have my own hookup to find." Her eyes bore into Natalie's: a challenge. Natalie huffs in response and storms off, but not before snapping her fingers at Luke to follow.

I'm still taking in the scene—*Did she really just snap? An actual snap?*—when Bronte breaks me from my reverie.

"Okay, then," Bronte says. "You guys want to watch from the bench?" And of course we do. We follow her over to where the cheer squad is huddled, their numbers thinned—understandably lots of court hopefuls coming from their ranks.

"Introducing the 2022 homecoming court!" a peppy voice I recognize from the daily announcements shouts over the music. The convertibles approach in an orderly line, each slowing to a crawl in front of the bleachers so the homecoming queen hopeful sitting atop the back seat can flick her wrist like the Queen of England while her escort ensures she doesn't go tumbling over the trunk of the car.

Three couples go by, radiant in powder blue, shimmering black, and toothy white convertibles. They're a stark contrast to Morgan, who looks pained, escorted by Caleb, still in his football uniform. Her seafoam-green dress sparkles under the floodlights, but she's straining to look happy.

"The cars are . . . a nice touch," I say.

Amber snorts. "Meggy Harper's dad owns the local car dealership. That's why she gets to go first, and in the best car, color-coordinated to her outfit. Natalie fucking hates her."

Speak of the devil, Natalie glides by. Unlike Morgan, she has no trouble delivering her best Miss America from-the-elbow wave. She's the last in the procession, as if the true queen has finally arrived. It's easy to picture her in a glittering crown, giving a tearful acceptance speech to the masses. I'm not sure anyone else ever stood a chance.

The cars park before a wooden stage right in front of the cheerleader bench. Bronte, Amber, and I have a front-row seat as each king and queen hopeful lines up at the foot of the stairs waiting to be announced. A yearbook photographer is on hand, snapping couples' pics before Principal Morris calls them up onstage for the big group shot. One by one, the crowd claps and cheers for each twosome until one is left: the shoo-ins for queen and king.

"Natalie Aurora Bergen and Lucas James Rinaldi!"

Luke ascends a step ahead of Natalie, offering a helping hand, which she bats away. She's enjoying the moment too much, pivoting on the first step, waving to the adoring crowd. A coquettish kiss is blown with a wink before she turns around. And then a gasp of shock carries through the crowd as Natalie goes down, hard. There's a loud ripping sound, a strangled cry.

"You tripped me!" Natalie growls, back on her feet in a flash. She jabs her fingers into Morgan's shoulder, sends her reeling a good half foot.

"What? I didn't trip you. I was ahead of you!"

"I felt something tug on my scarf! You fucking bitch!"

Natalie lunges at Morgan, but Luke and Caleb are quick to

step in between them. Luke whispers something into Natalie's ear that makes her turn, face a tomato red—with rage or embarrassment, who can say? Now the crowd is hushed. Then the first giggles begin.

And then Natalie's storming from the stage and off the field, a "Fuck all of you!" flying behind her as Principal Morris sputters at the mic. Luke, Morgan, and Caleb tear off after her, group photo be damned.

"Should we go after them?" I ask Bronte and Amber, but they're as shell-shocked as I am.

"Uh, no," Amber says after a few seconds. "There's enough of them."

Plus I see Natalie's dad making a hasty exit from the stands.

With teeth gritted, Principal Morris yells for the marching band to "Play, dammit," making for an abrupt and uncomfortable start to the rest of halftime.

The energy in the crowd shifts. The drama is over, and there are only fifteen minutes left for bathroom breaks, grabbing snacks, and so on. All that coffee shared with Amber hits me at once, so I excuse myself to find a bathroom. But then she and Bronte join me, saying they need to grab something from Bronte's locker. It takes forever to crawl along the bottlenecked corridor into the parking lot behind the field, and then I leave them at the athletic center. Natalie and co are long gone.

I check my phone. Nearly half my bathroom-break time has been eaten up by pure human traffic. And the line for the ladies' restroom snakes around the back of the stadium. It'll be ages. *I will not pee myself at a new school at the big homecoming game,* I tell myself. *I will find a bathroom. It's a big-ass school.*

I make a dash for the main building to beat the lines. But I'm foiled at the doors abutting the cafeteria; they're locked—likely to keep riffraff like me out after hours. Shit. Briefly I debate the Weston Annex, but I can see that the soaring glass windows in the distance are dark. I dance on the balls of my feet, getting more desperate by the second. Then I remember the pool isn't far. Maybe the doors are still unlocked from this afternoon's murder tour. Luke had bragged earlier about making over fifty dollars in tips. And a chlorine-filled bathroom is better than no bathroom at all.

I race down the field, and . . . success! I find the door to the pool not simply unlocked, but ajar. Cerulean lights refract onto the cinder-block walls. I squint in the dim wattage, the room nowhere near as bright as it was when Morgan and Luke put on their performance. Like a spy on a clandestine mission, I turn on my phone flashlight and use its narrow beam to guide my tiptoes alongside the pool and root out the blissfully line-free bathrooms within.

As I exit the locker room several minutes later, my relief is palpable. I suddenly couldn't care less if we win or lose the football game. Surely no victory could be as sweet as having an empty bladder. I'm swinging my phone beam back and forth to ensure the path is clear of floaties or stray goggles when I catch a dark streak on blue out of my periphery.

Someone's thrown a raft or something into the pool. I narrow in on it, step closer. Less raft, more person-shaped. A CPR dummy in a dress. I know this game.

"Ha ha. Very funny," I say, addressing my prankster. Frankly, I'm impressed that Luke was able to carry off the logistics. He would have had to run from the field to beat me, and known I was coming here.

Wait.

I inch closer to the body at the far end of the pool. A hollow, sour tugging at my navel slows me. The dress is seafoam green. And the "dummy" has hair. They don't normally have that, do they? The hair is a dark-brunette tangle, floating like seaweed. Fear strikes my core.

"Come on, Morgan. You're ruining your dress." I step closer.

Morgan stays put.

"It's not funny anymore." Another step forward. My head swims, dizzy, like I'm drunk. I am outside my body, watching myself approach. I know this sensation. *This isn't happening.*

I notice the Swarovski crystals. *Natalie.* I didn't see her when I came in. How didn't I see her when I came in?

They never tell you what dead bodies look like, how actors on TV can never get it right, because the light in their eyes makes it impossible.

I can't see Natalie's eyes. She's facedown in the pool, unmoving. But I know two things to be true:

There is no beauty in this drowning.

And another Seaview queen is dead.

My scream is swallowed in the glittering, glimmering blue.

CHAPTER ELEVEN

I sleep to forget.

I thought when my mother died I would stay up through the night, wanting to prolong the before from the after. But that night, much like last night after I found Natalie in the pool, I shut down the torrent of emotion with welcomed unconsciousness. I pushed down all the black thoughts, the repeating loops of finding her, running for help, sitting on the curb as police lights flashed across the school parking lot. Watching at a distance when they told her friends. *My* friends.

Morgan is my opposite. I wake to the evidence of her insomnia.

You there? [DELIVERED 2:02 AM]

sorry I can't sleep [DELIVERED 4:18 AM]

Maybe you could stop by the diner tomorrow? [DELIVERED 6:30 AM]

Natalie was her best friend, and I am now the closest person to her death. I can feel Morgan closing in on me like Cling Wrap. She'll want to hash and rehash Natalie's final moments, or at least the moment when I found her. We don't know how Natalie died yet. I have nothing to give her.

I'm dreading my police interview later today. They took my initial statement last night at the school, but Sheriff Morrow warned me to keep a clear schedule.

I pour a quarter pot of coffee into an oversized mug with a Pinterest affirmation emblazoned on the side:

Live, Laugh, Love

I'll pass.

"You want eggs, baby girl?" Maura pushes a plate my way, but the over-easy eggs remind me of ochre walls, and the smell makes my stomach flip.

"No, thanks." I butter a piece of whole wheat toast instead.

Maura does that grandmotherly concern thing, watches me astutely as I chew. "Should I call Dr. Shelby for another session? You've had a real shock—on top of everything you were already dealing with."

"I mean, her daughter just died," I say, "so, uh, I don't know if Dr. Shelby will be seeing patients."

Maura sucks wind through her teeth. "That's right. And the mayor, too. I wonder if he'll step down. The paper speculated."

She slides a copy of the *Seaview Register* across the table, the headline **MAYOR'S DAUGHTER DROWNED** screaming from the front page. On top of the surrealness I was already battling, now there's an actual, physical newspaper to contend with. How retro.

I skim the recitation of facts, measure them against my own murky memories, which my mind is already trying to block out.

SEAVIEW—The body of a student was discovered at Seaview High School last night, police said. The young woman, identified as Natalie Bergen, was the daughter of Mayor Bradley Bergen and prominent child psychologist Dr. Marisha Shelby.

A fellow student discovered the body at approximately 9 p.m. in the school's main building. Bergen, 17, was on the Seaview High homecoming court and, earlier in the evening, had taken part in the procession during halftime of the face-off between the Seaview Vikings and the Bay Town Tigers. The football game was subsequently canceled. A replay date has not been set.

Police did not release any details about the manner of death but did say they are treating it as suspicious.

I catch the byline: Laura Escano, Bronte's mom. I wonder if she'll want to interview me. Not that I'd be much use.

"You don't tell *anyone* what you saw tonight, or I can have you arrested and charged with obstruction," the sheriff had barked at me. His voice was gruff, but I barely noticed as I watched the dancing blue lights of the ambulance cast an eerie glow across the crowd. Like we were all underwater. I wanted to ask why it wasn't a hearse. Natalie was long gone; there was nothing the ambulance could do. But instead the sheriff lectured me about details I had no desire to give anyone, including him.

Natalie's mother wailed a dozen feet from me. When the EMTs wheeled her daughter's body into the back of their vehicle, Dr. Shelby's legs gave way. The mayor caught her, inches before she hit gravel, stony-faced as his eyes swept over the black body bag.

They didn't know what I knew. That the scarf wrapped around Natalie's neck, a gauzy white thing that had complemented her dress as she rounded the field atop that convertible, waving like a goddamn princess—no, like a *queen*—was pulled so tight across her neck it had left indents on her skin. Was it used to strangle her, or to hold her in the water?

My mind has been spinning a dozen scenarios, each more gruesome and horrible than the last. I'm on my second body since September, and I'm crumbling. It's different when you know the deceased.

I finish the article unsatisfied. It refuses to use the word *murder*, when it is obvious to me that's what we have. And here's Maura, sipping her coffee and eating disgusting, runny eggs, saying "poor girl" and "sweet dear," like Natalie's death is some abstract thing miles away from her.

But it's not. It's right here, uncomfortably close.

And it's exactly like *Killer Queen*, as if ripped from the pages of Maura's book.

I boil over. "You know, she was just like you wrote it," I say. Maura's eyebrows furrow. I keep on. "Natalie. Same place, same dress, same—" I stop myself from saying "manner of death," remembering Sheriff Morrow's instruction. "It was like the book," I say instead.

Maura considers me. "I thought you hadn't read the book, dear. Besides, you know I based it on a real murder. It was probably some crackpot copycat who watched the Netflix documentary. Or the poor girl accidentally drowned."

"How do you accidentally drown during halftime, by yourself, in a pool?"

Maura shrugs. "Maybe she was unhappy. I didn't know the girl, Celia."

Suzanne bustles into the dining room, hurriedly breaking our standoff. "Come on, the mayor is making a statement," she says, continuing into the sitting room and switching on the TV.

I don't know what I'd expected. A fancy stage, a background, a podium like press conferences in movies maybe. Instead, the mayor is on his front lawn looking like the world's saddest car salesman. His eyes are rimmed red, but his suit is crisp, his speech prepared. Dr. Shelby stands beside him with a thousand-yard stare.

"My beautiful daughter, Natalie Aurora Bergen, is gone," he begins, his voice shaky but resolute. "I'd like to start by thanking the sheriff and his team for their diligence and care during this difficult time. I have full confidence that they will get to the bottom of my daughter's unfortunate passing." He chokes a bit on that. Euphemisms for death are so strange. Unnatural. Why doesn't he just say *dead*? *Murdered*.

"Natalie was a light in the darkness," he continues. "A shining example to us all. She loved public service, her friends, her school, her community."

Well, she didn't love her friends all the time. I think back to the screaming match with Morgan. I know they're her parents, but between their statement and the article, no one is telling the truth. No longer able to take it, I slip away while Maura and Suzanne aren't paying attention. I head straight for Maura's office. I know she's prickly about me coming in here, but she also did say I could borrow any book I wanted. I locate my copy of *Killer Queen* immediately, still slightly out of sync with the rest of the books on the shelf.

I would've thought everyone—the police, the mayor, the newspaper—would have mentioned the connection to the book. But even though Maura's business is ubiquitous in this town, it strikes me that maybe most people in Seaview haven't actually read her books—except for Morgan. Because it's obvious to me Natalie's death was no accident. I flip open the book to where I left off: homecoming night. I skim until I find the passage.

> She looked so peaceful, floating in her perfect
> white homecoming-queen dress. Her crown
> made a home at the pool's bottom, glinting up
> through the shimmering blue. Melinda held
> her breath, watching the swirl of blond locks
> that fanned out from Cassidy's head like a halo,
> her body sprawled spread-eagled on the pool's
> surface. She wondered: Did Cassidy realize what
> was happening at the moment of her death? She
> hoped not. A shudder passed through her. She
> needed to get help, call somebody. The ceiling
> shook from the mass of bodies in the gym above,
> jumping up and down in unison on the chorus of

a Neil Diamond song. "Sweet Caroline." Melinda thought she might be sick.

Déjà vu. It could be the statement I made to the police deputy yesterday, with minor details changed. Blond instead of brunette. A white dress instead of seafoam green. And Natalie's hair looked nothing like a halo. It's a ham-fisted simile, besides. Dead people aren't angels. They're heavy and waxen and . . . gone.

I read the passage again, but this time I allow myself to do the unthinkable: replay last night. I push against my own instincts and play the scene like a movie reel that I can slow down, rewind, and fully take in. Compare and contrast.

There was no crown. Natalie hadn't won it yet. I read ahead to confirm another detail: yes, in the book Cassidy is strangled with a gauzy scarf from her homecoming getup.

I've covered the obvious, but there has to be more. I close my eyes, prodding through the dark to that place, remembering not just what I saw, but how I felt. Out-of-body, strange. I'd thought Natalie was a dummy. A prank. Why?

The scene felt staged. Just like Morgan's performance at the murder tour. You could easily mistake Natalie for Morgan, because of her hasty dye job. And I did, briefly. If Morgan had still been blond, her resemblance to Cassidy would have been fucking uncanny.

Natalie was killed and staged to echo Maura's book. I'm sure of it. And as my grandmother herself said, that was based on a real murder.

There is a copycat killer in Seaview. The question is, which murder were they copying: Cassidy's or Caroline's? Or both?

Enough. I fear my thoughts now, but they keep coming. An onslaught of the moments after I screamed, the sound so loud, full-bodied, and otherworldly that for a millisecond I forgot it was me. The images unfold in slow motion. Maura superfan Chris runs in. From which direction? The outside door, or from the school? I don't know. His sweater is mint green. *It clashes with the walls,* I remember thinking. He clutches my shoulders in his bony hands and shushes me. Tells me to calm down, it's going to be okay, we'll get someone. He walks me all the way to the parking lot, where we find a security officer. Chris has to explain. My words have left me.

Finally, I shake myself back to the present.

The first person on the scene with me was Maura's *fan.*

"Hey, Cecelia."

I shriek, eyes flying open at the sound of the deep baritone.

It's Ben. Just Ben.

"What are you doing here?" Adrenaline pushes an edge into my voice.

"Internship, remember? I'm assisting Maura today with some research. I would have canceled, considering, but I wanted to see you." He turns sheepish, won't quite meet my eyes. "Sorry if that's too much. I've been thinking about you nonstop since it all . . . but I didn't want to bother you."

"Oh?" Internally, I'm relieved that he didn't send one of the dozens of ignored texts on my phone. I couldn't deal. He'd anticipated I wouldn't be able to.

"Sorry," Ben says. "I just . . . I hate that you had to find her. I keep thinking about how awful that must have been for you. I found my mom. And I imagine you saw yours. . . ."

"Yeah," I say. A smile pushes at my lips. "Thank you for caring.

You know the last thing I would ever want to do is pull focus from Natalie's family. Ring theory, you know?" Ben nods. We both understand the reference: the person closest to a death is allowed whatever emotions they like, but those outside shouldn't dump their own emotions and issues onto that person. I'm glad I don't have to explain.

"What are you doing with that?" Ben points at the book. I snap the paperback shut. Ben's face is open, curious. Nonjudgmental. Still. I hesitate, thumbing the pages and creating a breeze on my face.

"Have you read this?" I hold the book aloft.

He tilts his head to the side, bemused. "Of course I have. I'd be a pretty shitty intern if I hadn't read Maura's books. Plus, I'm from Seaview. It's practically a requirement."

"Well, I seem to be the only one who is stating the obvious about what's going on. Surely they told her father."

"What do you mean?"

"It's a copycat murder. And one of Maura's creepy superfans was *there*, Ben. He was there, right after I found her. That's gotta mean something, right?"

Ben squints, like he's lost the plot. "Wait, *who* was there?"

"Chris! That guy you interrupted talking to me last Saturday. Peach sweater."

One week ago seems like an age.

"Business Card Guy?" Ben's putting it together but still looking at me sideways, as if he's unsure I'm all there.

"Yes!" I'd forgotten about that. Where did I put that card? Jeans pocket? Backpack? Both are upstairs. I'm halfway out the door before Ben stops me midstride.

"Where are you going? Slow down. Hold on. What's going on?"

I'm a million miles ahead of him. He'll just have to catch up. "Come on. His card is in my room."

I take the stairs two at a time, sprinting all the way up, with Ben on my heels. I find the card in the front pocket of my jeans. His Instagram handle—@thrillschillsbills—is easy enough to find, and I can see from his Stories that he was at Hotel Seaview as of an hour ago, enjoying a Continental breakfast.

Turning on my heel, excited by the chase—somewhere to start!—I notice Ben dazed in the doorway.

"Let's go," I say, grabbing my purse.

"What are we doing, exactly?"

I grin. Confusion looks good on him.

"Solving a murder."

CHAPTER TWELVE

Nothing puts a damper on a fancon more than a police presence. A cruiser sits in the porte cochere with a strained valet perched nearby, itching to move it. A wash of relief passes over his face as he realizes Ben and I are on foot. We parked on a side street.

Hotel Seaview bridges the gap between town square and beach, looming on the edge of the boardwalk like a Victorian mirage. It towers in gleaming white wood, with a spray of windows, like freckles on a face, and a warm cherry-brown roof sitting on top of the main spire. Inside, dark beams hold up a soaring ceiling. A wraparound rail reveals the second floor. But beyond all that architectural class, the décor is decidedly . . . kitsch. As though a sea shanty threw up, then collected dust for twenty years.

I'm equal parts bummed and vindicated to see the sheriff and his deputies at the hotel; seems I am not the only one to connect the murder scene to Maura's books. But it means they may have beat me to Chris. For a second, the reasonable side of my brain questions if it's healthy—safe, even—for me to throw myself into a murder investigation. Perhaps not. Still, this feels right. It's forward action. Doing something.

Ben startles at the door, observing Deputy Shields warily. I assess her from a different angle. Last night at the school when she took my statement, it was too dark to make out all the details of her features, but today I can see she's startlingly young—can't be much older than I am. She's Indigenous; she has high cheekbones, large brown eyes, and a Kewpie doll mouth. She's pretty. From the way Gabriel's grinning at her across the reception desk, I think he must agree. Not that I care.

I grab Ben by the arm and tug him into the lobby. He dragged his feet all the way here—metaphorically, since he drove—and now he's acting even less enthused. Too bad. I rush us past hotel check-in, looking for the con welcome table and, in the process, glimpse again the object of Deputy Shields's attention: Gabriel. I increase my speed double-time, hoping he doesn't see me—or us, really.

After tucking us into an alcove under the stairs, I check Stories. Chris was at a panel called "The Wicked World of Weston" twenty minutes ago. I spot a lone woman at a folding table with a black tablecloth thrown over it about a dozen yards away. Thirty-something, she sports shoulder-length dark-brown hair with a tasteful teal underlayer, a black con shirt, and a bored expression. There's no missing the slew of paraphernalia on the table—badges, lanyards, and brochures—which I'm hoping also includes a schedule and map. And you can't miss the sign:

BADGES REQUIRED TO ACCESS CON SPACES.
WE WILL CHECK. YES, WE MEAN YOU.

Time for a charm offensive.
I saunter up to the table and read the woman's badge.

Hi, my name is:
Diana Martinez
@hrhweston

I sense Ben following behind.

"Hi, Diana! I'm not registered, but I'm hoping you can help me?"

Diana turns from listless to on guard. She knows I'm about to bullshit her. Time to bring out the big guns. "I'm Maura's granddaughter, and *this* is her assistant." I indicate Ben, but when I turn to him, I see he's hesitating. None of that. We have to play happy couple. Two perfectly normal-looking and Maura-connected people are better than one.

I link our arms and pull him level with me. "We were hoping we could get a copy of the con schedule for her?"

Diana's spine straightens, and her eyes spark wide. "Oh my God, hi! Sorry I was grumpy. We've had a few reporters this morning, nosing in about . . . well." She jerks her head in Deputy Shields's direction. The young deputy is giggling with delight at something Gabriel's said. I resist the urge to roll my eyes.

"What's going on with that?" I ask instead, playing dumb. "Why are the cops here, I mean. I understand a girl died." Understatement of the year.

Diana leans in conspiratorially. "I don't know why exactly, but they got here about an hour ago, demanding our registration records and to interview attendees. They're waiting for the hotel to provide an interview room, and our head of con is trying to track down our lawyer so we can cover our asses."

Aha! I may have my chance with Chris after all, thanks to the con slowing them down and demanding a consult with a lawyer. The sheriff must have forgotten: These people literally devour crime fiction. They're not stupid. And perhaps one of them is too smart.

"Oh wow," I say. "So about that schedule?"

"Oh, yes! Let me get that for you!" She reaches down into the hidden recesses under the table and hands me a whole-ass program book. I thumb through it and am instantly overwhelmed.

"Actually, maybe you can just tell me where to go. I'm looking for someone at 'The Wicked World of Weston' panel? For Maura," I add hastily.

"That's on the publishing track," Diana says, and before I can beg for something more specific, like a page number, she grabs my program and opens it to a double-spread. "Map is on page five, but it's down one level, and look for the White Alder room. Elevator's over there, but it's old and slow as hell. I recommend the stairs."

"Thanks," I call, already moving away.

"Did you understand any of that?" Ben asks as we make for the stairs.

"We'll figure it out."

As we reach the landing, Sheriff Morrow strides into the lobby, with a person I assume is the hotel events manager, and they're making a beeline for his deputy. "Shields! Let's go!" the sheriff orders. I can't hide my smirk as the deputy jumps away from Gabriel like a kid caught with their hand in the cookie jar. But then Morrow swivels our way. His eyes widen with recognition, and he calls out my name. Before I'm able to respond, Ben grabs my hand.

"Come on!" We fly down one flight to the conference level and burst onto the landing in a fit of giggles. We draw stares from a few stray con-goers loitering outside the vendor hall—I hope because we're acting like idiots, not because they recognize me.

"Why are we running?" I ask Ben.

"Because it's fun."

"Why are you game, all of a sudden?" I say, breathless and giddy.

Ben shrugs, ducks his head shyly. "It's like going on an adventure with you. I think you wanting to interview a possible killer is bonkers, but as you seem determined, it's better if you're not alone."

Heat floods my cheeks as I stare straight ahead. I squeeze his hand tightly in mine. We don't want to linger. The elevator dings to our right, and as we slip down the hallway, I overhear Sheriff Morrow tell Deputy Shields to start taking alibis in the vendor hall.

According to the program book, the conference center is a giant L, and the publishing track is at the tail end of it. It quickly becomes apparent that all the conference rooms are named after trees. We pass Buckeye, Box Elder, Gray Pine, Giant Redwood, Black Walnut. It is the most NorCal thing I can imagine.

We arrive at White Alder just as the panel is letting out. I catch an easel next to the door with the schedule. There's a fifteen-minute break until "High-Stakes Settings" begins. Ten people file by, but no Chris.

Someone grabs me by the elbow, yanks on my arm *hard*.

"Hey, let go of her!" Ben bellows, and I whirl around to find Chris, all shell-shocked puppy in a lavender pullover. He really loves pastels.

"Sorry," he says to me. "I just wanted to say hi. So great to see you here." He's stepped back, but there's a tilt to his posture, like he yearns to come closer.

Even though I came here to find him, I am creeped out by Chris's sudden appearance. Instinctively I stick my hands in my pockets so he can't shake them this time. Ben hovers close, ready to play protector. If it weren't so regressive, I'd find it cute.

"I've been so worried about you since last night."

"Er, yes, I wanted to talk to you about that, actually."

Chris might as well be five and just informed that I got him a pony. He steers me into White Alder, now mostly empty but for a straggler or two staying put for the break. I'm relieved others are here. The three of us sit in the back row, by the water table. Chris offers me a plastic cup, but I decline.

"You know I'm a licensed psychotherapist, Cecelia," he says, his voice low and soothing. "What you experienced last night must have been a huge shock."

He reminds me of Dr. Shelby for a millisecond, before transforming.

"Did you know her?" he says. "The victim? I hear her name was Natalie. How good a look did you get at the body? Anything jump out at you?"

I am caught off guard. I thought *I'd* be asking the questions, but Chris's insistence has disarmed me. Suddenly, I am back to the parking lot last night. Vulnerable and scared.

"You have a lot of questions about something that's none of your business," Ben chimes in, saving me. "Weird that you were there at all. Cecelia says you were first on the scene last night after she screamed."

Ben tips forward in his chair, going for a tough-guy act, but it's diminished by the fact our chairs are all in a row. I worry he might fall out of his.

"I was. I'm just so glad I was there. Imagine if I hadn't been, you know?" Despite his gossipy bravado, Chris radiates sincerity. I find myself able to breathe again. I don't know what I expected. A confession? An evil laugh? I go for broke.

"Why were you there, though? You had no reason to be down by the school, or at the game at all. You're a massive Maura fan, and then you're right there when I discover a body that's just like in her book. Why?"

Chris's mouth forms an O of surprise. Ben and I tense, our two-man operation trying to predict Chris's next move. Would he flee? Could he hurt us? Were we wrong to try and get this close?

Then Chris's face falls into a wince, and he exhales with contrition. He fishes his hand into his cross-body messenger bag, pulling out a giant sheaf of paper.

"It's my novel," he says. "I wanted Maura to read it. I thought if I got close to you, you could put in a good word. I followed you last night. That's why I was at the game. Why I chatted you up at the pool last week." He thrusts a manuscript toward me and I catch the title page. *Death by Therapy by Chris Wang*, it reads. "It's a murder mystery, of course. About a, um, therapist. Maura might really like it, and if she does, maybe she could send it to her agent."

"Dude. Not the time," Ben cuts in, firm but with undertones of amusement.

I myself have to push down the chirp of an incredulous laugh. This is absurd.

"So you followed me from the football stadium to the school, and what? Waited outside?" I find myself oddly grateful he didn't follow me into the bathroom.

"Yes," he confirms, as though that were an entirely normal thing to do. "And then I heard you scream, so I rushed inside. I didn't see anyone, though. It was dark."

Chris pauses, seems to chew on his own memory. "Wait, you think one of Maura's fans did this? And you came here because you suspect me?" His laugh is sharp, cold. "Honey, I am not the cuckoo-crazy fan you're looking for. There are some psychopathic bitches in this fandom, trust me, but I'm not who you want."

He drops his voice, casts down his gaze. "It's actually not a bad theory, if you ask me. I've certainly wondered before if some of the fans were using Maura's books as . . . a primer."

"A how-to for . . . killing someone?" Ben throws a metric ton of skepticism into his tone.

"And get away with it. Not all of Maura's books end with the killer behind bars. Some of the best ones have an unsettling ending," Chris affirms. "Though of all of them, Cassidy was the sloppiest. The teacher was pretty obvious. Teachers and students is an overdone trope."

"Well, in real life, it wasn't the teacher," I hear myself say—echoing Morgan. "It was the janitor." I truly think about it for the first time: what happened fifty-two years ago. Like everyone else, I've been focused on Maura's story—hyperfocused. What about the real murder? The original.

I rise to leave, but Chris catches my arm.

"The person you want to look into is Reama Ayad. She was on the tour with us. Tall, dark hair, thinks it's the fifties. *Obsessed* with the books and every detail in them. If anyone could take it too far, blur the line between reality and fiction, it's her. Find out if she skipped last night's ball, too. Went to the school instead."

Like you, I think. But then Chris blanches, staring over my shoulder. I whip around, expecting the looming figure of Reama, but it's the diminutive Deputy Shields in the doorway.

"Mr. Wang, will you come with me?"

Her eyes flit over to me and Ben, drawing a frown. Chris audibly gulps before hupping to, though not without dropping his manuscript in my lap before I can protest or shove it back at him. And then my phone buzzes. Another text from Morgan.

> We need to talk. In person.
> I'm at Quinn's. Can you come?

I show Ben the text, and we share a nod, rising to leave. The deranged-fan angle may still have legs, but Chris's tip about Reama will have to wait. At least Quinn's is close.

Deputy Shields is loitering outside, nose pinched with disdain. Sea salt and must cling to the air of the narrow hallway. I notice the nearby bathrooms and assume Chris is inside.

"You shouldn't be here." Deputy Shields squares her shoulders, affects a power pose.

"You moonlighting with con security?" Ben asks, making a show of looking for her nonexistent con badge.

"Why were you talking to him?" she persists, ignoring Ben, lasering in on me.

"Ben and I were just passing through."

"Well, keep going. This is official police business, and witness tampering is a crime."

She's mostly bravado, her authority undermined by the scant few years separating us.

And yet . . . witness tampering sounds not good.

We'll back off. For now.

Next time I'll need to be more careful. Because I'm only getting started.

CHAPTER THIRTEEN

Quinn's is crowded. Amber's mom is on shift, flying between stuffed booths, cluttered four-tops, and the main counter. A party of five at the empty hostess counter glares at a solitary figure monopolizing a corner booth: Morgan.

We join Morgan at the table, where she is drowning herself in a milkshake. *Bold for breakfast,* I think, until I check my phone and discover it's after eleven. I resist the urge to order more coffee and instead help myself to a glass of water from the pitcher on the table.

"You okay, Morgan?"

Morgan rakes her gaze up from the frozen-strawberry confection. If she's surprised to see Ben here, she doesn't say. Instead, she shrugs.

"Sorry for all the texts last night," she says to me. "I was hoping someone would be awake. I kept having nightmares."

The nightmares won't stop. But now's not the time to tell her that.

Morgan considers us. "You got here fast."

"We were across the street," I say. "Good timing. What did you need to talk about in person?"

She cranes her neck, assessing the nearest tables for familiar families, turns back to us, looking to Ben with a frown. Shit.

"I can leave," Ben offers, sliding a few inches to the right.

"You being here might be perfect, actually," she says. "You work for Maura, right?"

"Yes?" Ben has a deer-in-the-headlights kind of look. "I'm her intern, technically. Gives me an excuse to hang around, learn the ropes."

"But you've read the books." Morgan is insistent.

"Of course."

I jump in, breathless. "You think it's a copycat."

"Yes!" Morgan's eyes shine with tears. "My mom keeps trying to calm me down, but she doesn't understand. Amber told me how you found her. She wasn't supposed to, but I made her."

"They haven't released the details publicly, but people are going to catch on. We saw the sheriff at Hotel Seaview, interviewing people at WestonCon. It's pretty obvious."

I hesitate. Should we tell her about Chris?

Morgan shakes her head. "No, you don't understand. They think they're simply solving a murder and won't listen to me. I spoke to Sheriff Morrow this morning. He dismissed me as some silly kid."

"Why?" I ask, at the same time Ben says, "You did? About what?" Morgan checks all around her again, beckoning us in closer. We both come down as tight as the table will allow. Morgan drops her voice nearly to a whisper.

"Natalie wasn't supposed to die. It was me. They were trying to kill *me*."

Morgan's confession is a physical thing, exploding like a bomb that pushes and carves out its surroundings. I spring back so fast my head hits the seat cushion behind me. Ben knocks my water glass over with his arm. Silverware clatters to the floor.

"You don't believe me?" Morgan's lower lip wobbles.

I'm torn between frantically grabbing for napkins to dry my now-soaked lap and reassuring her. "No, it's not that. It's just . . ." I give up on triaging the damp spot. "It's a shock. Right, Ben?"

But he scoffs at the idea. "That's absurd. You think someone *accidentally* drowned the entirely wrong person? How?"

"It's not *absurd*," I say, irritated I didn't consider the idea first. "When I found Natalie, I . . . I thought it was you." Morgan flushes. I continue making my case to Ben. "Think about it. Morgan and Natalie were dressed a lot alike. If it was a fan trying to act out some fucked-up fanfic, it would have been easy to mix them up. They only saw the homecoming court from the stands."

Morgan is nodding along like she's hypnotized.

"You told the sheriff you think you were the intended victim?" Ben asks, not yet convinced.

"Yes! And I told him I need protection, because I'm not safe. They're going to realize they got Natalie by mistake. Because of the hair." She tugs on a brunette beach wave and gives a high-pitched whine. "Why did I dye my stupid hair? It's obvious what happened."

"It's . . . compelling," I finally say. "How *did* you two end up in near-identical dresses?"

It's a coincidence piled on top of a coincidence. Could Morgan have really been the target? Natalie or Morgan. Morgan or Natalie. This murder investigation just got more complicated.

Morgan grimaces. "I don't know," she eventually says, a little too evenly. "But from behind, we'd look the same."

Almost. I'd spotted those Swarovski crystals easily enough. But perhaps someone with a murderous agenda, high on the adrenaline of the hunt, wouldn't notice. They'd only see a seafoam-green gown and long dark hair.

"What if they realize they got the wrong person and come after me now?" Morgan whines. "They could try again tonight. The actual night of homecoming."

"The dance has been canceled," Ben throws in.

"I know," Morgan says. "But *symbolically*."

"I'm sure if the sheriff didn't take it seriously, it's because they know something we don't," Ben says.

I can tell he's trying to reassure Morgan. Which is sweet, but I'm not so sure. It's a tiny town. . . . Does Morgan really think the sheriff's department has a protective detail available?

"Like Cecelia said, they're interviewing everyone at Weston-Con, so if it was a fan of the books, they'll catch them," Ben adds. "I wouldn't worry." He reaches across the table to pat Morgan on the hand.

Morgan isn't placated. "I'm not *stupid*. There's a whole other possibility. A worse one."

My brain has been clicking together the pieces Morgan's working with. Things I've wondered, too. "The book was based on a real murder," I supply.

Morgan nods emphatically. "Of my great-aunt. Who I look a lot like. When I'm blond, at least." Morgan drops her voice to a whisper. "I know nobody talks about it in this town, but my grandpa thinks Joe Bedecki is innocent."

"Who's Joe Bedecki?" I ask as Ben draws in a sharp breath. He and Morgan share a look. Yet another Seaview secret.

"The janitor," Ben says. "The killer," he adds for my benefit. "He was convicted. They found evidence in his office. A pair of her panties."

"Panties?" He gets a healthy dose of side-eye from me.

"That's how they put it on true-crime shows," he mumbles.

"Who did your granddad think it was?" I narrow in on Morgan.

"I don't know. He just always rants about it, though only when he gets really soused. Like on Thanksgiving. Super Bowl. Times like that."

"Wait, he's *alive*?"

"Uh, yeah, of course. He was Caroline's younger brother. He's like sixty-five."

For some reason, when thinking *fifty-two-year-old murder,* I envisioned something far away, untouchable, under glass. Like one of those cold-case documentaries full of black-and-white images and slow-motion reenactments. But of course Maura was there, too . . . and I live with her. The people in this town are closer to Caroline Quinn's murder than I realized.

Morgan's phone rings, and she picks up, already sliding out of the booth.

"Caleb, oh my God, hi. I have to tell you my theory!"

She heads outside the diner to take the call, leaving Ben and me alone. In an alternate reality, it could be a date. Instead, here we are, sitting stiffly side by side, investigating a murder—possibly *murders.*

"So what's next?" Ben inquires. "What are you thinking?"

"Reama," I reply. "The fan Chris mentioned. We have to get back into WestonCon, ask around."

"Deputy Shields wasn't happy to see us there."

"It's a public place. For all she knows, we're huge fans checking out the con. We'll be careful."

"You're serious about all this?" Disapproval tugs his mouth down.

"Yeah, why?"

"It's just . . . are you actually planning to, what? Investigate Natalie's murder? Why? You barely knew her. Barely know any of us, really. You've only been here two weeks."

"Less than two weeks, technically," I crack, seeking a bit of levity. I'm nervous, trying to put words to what's been driving me since the beginning.

But then I decide to lay myself bare. To trust that Ben will understand. "It's something I can do. Natalie was murdered. It's not cancer, or a house collapsing, or some other horrible, awful thing that sometimes happens and you have to accept it and move on. Someone *did* this. And I can do something about it. Help Natalie find justice." I search his face for understanding. "You didn't throw yourself into something as a distraction after your mom died?"

"Nothing as weird as a murder investigation, no. But . . . I guess I get that." He exhales deeply, dramatically. I brace myself for his reaction, but then he blesses me with that brilliant lopsided grin. "Look, I'm happy to be your girl Friday on this one, but I'm going to need more coffee. You want?"

"Yes, please. With soy creamer and two sugars."

"Uh, don't think they do fancy creamers, but I can get you some half-and-half."

"That's good. Thanks."

While awaiting my caffeine fix, I let my mind wander back to the matter at hand. Morgan's not wrong. A stranger could have easily mistaken Natalie for her.

But that makes it all the harder. There's not only the motives for why someone would want to kill Natalie to consider, but why someone may have really been after Morgan all along. I track through it in my head.

Morgan is the one with a double connection to both fictional Cassidy and the very real Caroline. If I were going to commit a murder based on either one, Morgan would be the perfect victim.

Then there's her grandfather's theory.

A few seconds with Google on my phone, and I've got a page of search results for "Joe Bedecki." His last appeal was twenty years ago. There are a few mentions of him in anniversary pieces, reviews of the Netflix documentary, and an article on an old crime blog with photos from back then. And I hate to admit it, but 1970 Joe was a snack.

Was Joe a patsy? If he didn't kill Caroline Quinn, the real culprit could still be alive—and in Seaview. But can you copy your *own* crime?

I have so many new questions: If Natalie's death *is* connected to the original Seaview killer, why did they wait so long to kill again? Why choose Natalie as their victim—and why *before* homecoming? If the symbolism involved the homecoming queen, they were a day too early. Queen presumptive isn't exactly the same.

"I see your brain literally ticking," Ben muses. He has returned with two white mugs in hand, both with faded gold Quinn's logos etched on them. "I ordered us grilled cheese and soup, as well."

"What if I don't like grilled cheese?" I tease as he slides in next to me.

"I stalked your Instagram. Paired it with tomato basil and everything."

"Thank you," I say, flattered he'd look me up. I warm my hands around the hot mug and then walk Ben through my jumble of thoughts. All the potential threads. We land back on Joe Bedecki.

"You didn't seem surprised when Morgan said he might not be guilty," I say. "You really think there's some grandpa out there who's a secret murderer and may have done this, too?"

Ben snorts. "Alternate suspects for Caroline's murder have always been out there in certain circles. But no one really believes them, and Sheriff Morrow isn't going to go poking around an ancient closed case to solve Natalie's murder. He's a good ole boy. He toes the Seaview line. That means tiptoeing around the mayor about his daughter." Ben's mouth is a taut line, like he's itching to drop another bomb on the table.

Amber's mom drops a tray of food instead. I jump so hard my thighs bang on the underside of the table. Liquid red sloshes over the edge of my soup bowl.

"Sorry," I say to her, noting for the first time that her name is Stephanie, per her teal name tag. I use the last of our napkin supply to clean it up.

"No worries. And sorry I didn't make it over here before, but Ted expedited your food as an apology. We like to take care of Morgan's friends. And Amber's." She finishes moving our plates over from the tray and bustles off to another table, where a patron is literally snapping their fingers at her. *What's with the snapping in this town?* I think. Then: *Maybe there will be another murder soon.*

Needing to clear my head, I turn my focus to the food. I grab a spoon, and hot, glorious tomato soup glides down my throat. Ben crunches into a grilled cheese triangle, and ooey-gooey cheese drips down onto his plate. Before I can forget, I pluck a ten-dollar bill from my wallet.

"No, it's on me," he insists.

"I can buy my own lunch," I say. "In fact, after our last date, I should really be paying for you. . . ."

Ben acquiesces, but only on my half. "No, this is good."

"Thanks. It's a matter of principle. Plus, you should really milk me for all I'm worth. I've got Maura Weston bucks now, and you're running around in a Viking head to make extra cash."

"You're my sugar mama, then," Ben teases back. "I can finally quit the mascot hustle."

If this were a movie, we'd kiss now: romantic diner-booth make-out following flirty banter. My heart is pounding, the intimacy terrifying, but . . . I think I want it. I lean forward, curl my lips into a smile that I hope says *Come closer.*

It does. He does. I lick my lips so they're not sticky with soup. I inch nearer.

And then his phone rings. We both startle, the spell of the moment broken.

"It's Maura," he says. "I have to take it."

It readily becomes clear that he has to go. He's on duty today. *Sorry,* Ben mouths to me as Maura squawks in his ear. I can hear her through the phone. I think I catch a grocery list. I don't think food shopping is an essential part of book publishing, but what do I know?

I return to my own to-do list as I shove the last of the grilled cheese into my mouth. The most logical next step is to go back to the hotel, try to dig around about Reama and anyone else in Maura's fandom who might be shady.

Five minutes later, and Ben is still on the phone. We can both take a hint. He mouths, *Goodbye,* grabs the rest of his grilled cheese for the road, and departs. I watch him out the front door, which is when I notice that Morgan's no longer there. I've been abandoned twice over. Kind of kills the crack-investigation-team feel. Just when I think it can't get more surreal—or depressing— Luke steps into frame, beckoning his latest tour group to the diner window. The murder tour is back in swing not even twenty-four hours after an actual murder. It's disgustingly callous. At least he won't be ending with a reenactment at the school pool this time.

I hope.

"You finished, hon?"

Amber's mom appears, refilling my coffee and pointedly ignoring the spectacle outside. I hand her the black folder with my shiny new credit card, courtesy of Maura (by way of Suzanne). So much for going Dutch.

Stephanie makes to run the card, but a jingle at the door alerts both of us.

"Kyle," she offers tightly.

"You know how I like it" is the sheriff's hello. And then he slides into the booth across from me, as though we'd scheduled the meeting. Stephanie makes a disgruntled sound in the back of her throat, then goes to fulfill his order.

"The coffee at the hotel is garbage," he says with a shrug. The smell of his sweat travels across the booth: a sour tang, from too much booze and not enough sleep.

"We're both coming from over there. For some reason," he continues. There's warning in his tone. Passive aggressive with a side of sarcasm.

"I had to run an errand for Maura." I blink at him.

"Well, I'm glad to catch you." He runs a hand through graying blond hair. I see shades of Amber in him, though he's oddly softer, despite being a cop. Amber's a boss-ass bitch. On cue, her mom tells the snapping Karen not to do that to her ever again. And then she's standing over us, passing me my check and slowly pouring black coffee into a chipped white mug for her ex-husband. Listening in.

"I'll need you to come down to the station this afternoon for your formal interview. We're one street over, on Pleasant Drive."

"Oh, sure. Of course. I'll be there with bells on."

"Hmph." Sheriff Morrow sips his coffee with a grimace, though he makes no move to soften the bitter brew.

"Anything else for you?" Stephanie asks.

"Just some privacy."

"Do I need to call her grandmother? She's under eighteen, Kyle."

"Leave it, Steph. She's not being questioned as a suspect. It's fine."

He says that, but I'm not so sure. Stephanie reluctantly departs, but her fierce gray-blue eyes never leave our table, ready to come to the rescue should I need.

"I heard that in the course of your . . . errand, you also found the time to speak with Chris Wang. I can't have you interfering in this investigation, Cecelia. You're both witnesses. That's the kind of thing a defense attorney can run wild with."

"I'm sorry," I say, and I genuinely am. The last thing I want to do is hurt Natalie's case, but the cops don't seem to be investigating the right things. "I didn't know. I was . . . trauma bonding," I spit as an excuse. "Needed to go over it again with someone who was there."

"Well, then, I'm glad you had that opportunity. But know that if I see you again talking to any persons of interest, I'll have to take you down to the station and charge you. And those sorts of things don't look good on college applications, I hear."

Sipping tomato soup as I press my lips together and nod, I try to look unfazed, despite his threat. And he *is* threatening me, which means he's smarter than I gave him credit for. Yes, yes. He won't see me.

That's what the back door is for.

CHAPTER FOURTEEN

The back door is locked. Hotel Seaview takes security seriously, it would seem. And the lobby is clearly out of the question. I could sneak past the valet, but Sheriff Morrow's deputies are camped out in the lounge. I've waited nearly twenty minutes by the dumpster behind the building for an employee or even a con-goer to pop outside for a smoke, but no luck. While this is a low-traffic alleyway, it's not even a hundred yards to the sand, and the employees from the beach-facing stores could come out at any moment, finding it suss as fuck that I'm here. One can only pretend to play on their phone, waiting for someone, for so long.

I could come back later, but I'm *right here,* and the con ends tomorrow. Time is precious.

I pace the alley, eyes searching the building, grasping for a brilliant idea but only finding doubt. Like Ben said, I'm a seventeen-year-old, not a police detective. But the fog of purpose pulls at me. If you're doing something, you don't have to think too hard. Feel too much.

I spot a window that's cracked open an inch and sprint toward it. The sill sits slightly above my head, so it takes some serious stretching to get my fingers purchase on the window to push it up. I reach. *Come on, come on, come on.*

"What are you doing?"

I lose my footing and career backward, but instead of hitting asphalt, a pair of hands steady me. I whirl around, tracing hands up to biceps up to . . . Hello.

"Gabriel, um, this isn't what it looks like?"

"It looks like you were trying to sneak in via that window. You know we have a front door, right? No criminal activity or acrobatics necessary."

"It's a long story." My voice lilts. "What are you doing here? Ew, you don't smoke, do you?"

"Not cigarettes, if that's what you mean. I got roped into trash duty. I could make a joke about sneaky journalists here, but it would summon my mom instantly, and then she'd probably hire you. She loves tenacity."

"You think I'm rooting around for a story?"

"You're not? I've already had to wrangle someone from the Mendocino paper. I expect the Bay Area reporters next. Dead rich girl is a big story, and everyone and their mother is circling the psycho-fan angle. Figured you'd joined the school paper."

Disappointment streaks through me. And here I thought I was a genius for calling the copycat angle.

"No, it's . . . weirder than that. I discovered the body, and you know who I'm related to. I have questions for some of the people at the con."

Gabriel eyes me shrewdly. "I'll let you in if you promise not to do anything illegal. I need this job."

"Thank you!" I follow him to the door like a duckling, finding myself in a generic-looking hallway, not half as historically wood-paneled and wallpapered as the spaces I was in earlier. This corridor is for employees only, and Hotel Seaview gave up on keeping it pretty decades ago. Ancient paisley paper swells on waterlogged walls. The smell is a mixture of mold and phantom trash, which makes Gabriel's woodsy smell pop out. I almost ask him if it's natural or Axe, but I refrain. TMI.

He walks me back to the public domain, halting outside a staff break room a few yards from the doorway that leads into the basement conference area. I catch his eyes flicking down at my chest. We both jump into the embarrassment shuffle, clearing our throats, looking at the walls. But then he surprises me. Points dead center.

"You don't have a badge."

And now I'm mortified all over again, for assuming he was checking me out.

"Hence my windowsill acrobatics, yes," I cover by way of sarcasm.

"You'll need help getting into con spaces without one." Gabriel is serious without fail. "What exactly is your plan?"

"I figured I'd bat my eyelashes and mention I'm Maura's granddaughter."

"Or I can take you in the service tunnels. There are corridors that run behind the con spaces. Makes it easier to avoid Sheriff Morrow."

My eyes widen. "Word gets around, huh?"

"Deputy Shields is chatty."

"Is the sheriff really that bad? He has some pretty aggressive dad energy."

Gabriel's grimace speaks volumes. "I'm not the best person to ask, given I'm not this town's favorite son. Poor and brown, quite the combination. Mysteriously pulled over at regular intervals. So if you ask me? Steer clear of the sheriff. The whole department, really. They're washed-up jocks and playground bullies, given a badge and stuck in a town where not much happens . . . or at least hadn't happened for fifty years."

Sheriff Morrow's threat echoes. I need to be careful.

"Even Deputy Shields?" I ask. She has a riled-up-kitten energy. Hard to picture her as a backwoods cowboy cop. "I saw you two earlier all friendly," I rib him just a bit, and Gabriel's cheeks go adorably bright red.

"She's a family friend. And, yeah, one of the better ones. My mom uses her as a source sometimes. Shit. I didn't tell you that."

"A family friend who likes a glow-up and doesn't much care for age-of-consent laws?" I waggle my eyebrows comically.

"Gross."

"Oh, I agree. Just because she's a woman, doesn't make it cool. In hindsight, I probably should have rescued you. . . ."

"I would have liked that. You, swooping in to save me."

I perform an exaggerated, chivalrous bow, and Gabriel pretends to swoon. I dive to catch him, and we end up chest to chest. And then we both go still.

"So these secret passageways?" I squeak.

"Follow me."

We pass through Victorian sea-shanty land once more, though only briefly. Gabriel taps his employee badge to a key reader next to a heavy wood door. Inside, an industrial hallway Ts out into a long stretch that I realize perfectly aligns with the large ballroom directly across from the stairs—the vendor hall.

"Was this always here?"

"No, they retrofitted it in the nineties. They host a bunch of self-help and multilevel marketing conferences throughout the year. And WestonCon, of course."

I wonder if that's where Maura got her *Live, Laugh, Love* mug from. It doesn't seem very her. Maybe Suzanne picked it up.

I take a step toward the double doors, behind which the hustle-bustle of the vendor hall is audible. "Shall we go in?"

"Right. Yes." Gabriel beeps his key card at the lock, and we quietly slip inside. Not that our manner of entry matters—the din of noise covers the click of the door behind us. We emerge between two booths, one selling tasteful watercolor paintings of Seaview landmarks immortalized by Maura's books, the other stuffed floor to ceiling with T-shirts, hoodies, hats, dresses, and even body pillows adorned with anime-style renderings of her characters. There's a blonde in a flowy dress and wet hair, who must be Cassidy. A shiver runs down my spine.

"So what now?" Gabriel breathes into my ear.

Right. We're back to that issue. I have no clue what I am doing. But then I spot a familiar face and make a grateful beeline.

"Diana! Hi! It's me, Cecelia!"

Diana from the reg desk looks up from the selection of handmade purses she was perusing. They're made from Maura's paperback covers from the eighties.

"Hey, funny seeing you here." She's half-hesitant, glancing to my chest, though she knows I don't have a badge. Then she sees Gabriel. "Hey, hon, you on a break?" They hug.

"You know each other?" I look between them, confused.

"Oh, this is my godmother," Gabriel says.

"I also work with the mayor and the town archive. I should

have properly introduced myself this morning." She formally offers me her hand for a shake. I take her in with new eyes. This isn't just some Maura superfan—though obviously she is, considering she's on con staff—she's a local.

"Did you get what you needed for Maura? We're expecting her for the afternoon keynote any minute now." She checks her cell phone. "Oh God, the reception here sucks. I've missed a call from my cochair."

"Before you go—" I practically lunge for her, grab her arm. Then I realize how creepy that is and let go. "Sorry. I'm trying to find out more about Reama? She was at Seaview High last week for a reenactment of the Cassidy scene from Maura's book. Someone said . . . Well, they suggested I ask around about her."

Diana transforms into archivist mode, looks from me to Gabriel, lips pressed together in a hard line. "I can't imagine what they meant by that. And practically everyone here has attended the reenactment at least once. Why are you asking?"

"Cecelia is still reeling from finding the body," Gabriel says, jumping in. "She found Natalie, you know. She needs closure."

"Oh, you poor dear," Diana says, hawkish gaze warming. "You shouldn't listen to gossip, though. What happened to Natalie Bergen was a tragedy, but it has nothing to do with anyone here. Which I tried explaining to Sheriff Morrow more than once already." A walkie-talkie on her hip squawks. "I have to go make sure we're set up for the keynote lunch. If you two are hungry, I can sneak you in, if you like."

Gabriel and I both make our excuses. I'm full, and I sense he's allergic to all this Maura worship. Diana departs, though not before throwing me one more scrutinizing look, tinged with pity.

"Well, that was a bust," I say. "I think maybe I'm bad at this whole girl-detective thing." It started so well with Chris, but I'm increasingly unmoored. Unsure.

"Excuse me."

We turn to find a twentysomething brunette dressed as Hazel the waitress from one of Maura's book series. Their badge says SKYE, THEY/THEM, and their body language says *I don't want to talk to you, but for some reason I am.*

"You were asking Diana about Reama?" They dart their eyes all around.

"Yes!" I perk up. Finally this is progress.

"I don't know who you talked to, but Reama has a bit of a polarizing reputation around these parts." Skye seems to consider their words carefully.

"What does that mean?" I prod.

"She exposed a con artist and pissed a lot of people off. And sometimes she advocates for death of the author, which makes the diehards upset."

"She wants Maura *dead*?" That's Gabriel, who's now rather keen on my whole investigating schtick.

"No! 'Death of the author,'" Skye says again, as if that clarifies things. "It means she advocates for divorcing the author from the work. Some fans love the books but don't love everything about Maura, or everything she does in every book. Reama gets a lot of flak because she dares to criticize the thing she loves."

"Got it," I say, thinking about what Chris had called her: a fan who took her love of the books too far. But it sounds like Reama has issues with the books, if anything. "What's with the con artist?" I ask.

Skye rolls their eyes. "The grifter was working on a very popular fic before Reama exposed them for scamming people out of tens of thousands. They ran multiple GoFundMes and lied about things like a house fire, cancer, bankruptcy. Then they ghosted, so now it's an abandoned WIP and Reama's the bad guy."

A new theory forms: Is Reama trying to take down the fandom as an act of revenge? Ruin it for everyone with a grisly copycat murder?

As if Skye can see the wheels in my mind turning, they add, "You know, if you want, you could try talking to Reama yourself. She's over there."

Skye points across the vendor hall to the bookseller booth, where, indeed, Superfan Reama is browsing. For a potential killer, she has great style. She's wearing a vintage dress in baby-blue gingham, with the cutest cat-shaped handbag. I turn to thank Skye, but they've wandered off, blending into a crowd of similar-looking Hazels.

"Shall we?" I don't wait for Gabriel's reply, and he follows regardless. My feet carry me over before I can second-guess myself. I move next to Reama as she browses a towering stack of books. I run my fingers over limited-edition paperbacks, companion guides, and various mystery titles by read-alike authors. Reama looks over to me, and we lock eyes for a microsecond. Hers narrow. My heart jumps into my throat, but my brain does me a solid.

"Which one's your favorite?" My voice squeaks a bit at the end, nervousness bleeding through. I clear my throat and say more evenly. "Like which one do you recommend to a relative newbie?"

Reama tilts her head. "Cecelia Ellis is a newbie to her grandmother's catalog?"

A cold itch crawls up my back, at the way people know me

now, or presume to know me, by association. Reama looks me up and down and seems to find me wanting.

"And you don't have a badge," she scolds.

"Yes, I'm not a big mystery reader. I'm here with—" I whip around but find that Gabriel has abandoned me for a nearby booth handing out samples of themed baked goods. "My friend works at the hotel," I settle on, turning back to Reama.

She hums under her breath. "Plus you're Maura's grand-daughter, so you can do pretty much whatever you want." Reama's tone is bright, but there's bite behind it. I steer us back to safer waters.

"Well, I'm new to all things Westonverse and could use some recommendations. I've only read the one on the boat."

Reama tsks with distaste. "Not the place I'd start. The twist was—"

"Obvious?" I finish for her.

"Yep. And the heroine was frustrating. The alcoholic schtick gets old fast. Right. Well, I'd start with the Hazel Minty Mysteries if you like cozies, or if you're into cooking." She picks up a paperback with a gingham pattern on the edges and a picture of a waitress with a magnifying glass. "Every book comes with a couple of recipes."

"What the heck?"

She waves me off. "It's a whole subgenre, and everyone loves Hazel solving crimes with her librarian best friend, Ginger. Plus, there's a hot-baker slow-burn romance. But if you prefer darker, Maura's Gothics are pretty good. I like the one with the hotel and the backstabbing family. They're over there." She indicates a shelf off in the corner of the bookstore booth. "However, you can't go wrong with the straight-up-commercial murdery ones, and seeing as you live in Seaview now, *Killer Queen* is a no-brainer."

Reama hands me a copy, a different edition from the one at Maura's house. Newer, with an eerie image of a girl in a white dress floating in a black abyss. Images of Natalie strobe through my mind.

"Is it your favorite?" I ask, quickly pulling the book to my chest so I don't have to see the cover. So far Reama may be a superfan, but she doesn't seem dangerous. I'm more inclined toward Skye's interpretation than Chris's.

Reama tuts. "It reads like a first novel. Though the newer editions include some smoothed-out prose, I noticed. But it's essential reading in this town. Especially considering."

"You mean the murder?"

"I heard you found the body. What are the odds?" Her dark eyes sparkle at me. This feels like a trap.

"It was as terrible as you'd imagine," I say. I'm about to put the copy of *Killer Queen* down when I catch the bookseller's death glare. So I pull out my wallet and pay for it in quick order, then shove the book deep into my pack. And then I'm back on Reama, not even attempting subtlety at this point.

"What about you? Did you go to the ball last night?"

Reama's shoulders stiffen. "Why do you ask?"

I give an exaggerated shrug. "I heard it was a banger."

After a beat, Reama makes a show of checking her phone. "The keynote luncheon starts in ten, and I need to hit up the bathroom. It's been nice chatting. Hope you enjoy the book!" She tosses the last bit over her shoulder, already on her way.

I retrieve Gabriel, the corner of his mouth smeared with chocolate, and drag him by the arm into a dead spot of traffic so we can talk. "She's hiding something, for sure. Dipped out as soon as I brought up the party last night. And *she* brought up Natalie's murder. Me finding the body. She gives me the creeps. But I . . . don't know what to do next."

Distress washes over Gabriel's face. "Look, I cannot lose this job. My car and the gas in it are my sole responsibility, and I cannot be the senior without a car next year."

"Do I sense a 'but'?"

"Yes." And he exhales deeply. "Come with me."

We don't bother with the secret passageway, instead weaving our way through the vendor room, out into the hotel, and upstairs.

"Wait, I can't—" I tug Gabriel back at the top of the stairs, peering around a wall post into the lobby where the deputies are.

"Stay low," Gabriel instructs. "And if they say something, I'll say you're my girlfriend. We can kill two birds with one stone. Deputy Shields may finally get the message."

He's off before I can protest further, and I have no choice but to follow. Crouching, I shield the right side of my face with my hand and move as quickly as possible. Gabriel flips up the partition to the reception desk, and I slip through, flattening myself down against the wall. Then I crab-walk into a cubby-sized office, where Gabriel slides into a chair in front of a sizable screen.

"So what's the 'but'?" I say.

Gabriel shakes the mouse to wake the screen.

"But the WestonCon party in question was held in the main ballroom," he says, "and we have all their entrances and exits on video." Gabriel double-clicks on one file folder, then another, then another, until a long list of files comes up. "Which I pulled for Sheriff Morrow not an hour ago. Shields has been watching the vids on a laptop, with the badge checkers from last night, ever since." He opens a drawer with a flourish, pulls out a thumb drive.

"Give me five minutes, and you'll have it, too. You can find Reama's entrances and exits yourself, see if she has an alibi."

"Shit, seriously?"

"Just remember, *I* didn't give it to you."

"Can't we look now?"

"There's no time. The party was four hours long, and I don't want to get caught." Gabriel's eyes dart to the doorway.

"Four hours?" That's a lot of footage to watch. A preemptory wave of boredom rushes over me.

"At least you know who to look for." He jerks his head in the direction of the lobby. "Sheriff Morrow's team is creating an interview list by process of elimination. You simply have to check if Reama went in, and when."

"Or never attended at all," I say, picking up the thread. "You're rather observant, aren't you?" I perch on the edge of the desk. Gabriel blushes.

"No one pays attention to the staff. They'll say anything in front of you. Especially if they see you as a stupid kid."

"You're not a stupid kid to me." The room stills with my sincerity. I want to be embarrassed, but I can't deny its truth, nor the way my stomach drops when Gabriel's eyes find mine.

"I don't pay you to flirt, you know," comes a voice from the doorway. I jump so hard I knock my elbow on a file cabinet next to the desk. I rub it, biting down curses, and raise my eyes to the interloper. I recognize her from Maura's party. So this is the woman with questionable taste in sailor paraphernalia.

Gabriel doesn't bother to respond to the barb. "Cecelia, this is my boss, Elaine. She owns Hotel Seaview."

"And it only took every male family member dying for it to happen," she says. "Fuck the patriarchy."

"We've met," I say. "And now I see why you're friends with my grandmother."

Elaine gives a throaty laugh. It makes sense. Cool-grandmas squad.

"We've heard all about you. Vanessa's baby girl. Spitting image, too. I think I even caught *her* in here with a boy or two when she was your age."

"Wait, she worked here?"

"Oh yes. Though 'worked' might be a stretch—I caught her daydreaming in the rooms when she was meant to be cleaning. But she was a good girl." Then Elaine's face scrunches up, like she's walked into a bad memory. She says nothing, though. I wonder if she's thinking about how my mom turned out. Estranged from Maura. Dead at forty-two.

"Gabriel, dear, I noticed you put that 'Back in Fifteen' sign up twenty-five minutes ago, so wrap it up in here, okay? My only request is no sex in the office, please."

I nearly choke on my own saliva. Then Elaine departs, and Gabriel mumbles something about a few minutes more, and I need to get out of this stuffy back room. The reception desk is cooler and doesn't smell like stale Fritos, but it does bring me face to face with the sheriff.

"Funny seeing you here again," he says wryly.

"I was visiting Gabriel," I explain innocently. "I have time to kill until I need to be at the station, you know. Do you need something? Maybe I can help you." Well, now I'm just being cheeky. But it's kind of fun.

"I wanted to follow up on our request for a conference room, but I'm guessing you can't help with that."

"No," I say, smiling.

"Why don't I move up your interview, since you're just burning daylight. We can walk over to the station now. We're not set up to start interviews here yet."

It takes significant effort to keep my panic from showing. ". . . Sure. Of course. That would be great. Let me say goodbye to Gabriel."

You can see straight through to the office from reception, so there's no privacy—not for a proper update, nor for a handoff of the USB, even if it were ready. Which it's not. Gabriel offers a subtle shake of the head, passed off as a stretch and hair tousle.

"Put your number in my phone. I'll text you later," I say, knowing the sheriff can hear me. Gabriel obliges, typing out each number slow as can be.

"Let's go, Weston," the sheriff barks.

"My last name is *Ellis*." The ice in my voice is unmistakable. But the sheriff's message is clear: we're out of time. I acquiesce and go out to the lobby to join my police escort. We're nearly to the door when my name echoes through the room. Gabriel runs over to us, shoots a nervous look at Sheriff Morrow.

"I just wanted to . . ." He laces the fingers of one hand through mine, pulls me in close, away from the sheriff. Strokes my cheek and then leans in to kiss it. "Goodbye, Cecelia."

His lips are soft against my skin. The intimacy of it trills through me. I'm so distracted by the kiss—on the cheek, but *still!*—that I almost miss the tug of pressure on my coat pocket. As Gabriel jogs away, I push my hands inside. The flash drive is there. *Yes.*

I turn for the door, ready to spin excuses for the sheriff, but he's not the only one looking at me with confusion.

Ben appears to have some questions, too.

CHAPTER FIFTEEN

Shit, fuck, and damn.

"Ben! Hi! And Maura. And *Suzanne.* Here for the keynote?"

My grandmother removes a pair of oversized sunglasses, surely superfluous in overcast Northern California in October, her expression bemused. "And what a way to kick off the day. Again." She smirks. "Benjamin, I'll meet you in the ballroom," she says, and she swans off, Suzanne in tow. My grandmother loves an entourage.

Even Sheriff Morrow defers, saying he'll wait for me outside. I pull Ben to the side of the lobby, away from Deputy Shields, who is gawping on the couch.

"It's not what it looks like," I start.

"Well, it looked like a brush pass, so I hope that's what it was, because I prefer that to the alternative."

"Wait . . . what?"

"He put something in your pocket, no? What was it?"

I'm baffled. Ben . . . doesn't appear to be jealous or upset. Dear God, he's perfect. Giddiness rises up from my stomach. "It's a thumb drive with video footage from the ballroom last night. All the comings and goings of everyone, so we can figure out who has an alibi and who doesn't."

"Wow. Solid assist from Escano. I have to finish up with Maura, and you apparently are going with the sheriff, but let's meet up later to go through the video. Make a date of it?"

"How romantic! Combing surveillance footage together."

"Better than you doing it alone."

"Definitely." I lean in, and out of obligation or want, or maybe something in between, I kiss him on the cheek. A mirror of a moment ago, reversed. I ignore how perfunctory the gesture feels. I'm saving the best of our firsts for when a lobby full of hotel guests and police personnel aren't staring.

I join Sheriff Morrow outside, and we make the short walk to the police station in silence. Amber gestures at me from behind the check-in desk.

"Hi, Cecelia," she says, proffering a clipboard and pen. I have to sign in.

"Holding down the fort, sweet pea?" her dad addresses her, to a hearty eye roll.

"Dad, I'm on the clock. Call me Amber at least. Miss Morrow is better."

"Well, *Miss Morrow,* we are going to be in interview room B, and I think we would both like some fresh coffee. If you wouldn't mind."

Amber gives a little salute and hops over to a Keurig, while I follow Sheriff Morrow past reception through an open double doorway into a bullpen. An overgrown boy with a comical mustache looks up from a cluttered desk in the corner, furrowing his brow at me. Infinitesimally, his head tics to the right at a dry-erase board with my face on it. And Natalie's, Luke's, Morgan's, Creepy Chris's, even Mayor Bergen's . . . They've pulled down a selfie I posted to Instagram a few weeks ago and printed it on cheap white printer paper. I'm on a police murder board. Wow.

Sheriff Morrow catches me staring. He clears his throat noisily and urges me to follow him.

Interview room B is on the left, a narrow, beige space with a single table and chair, except for a more comfortable rolling chair resting against the wall. The sheriff gets the rolling chair. I sit down on padding that may have once been a bright purple but is now a faded maroon, with grooves where many butts before mine have sat. Up in the adjacent corner is a camera. I've been transported into one of those ID channel murder shows my mom loved marathoning. Now I realize if this story ever gets dramatized for TV, that footage of me in this chair may make it on air. I sit up straighter.

Sheriff Morrow is thorough. Starts me in the morning and walks me all the way through to finding the body. He doesn't write anything down; no, every ounce of his attention is on me. He's casual—too casual—and blunt when I make self-deprecating jokes, like how *of course* I picked the worst possible place to pee. We discuss the fight between Natalie and Morgan, and betrayal stabs through me as I repeat Morgan's ominous words:

Maybe it's someone else's turn to win for once.

God, she didn't mean it literally, did she? No way . . . Morgan's the one spinning an alternate-victim theory.

Unless that's a cover, a nasty voice inside me whispers.

"What about Morgan?" I blurt. "She told me the killer might have been targeting *her.*"

The sheriff turns icy. "I'm the one asking the questions, Miss Ellis. Need I remind you about our conversation earlier today? I don't like how you seem to be going out of your way to discuss this case with other witnesses. And Morgan Quinn has always had an overactive imagination. I don't need her, or *you,* meddling in this investigation."

His dressing down brings wicked heat to my cheeks, but also a surge of defiance. *I got to Chris Wang first. I'm on top of the Reama lead. What do the cops have to show? I'm taking Morgan seriously.*

"I understand," I say, pretending to be properly chided. But inside my head, the wheels are turning. *Luke was Natalie's escort on the field—surely why he's on the board outside. I need to talk to him. Piece together a timeline of where Natalie went after the car procession. Ooh. I need my own murder board.*

There's a knock at the door, so well timed I suspect the person on the other side had to have been listening. It's Amber. She offers a fresh cup of coffee to her dad, and a tight-lipped smile at me.

"Deputy Shields is back," she says. "With a couple con-goers in tow."

"Right. Is there anything else you want to tell me, Cecelia?"

"Nope," I say, already moving to leave. Gabriel's thumb drive is searing a hole in my pocket. When we reenter the bullpen, I notice that the young cop from earlier is gone, leaving the murder board empty and unguarded.

"Where's the bathroom?" I ask, already moving away from reception.

"It's down there to the left." Amber points as they go to meet Deputy Shields and Mustache Deputy, who I see corralling a group of Maura superfans to sign in. I recognize a few people who were at the reenactment on Saturday, plus my old friend Chris.

I maneuver carefully, doing a head tuck and a whirl, the first so Chris doesn't spot me and the latter so I can appear to be heading bathroom-ward while I double back. I zip past the open doorway and flatten myself against the near wall. I only have a minute, at best.

The murder board winks at me. I'll be visible if anyone in the main office looks away from the group of con-goers. I ready my phone, tapping into the camera app, and steal closer. I'm ten feet from it, then five. I raise my phone horizontally to snap a pic . . . but, shit, I'm too close. Edging back, back, I *almost* have it in frame when there's a sharp pinch in my hip, then the whoosh of papers flying. I've hip-butted into Mustache Deputy's desk; I whip around and check my six, to find reception empty. Shit. Tapping hurriedly, I hope I've got the board in focus for the shot, but there's no time to check before I dive behind the deputy's desk and surreptitiously gather the files from the floor. Above me, someone clears their throat.

"Found it!" I right the folders on the desk and hop up, phone thrust forward triumphantly. Mustache Deputy does not appear amused. "Slippery fingers, whoops. Sorry for messing up your desk." I talk so fast he's unable to get a word in before I dart around him and power walk toward reception. In my periphery, I see Maura's fans being led into individual interview rooms.

Amber stops me at the front desk, with arms crossed over her chest and a calling-bullshit expression.

"I admire your gumption, but that was stupid," she says. "Deputy Rodriguez is going to tell my dad."

"I lost my phone." I shrug.

Amber hums, not believing my lie. "Like my dad said, they're professionals. You should leave this to them."

"You were listening at the door!" I point at her, my own gotcha moment.

"And you were taking pictures of the murder board. Which was completely unnecessary. I got photos hours ago on my DSLR. I can send them to you." She produces a camera from under the reception desk and waggles it in my direction.

"Now who's leaving it to the professionals?"

"Technically, I work here." She holds a beat. "But I'm not interrogating people at fan conventions and entertaining Morgan's wild theories."

"You're the third person to tell me Morgan can't be taken seriously. Care to enlighten me?"

Amber tucks her camera into her backpack, then swings it over her shoulder. "It's not deep. She's a drama llama. In ninth grade, she was *convinced* Seaview had a serial killer, and spent my entire birthday party making her nonsensical case to my dad. She's no longer invited to our house, and he's been wary ever since. And Morgan's always been sensitive about Natalie." She turns off the desktop computer, indicates I should follow her out. Guess we're leaving together.

"I thought they were best friends." Though how Natalie left Morgan out in the cold during Spirit Week dances through my mind.

"Natalie wasn't always easy to be best friends with," Amber says ominously, pushing open the front door.

We burst out into crisp, salty air. I keep forgetting we're only blocks from the ocean. I peer up at the sky, which is a stony gray. I've left perpetual sunshine for unrelenting gloom. There's a metaphor in there somewhere.

"Cecelia! I've been so worried about you." Bronte bounds up to us, practically tackle-hugging me, solid and strong. I angle into her embrace. "I texted you this morning but didn't hear back. Are you okay?"

Amber snorts. "More than okay. She's on the case."

"What does that mean?" Bronte looks to me, and all I can do is push down my burning shame with a shrug.

"She's meddling in my dad's investigation," Amber says.

"But *you* do that all the time," Bronte counters. I could kiss her if she weren't, well, Amber's girlfriend.

"I mean, sure, yes," Amber stammers. "But I'm more subtle about it. I caught her photographing the leads board. And she's been listening to Morgan."

This again.

"Will you guys tell me why it's so unreasonable to believe Morgan? It's a compelling theory. She looked *identical* to Natalie. The killer could've meant to target her instead."

"Sure." Amber scoffs.

"Amber!" Bronte scolds, but softens as she looks my way. "I know it's probably the last place you want to go right now, but Amber and I were going to walk back to the school to get my stuff. I had to leave everything in the locker room after they cordoned off the place last night. You want to come? We can chat on the way."

The scene of the crime. One side of me worries about reliving the horror of last night. How was Natalie killed only last night? But a sick, twisted part of me is elated to investigate.

"Yes," I answer, too quickly.

"How's he been?" Bronte asks Amber, both a step ahead of me and at a volume begging privacy. But I can't help but overhear.

"He's stressed as fuck, guzzling coffee because he's smart enough to know now is not the time to be drinking. Though I'm sure tonight will be fun."

"You won't be there to take care of him, though. You're staying with me. It's decided. Screw his weekend."

Guess I didn't imagine the smell of booze on the sheriff. Amber snorts, but the way she holds on to Bronte's hand tells me she's appreciative. I feel a pang of jealousy, instantly wishing I had someone to confide in like that. Gabriel's face appears in my mind, but I shake it away quickly, guiltily. Ben. I like *Ben*. One dumb kiss has me rattled. That's all it is.

Amber seems to remember I'm behind them, left out of the conversation. She waits a step.

"Here's the deal with Natalie," she says without preamble. "Everyone has a Natalie story. She was divisive. Even among her friends."

Bronte coughs, glances sidelong at her girlfriend as though she's saying too much, but Amber doesn't cede.

"Come on, Bron, you know I only put up with her because I love you. She was shitty to me for years, and that's in spite of our dads being friends. She told everyone I was a raging lesbian in seventh grade, made me a social pariah."

Bronte opens her mouth as though to speak, but Amber barrels on.

"So I *was* a raging lesbian, but that's not the point. Natalie weaponized shit against people all the time. Morgan can be extra, but she's harmless. Someone *killed* Natalie because they had a reason to. It's obvious."

I'm not ready to completely disregard the Morgan mistaken-identity theory, but Amber makes a compelling point. Natalie's own friends think someone did her in on purpose. That can't be ignored.

As we come up on the school in the light of day, I can see properly the chaos of last night. Yellow police DO NOT CROSS tape cordons off the pathway that leads to the pool. Twisted, foot-trodden bags of popcorn and paper cups litter the ground. A game, abruptly halted, the custodial staff banished by police presence, orders not to disturb the scene. I spot a lone figure with a push broom and a dustpan scooping detritus into a giant trash can.

We cut past the main school building, past the Weston Annex to the back quad, where a squat, red-faced, and balding man paces, hovering over a cluster of students crouched low in front of a bench. As we wing closer, I realize they're placing flowers on the ground, near a cardboard sign that reads RIP, NATALIE.

"And it's the Caroline Quinn Memorial Bench," Amber notes dryly. "Apropos."

Bronte ignores the quip and steers us to the athletic center, which is, thankfully, free of yellow tape. "This should only take a minute," she says, testing the door handle, which doesn't budge. Bronte is nonplussed. She angles her head in the direction of Pacing Dude, checking that he's not looking as she pulls a large, clunky key from her bag. Then her eyes flick up at the roofline. I follow her gaze and find the round bulb of a security camera peering down.

"They don't check the CCTV unless something goes missing or gets stolen," Bronte says as she slides the key into the lock and we slip inside.

Or murdered? I'm sure they're checking the feeds from last night. If only I could get my hands on the footage. Add it to my watch party with Ben later.

"Who is that guy?" I ask. We're in a nondescript hallway, walls beige cinder block and the hollow dripping sound of a leaky shower hinting at the locker rooms beyond.

"School resource officer," Amber supplies. "Or rent-a-cop, as my dad calls him, though it's literally an official full-time gig. But old Will's a decent enough guy, even if he can be overzealous about petty shit."

"Like breaking into the school on a Saturday? Do all the cheerleaders have a key?"

"My phone is locked in here, so they can suck it." Bronte makes a beeline for the girls' locker room, and I don't miss how she avoids the question about the key. A crooked line of yellow tape cordons off the back row of lockers, and I can't help but think it's strangely in sync with the school colors. Bronte ducks under with the practiced grace of an athlete, going right to a purple locker at the end of the row.

"Which one is Natalie's?" I ask, figuring that's why the tape is here. They were searching it. Bronte points at an open door in the middle of the row. Inside, I find a half-used bottle of body glitter, a pair of pom-poms, and a tatty pair of sneakers, but not much else. Not even her cheerleader uniform, which surely she took off last night to get into her dress. Did the cops take it?

"Bron," Amber says in a warning tone. "Do they know about the other locker? Shouldn't we tell them?"

"Other locker?" I ask, but they ignore me, in their own world.

"Does it really matter?" Bronte, nervous, bites her lower lip. She finishes up with her locker, slams it shut, a beat-up canvas grocery bag now slung over her shoulder.

"It might. Should we?"

And now they look at me even as they still talk to each other.

"She's already all in," Amber reasons. "If we find nothing, it doesn't matter. But just in case. It's what my dad would do."

"This is idiotic," Bronte says, but it doesn't stop her from following Amber back under the tape, out into the hallway. And I follow—toward the entrance, to a dingy and dark corridor to the left and a heavy wooden door that has names and invectives carved into it, some with decades of wear. PEDO jumps out at me.

Streaky white residue covers the other half of the word, like some-one slapped a sticker over it at some point, only to have someone else peel it off.

Bronte produces the key again, the one she's avoided explain-ing to me, and lets us inside. It's a windowless room—pitch-dark, until Amber finds the lights. Likely a junk room, maybe once an office. There's a beat-up desk in the corner and an ancient TV collecting dust on top of an old filing cabinet. I can't put my fin-ger on what is disturbing me, but something about the room is unnatural—as though someone other than us is here. I see that the condensed rows of lockers on the other side of the room are dust-free, recently used.

"Natalie had a secret locker in here," I put together. "Why?"

"Because why not?" Amber says with a shrug. "The cool kids have been using this place for decades. Our parents did. It's the best place to store contraband, or shit you don't want stolen."

"Like a dress?" Bronte's voice wobbles. We didn't even hear the locker open.

"Holy shit," Amber says as her girlfriend stumbles back, as far away from her discovery as she can.

But I'm pulled forward in a zombie walk, my eyes drinking in every detail.

A baby-pink homecoming dress hangs from Natalie's locker, crinoline innards spilling out of deep slashes. And a message scrawled across the chest in lurid red lipstick:

FUCK YOU.

CHAPTER SIXTEEN

For the second time in twenty-four hours, I'm huddled in the Seaview High School parking lot, surrounded by law enforcement. Amber insisted we call her dad, as this was "serious shit." She's right. It's why I was sure to get a photo on my phone before SRO Will trundled over and started shrieking about protocol and contaminating the scene. I keep pulling it up on my screen, eyes raking over FUCK YOU in Lady Danger red, the mashed tube of MAC lipstick placed boldly on the shelf, so Natalie would know it was personal. Fuck you. Fuck your lipstick.

Did Natalie see this before she died? Did she know someone was out for blood?

It changes everything. Confirms there was nothing accidental about her death.

"Hey. You okay?" Bronte rubs my back as we watch Amber across the parking lot, father chewing her out for even being in a position to discover key evidence. *Meddling.* Every so often the sheriff gestures over in my direction, fury etched across his features.

"Is *she* okay?"

Bronte's mouth is a firm line.

"He can be an ass. But he's not violent, if that's what you mean."

We watch the rest in silence until the sheriff storms into the athletic center and Amber approaches us in a brisk walk.

"Come on," she says, barely pausing her step. Bronte and I hurry behind her. "I need a fuckton of cookie dough and some strong weed after that."

"Amen," Bronte says.

I don't know why I'm surprised that Bronte likes to smoke, but I am. She's so squeaky-clean. I remind myself weed is legal in California and not a big deal. Everyone probably does it. Even if I'm no expert.

"Are we going to Luke's?" Amber asks.

"You know we don't have to go to his place for good weed," Bronte says.

"Yeah, but Morgan wants us there. She says she can pick us up."

I try not to act as hurt as I am that clearly I am missing information. They notice anyway.

"Sorry. We're so rude," Bronte says. "You're not on the group chat, but you're welcome to come. Luke is having a hang at his house tonight, so we can process everything with Natalie together."

Amber snorts. "And because Morgan's convinced someone's going to murder her tonight."

"I don't want to crash your party," I protest. I'm not on the group chat. Not really part of the group. And yet I can't stop thinking about the other photo on my phone. Blurry but not so much so that I can't make out the word the cops wrote in red dryerase marker, and circled—twice.

With lines drawn connecting it like a spider's web to several images: the mayor, Morgan, Luke. A party at Luke's house may be too good to pass up. A chance to prod everyone about their whereabouts when Natalie was killed. Suss out motives.

Bronte either senses my hesitation or her default setting is peacemaker. "It's not exclusive. Knowing Luke, he invited Caleb, too. The more the merrier. We'll go from my house."

And I realize we've wandered far afield of Maura's Victorian at this point, and we must be nearly to Bronte's. The street is unfamiliar to me, with cracked sidewalk slabs and straw-colored, sunbaked lawns running up to boxy ranches begging for upkeep. Bronte and Amber head up the driveway of one of them, bypassing the front walkway, to lead me through a carport and in through the side kitchen door. The inside is dated but well loved, the ancient cabinets freshly painted a soothing sage color, the fridge boasting old report cards and childish artwork. It's a house you can't help but love and feel loved in. Amber helps herself to a can of soda from the fridge, but before she can even offer me one, a high-pitched honk comes from outside. Morgan's here.

We pile into her hand-me-down but lovingly maintained VW Golf (the Obama/Biden bumper sticker gives a clue to the car's age). Bronte and Amber claim the back seat, so I've got shotgun with Morgan. She raises an eyebrow as I slide into the front. It smells like cherries, and Taylor Swift blasts on the stereo.

"Thanks for coming with me, guys." Morgan sniffs. "I don't want to be alone tonight."

I try to assess whether it's a performance. Morgan *is* an actress. But so was Natalie.

"Where does Luke live?" I ask as we fly past everything familiar, heading away from town, merging onto the 1. The sun sets in glorious peach and purple streaks behind the line of the coast and the rising tree line.

"Rinaldi Wines," all three girls sing. It must be a television jingle, a group in-joke I'm missing. But that's the last semblance of humor in the car. Morgan's white-knuckling the steering wheel, as on edge now as she was this morning. Amber and Bronte chat in low voices in the back seat.

My phone buzzes with a text. Confetti explodes in my chest when I see it's from Ben.

> Finished with Maura. Hang out tonight?
> You, me, hours of surveillance footage?

And immediately my insides deflate. I completely forgot about our plans.

> Hey sorry can't. Going to Luke's with Bronte, Amber, and Morgan. Tomorrow?

> Wow, am I dating a popular girl?

> Yes so better try and keep up 😊

> 💀

I'm drawn back to the Photos app. Back to that police board and what it has to say about my company for the evening.

My eye catches on a messy scrawl next to Luke's picture—it's off to the side that's hard to make out, though the bright-red

154

marker used signals its importance. I tilt in close to the screen and squint: *Cagey about alibi.*

Now that's odd. Why didn't Luke tell the police where he was after Natalie left?

Another slash of red jumps out from next to Mayor Bergen's headshot. *Overheard screaming at victim before game.*

You know what they say: if the mayor was willing to scream at his child in public, who knows what he was willing to do behind closed doors.

We pull off the highway onto a narrow two-lane road, which winds through landscape that alternates between scraggly fields and dense trees and brush until we reach a driveway announced by dual lampposts. *Rinaldi Wines* is etched into a wood sign at the right of the drive. We pass through the gate, swung wide open as if in anticipation of us, and then pass two dozen vehicles parked haphazardly on the sweep of grass near the house. The side yard is lit up and crowded with laughing partygoers.

"It's . . . bigger than I thought it would be," I remark, peering past the makeshift parking lot to the vineyard. Someone's strung fairy lights along one of the paths, and I can make out several people in fancy dress, strolling.

"It's a wedding," Morgan explains. "They host them year-round. Our party is back here." She pulls past the main house, a soaring Queen Anne with all windows ablaze, down a driveway marked PRIVATE. We park in front of what I think is the guesthouse but reads minimansion to me. This second house, behind the first house, was presumably built so Luke's family could reside close by while wedding guests took over the picturesque Queen Anne. We enter the Mediterranean ranch, where we are greeted with an open-plan living area with soaring wood beam ceilings and Luke stoned on the couch. He toasts us with a White Claw and slumps into the buttery leather cushions with a dopey expression on his face. Then he gestures to the nearby kitchen island cluttered with bottles and a towering plate of brownies I assume are the "fun" kind.

"Take your pick." Luke registers my discomfort. Delights in it. A sour spike of unease hits my stomach. I seek shelter behind the girls and pour Diet Coke into a Solo cup, adding a splash of vodka to fit in. Everyone else grabs a beverage and a weed brownie, and we arrange ourselves around Luke on the couches. I'm relieved when no one comments on my lack of sweet treat.

"How's the case going, Amb?" Luke jumps right into it. Amber's mid–brownie bite, chocolate coating her teeth, as she freezes, mouth open.

"Uh, it's fine. I can't really talk about it. My dad will kill me. He's being more aggro than usual, because . . . well, huge important murder case."

"You can't tell us anything?" Luke presses, mellow high be damned. Like recognizes like. He's fishing. But I think we have very different motives, he and I.

"No." Amber is firm, and she throws me and Bronte a beseeching look for good measure. We're *not* telling them about the dress. Got it. But, God, I itch to see how Luke and Morgan would react. Lipstick ruination doesn't seem Luke's style, but Morgan's squirming.

Come to think of it, though, any of the homecoming-queen hopefuls could've been pissed at Natalie's assured win. Except not everyone had a mysterious key, did they?

I can't ask about it now, but I file it away to press Bronte about later. As game as Amber seemed earlier, her father must have said something to scare her off.

But Amber is saved from further questioning, because Morgan cracks, the first to cry.

"I can't believe this is happening. I miss her. But I shouldn't have to miss her! Natalie should be here. We were supposed to be pregaming right now—at her house, before the dance."

"Do you think they'll reschedule?" Luke coughs, tacks on: "In honor of Natalie, I mean."

I'm reminded of Luke's murder tour this afternoon, back on schedule. Now he's worrying about not having a stupid school dance?

"That's a good idea." Morgan sniffs. "I'll talk to Principal Morris tomorrow. Doing something for Natalie. She loved homecoming and prom."

Everyone turns wistful. The makeshift memorial has begun.

They take turns telling stories: How Natalie could be so thoughtful. Never forgot a birthday. Knew exactly what you were thinking sometimes.

"Yeah, but sometimes she knew . . . too much," Bronte says, exploding into giggles. Amber snorts, catching the funny bug.

"Pick a little, talk a little," she rattles off, and the group repeats the phrase. It tugs at my ear, familiar.

"God, don't remind me!" Morgan practically explodes. "She didn't speak to me for two weeks when I got the lead in *The Music Man.*"

"Oh, I meant more that she was a huge gossip," Amber retorts. "First person to know about my parents' divorce and spread it like wildfire." She launches into an uncanny impression. *"But, Amber, everyone was going to find out anyway. Why are you mad?"*

My interest in the conversation piques, hoping an airing of grievances means Luke or Morgan might burst out with a confession. Instead, the conversation returns to raucous retellings of junior-prom high jinks and the postparty rager at Natalie's beach house. More memories and in-jokes I'll never have, because I wasn't here. I don't *belong* here. I can't keep up, and I don't want to pretend to try. My eye is drawn to a white-embossed Viking on a shiny purple cover on the coffee table. A yearbook. I stretch over the glass table to reach it, fingertips grazing the leatherette cover and dragging it toward me. *2021–2022* reads the spine. Their junior year.

The early pages are littered with candids and group shots: from pep rallies, the caf, club meetings, on the quad. Natalie's megawatt smile and silky blowout pops on nearly every page. With her nearly always: Morgan, Luke, Bronte, Amber . . . and Ben. A view into a strange past. An alternate universe before Ben's mom died and his grandfather sued the city. They're a clique. I already knew it, but it's different to see in front of me.

They expand their ranks for homecoming. Everyone dazzling, in gowns and tuxes, beaming as they emerge from a stretch limo. Morgan's escort from this year, Caleb, and Bronte's brother, Gabriel, in the mix. Some girl with stunning red hair in a bombshell crimson dress on Ben's arm defies every rule about red on red. In another candid, Natalie's eyes shoot lasers in her direction—I assume for showing her up on the dress front. As for Ben, he looks fucking hot in his tux. Jealousy coils in my gut at this unnamed girl. I want to be her, to project myself onto the pages, so I can belong to the group, to this place, and to Ben before death cast its pall over everything.

Another spread catches my attention; the drama club performed *Into the Woods* last spring. I know the musical well—it was our fall show sophomore year at Pasadena Central. Too nervous to audition, I jumped into costume duty. It's obvious here who's who: Morgan as Cinderella. Luke, her prince. Gabriel surprises me as the baker. Ben, too, as the other prince. And the witch: Natalie. That must have burned Morgan up inside. Sure, she got to play the headline princess, but Natalie got the showstopper. I think her gown at the end is designer, too. Doesn't look like a high school costume prop.

Interesting how two of the murder suspects have a background in drama.

"Tell me about it." Luke's slurred words pull me out of my reverie. Morgan's eyes are puffy and she sniffles at intervals, but Luke's are fiery. He's messy, drunk, sad, and fixed on me. "Finding her," he elaborates. "We all want to know, but they're all too chickenshit to ask. That's why you're *here,* isn't it?"

Now I'm in the hot seat, and though the last thing I'm keen to do is relive last night again, I understand the opportunity for quid pro quo. So I tell the story again, skipping the finer details of what it's really like to find a body. Some things you don't share.

Luke narrows his eyes. "Why *that* bathroom? It's weird."

"And I think it's weird how drunk off your ass you are," Amber jumps in.

"What does that mean?"

"It means that I find it *weird,*" she throws his word back at him, "that you've been dodging my dad all day and refuse to be interviewed about your alibi."

"Are you accusing me of something?"

"Are you accusing *her* of something?" Amber keeps pointing at me, and I wish I could sink down into the leather cushions and disappear.

Morgan protectively puts her arm around Luke's shoulders. "Amber, what the fuck is your problem?"

And that sets off Bronte. "Don't talk to her like that! Cecelia was in the wrong place at the wrong time, but we don't even know where you two were. Morgan, *you* should have been in the locker room with us, changing into your cheer uniform, but you weren't."

"It's none of your business where I was!" Morgan screeches. Heels clacking noisily, she rockets across rust-red tile to the front door; she slams it behind her.

Luke scowls at Bronte and Amber before taking off after Morgan.

"Shit. I shouldn't have done that." Amber moans, head lolling on the back of the couch. She's out of it, but present enough for regret. *"Don't meddle, Amber. Jesus fucking Christ,"* she mimics sternly. I recognize her dad in it. "I think I'm going to be sick."

Bronte expertly jumps into caregiver mode, hauling Amber up off the couch to what I assume is the bathroom. I catch her muttering as she goes: "Fucking Rinaldi shit-quality weed."

And then I'm alone.

With Luke's phone, it would seem.

It's sitting on the coffee table, winking up at me.

Should I snoop on Luke's phone?

Yes.

But when I pick it up, it prompts me for Face ID. Shit. What was I thinking? I don't know his passcode, either.

There are other ways to get into a phone, however. Especially when its owner is hella stoned *and* drinking.

A plan forms in my mind. Plate of brownies in hand, I slip out onto the front porch, looking for Luke and Morgan. I find them on the porch swing, Morgan hiccuping the last of a crying fit.

"Time for another?"

And it's that simple. Luke and Morgan each grab a brownie and follow me back inside, where a green-looking Amber is on the couch.

"Malibu and Coke is the devil," she croaks.

I nod as though I understand. "Hey, can I use your phone to call my grandma?" I ask Luke, already holding out the phone to him. "Mine is dead."

It seems more plausible than grabbing his phone and pretending to take a selfie.

"Uh, sure." He unlocks it and hands it to me. I make a show of going to the dial screen and punching in numbers. And then I pretend to dial. Hold the phone to my ear and walk out into the yard for some privacy. The music from the wedding works well to muffle any noise.

Charade over, I tap to the home screen, not even sure what I'm looking for. I start with the photo roll. And there's Natalie. A selfie of her and Luke from last night. Natalie the way I'd prefer to remember her, striking in seafoam, Luke mugging beside her. The way the camera is angled, Morgan is visible in the background, scowling.

I go back to the home screen, try Luke's messages. Maybe his halftime hookup texted a meeting place. Or a thank-you—if he's as good as he says he is.

There are no messages from any strange girls close to the top, only the group text Bronte mentioned, and individual threads with Morgan, one with Caleb. And fourth from the top, a chain with a dead girl.

Natalie.

I tap, sucking in a breath. My eyes rake over the iMessage chain, her name at the top, and in the texts as well.

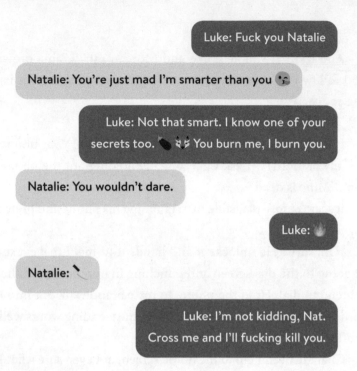

Luke: Fuck you Natalie

Natalie: You're just mad I'm smarter than you 😏

Luke: Not that smart. I know one of your secrets too. 🍆 💦 You burn me, I burn you.

Natalie: You wouldn't dare.

Luke: 💧

Natalie: ✒

Luke: I'm not kidding, Nat. Cross me and I'll fucking kill you.

"You all set?"

I jump with an undignified shriek.

"Luke, you scared me!"

He's at the edge of the porch, watching me.

"Thanks, I'm finished," I say, covering for the fact I very obviously was not on the phone just now. Hastily, I press the home button, hand Luke the phone, and follow him inside. I slip back onto the couch, mind reeling with Luke's last words to Natalie. He said he'd kill her.

He said he'd kill her the night she died.

CHAPTER SEVENTEEN

I don't want to be here anymore. Should never have come. Everyone is high or drunk, or both. No one in any state to drive, least of all Morgan, who brought us here. The room is suddenly claustrophobic, and I can't make eye contact with Luke. *I'll fucking kill you. I'll fucking kill you. I'll fucking kill you.* The text loops in my mind.

My distress is a homing beacon for Bronte's concern. "Is everything okay?"

"Yeah, I have to get home for curfew," I lie smoothly. "Do Ubers or Lyfts come out here? If I could use your phone, that is," I add as I catch Luke's probing stare.

"Unfortunately, not really." Bronte worries her lip. "And we promised Morgan we'd stay with her. Since she's scared, you know? I didn't think about whether you'd want to spend the night, too."

A roar crescendos somewhere far off. Amber rallies and sits up, cocking her head like a meerkat.

As though possessed, she raises her hands in the air, waving them with frantic enthusiasm. "Y-M-C-A!" she slur-sings to Bronte with a giggle.

"Oh!" Bronte perks up. "The wedding! Gabriel can drive you. He's working next door. Hold on."

Ten minutes later, I'm crunching over gravel toward the main house, the tight coil of unease within releasing with each step, like a low-pressure valve. I have never been so relieved to leave a party. And when I find Gabriel waiting by a dusty Kia parked next to the kitchen entrance, my insides swell with warmth.

"Exactly how many jobs do you have? I seem to run into you everywhere."

Gabriel opens the passenger door for me and then jogs around to his side.

"Officially, two," he says, sliding behind the wheel. "Catering lands me all sorts of interesting places."

"I feel bad asking you to leave work early to take me home. I didn't think Bronte would tell you to do it *now*. I could have waited."

"Nah, my shift was just ending. My boss knows my mom expects me home by eleven, so I don't work closing."

"Bronte doesn't have a curfew, too?"

"Special dispensation for friend death. Or something." Gabriel turns the key in the ignition, engine sputtering to life with a wheeze. "Speaking of . . . you okay? I've been thinking about you all day. Bit surprised to see you here, actually."

God, was that this morning? The memory feels far away, though the phantom burn of Gabriel's lips on my cheek flares up anew.

"I think I got pity-invited to their group-therapy session. Or I was asked along to rehash how I found the body."

We bump down the drive and slip away into the black night. I'm not used to it out here. Without the congested sprawl of the city, the landscape descends into true darkness. It's both eerie and peaceful.

"If it was Bronte, I'm sure it's the former." Gabriel's eyes are focused on finding the main road in the dark. "Not that she pities you! But my sister is the kind of person who likes to take care of people. If it was Luke who invited you . . . well, that's another story."

"One you want to tell me?"

Gabriel strikes me as observant. The patient hotel clerk, the silent waiter, the ignored younger brother. Gabriel's *seen* shit. We glide onto the highway. Gabriel flexes his fingers over the steering wheel and sighs.

"Nothing special. He's like every other rich asshole at school. Ridiculously entitled and hopelessly clueless as they move through the world."

"Was that Natalie, too?" I hazard a guess.

"More or less." But he doesn't say anything else, and it's not enough.

"Amber and Bronte got into a minifight about it earlier," I say. "Amber's sure plenty of people had a reason to kill Natalie. Any idea what that means?" I dangle it like bait.

The muscles in Gabriel's jaw tense. "Natalie always got what she wanted, no matter the expense." He reaches for the radio, turns it on, ending my inquiry. Country music blares through the stereo. Not what I expected of him.

I debate my next move carefully as we make quick time back to Seaview proper. At this hour, with zero traffic, it's a brisk ten-minute drive.

Gabriel's a potential ally, someone who knows a lot about this town and has already done me more than one solid. But by the same token, he's an unknown entity. Everyone in this town is. I have to go with pure gut instinct.

"Can you tell me at least if Natalie was dating anyone in particular? Any notable ex-boyfriends? Or drama with Luke?" Luke's texts implied that Natalie had a secret hookup. Romantic history could be important.

"I wouldn't call it drama. They dated years ago, but in that stupid way you date when you're in ninth grade. I don't really count anyone I hooked up with back then, do you? Plus, they stayed friends. Obviously."

I ignore the question directed at me—I didn't have my first proper boyfriend until junior year, and he turned out to be a real fuckboy. I am not confessing that right now. And more critical is Gabriel's news: Natalie and Luke were *exes*. "So Luke and Natalie dated each other?"

"In fairness, Luke and Natalie have dated everyone. Natalie and *I* dated for like five minutes. It's a small town. Not a ton of options."

I look at him involuntarily, my insides squeezing. *Gabriel and Natalie.* He catches me and smirks.

Without warning, I watch the hood spin left as my ribs crash into the door handle. Then I'm weightless, like the ground is missing beneath the car.

"Shit!" Gabriel releases tension on the wheel as we skid across Beach Avenue, coming to a rest in front of Seaview Harbor.

"You okay?" he asks, watching me carefully.

"Yeah, I'm fine," I answer before I'm fully sure that's true. "Did it rain?" Confident nothing is broken, I search for signs of a storm, but in the wash of the streetlights, I find the nearby buildings bone-dry.

"It's the tide," Gabriel explains, tongue poking through his teeth as he concentrates intently on the road. "And we're already in it." I don't know what he means until the tires squeal a wet, phlegmy cough. The puddle we rode into is now a miniriver, threatening to sweep us away with it.

"It floods down to the harbor all the time. Only gets really bad once or twice a year, though."

I'm tense, bracing my feet against the floor mat, but Gabriel's voice calms me as he inches to the other side of the stream.

"Is that why the staff room at Hotel Seaview smells so bad?"

Gabriel laughs as if I were joking. "That and Elaine's insistence on microwaving fish for lunch."

His warmth fills the car. Fills me, heating me from within. And then we're through, the country station impervious to our anxious giggles.

It's only later that the term *managed retreat* pops into my mind, but we're already in Maura's driveway, coming to a stop dead center of the house.

"Thanks for the ride."

Gabriel nods, but I can tell something's on his mind.

"Listen," he says, turning to me, his expression stormy but his tone kind. "I know it must have been traumatizing with everything with Natalie. You know I get it. We've both lost parents. Death is a shitty vortex. I'm not judging you for the sudden obsession with Natalie, considering. Just be careful, okay?"

"Of course." I ensure that I sound casual, chill, and I offer a wave once I'm out of the car. But then he doesn't drive off. He's waiting to see that I get inside, I realize. I make my way up the porch steps at almost a run.

"You're a real social butterfly," says a gruff voice. I nearly jump out of my skin. Suzanne moves the vape from her mouth and blows out sweet-smelling smoke. I take a step back. Nasty habit.

"It's been a whirlwind day," I reply, hesitating at the front door. Gabriel is still idling in the drive, so I offer a thumbs-up I immediately regret, but the car rumbles away. I take a seat next to Suzanne on the wicker love seat. "Were you waiting up for me?"

"Something like that. After last night, your grandmother wanted to be sure you got home safe."

"What if I'd shown up at two a.m.?"

"Then you would have found coal in your cereal bowl tomorrow morning."

"That's . . . both random and terrifying."

Suzanne's laugh is throaty and warm. "I was joking, regardless. I'm a night owl, so it's no big deal. I did warn your grandmother, however, that you might need boundaries. You may be almost eighteen, but she can't treat you like an adult houseguest. For both your sake and mine, let's say you endeavor to be home by midnight most nights, okay?"

"Then I'm early." It's barely past eleven.

"Precisely. Where were you that Gabriel Escano gave you a ride home? I'm surprised you weren't with Benjamin."

Heat creeps up my neck and into my cheeks. "It was a coincidence. We were at Luke Rinaldi's. The girls invited me over there for a memorial thing. Kind of."

Suzanne exhales deeply. "Good for you being the belle of the ball, but I say better not to entangle yourself with anyone in this black hole of a town. You'll be off to college before you know it. Don't need the dead weight."

Hearing words my mother surely would have said has me feeling a certain way. Both empty and full at the same time.

"Next time, you call me. I'll pick you up anytime you need. Even after midnight. Okay?"

"I will. Thanks, Suzanne." I leave her to finish her vape, and ascend to my room as quietly as I can manage, though the thunderous snores from Maura's room render the effort courteous but moot.

I'm exhausted, but tonight there's no turning in early to forget. I fish Gabriel's thumb drive from my bag and get to work, copying the massive video files over to my hard drive to reduce lag.

The file names are cryptic, a string of nonsense letters followed by time code and date. Gabriel's already saved me stress by only transferring the time codes I need, but there's a file for each different camera position. I click on each one to scope out what I'm looking at: ballroom main entrance, ballroom back-door exit, ballroom side exit, angled view of ballroom hallway from the lobby. Four hours of footage for each. Holy hell. I am definitely getting eyestrain. And no sleep.

I start on the lowest-hanging fruit: ballroom main entrance. The event started at almost the same time as the homecoming game—around seven-thirty. I think about the police timeline. The court procession ended at eight forty-five—at least that's around the time Natalie stormed off. I found her body around nine. I'm looking for someone who either left the ball early or never showed up at all. A needle in a haystack, basically. But at least it means only trudging through the first hour of footage. And I'm only looking for Reama. It's all I can do—I don't have the attendee roster or a member of WestonCon staff, like the cops do. I push down the fleeting thought that maybe I've lost my mind. What had Gabriel said? *Death is a shitty vortex.* It is, but I'm desperate, clinging to something I can control.

Like watching an hour of mind-numbing video of a door. The footage is in color, and it's hardly HD but not the grainy low-res black-and-white stuff I'd expected. Still, I'm bored quickly, so to keep from falling asleep I turn it into a game, ranking the fashion choices flowing into the ballroom as "yes" or "mess." I'm hard pressed to find a yes among the many poufy sleeves, Day-Glo colors, and overteased hair, until my brain cells properly power on and I realize it's a theme ball. They're decked out in eighties decadence and dressed as Maura characters. I recognize a few from the descriptors Luke gave on the tour.

It makes it harder to spot Reama among the throng, but then I blink, and there she is. It's unmistakably her—she's taller than average, and also pointedly not dressing to the theme. She's stuck in her own decade, in a dress likely pulled from the back of her closet. It's body-con, very early 2010s, but I have to admit the formfitting turquoise dress is a yes. And she's coming out of the ballroom instead of going in—either I missed her, or she was inside before the clip began. Or came in another way. I watch her eyes dart to either side of the door. Then she stands and waits a moment, tapping a foot impatiently. Waiting for someone. I check the time stamp: 8:25 p.m. It's fifteen minutes to the school, at worst, meaning if Reama is about to leave, she could have feasibly made it . . . but she isn't leaving.

She seems to give a start, but stops and pulls a phone from her clutch bag. Something on the screen annoys her—I can see her eye roll from here. Then she walks out of frame, veering off to her right, away from the lobby. *Away* from the school. Hastily, I bring up the side hall video feed, clicking to the same time stamp and begging under my breath for her to wander into frame. She does, but then streaks right past the door at a rapid clip. Moving where, though? I try the only video feed left: back exit. It's a familiar sight; I can make out the window I attempted to climb into, as well as the staff entrance one level down. The camera is angled to take in a full view of the back of the hotel. The video quality takes a nosedive; most of the alley is pitch-black, and the lights that illuminate the building blow out the footage, so it's too bright and yellow in places, grainy shadow in others. But I can make out Reama clopping down the stairs, into the alley.

She approaches a car, low and long like a station wagon, pulled into the shadows. Reama bends into the open window to chat with the driver. It's difficult to make anything out beyond basic shapes; everything is shadow and light, though when the driver leans forward as they talk, I catch a curtain of hair. The driver passes something to Reama—a file?—and then blows a long drag of smoke out the window. Nasty habit.

Reama returns the way she came and the car pulls off, gliding through a patch of light on the way. Dark-colored Subaru.

What is Suzanne doing meeting Reama behind Hotel Seaview the night Natalie died?

CHAPTER EIGHTEEN

Ben watches the video clip three times, squinting at the screen with his head tilted to the side.

"You're sure that's her?"

"That's her car."

"A lot of people drive Subarus," he points out.

"There's also the hair, and the vape. I'm sure of it."

"All right, *say* it's her. But how does that factor into . . . that?" He gestures at my mess of note cards, Post-its, and printed-out Instagram profile pics strewn across the bedspread. Amber sent me the high-resolution—and much more in-focus—pictures from her camera of the sheriff's board, so I've got everything they do, plus a few of my own threads.

I stop pacing behind Ben at the computer and cross to the chaos. Reama's headshot is up by my pillow, next to an index card that says *obsessive fan?* and *secret meeting with Suzanne?* But he's right. I have no clue how she or my grandmother's assistant fit into Natalie's murder. I traced Reama back inside the hotel on the clips. She disappeared off feed for less than ten minutes, presumably to do something with the file Suzanne gave her, and then returned to the ballroom at eight-fifty. She doesn't leave again, and had no time to get to the school and back. She didn't kill Natalie. Seemingly, it's a dead end.

But what I saw on that video was weird. And while Reama might have an alibi, Suzanne doesn't. If she was speeding off in her Subaru at eight-thirty, she could have just as easily driven home as to the school right in time to kill Natalie. Why, though? It's a paper-thin theory.

Luke, on the other hand . . . I unstick the Post-it where I did my best to re-create the text chain I saw, walk it over to Ben. "He texted that right before she died."

" *'I'll fucking kill you,'* " he reads out in a low murmur. "And he hasn't given the cops his alibi yet?"

"Nope. I'm kind of floored they let him fuck around all day yesterday, and didn't make him submit to questioning."

"Luke's my friend, but he's also a Rinaldi. It's the same reason they haven't talked to the mayor. Golden families with a lot of po-litical power can sway a recall or reelection campaign in a way the sheriff wouldn't want. They're handling them with kid gloves." Ben gets up from my computer chair, returns the Luke Post-it to the cluster at the foot of the bed and eyes the writing next to the mayor's photo. Overheard screaming at victim before game.

"Do you think Amber will feed you updates from her dad? This is a lot of ground to cover. It would help if we knew what to prioritize, and, well, we're hardly going to be able to interrogate the mayor." I don't miss the way Ben's expression goes hard as he eyes the mayor's smug grin in his official headshot.

"I don't know about Amber. Her dad laid into us pretty hard about the dress. I think I have to be careful playing detective in front of her. I don't want to put her in a precarious position. She was too high last night to notice me snooping in Luke's phone, but I think Bronte saw me."

A wounded expression flickers over Ben's features.

"What is it?" I pat the lone clear space on the bed next to me. Ben obliges but ducks his head to the side, hiding his hurt. I ache for him.

"I thought I'd hear from them, now that she's gone." His voice is small, lost. "God, that sounds bad, but, I mean, we were all friends. This horrible thing happens, and they throw a . . . grief party and invite you but not me?"

"Technically, I wasn't invited. I crashed."

I get a withering look. Right. Not the point.

"I'm sorry they didn't ask you to come. I don't know them that well, but I'm sure if you reach out, you guys can talk."

Ben lets out a snort. "Luke's ignored all my texts. Maybe he thinks *I* did it." There's a pregnant pause. "Maybe he knows I'm wondering if *he* did it."

"You are?"

"He was her escort in the procession. The last person to see her alive. Of course I've wondered. And then those texts?"

"And why would he think you did it?" My voice shakes. I'm afraid to hear the answer. But of course anyone there, who knew Natalie, who disliked Natalie, is a suspect.

"Natalie . . . had a twisted sense of humor," Ben says. "I loved that about her. Nat was a good time." A cloud passes over his features. He means it. Ben cared about her, even if she had stopped caring about him. "There was . . . an incident at the end of last year. She was upset about the lawsuit. She, uh . . ." Ben gulps, his face going a mottled red. Fastidiously avoiding my gaze, he lets it out in one rushed breath. "She started a rumor that I was, uh, pleasuring myself with the mascot head. I wasn't! To clarify."

"Wow." I picture it momentarily and find a flash of embarrassed heat rushing through my body. But then I can't help laughing. "That's ridiculous, though. Who would believe that?"

"You'd be surprised," Ben says dryly. "But you see why I avoided her and her family like the plague."

"Did Natalie target anyone else?"

"Not publicly, but it looks like she was even awful to her close friends, judging from Luke's texts. Who knows who else bore a grudge."

"Morgan," I suggest, fingering her Post-it. "She lacks an alibi, and there was tension over the dress. *And* she definitely has a personal connection to and in-depth knowledge of the *Killer Queen* murder scene."

"Luke does, too, though," Ben says, "given the murder tour. . . ."

I picture them all running off the field, into the parking lot. But what next? Logically, the whole thing is murky. Why would Natalie go to the pool with either of them? Or anyone else, for that matter?

"What are you thinking?" Ben's watching me curiously.

"Why was she at the pool? It's weird, right?"

Ben shrugs. "Maybe she was hooking up with someone."

"Halftime hookup," I say without thinking.

"That's a cute name."

"Yeah, it's what Luke calls it." And we're back on Luke. And the logistics are still hinky. "How long is halftime? After the homecoming-court procession specifically. There were, what? Fifteen minutes left, if that? Not much of a hookup when you have to go all the way to the main school building."

"But private. No one goes down there during a game."

No one but me. I try to visualize it, grasp at my own memory of how long it took to get there. It passes through my fingers like sand.

"Let's go there. To the school." The idea hits me like a shot. I grab my sneakers, sit on my bed to put them on. Ben gawps at me.

"It's Sunday."

"I know. The day of rest. The place was still swarming yesterday, the school resource officer haunting the parking lot. I couldn't get to the pool. But I bet it'll be quieter today. Plus, it's raining. I want to test the timeline. And who knows, maybe we'll find some clues."

Ben hesitates. "I'm sure the cops have been all over it already. . . ."

There's a double rap, the kind of knock meant more as a statement than a request. Maura flings open the door. "What are you two getting up to in here?" She stops in the entryway, taking in me with my shoes on, Ben hunched over my laptop, the mess on the bed. "When I was your age we got straight to it, but solving a murder together works, too. Morbid, as far as foreplay goes, but they say your generation is all newfangled, don't they?"

"Who says we're solving a murder?" My voice practically squeaks. Maura casts me a no-bullshit side-eye.

"Sweetie, I write mysteries for a living. Which is why I have all the supplies downstairs for a good old-fashioned murder board. That's what you need. Grab that mess and follow me. I'm not hoofing those stairs a second time."

Maura leads us to the ground floor, where she snaps at Ben to raid a nearby closet. "You know the one," she says, and he does. A minute later, he wheels a giant wooden corkboard into Maura's office, a plastic bin tucked under one arm. In short order, my grandmother helps us marry my scribbled note cards and Post-its with her supply of thumbtacks and colored string, creating a map of suspects. It's glorious. But then she frowns.

"Why is Suzanne on here?" Maura squints at the blue index card. "*'Gave file to Reama night of the murder,'*" she reads aloud. Then she laughs. "Oh, sweetheart, you've really twisted yourself into a pretzel, haven't you? Tilting at windmills. I sent Suzanne to the hotel to give Reama an ARC of my next book. Let's take her off before she sees it."

"Oh" is all I can say, slightly abashed. The answer was so simple. Did I really want to see the worst in Suzanne? With Reama and Suzanne cleared, it's looking more and more likely that one of Natalie's friends—or family—did this. I zero in on the mayor's image on the board. Could a parent really kill their own child? It depends. Why were they screaming at each other before the game? I remember the mayor in the stands, cool as a cucumber. Cold, even.

"Let's go," I say to Ben. The school is calling me. I feel its gravitational pull in my gut. I need to be where it happened. Maybe mystery-solving skills are genetic, and Maura's legacy is pushing me in the right direction.

"We're going for a walk," I say. Ben blows air from his lungs, hauling himself up. I've worn him down. Good.

"Today a walk with Benjamin, last night a car ride with Gabriel." Maura winks at me before turning to Ben. "Better bring your A game, Benjamin. She's a keeper, but she's popular. The apple doesn't fall far from the tree, eh?"

"Bet you were the most popular girl in school in your day, Maura," Ben says, sweet-talking my grandma, of all things.

"I broke some hearts." Her smile is sly. Both of them seemed to have skipped right over the part where she hinted I'm hooking up with Gabriel *and* Ben. For his part, Ben's either unbothered or has an incredible poker face.

"Have a good walk, you two," Maura says, settling down behind her lovingly scuffed MacBook.

Soon our feet slosh through soggy, decaying leaves on the drive. The day is gray and foreboding, a misting rain coating us almost immediately. I pull tighter into my paltry SoCal excuse for a jacket, too stubborn to admit I'm underdressed. We hang a right past the driveway, walking down the middle of the road. Maura's street doesn't have sidewalks.

"Gabriel drove you home last night?"

I wince. And there it is.

"Yeah. He was at the Rinaldis', working a wedding. The timing worked out."

"And he gave you the thumb drive with the video footage yesterday."

It's pointed, how Ben says it—petulance mixed with wariness.

"Are you jealous?" I half tease. Half hope. God, that's regressive, but I love the pang of desire I feel at the idea of being wanted badly enough to inspire jealousy.

"No," Ben says quickly. Too quickly. His glasses have fogged over, but he doesn't move to clean them.

"A little," he concedes. "But it's not only that. Gabriel's been showing up a lot for you lately to be helpful. I know you don't read Maura's books, but there's one about this phenomenon: sometimes the killer inserts himself into the investigation."

"It's not like I'm a cop."

"No, but you're the girl who found the body and has decided

to take things into her own hands, and he knows it. Or maybe he likes you. And maybe that makes me a bit jealous. A bit." He winks, and my knees turn to jelly. "But maybe you should be careful."

"There's no way Gabriel's a killer. He's . . ." I almost say *a good kid*, but I'm only a year older than he is, and how patronizing is that?

"Nice?" Ben supplies, then shrugs. "Nice people can do awful things. And Gabriel's not all good. He got suspended for punching someone a few years ago. He's got anger issues."

I chew on Ben's theory. Ludicrous, surely. But Gabriel was at the game—he's a football player—and could have done it as easily as anyone else. Luke or Morgan. They're on the board. Should Gabriel be, too? Should Ben?

"Not that I'm accusing you," I say. "I'm not. But . . . where were you?"

I hold my breath, waiting for Ben's reply.

"Where I am every halftime. In the locker room, trying to cool down out of that stupid mascot head."

I stop an intrusive thought that now lives in my brain rent-free, courtesy of Natalie's rumor about Ben and that giant foam head.

"So you know who was in the locker room and who wasn't?"

Ben nods. "Gabriel wasn't there."

And Bronte says Morgan was missing from the cheerleaders, too.

The long stretch of Maura's street ends, giving way to a neat row of houses with a proper sidewalk in front. The edge of the Seaview High parking lot is visible a few blocks off. We walk the rest of the way to the football field in companionable silence.

"Is there a plan?" Ben asks.

"Everyone keeps asking me that," I mutter, scanning the area. Yellow police tape still cordons off the lower stairs that lead to the pool, but otherwise, the place is deserted. The shrine has grown, a mound of bouquets and teddy bears now limp and wet at the foot of the Caroline Quinn Memorial Bench.

"This way." I take off, leading us to the field proper. I do a turn, sizing up the stands, identifying my approximate position, then come back around, point.

"The procession started there." I power walk the path the cars took. They would have let the court hopefuls out in a side parking lot behind a squat cinder-block structure.

"What are we doing?" Ben jogs to keep up with me.

"Timing it."

"Why?"

Because I need to keep busy. Keep following threads. Put myself in Natalie's shoes. Crowd the other thoughts out of my head.

"Because we need to know how much time the killer had," I settle for, pushing against the mist-turned-drizzle, rounding the athletic center, and pausing to orient myself relative to the main school building. We're on the rear end of the tennis courts, and if Natalie took the long way around them she would have avoided the view of food-truck lines and the security officer. I check my phone for the time before moving on. City-trained, I'm an aggressive walker on my best day, but I take it slower—one, because of the rain, which has turned the grassy path around the back of the property a muddy slip risk, and two, because Natalie was in heels.

"Four minutes," I confirm as we reach the old pool door, the one I'd found ajar on my quest for a free bathroom. We huddle under the slant of the school roof to save ourselves from the downpour, and I do some mental calculations. I was stuck in the bottleneck in the stands for a good four minutes, then it took me five to get to the bathroom. That gives Natalie's killer a tiny window—six minutes?

A chill runs down my spine. The murderer was there with me, or close by. Maybe even finishing Natalie off while I used the restroom.

"What are you thinking?" Ben asks.

"That it takes three minutes to strangle someone," I say darkly.

Ben tests the door handle. And it opens.

"Shall we complete the circuit?" Ben steps into the pool building, but I hesitate on the threshold. She's in there. I can see her already against the dark of my eyelids. Floating. Ben's right. We should follow Natalie's trail to the very end. We owe it to her.

I step inside and am enveloped in darkness. Ben locates the switch so we don't stumble into the pool. And . . . it's just a room with a pool. Empty.

Ben walks the perimeter of the water while I keep to the doorway. I try to imagine Natalie coming here for a hookup. It's not an ideal place for it. The bleachers are metal and it smells of chlorine. And the bathroom is, well, the bathroom. Why here?

Convinced there's nothing left to learn, I move back outside.

And I find a bouquet of flowers set beside the door. A crowd of golden marigolds and peach roses, with a card, dead center, screaming with a message:

FORGIVE ME

Natalie's killer was here.

CHAPTER NINETEEN

"Ben!" I shout, but already I'm running to the edge of the building, eyes desperately scanning the path for the culprit. By the time Ben catches up to me, I'm at the base of the stairs to the parking lot. "Look!" I brandish the flowers. "It's them. The person who killed Natalie left flowers for her. They had to have just been here!"

I dash up the stairs, not waiting for Ben to follow. We were only inside for a few minutes. They have to still be here. I rush through the courtyard, cutting across to the parking lot when I see them. A figure in a dark raincoat, hood pulled up.

"Hey!" The rain swallows the sound. They're almost to the sole car in the lot, a black pickup truck. Getting away. I break into a sprint, ignoring the burn in my lungs after the first hundred yards. I'm hardly a runner, but I make up the distance between us well enough. I catch them with key in lock, slow myself to a stop, and, wheezing, second-guess everything. Up close, they look harmless—their shoulders slouch, and I caught them lumbering the last few feet to the car. This isn't a fit killer with the strength to grip a young girl's neck for three minutes straight. But if they are, somehow, the murderer, should I even be this close? *Why the hell do I never think of a plan?*

My audible gasps for breath make the decision for me. A be-wildered Frank Quinn turns at the noise and blinks at me from the recesses of his rain hood. "Yes?" His voice bears the wary edge of uncertainty.

"Hi, uh, sorry to bother you," I rasp. "Did you leave flowers at the pool door?"

"Yes, why?"

Frank Quinn. Grandfather of Morgan. Brother of Caroline—who also died in the pool. "Is today the anniversary?"

He nods, and embarrassment washes through me. I kicked up a paranoid fuss over a bouquet with a note. This isn't a movie. Of course Natalie's killer didn't leave a flower arrangement.

I can sense Frank has more to say, but his eyes soften as he takes me in. "You're getting soaked. Come on." We head for the field, where the stadium seats create a dry overhang. And as we corral ourselves underneath, Frank removing his hood as I shove my hands deep into the soaked pockets of my jacket, Ben jogs up. Sans panting, I note. Ben's in shape.

"What's going on?"

"This is Morgan's grandfather," I say. "It's the anniversary."

Ben does some mental calculation. "Oh, right. October six-teenth. I forgot. Hi, Mr. Quinn." He dips his head in a gesture of respect.

"Benjamin. I presume your grandfather is well?"

I feel doubly silly having attempted to introduce them. Of course they know each other. Ben asserts that, yes, his grandfather is fine, and I stare at my feet. Flex my toes. My shoes are soaked through, and I wonder at a trip that's accomplished little more than freezing me through. I've discovered that Natalie wouldn't have had time for small talk with her killer. So what?

"Did you find what you were looking for?"

I startle to attention, finding Frank looking at me beseechingly. "What?"

"We've all heard that you found the poor girl. I imagine you came for closure."

"Something like that," I say.

I watch the rain glisten on the grass, and I think about how Frank must feel. Fifty-two years ago, his sister was killed at this pool. Every year, for *fifty-two years,* he's put flowers on that spot.

Did he ask for forgiveness every time? The question pushes up my throat before I can stop myself.

"Why the message on the card?"

Sadness clouds Frank's eyes, tugs down on his mouth. "I was her brother. It was my job to protect her. And I was there. Too preoccupied with someone's illicit flask to notice her go off."

"With Joe Bedecki?" I prod.

Frank turns hard, no longer warm and fuzzy.

"Morgan says you don't think he did it."

Frank's mouth twists sourly. "Doesn't matter what I think, does it? No one's ever listened to me."

"The evidence was pretty clear," Ben says, defensiveness in his tone.

"Were you there, boy?" Frank snaps. But then he exhales, long and sorrowful, as though he is more tired than he is angry. He turns to me, calmer now. "Why are you on about it?"

"If you don't think they caught the real killer, then that means he may still be here, in Seaview."

He shakes his head. "Sure. But they'd be as old as I am. Older, since I reckon it wasn't a fellow fifteen-year-old that strangled my sister. It takes a lot to kill a person. I certainly don't have it in me."

Frank is right, but still. The original murder niggles at me, like there's something *there,* but I can't yet see it. The superfan angle is DOA, with Chris ruled out and Reama with an alibi. Still, someone's copied the book, or the original killing, for a reason. Misdirection, I guess. But *why?*

We huddle close to the wall as the rain intensifies, half the parking lot now rendered a lake. But Frank doesn't make a move for his car as I expect. He eyes Ben.

"I'd offer a ride," Frank says, "but I'm going in the opposite direction. I reckon a gentleman might dash off back to Maura's to grab his car so he might save his girlfriend from getting fully soaked."

Embarrassment licks at my insides, and before I can stammer a protest, Ben tells me he'll be back in five minutes and takes off in a jog.

"I'm not a damsel in distress," I tell Frank, annoyed. "I can handle walking home in the rain."

Frank takes my chastisement in stride. In fact he appears downright amused. "It'd be a shame if you did after I went to all that trouble to get us the opportunity to speak alone."

I feel a burn briefly from the censure, but then raw curiosity takes its place. "What did you need to say that you couldn't say in front of Ben?"

"He's a good kid, but family runs deep in this town, and his grandfather was the sheriff when Caroline died. To suggest a bungled investigation would cause more problems than it's worth. So keep this to yourself. Joe Bedecki was the easy collar, and the sheriff's office has always liked it easy."

" 'Easy collar' how?"

"Joe's family was poor, and he'd gotten into trouble with the law more than a few times before he landed the janitor gig. He was young, handsome, known to flirt with the girls at school. They narrowed in on him right away."

I want to say that it's creepy for a grown-ass man to be known for flirting with high school girls, but more than anything I want more information. And Frank clearly has more to say.

"Look, I wanted whatever fucker who killed my sister to burn, don't get me wrong. But who keeps incriminating evidence like a pair of underwear in their work locker? What a goddamn moron. It always screamed planted evidence to me. Caroline knew Joe—of course she did. She was sweet as sunshine, chatted up all the school staff. Didn't care if you were a Nobel Prize winner or the school janitor. But she never said a word to me about Joe being inappropriate, making her uncomfortable. I don't buy that they were an item and he killed her over it."

I digest Frank's words. He's right about the underwear, but wrong, I think, about Caroline's confidence. What teen girl would tell their younger brother if they were being harassed? Or tell anyone at all? People tend to blame young, pretty girls for their harassment rather than the virile young men perpetrating it. The #MeToo movement has made a lot of difference, but it's not magic. And Caroline died in 1970. If Joe Bedecki were creeping on her, she likely wouldn't have told anyone. Except . . .

"But someone told the cops Joe was messing with your sister," I say. "Must have, if that became the dominant narrative?"

Frank looks at me. "It was Maura, actually. Caroline was her best friend. She found the body, too, like you and young Miss Bergen the other night. Your family must be cursed."

I rock back on my heels. Maura found Caroline in the pool? Why didn't she say? I think again about the scene in *Killer Queen*, knowing now that it was based on real life, like Maura could exorcise her demons through fiction.

"I always thought Maura made it up to punish Joe. She'd make eyes at him, but he kept on trying it with Caroline. She was jealous."

Suddenly, I know exactly the type of boomer Frank is. The misogynist kind.

"What's your alternate theory, then?" I ask, sandpaper edge to my voice. "If you don't think Bedecki did it."

"Everyone loved Caroline, so I don't know," he answers unhelpfully. "It just never sat right that it was Joe. My best guess: probably some out-of-towner psycho who was in and out before anyone bothered to look, so the sheriff pinned it on the nearest guy they could. Lots of serial killers in Northern California in the seventies, we came to find out."

I look to the bend in the parking lot, willing Ben's car to appear. I'm cold, wet, and let down. While it could be possible a serial killer rolled into Seaview in 1970 and happened upon Caroline, what are the chances he did so again two days ago to randomly murder Natalie? It doesn't make sense. Frank's theory is interesting, but not likely. Another dead end.

"If you don't believe me, talk to Grace." Frank nods at the building. "Works right here at the school, in the front office. Joe is her brother. She'll tell you. We're the only two folk who don't spit his name like a curse."

Grace. I remember her from my first day. Maura breezed into the front office and ordered Grace around like her pet. She was sweet, walking me to class. To think she carries this pain with her, working in the very place where it all went down, helping the children of people who have painted her brother as a murderer. Of course, maybe her brother *is* a murderer.

Ben's wheels splash into the lot. "Thanks for sending him for the car," I say, "and for the information." I offer my best grateful-young-person expression, and, with a salute, Frank makes a dash to his own truck.

I duck through the downpour and into Ben's passenger seat. A warm car never felt so good. Ben must have run into the house; I'm glad to see him sitting on towels, with one thrown over his shoulders, dark-blond hair dripping rivulets of water down his neck onto the white terry cloth. His glasses are streaked with half-dried droplets.

"My knight in shining armor."

"In needs-a-wash Toyota, more like," Ben quips back. Then he wrinkles his nose. "So what was so important to say to you that Frank needed to send me off?"

"You don't miss a beat."

"My mom always said I was too smart for my own good." A grimace flashes across Ben's otherwise-easygoing face. I reach over, place a reassuring hand on his shoulder. It's a familiar sensation to me: the fond memory that brings on the grim reminder. He drops one arm from the wheel, finds my left hand, and threads our fingers together for the rest of the drive. It's intimate, and I think how Frank called me Ben's girlfriend, and how neither of us protested. I squeeze his hand, run my thumb over the back of it.

"Frank spun some theory about a traveling killer. I don't think it fits. Oh, and he called my grandmother a jealous harpy."

Ben snorts. "Maura would take that as a compliment."

"Did you know that she found Caroline's body and was involved in the investigation?"

"Well, yeah. It's pretty known here. And Grandpa was the

sheriff. He and Maura are friends. How do you think I got the internship?"

"Right." We pull into Maura's circular driveway, rain beating like a timpani on the car as Ben slows to a stop and puts us in park. He has to let go of my hand to do it; my fingers tingle in his absence.

"Thanks again for picking me up," I say. "And for everything. Indulging me."

"I'm enjoying it. Being your partner in crime-solving."

"Me too."

Neither of us makes a move to leave. There's a heady tension, like yesterday in the diner.

"Your hair is driving me crazy," I say, grabbing the towel on his shoulders. "May I?" With Ben's consent, I ruffle his hair with the towel, then comb my fingers through his drying curls to arrange them artfully. "There." For good measure, I nudge his glasses half an inch up the bridge of his nose, and whisper my fingers over his jawline.

I'm close to him now. The center console is digging into my side. Ben finally gets the message, meeting me halfway, hand on my forearm, inching higher. I lick my lips and give the tiniest of nods, and Ben closes the gap.

We rocket past a chaste pressing-together of lips to equal parts electric and awkward. The latter slips steadily away until we're all heat and breath and pressure and *more*. Only *more* can't be *now*; it's midday Sunday, in a car, in my grandmother's front drive. So I break away, lean back, winded, assessing my handiwork with an uncontainable grin.

Ben's cheeks flare adorably red, his lips kiss-swollen and his glasses thoroughly fogged. He clears his throat. "That was epic. And, trust me, I want to go inside with you and use your bedroom for activities other than working on a murder investigation. But I need to go. My grandpa needs me to do a grocery run."

"And I should probably spend some quality time with my grandmother. We are so cool."

"The coolest kids in Seaview." Ben gives a sage nod.

"See you at school tomorrow?"

"Definitely. I'm guessing you have Luke's alibi on your agenda?"

"You know me so well. I want to know what Natalie had on him. And then, yes: Did he have a halftime hookup or not?" I wonder if Luke gave his alibi to the cops today. I should text Amber, see if she knows.

"He definitely wasn't in the locker room," Ben says. "And like I said, I don't remember seeing Gabriel, either." His look is loaded. An image of Gabriel's strong frame pops into my head, unbidden, but I shake it away, unlock the passenger door, and swing it open, thrusting one leg out into the rain.

"I'll see you tomorrow." I offer one last shy smile before dashing up to the porch.

Inside, I pull my waterlogged sneakers off with a relieved sigh; the soggy socks follow, and I shove them into the shoes, leaving them by the door.

"Celia, that you?" Maura calls from the dining room. I wend my way through the front sitting room and find her bent over the beginnings of a giant jigsaw puzzle. Elaine, from Hotel Seaview, is next to her, rapidly sorting pieces into different containers. Peak grandma right here. Elaine is nursing a gin and tonic, and Maura's on what must be her eighth coffee of the day.

"Join us, sweetheart." Maura pats the chair next to her.

Elaine squints at me as I take a seat. "It's simply uncanny how much she looks like Vanessa."

"Does she?" Maura tuts as she fits an edge piece. "I think she takes after me. That gorgeous wavy mahogany hair. Vanessa's was dishwater brown and frizzy more than anything."

I would've said warm brown and wild, but it's true my mom used to say she wished her hair were a richer color, like mine. With Maura's current gray, I didn't realize who I'd got it from.

"So . . . puzzles?" I say, attempting to change the subject. My mother is a sore one.

"Don't knock it until you try it, girly," Elaine says with moxie. "Maura and I have been doing our weekly jigsaw for going on ten years."

Maura slides the box my way. It's an idyllic scene of a cabin on a cliff, with brilliant pink, purple, and yellow flowers cascading down to the choppy sea. Pretty, if on the cheesier end of the art spectrum.

"You're welcome to join us," my grandmother says. "I'm surprised young Ben didn't come in, though. How was your walk?"

"Ben?" Elaine says with some interest. "Yesterday it was Gabriel."

"My girl's popular," Maura says, a wink in her tone.

"Walk was good," I say ignoring that *of course* Elaine already knows about my drive with Gabriel. "We ran into Frank Quinn at the school. He was leaving flowers for his sister." Elaine's presence is mildly inconvenient, but it won't stop me from asking my burning questions. "He said you found her body, back in the day. Thinks we must be cursed."

Maura barks a laugh. "He said that, did he? Frank's always

loved sensational conspiracy theories. But, oh, Cecelia . . ." She grasps my shoulder with her hand, squeezes reassuringly. "That's why I hate what's happened to you. I know what it's like. The way it haunts you."

"That's why you wrote the book?"

"They say write what you know," Maura replies darkly.

"Frank also said you told the cops about the pervy janitor. And his sister is Grace, the administrative assistant at Seaview High."

"Lordy loo, Celia, are you on a tear. Yes, I told the sheriff about Joe, but Grace has never held that against me. Her brother did something truly awful in the name of passion, and she understands he's paying for it."

"That's the Joe she mentioned my first week?"

"Oh, yes, he's rotting in a prison about three hours' drive from here."

"Sometimes I take Grace down there for visitation day. Poor dear." Elaine gets lost momentarily in her own saintly pity before turning on me with some interest. "But why are you interested in Caroline Quinn and Joe Bedecki?"

"Cecelia's been bit by the amateur-detective bug, fancies herself a protagonist from one of my novels," Maura answers. "If she's asking about Caroline and Joe, it's because she's connected it to Natalie's death. She's got a murder board started in my office and everything. Your favorite politician's on it, in fact."

"Oh, is he?" Elaine singsongs. "God, wouldn't that be juicy as shit if the mayor killed his own child?"

Maura catches my confusion.

"Managed retreat would see Elaine's Hotel Seaview sold off and demolished to make way for the sea," Maura says.

"Fuckers," Elaine spits. "I finally outlive my brothers to run the place, and they want to tear it down. So we get a little basement flooding once in a while. It's fine."

I think about Gabriel and me coming through a stream in the middle of the street last night.

"What's on your murder board about Mayor Fuckerino?" Elaine inquires of me gleefully.

"He got into a screaming argument with Natalie before she died. That's all I know."

"Well, dear," Maura says, sitting up from the puzzle and fishing out a notepad from a side-table drawer. "Lucky for you it's not all *I* know. I was curious about your quandary, so I made some calls. Diana heard from Mark, who heard from Lorraine Hardy, that the dispute was over Natalie's homecoming dress. Cost a mint, apparently, and sweet Natalie went behind Daddy's back and charged it to a credit card. He screamed at her in the parking lot at the school before the game, and Lorraine's son Caleb heard the whole thing."

Go, Grandma, helping out with the murder investigation! It's not earth-shattering—a dispute over an expensive dress—but it is interesting. If Natalie's dad was willing to lay into her in semi-public, what could he do behind closed doors? It's something to consider.

I find myself joining the jigsaw-puzzle squad. We work primarily in silence, with Maura and Elaine falling into a snappy patter every so often about some town gossip, a colorful hotel customer, the publicist Maura hates.

I use the time, the headspace granted by the intersection of mindless sorting and the assurance of pattern and order to catalog where things stand. Luke, Morgan, Mayor Bergen . . . prime suspects. Well, Morgan, barely—my gut tells me it's not her, though who knows. My gut says all sorts of things about Gabriel, too, and it's bugging me what Ben said: that Gabriel has been awfully helpful. The biggest mystery is Natalie: who she was and what her relationships were with people. I was only in her orbit for a week, but I felt that pull. Natalie, a sun to everyone else's planets. Who did she burn?

Elaine patters off to the TV room to refill her G&T, and I find my grandmother frowning in my direction.

"This whole murder thing isn't good for you. You've had a storm cloud over you for the last hour, Celia. I think you should see Dr. Shelby."

"I'm fine," I snap. "And I already told you. Her daughter died. I can't go see Dr. Shelby, even if I wanted to."

Maura purses her lips. "I was hoping I wouldn't have to strong-arm you, but I am the adult here. I need to look out for your best interests now that your mom isn't around. I called Dr. Shelby earlier. You have an appointment tomorrow after school. She was happy to take you. Suzanne will pick you up from school and take you over. It's all arranged."

Well, that's fucked-up, I think, but maybe I'm a hypocrite. There are all sorts of ways to process grief. I'm one to talk, throwing myself into amateur-detective work. Perhaps work of a different kind offers Dr. Shelby the same solace.

But Maura's meddling also means I'll have to rehash the details of finding Natalie to her own mother. Dance around what I'm doing in the wake of her death: Poking around. Exposing secrets.

Losing myself.

CHAPTER TWENTY

I set foot on campus Monday and feel the target on my back. All over, really. Anywhere people catch a glimpse of me. Their eyes rake over my face; whispers follow behind me when they think I can't hear. *She found the body.*

But soon a new word, breathed low in the halls between homeroom and first period, reaches my ears: *sheriff.*

And then there he is, center court behind the podium in the gymnasium, at an impromptu assembly called at the end of first period. "My staff and I are working tirelessly to explore all avenues of inquiry," he says. "We ask for everyone's patience and remind everyone to please not disturb the scene of the crime." His hard gaze sweeps across the bleachers, lands on me. I shift in my seat, shame burning up my neck. But the sheriff moves on. He can't know what I've been up to. There's no camera by the pool's back door. I checked.

"We'll be conducting interviews all day in the library. Some of you will be called down to speak to us."

I follow the sheriff's eyeline right to Luke, sitting two rows in front of me. Satisfaction pulses through me to see him squirm.

"But we encourage those with information—about the victim, the night in question, anything that may be relevant—to come forward. My deputy is available to speak with anyone on a walk-in basis."

Said deputy is Shields, who tugs at the collar of her stiff uniform, looking kiddish next to the handsome-if-weathered sheriff. And she avoids looking directly at the crowd, instead finding fault with her fingernails.

"Hey, Sexy Lexie!" rings out from behind me.

I twist around and locate the source: a crop of stoner kids, sniggering, and one girl with the same high cheekbones and dark eyes as Deputy Shields, glowing with embarrassment. Younger sister? Shields probably only graduated a year or two ago and is now playing big bad deputy in front of her peers.

The teasing turns her defiant; she stares hard, straight ahead. At Gabriel, I realize with a sour spike. They share twin nods. *A family friend.*

Principal Morris steps up to the mic to finish. "There is also a grief counselor available to see those who wish to talk to her. If you need to leave class to speak to someone, you may, but we will be monitoring student activity in the halls and the parking lot, so this is not an opportunity to leave campus or skip."

With that stern warning in the air, we're released back to class; I'm caught in the riptide of students funneling out of the gym when I see Luke and Morgan, tucked into an alcove under the stairs, heads bowed together in serious conversation. I exit the stream of traffic, double back, and pretend to be tying my shoe in convenient proximity to the stairwell. I can barely make out their hushed words.

"They can't find out." Luke is tapping his nervous fingers on a yellowing trophy case so insistently the glass rattles. "I'll be royally fucked. So will you."

"They don't know," she practically pleads. "They can't."

Luke is slick and assured as ever. He looms over Morgan, and I can't help the panic that spikes through me on her behalf. *I'll fucking kill you.* And then Natalie *died.*

"Stick to the plan," Luke warns. "It'll work."

There's a rush of air as Luke flies past me. My spine stiffens in fright, but my eyes remain glued fastidiously to my laces, praying he didn't notice me. *What are they up to?*

Before Morgan can find me crouched without an authentic excuse, I rush to my next class. But the question pokes at me all through second period and into third. I'm sure I bomb Mr. Diaz's pop quiz in AP Chem, because I can barely focus on the screen. Each time the intercom crackles to life, calling a new student for questioning, my curiosity intensifies. The third time, it's Luke's name that's read out. *Please report to the media center,* the scratchy voice pages.

My hand shoots into the air. It's not hard to put a noticeable wobble in my chin as I ask to see the grief counselor. I need only to think about my mom for two point five seconds, and soon I'm flying down an empty hallway. I'm running on instinct as I slip into the library and immediately disappear into the stacks. To the left, tucked into a corner, is a circular table where a thirtysomething woman in a bargain-store suit sits. There's a cardboard sign made with fading markers that reads GRIEF COUNSELING taped to the front of the table.

Shit. I want the other side of the library. I dart past a bank of public computers and a row of yellowing celebrity READ posters to where Sheriff Morrow and his deputies have commandeered a cluster of round tables.

Luke's tense, at a table near the circulation desk, which is, blissfully, librarian-free. If I make a break for it, I should be able to use it as cover and listen in.

I'm getting good at the crouch-and-run, becoming a practiced snoop. Before I know it, I'm behind the desk, Luke's cocky drawl floating into my ears.

"I don't know what you want me to say. We came off the field, Natalie ran off, and I didn't see her after that."

"And what about her dress?" the sheriff asks, with a nonchalance that makes it clear this is strategic. A game.

"It was green, with sparkles," Luke answers. "She died in it."

"You know she was wearing it when she died?"

There's a biting laugh, and an incredulity in Luke's tone that speaks volumes to the *Are you stupid?* look I'm sure he's wearing. "Because it was in the paper? Because Cecelia literally found her and we're friends?"

Now that's a stretch.

"She wouldn't have had time to change anyway. That's obvious," Luke continues. He's still leading with confidence, but underneath there's an unmistakable rattle. "What the fuck is your thing with the dress?"

The sheriff doesn't scold Luke for language, as I expect. There's a pregnant pause, purposeful, and then: "What about this?"

There's a slow scrape of something being slid across the table. I ache to take a peek, but the only thing more dangerous than Luke finding me is having *both* the sheriff and Luke discover me.

"I did *not* fucking do that."

"And where were you during halftime? After the procession."

The air is pregnant with Luke's pause. It takes on a static kind of charge, mixed with old-book smell. He sighs.

"With Morgan Quinn. Hooking up. We snuck off to the theater to . . . you know."

Morgan was his halftime hookup?

It's all I need to hear. A whole fucking weekend being cagey about his alibi for *that*? Did Luke really think anyone would care he's dating Morgan? Natalie is *dead*. Leave it to the popular asshole to be ashamed of his hookup. Because Morgan's not as rich and hot as he is? Fuck him.

Back into the stacks quick as I can, I find my way into the deserted hallway. It's always strange to be in the halls alone, even when I know a bustle of activity is feet away, behind the closed classroom doors.

I'm pulled to the display case like a magnet. I hover my fingers over the glass, as if to reach out and touch the artifacts within. Angelic Caroline immortalized in black and white, her crown next to her photo, winking at visitors as they pass. It's exquisite, until I remember that she died with her crown. I imagine Natalie will be added to the display soon. Fallen queens of Seaview, forever behind glass.

"She was beautiful, wasn't she?"

I startle, turn. Find a short cardiganed woman at my shoulder. Grace.

"Hello, dear, what are you doing out of class?"

"I was, uh, I was in the library for grief counseling. I was headed back to class, but I got distracted. . . ." For a moment, we both look at the faded picture in silence.

"Frank Quinn told me about your brother," I say in one breath. "I'm sorry to bring it up," I say, trying to backtrack. "I know it's sensitive. I've been learning about everything with Caroline. . . ."

The set of Grace's mouth is grim, but her eyes aren't unkind. "I wish Frank hadn't dragged it all up again, but I understand your curiosity, given the circumstances," she says. "It's funny. You and Vanessa are so similar. I was so sorry to hear about your loss, hon.

I should have said it when we met, but I didn't want to ruin your first day."

"You knew my mom?" I hate how small my voice sounds. Childlike. But even the most tenuous connection to her is potent.

"Of course. I've been here a long time. It would have been twenty-three, twenty-four years ago she was in here asking me similar questions for her paper."

"What do you mean?"

"You didn't know? Vanessa did a big research report for AP Psychology on Caroline's death, and on Joe. She asked smart questions, your mom. I half expected her to end up in journalism."

"She was a social worker," I supply.

"That fits," Grace asserts fondly. "She had a big heart."

"Can you tell me more about what she asked?"

"Oh, goodness." Grace exhales fully. "It was so long ago. Mostly about Joe, from what I recall. What he was like, what he'd said about that night. I was fifteen, so I didn't know Caroline much at all, but Joe was my big brother."

"How old was he when it happened?"

"Twenty-one. Prime of his life. And, well . . ." She frowns, surely thinking of her brother sitting in a prison cell all these years.

"Big age gap between you."

"Oh, yes, I was an 'oops baby,' as they used to call it. They're kinder now." Grace chuckles to herself. "But Joe, he was a good big brother. Babysat me a fair bit when I was young. Then he became a teenager and started on the path that led him to where he is, as it goes."

"Did something happen?"

"Not especially. He fell in with the wrong crowd in school, got fired from the Hardy lumberyard for stealing, and then ended up here, working as a janitor. You know the rest."

"I don't, really. All I've heard is speculation. And what was in my grandmother's book. The older man who wanted the homecoming queen so badly he lashed out when she spurned his advances."

"Your grandmother's book is fiction." There's steel in Grace's answer. She looks me up and down. "Since you've been talking to Frank, you know we don't believe the police theory, which became the prosecution's theory that put my brother away."

And my grandmother's theory, I dare not say. But it's like Grace sees right through me. There's a glint of knowing in her eyes.

"I made my peace with it long ago, as best I can." Grace tugs her sweater tighter. "Only way to keep on living in this town. And now all we can do is pray the police have improved their skills in the past fifty years, for poor Natalie's sake."

It all comes back to Natalie. This town and its legacy of death.

"You should get back to class," Grace says, gently, like she's worried about me.

Maybe she is. Maybe *I* should be more worried. I take one last look at Caroline. She had her whole life in front of her. Like Natalie did.

Someone killed them. Snuffed them out like candles and discarded them like trash.

Luke was with Morgan. Joe Bedecki might be innocent.

I don't know where to go next. What to do. I'm just a stupid teenage girl hurling myself against the bitter tide of death: cold and inky black and crushing. You can't always have closure.

But I know someone in this town is a killer, and I have to find them.

CHAPTER TWENTY-ONE

Suzanne's Subaru idles at the curb after school, ready to ferry me the few blocks to Dr. Shelby's.

"You all right, dear?"

For the second time today, I find Grace behind me, squinting down from the top of the stairs.

"Yeah. That's Suzanne, my grandmother's assistant," I explain. "She's driving me to therapy."

"Oh. I didn't recognize her car," Grace says. "Well, I saw you walk out and wanted to check on you. I know you've had a hard few days. I'm glad to hear you have someone to talk to about it all. Stay safe." And she pats me on the head like I'm a cocker spaniel. It's an odd exchange, but I can't deny it's nice to have someone looking out for me.

The Subaru honks. Time to go.

Suzanne is no less smothering once I'm belted in and we roll out of the parking lot.

"Were you okay at school today? I heard the police were there."

"It was fine," I mumble. "They already spoke with me on Saturday, so I wasn't called in." I decide to skip the part where I snuck in to listen in on other interviews. Suzanne's smarter than that, though.

"No updates for your murder board, then?"

I keep my eyes glued to the blur of houses beyond the passenger-seat window.

"It's good, keeping your mind sharp," she continues, undeterred by my silence. "Solving real-life crimes can be an exercise in frustration, futility. But it keeps your brain ticking. We can go over your notes when I drive you home after your session."

We pull up in front of the Shelby-Bergen house in no time at all. It's still cookie-cutter perfect, the lawn sun-dappled and green. At odds with the specter of death I know I'll find inside. A family grieving.

"If it were me, I'd try to get my hands on the CCTV video from the school," Suzanne says, prattling on as I throw open the door, stick one foot out. "Surely they have it. That's what the police will be looking at, too. Just a thought."

"Thanks." I punctuate my statement by slamming the door behind me.

It's a good idea, but I don't remember inviting the entire Weston household into my investigation. I do, however, remember the eagle-eye cam Bronte pointed to outside the athletic center. Maybe that video could show me who went off in the same direction as Natalie and when. How to get it is another question.

I knock with three quick raps, my dark hair reflecting in the warped triptych of glass cut into the door. Doe eyes, rimmed red, greet me on the other side.

"*Morgan?* What are you doing here?" I ask.

Morgan runs fingers through her hair.

"What do you think?" She sniffs.

"Your police interview didn't go well?" Her name had crackled through the intercom about an hour after Luke's. And now here she is, fitting in a quick session with Dr. Shelby, much like I am.

Morgan's face crumples. "They won't leave me alone about the stupid dress. Natalie could be a selfish bitch, and, yeah, I was mad, but not enough to *murder her.* That's outrageous." Fury melts into shame as Morgan catches my searing gaze.

I can't help it. Her anger is enthralling.

"God, I can't believe I said that," she mumbles. "Please forget I said that."

"You're allowed to feel your feelings, whatever they are," I say, trying to reassure her, therapy mode rubbing off on me. Then I switch tacks, because I can't pass up the opportunity to clear up Morgan's alibi. "So you fought, and then what? Where did you go?"

Now she squirms, refuses to look at me.

"I can't."

"It's weighing on you, whatever it is."

"They think whoever destroyed it did it as a warning. That they must be the killer as well. But I could never hurt Natalie, I swear."

"A warning? You mean . . . the dress?" The pink dress we found in Natalie's secret locker. I remember the scratch on the table when the sheriff showed something to Luke. *I did* not *fucking do that,* he'd seethed. "That was *you?*"

Morgan nods, fresh shame spreading across her cheeks.

"I was so mad. I wanted her to suffer, just a bit. But then she died, I mean . . . *God!*"

Grief washes over her, and I know Morgan's a drama kid, but I don't think this is acting.

"So that's where you went after the procession. To the secret room to mess with the dress. So you have a key?"

Morgan nods again. I wait for her to mention meeting up with Luke, but she doesn't. Instead, she swings her backpack off her shoulders and around to her front, unzips the smallest pocket, and fishes her fingers inside until she finds something.

A key, very much like the one Bronte used the other day. Twice the size of a normal house key, it's a gold color, with a square fob embossed with the words *do not copy.* "Natalie had them made for each of us. Me, Bronte, and Luke. It's a master key for the school."

"Not one for Amber?"

"Natalie could only get four made on the DL. Or so she said. Amber shared with Bronte anyway. Here." She presses the key into my hand, the metal warm. "You can keep it. I don't want it anymore. It's cursed."

I follow the thread Morgan's started. Every other door at school was locked, except for the pool doors, found ajar.

"Is that how Natalie got into the school that night? With her key?"

The set of Morgan's mouth is grim.

Four master keys. Bronte seen by dozens of people in the locker room. Morgan slashing Natalie's dress in the secret room. And hooking up with Luke?

"Cecelia, you can come on in." Dr. Shelby emerges from her office, kind but weary eyes traveling to Morgan. "Would you like to stay, sweetheart?"

But Morgan's already out the door.

"Wait!" I call after her, signaling to Dr. Shelby that I'll be right back before I rush out onto the porch. "After you vandalized the dress, did you hook up with Luke?"

"Uh, yeah," she answers hastily, eyes downcast. "See you to-morrow."

Liar, my brain screams as I watch her walk away.

Four master keys. Two accounted for. One liar. And one dead girl.

✦

Dr. Shelby seems fine. But I know better.

Her smile is thin, strained. Fake-it-until-you-make-it vibes. She's in the numb phase, going through the motions of normalcy. Painfully relatable.

That's what makes this excruciating. I know my pain will trigger more grief in her. What was Maura thinking, setting this up?

Yet here I am on my therapist's couch, and her opening volley is frustratingly opaque: "Do you know why you're here?"

Oh, all the possible ways to answer that question. I start simple.

"My grandmother called you. I asked her not to, for the record."

"I don't mind," Dr. Shelby says. "It's my job."

"And throwing yourself into work is a valid coping mechanism," I say, parroting back at her something she said to me last week.

"Indeed," she responds. "So how are you feeling?"

A loaded question.

"I don't know how to answer that."

"Honestly, I would hope."

I remain silent.

"You can talk about Natalie. It's understandable you'd be experiencing a range of emotions after discovering the body."

Is it appropriate to ask my therapist if her detachment is healthy?

While I debate whether or not to answer, my eyes crawl the room, travel up the bookcases, trying to grab a title or two. As if the *DSM-5* would psychically confer answers. A glimmer catches the corner of my eye. Upper-left-hand corner of the room, tucked at the top of a bookcase. A camera.

"Tell me what you're thinking."

I nearly jump out of my skin.

"Like I'm being watched," I blurt, the first thing that pops into my head.

Dr. Shelby nods sagely. "It's natural for people to have interest in anyone connected to a death like this. To have questions."

I ignore her, wondering instead if it's common to have a camera in a therapist's office. *Does she play back the video of sessions to review her advice? Does she make notes for our next meeting? Is . . . is someone else watching?* My mind swirls with the million things I cannot say, so I deflect to something safe.

"I miss my mom."

And Dr. Shelby lets out a rush of air like a punctured balloon, as though relieved I don't want to talk about her dead daughter. I barely half listen as we navigate the passage of acceptable grief. My mom's death is still an abstract, waxen thing. Fuzzy around the edges. I can't connect to it in any real way. But the camera. The camera is here *now.*

After fifteen minutes push by, Dr. Shelby tells me to sit in my feelings, but all I can think about is that Luke lied about his alibi. *I'll fucking kill you,* he texted Natalie. Her father screamed at her before the game about a too-expensive dress. The dress she died in. Morgan smeared *fuck you* on it in red lipstick. Amber, sure

Natalie was the intended victim. This house, this family, is too good to be true. Who was Natalie really?

My eyes flick back up to the corner of that bookshelf, to the eagle eye peering down. It can't be legal to record sessions without client consent. I know it's not. So why is it there?

Where does the footage go?

There's a knock on the door, sharp and insistent. Dr. Shelby furrows her brow.

"Please excuse me." She crosses to the door, opens it a crack.

"The police are here." Her husband's voice carries. "They have more questions."

Dr. Shelby turns back to me. It must take considerable effort to force calm into her words. "I'll just be a minute."

I hope it's more like ten. I rocket off the lounger to her desk, where I pray she doesn't password-protect her desktop.

A dull ping tells me she does. Shit.

I race over to my bag and pull out my phone, Google "Natalie Aurora Bergen," and hope for an obit. (Who even am I?) And there it is: her date of birth. I type the numbers into the prompt box, fumbling through a few variations until the third one works. Month, date, no year.

A minute or two ticks by, and I don't find any camera software, no depository of files. I scan my surroundings, desperate for a next move. I spot it. Dr. Shelby's office must have been a dining room, because the door at the other end takes me into the kitchen. Left or right? Upstairs or further explore the main floor to see if the mayor keeps a home office?

But then I hear the low rumble of voices to my right, Sheriff Morrow's baritone slicing through the walls. Upstairs it is. I careen past a waterfall countertop to a back stairwell. Soon the second floor stretches before me. Though the master calls to me, I doubt I'd find a smoking gun in Mayor Bergen's room. That leaves Natalie's pink palace.

Inside, golden afternoon light streams through the window, still but for the fine particles of dust cast into its beam. Natalie could be down the hall or in the kitchen, sure to return any moment now. Even though she had her cool-girl room at the beach house, this place oozes with her—with the *Breakfast at Tiffany's* poster on the wall, a pair of purple-and-gold pom-poms hanging from the back of the door, a dried corsage from junior prom in pride of place on her corkboard.

My mind conjures up a vivid picture: Natalie sitting at her computer, turning off the monitor when I came in last week. In the now, I wiggle the mouse, and the machine groans to life, a home screen cluttered with icons greeting me. There's a folder labeled *Nanny Cam.*

Natalie doesn't have any siblings. Didn't.

A double click brings up a folder of video files. Hundreds of them, named with long strings of letters and numbers. It reminds me of the security files Gabriel put on that thumb drive for me. But there are subfolders, too. Dozens of them, labeled with names. The first few are unfamiliar, and then several are too close for comfort.

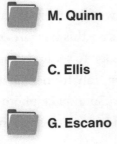

M. Quinn

C. Ellis

G. Escano

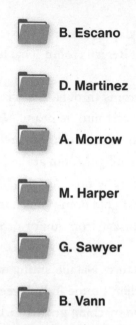

B. Escano

D. Martinez

A. Morrow

M. Harper

G. Sawyer

B. Vann

And on and on and on.

My name is a siren call. There are two files inside: one video and one text. Video first. A double click pulls up footage of my therapy session from last week. In the text file, there's only one line: **Will hopefully talk more about her grandmother.**

Heart thumping and sound rushing in my ears, I open a slew of text files from the other folders. They're carefully annotated, session after session, a catalog of everyone's innermost thoughts and juiciest secrets.

Save everything, my brain screams.

I scan Natalie's desk, try the top drawer, but there are no stray USB drives or anything I could use to save this treasure trove. A click on the email icon prompts a message to set up Natalie's account. She must have used this desktop only for her spying. No opportunity to email myself things, I snap a quick photo of the screen, then tiptoe to the door, listen. There's a low hum of chatter, but no one is shouting my name. I have a few more minutes, I hope.

Back at the desk, I open each of my friend's files, and a few random ones that catch my eye, for good measure. I take a picture of the notes inside.

A. Morrow: Stress over dad doing something shady at work that she can't talk about but has to keep secret from Bronte? Need more, but could be useful to have something on the sheriff. Daddy might like it, too.

B. Escano: Stole AP Chem final answer key for Addison Harper sophomore year. Racked with guilt. Get her to do same for me? Or use it to make sure she doesn't run against me for homecoming queen? (YES!)

B. Vann: His mom caught him jerking off to some anime shit—omg, DYING. Lots of low-self-esteem garbage about his dad leaving. Shit. Stopped seeing Mom after I teased him. Need to be more careful.

M. Quinn: Goes on and on to my OWN MOTHER about how stressed she is by "a certain friend." Met someone new who makes her feel pretty and special and good enough—WHY HASN'T SHE TOLD

ME ABOUT THIS?! Told her ALLLL about the dress she's sewing for homecoming :D Find out who and, if they're embarrassing enough, get free food and drinks at Quinn's!

G. Escano: Has some side hustle he's conflicted about. Never reveals what. Make him regret dumping me. But need to find out what he's hiding . . .

M. Harper: Raging eating disorder. Huge discount on my Audi :D

G. Sawyer: SO ANGRY about her brother Joe. Jesus, lady, give it up. Thinks Principal Morris is a moron. LOL, yes. Get on her good side and leave campus whenever I want!

In the margins, Natalie noted exactly how best to use her friends' secrets against them. What she could get if she were to turn the screw, ever so slightly.

Suddenly, I know exactly who Natalie was:

A fucking snake.

CHAPTER TWENTY-TWO

I bounce on the balls of my feet in front of Ben's small bungalow. It must have once been glorious, but it has aged poorly. The exterior paint's been scrubbed raw by salty sea air; its roof tiles are bleached by the sun and peeled up toward the sky in places. The yard has been recently mowed, but there's nothing in the way of landscaping to help the run-down look of the place; yellowing weeds sprout up between the flagstones that wend their way to the front door, which is a fading rust color.

I shake my phone in my hands as I wait for my text to Suzanne to send, telling her I no longer need a ride home. How could I go home after knowing what I know about Natalie? Finally, the text is delivered, and I give a tentative knock on the door. Before long, a murky shadow moves behind the grid of windows cut into the door.

"Hi." Ben is sheepish as he opens the door. "Sorry you had to come here. I'm on cookie guard, unfortunately. Grandpa's being defiant, and if I leave, he will eat an entire sleeve of Oreos and fuck up his blood sugar."

I start to offer that the solution might be not buying Oreos, but Ben cuts me off. "I don't buy them, and if I throw them out, he buys more. He figured out how to use Instacart last year, and it's been mutiny ever since." Then he takes in my wild eyes, the impatient tapping of my foot on the porch. "You found something."

It's all the invitation I need to grab him by the hand and blaze inside. Before we can find somewhere private where I can burst, his grandfather shuffles into the room, assessing me sharply.

"She is pretty, isn't she? Runs in the family." He thrusts out an age-spotted hand at me; his handshake is firm and sure. His gaze is so direct I practically drown in the blue of his eyes. They're identical to Ben's but wiser. "I'm Dick."

Ben groans, but Dick's having none of it. "It's my name. I can't change it just because your generation has a filthy mind."

"Technically, your name is Richard," Ben counters.

"No one's called me that since my schoolteachers during roll call. Suck it up."

"Nice to meet you, Dick," I say, doing a small curtsy on perverse instinct.

"Well, you two run off, then. I have Judge Judy to keep me company. And Oreos." His baby blues twinkle; Ben's remain flint.

"Very funny," Ben replies. "If you go into diabetic shock, I won't help you."

"I'll leave all my money to the humane society."

"I'm sure they'll appreciate your ten dollars."

And then they break into laughter: a relief to me, as for a moment I was unsure whether it was banter or a brawl.

"We'll be up in my room," Ben says. "Take notes on any juicy cases for me."

I follow him up the stairs, and even though he's been in my bedroom, I have to swallow down a nervous lump in my throat as I walk into his. But then it's surreal. Ben's room is strangely impersonal—like a hotel room. And then I remind myself that of course it is; Ben only moved here earlier this year. I think of my own sparse guest bedroom, and warmth blooms in my stomach: empathy, pity, kinship.

I shut the door behind us, recline against it. "I have so much to tell you, but—" My voice hitches. Ben's room suddenly shrinks.

He is watching me intently, and I realize how close he is. And how I want him closer. I pull him in by his hoodie pockets, go in for a kiss. Ben smiles against my lips, leans into me, and his hands slide up my back, rushing heat into my cheeks. We push off from the door, walking backward toward the quilted double bed tucked under the slant of the roof, but I come to my senses before we go further.

I pull away, smacking my head on the low ceiling. "Ow!" I give a nervous laugh, more embarrassed than hurt. "Seriously, I have to tell you what I found at Natalie's house."

"Sorry, sorry." Ben throws his hands up in surrender. And, God, I love the way his kiss-swollen lips quirk into a sly smile, like he's not sorry at all and is in fact waiting for an opening to resume.

Much as I'd enjoy that, this Natalie thing is serious. I sit up, cross my legs under me, and fill him in. And much to my shock and consternation, he *doesn't appear surprised.*

"I suspected," Ben says with a shrug.

"What the fuck? Why didn't you tell me?"

I get a side-eye. "And give you more reasons to suspect me? You're digging into people with beefs against Natalie. If I'd told you that I thought she was eavesdropping on private therapy sessions in order to blackmail people, what would you have said?"

"I would have said, 'Holy shit, that's huge, that's motive. We need to find out who she was blackmailing!' And she wasn't blackmailing you, was she?"

He shifts.

"Ben!"

"She wasn't! But she had said things, referenced things to me that only Dr. Shelby knew. That's why I had a feeling. But I thought everyone would write me off completely if I said anything."

The pieces slot into place quickly: Natalie's entry on Ben mentioned his mom; it was followed by a note about him no longer attending therapy.

"That's the real reason you didn't want me seeing Dr. Shelby," I say.

Ben hesitates, then nods. He hauls himself up from the pillows, mirrors my posture so we're sitting across from each other like in a campfire circle. "I saw her years ago, before my mom died, and when Natalie had specific ammunition . . . I knew when I needed to see someone again, after my mom, that there was no way in hell it would be Dr. Shelby. Natalie had this way of always having people under her thumb. Now we know why. I didn't want her to have anything on you."

His outburst makes sense now. And to think I'd gotten so annoyed at him, when all he was trying to do was protect me!

"Well, she had plenty to hold over others. Almost everyone at school had files. There were notes in some of them about the favors she could get out of people. Free shit."

"Blackmail," Ben supplies.

"Low-level, but yeah. I didn't have time to go through everything, but I'd bet she was asking for real money from some peo-ple. I only looked at files for the people I know, but imagine if she had ammunition on any of the adults in Seaview. People with real money and clout."

"What else do you remember? Anything specific?"

"I took some pictures." I show him the master list on my phone, three photos' worth of names. Ben bites his lip adorably as he scans. I scoot so we're side by side and I can watch the screen. Landing on his own name, he frowns.

"She must have started doing this freshman year. That's when I saw Dr. Shelby. You didn't, um, read the file, did you?"

"No!" I lie, to spare him the embarrassment, though now it's a priority to wrest my phone back ASAP. If he swipes forward too many photos, he'll see a blurry rendering of his adolescent secrets.

Suddenly, Ben gasps, and my heart leaps into my esophagus.

"That's the mayor's assistant." He points to *D. Martinez*. "And she's got at least two deputies, plus Principal Morris and the city comptroller here. Plus all her friends. Wow."

I hold out my hand for the phone before Ben can swipe fur-ther. I look over the list again myself, for good measure.

"There's no Luke," I say, realizing it now for the first time.

Ben laughs to himself. "Luke thinks therapy is stupid. Or maybe it's only Dr. Shelby. He says she has a 'Stepford wife' energy."

"Or maybe he knew what Natalie was doing and wasn't willing to risk it?" I propose. "But Natalie found out his secrets anyway."

"She had her ways," Ben intones somberly.

I throw myself down onto Ben's bedspread dramatically with

a groan. "I wish I'd had more time to read the files. Or make copies. Or *something*. Do you think it would be crazy to break into the Bergens' house? Or the school?"

"Uh, yes. But why the school?"

There's so much to catch him up on. I tell him about the camera outside the athletic center, Suzanne's tip about the CCTV, Luke's alleged alibi, Morgan's contradicting it. How I want to check if anyone followed Natalie toward the school.

"Morgan gave me a school master key," I finish, and Ben's eyes go wide.

I pull up onto my elbows. "We have to eliminate some lines of inquiry. We've got a list a mile long, thanks to Natalie's therapy blackmail scheme, plus Mayor Bergen, plus Luke."

"Have you talked to Amber lately? Can't she help fill us in on her father's leads?"

I fish my phone out of my bag and find a message from Amber. She must have texted while Ben and I were kissing. Hastily, I sit up fully and smooth down my shirt, slightly ashamed that I let hormones distract me from the task at hand. "The mayor says he was by himself on a smoke break when Natalie was killed," I read.

Ben snorts. "Who smokes anymore? And the mayor? He's all about his image."

"It *is* convenient he happened to be alone at the critical moment. No way to prove it either way. Unless he's on the surveillance footage."

Ben coughs. "You should write down everything you remember from Natalie's computer before you forget." He hops up to fetch a notebook and pen. "I can start asking around. See if Luke will be straight with me."

"So that's a no to breaking and entering?"

Ben freezes. "Maybe let's see if there's a less illegal way to sneak into the front office tomorrow. I think we need to be careful."

I hum with assent. Getting caught breaking and entering by an already persnickety sheriff would be bad.

I write down as many of the names as I remember from Natalie's files, and the barest wisps of detail. The few blurry pics I was able to get on my phone help with a few. Ben identifies some of the initials that meant little to me. *M. Harper* is Meggy, of *dad owns the local car dealership* fame. *G. Sawyer* is Grace, the school administrative assistant.

"Her name isn't Bedecki?"

"She got married, I guess."

"Dr. Shelby has a lot of clients, huh?"

"Told you. It's a one-therapist town. And everyone acts pristine and perfect, but this place has as many fucked-up people as anywhere else. Maybe more."

"Anyone she had dirt on is a suspect," I say, looking over the final list. "Including the sheriff, potentially."

Ben's brows quirk up with interest.

"Amber's file said her dad was doing something she had to keep from Bronte. And I didn't have time to look at the others, but you said several deputies are on that list. This is a game-changer. We can't trust the police."

"You can't tell Bronte and Amber, either," Ben says. "I know you trust them, but this is big. Amber would protect her dad, and Bronte her brother. Or herself."

I shake my head. "Bronte and Amber both have alibis." I have trouble believing in some grand murder conspiracy involving my friends—well, *those* friends—but the note next to Gabriel itches at me. Doing something shady for money. Where was he during halftime?

My phone buzzes with a text. It's from Maura, but I'm confused. It's like a drunk panda hit Send.

> Cecil come home. Suzanne I'm accidental.

I hand my phone to Ben to see if he can decipher it. His eyebrows rise above the rim of his glasses.

"Wow, you got an actual, real-deal Maura text. That right there is the result of Maura trying to figure out a smartphone and some rogue autocorrect. But . . . I think Suzanne was in an accident."

A ding signals a text for Ben as well.

"And she needs me to drive her to the hospital. Shit. Let's go now. I'll take you home."

✦

There's a pit in my stomach that sprouts in the car and takes root once we're home. I rush up the front steps to the Victorian mansion.

"You stay here, sweetheart," Maura says to me as soon as we walk in the door, leaving no room for protest. "It's a school night, and I don't know how long I'll be at the hospital." She's already got her coat on and her purse, makes a twirling gesture with her hand, and Ben goes right back out onto the porch on cue.

"Do they know what happened? Is Suzanne okay?"

"They wouldn't tell me much, but it appears her brakes failed. She's in pretty bad shape, but don't worry."

That's it. Maura pats me on the arm reassuringly, an empty gesture.

"Her brakes . . . failed?"

"That's what the sheriff said. I really must go." She pecks me on the cheek. "There's food in the fridge. Don't wait up."

I couldn't eat if I tried; my stomach churns. Suzanne was supposed to pick me up from therapy. *I* was meant to be in that car.

And brakes don't just fail. At least that's what movies and TV have taught me. I Google it and find that 5 percent of car accidents each year are due to brake failure. Over three hundred thousand. I don't know if that makes me feel better.

I trudge, shell-shocked, up the stairs, hesitate on the third-floor landing. My mom's room calls to me.

Inside is frozen, the same dusty picture I left the other week. But on the other side of a murder, reeling from bad news, I see it with new eyes. My mom used to read magazines on that bed. Change in that closet. Type her papers on that computer.

Papers about the Caroline Quinn murder for her AP Psych class. I'm too curious not to pry. I'm not naive enough to expect her ancient PC to turn on, so instead I riffle through her desk drawers. I saved every paper I ever wrote, and my mom told me more than once that she used to, too. The question is whether Maura threw them out. But this room doesn't look like it's seen spring cleaning in decades.

The papers aren't in her desk, so I cruise her bookshelves, and finally I get on my hands and knees, peer under the bed. There's a plastic storage bin just out of reach of my fingers. I lie down on my stomach, ignoring the inch of dust sticking to my cheek. It takes some contorting, but I stretch my arm until—yes. I manage to hook the edge of the bin with my index finger and fish it out.

Inside is a treasure trove: Spiral-bound journals, laminated school agendas, and weathered folders labeled by subject. AP Brit Lit, American Lit, AP Gov, and there! AP Psych. I expect yellowing paper, faded words, but the thick printer paper's been locked up tight for twenty-plus years, so other than the ink now looking a bit closer to navy blue than black, it's none the worse for wear. It's surreal to see my mom's name typed neatly at the top left corner: VANESSA ELLIS, 12TH GRADE.

I skim the paper, titled "Small-Town Justice: Mob Mentality and the Caroline Quinn Murder." There are names I expect to see: Caroline Quinn, Joe Bedecki, Maura Ellis, Grace Sawyer, Sheriff Vann—Ben's grandfather. But one name confuses me: Mayor Bergen. In 1970. The Mayor Bergen I know, Natalie's dad, can't be older than fifty, so the one my mom was referencing during the original murder investigation has to be related to him. Father, uncle, or grandfather. A town dynasty.

And a quote from Grace: "They needed someone to be guilty, fast, and my brother was convenient."

Natalie is dead. Suzanne might be, for all I know. A copycat murder. Suddenly failing brakes. Two victims connected to two people responsible for putting Joe Bedecki away. A note in Natalie's blackmail file: *SO ANGRY about her brother Joe.*

Bile rises in my throat as I realize two things: It *was* supposed to have been me with Suzanne. Maybe it's not people *connected* to those involved. But people *related* to them.

And Ben might be next.

CHAPTER TWENTY-THREE

Ben doesn't answer any of the half dozen texts I send overnight, and just as I'm pondering whether a seventeen-year-old can have a heart attack, finally my phone buzzes.

> Suzanne's out of surgery. Maura wants to stay the night and I can't talk her out of it. You okay? What's so urgent?

Of course I didn't text my wild theories to Ben, but I did say we need to talk ASAP. However, in the hours since I read my mom's paper, doubt has settled in. It *is* a wild theory that Grace is coming after us in some fifty-year-delayed revenge plot against the next generation. We don't even know that someone tampered with Suzanne's brakes.

But what if.

I've been looking for an explanation as to why Natalie's murder was staged as a copy of my grandmother's book, of the original murder, and if it's a message from Grace—*you will all pay*—that would explain it.

I picture her, a sweet old lady in a cherry-red cardigan. But then there she is, hovering over my shoulder at the top of the front steps, the twist of her nose at the sight of Suzanne's car. Asking me pointed questions. Cataloging my responses.

Like a plot out of one of my grandmother's books. It beggars belief.

And so I text Ben back—**false alarm, just freaked out**—and fret, waffling between absolute belief in my theory and mocking self-doubt. I need to do more research, get a better handle on Caroline's murder and Grace herself before I go warning Ben of some imminent attack. He'll think I've lost it, and that I'm definitely not girlfriend material. Plus, there's still the whole blackmail thing. Plenty of reasons for Natalie to wind up dead.

But what if . . .

I Google "Caroline Quinn murder" on my phone on the walk to school, nearly get hit by a car when I step off the curb with eyes glued to the search results screen. Imagine the utter waste, dying for basic information. Every link I click regurgitates the same facts I already know, that any fan of Maura's work knows: Caroline Quinn was found strangled in the pool not an hour after being crowned homecoming queen. Janitor Joe Bedecki was convicted a year later and sent to prison for life.

There are a few Reddit threads on r/UnresolvedMysteries with some mild conspiracy theories, but nothing of real substance. The sheriff did it, Mayor Bergen, secret boyfriend, secret girlfriend, principal, homecoming-queen runner-up, even Maura. The runner-up theory is compelling. I make a mental note to find out who it was.

Strangers on the internet are no match for an actual history buff in Seaview proper, and I know it—which means if I really want to get anywhere, I have to betray Ben. I know he said not to trust anyone from Natalie's blackmail files and he has his own theories about Gabriel, but he's the first person who comes to mind. No one is more obsessed with the history of this town than he is. Ben may have him cornered on the murder market, but this side investigation needs to be my secret until I know more.

A car comes up behind me, honking. I check that I'm on the sidewalk, not in anyone's way. I'm good, which can only mean . . . *Ben.* I turn to greet my beat-up Toyota chariot, but it's a sleek silver Mercedes idling at the curb, window rolled down, Luke behind the wheel.

"Get in," he says as the locks give a soft clunk. Luke is smiling, in that sure, winning way of his, but his eyes hold a test.

"No, it's okay, We're nearly to school." I'm breathy, high-pitched, unable to keep the nervousness from my too-sunny protestation.

"I insist."

This is do-I-suspect-you-of-murder chicken. I won't be the first to flinch.

"Thanks," I say, pitching down into the passenger seat. It's almost unsettling how low it is to the ground. Whoever rode shotgun last was shorter than I am; I have to locate the button to the right side to make myself more legroom.

"You usually get a ride to school with that woman, don't you? The walking L.L.Bean catalog with the vape."

"Suzanne," I say tightly.

"Right." Luke eases the car forward. He drums his fingers over the steering wheel to some phantom rhythm. A song only he knows. "I heard about her accident. That sucks."

"Word travels fast in this town."

Luke snorts. "Yeah. Except when it travels real slow."

The sound of tires cruising over asphalt fills the car. I start a silent countdown. Thirty seconds to the school parking lot. Twenty.

"She the one you called the other night, on my phone?" There's an accusation under his innocuous question.

"Yeah." The hairs on the back of my neck have gone electric. The call log. I never actually dialed out on Luke's phone. He must have checked.

The car rolls to a stop. We're at the end of the student parking lot, far from the drop-off line and most foot traffic.

"Well, luckily, Gabriel was there to drive you home. So it worked out," Luke says, turning off the ignition. "Did you tell Ben?"

I can't stop the laugh that rips from my throat. Was all of this Luke bro-coding for Ben?

"Of course he knows," I say, pushing mild offense into it. Then I'm all wide-eyed innocence. "Don't you tell Morgan everything?"

Confusion ripples across Luke's face. "Morgan? Why would I tell her everything?"

"Isn't she your girlfriend? You were hooking up with her during halftime, right?"

He tenses up, and I enjoy it very much. Let Luke be cowed by me. Serves him right after all his theatrics. "Thanks for the ride. See you later."

✦

School is almost normal, save for the announcement that deputies and the grief counselor will once more be available in the library. No sheriff, though. Has he moved on to stronger leads? I long to know what they are. Is he on to Grace, too? I'm restless all morning, but it isn't until lunch that it strikes me there are clues I can put together right now. I'm keen to avoid Luke anyway, so I skip the caf altogether, instead finding myself back in the library.

It only takes five minutes of wandering the stacks to find it: the yearbook archive. Better than waiting to go home to sneak into Maura's office to check hers. It didn't even occur to me last night. I pull the 1970 edition off the shelf and plop down on the floor, opening it to the homecoming spread near the front.

Caroline has a gravitational pull: dolled up in the court-processional, held all those years ago on the same chilly football field, and in the same winning photo that sits in the display case, resplendent in white. Below the group shot, in small print, is everyone's names, left to right, consolation prizes listed in parentheses.

Maura Ellis (2nd runner-up)
Elaine Rogers (1st runner-up)

Maura was robbed, I think, as I study the first runner-up for signs of murderous intent. But she's linked arm in arm with Maura, beaming at the camera. Seems sweet as pie. And familiar. Is that—Elaine as in Hotel Seaview Elaine? It must be.

I replace the yearbook on the shelf. *Skip school or stay?* I ponder, creeping close by the doors, but then Grace appears in the front office window, watching. Her eyes narrow. Surprise that I'm alive and well? Or suspicion that I might make a break for it?

Fine, I'm not that daring. After school may be better timing for a visit to Hotel Seaview anyway. Perhaps my local history buff will be on shift, as well.

He's not. I find the front desk of Hotel Seaview staffed not by Gabriel, but by a middle-aged man so engrossed in his phone I stand there for a good minute and have to clear my throat loudly before he takes notice.

"Is Elaine here?"

His eyes narrow. "Who's asking?"

"Jason, why are you grilling her?" Elaine appears in the office doorway. "Can't you see she's harmless? And gorgeous as always. Come here, dear."

I can't help but smirk as I glide behind the desk to join her. She closes the door behind me. I hope she still thinks I'm gorgeous after I'm done.

"What do you want, sweetie?"

"This is going to sound odd, but it's about Caroline Quinn."

Elaine cackles. "In this town, not that odd. What about her?"

"You were first runner-up for homecoming queen that year. Were you mad they didn't crown you queen after she'd died?"

Elaine's brow furrows. "All right, that is an odd question. Why would I want a dead girl's crown? Even if they'd offered, I'd have refused. I'm not stupid. This town mourned her like she was a saint."

"She wasn't?"

Elaine nails me with a thousand-yard stare. "Are you? Is anyone? We all have sharp edges and dirty little secrets. Caroline was no exception. She liked gossip, flirting, a little healthy one-upmanship among friends."

"Flirting with Joe Bedecki?"

"Him . . . and others. Like we all did. And I did not limit myself to boys, I'll have you know, though it was the seventies and we didn't exactly talk about it. Your generation is far better off in that regard."

"Do you think Joe did it?"

She waits a beat, as if searching for the words. "I believe a lot of different kinds of men can behave shockingly, strangle a girl if he's in the mood for it. Joe was one I wouldn't put it past. He was a dish, though maybe that was part of it. Beware the hot ones, dear. They get away with murder. Sometimes literally."

"Grace doesn't think he did it."

"She told you that?"

"She did. And my mom didn't think Joe killed Caroline, either. I found a paper she wrote on the murder."

"That old chestnut. I remember her running around town like Nancy Drew, annoying the shit out of her mom. She found the same thing you will. Joe was good for it. Skulking around the school during the dance. Her underwear in his locker."

"Were there any other suspects, though?"

"Honey, I was a teenage girl caught up in my own melodrama, so I wouldn't know. You'd have to ask the sheriff about that. It was less than a week, and Joe's name was all over the paper, arrested for murder."

Ben's grandfather. Which might tip off Ben. Great.

Or maybe not. Time to visit Amber at the police station.

✦

"Should have guessed you'd stop by to keep me company," Amber says with some amusement when I walk into the station. And then with a deep sigh: "I can't really help you anymore, though.

I've already done too much. My dad is on the fucking edge, keeps barking at me to reassure him I haven't told anyone anything. All the files are on lockdown, too."

She means Natalie's files, but I'm not here for hers. "What about older records?" I ask instead. "Like, *really* old."

Amber narrows her eyes. "Jesus, Cecelia, what are you into now?"

"The Caroline Quinn murder," I mumble. "I'd like to look at the original files, especially interview notes for . . . select people." I don't want to mention Grace, or Maura. Tip my hand. Amber and I share a nosy trait, but I know this thread of inquiry is a reach: that a sixtysomething woman is murdering people, or attempting to, in an act of decades-old revenge.

But since Grace was more candid about her feelings with my mother twenty-three years ago for her paper, what might she have said to the cops in 1970? If she was interviewed at all. I need to know what other suspects they had. If they even investigated beyond Joe. That may determine whether the sheriff would be in Grace's sights—and, by extension, Ben. The pattern is the grandchildren of the people who put Joe away. If it's actually a pattern.

"Please, Amber." I'm practically begging now. "If I don't figure this out, more people might be hurt."

Amber's shoulders sag. "This is the last time. Follow me."

We slip down a dank hallway off the lobby, past a warren of scuffed doors, a graveyard of pre-open-plan efficiency, until we reach one marked RECORDS. Amber unlocks the door, and I'm hit in the face with so much must and mold it wrenches a cough from my throat.

"Yeah, no one comes in here much, and none of the really old shit is digitized. Be careful, and don't let anyone see you. My dad's in an interview, but he'll be done soon."

The door clunks behind me, and I must be imagining the way the air seems thicker, the room smaller, now that I'm shut in. Despite the claustrophobia, I lock the door, just in case. I shake off my trepidation and make my way over to the nearest filing cabinet: tall, ancient and creaking. The label slipped into the front placard is yellowing and cracked, ink smudged and faded, but I can make out the year span: 1938–43. Wow, deep cut. The second cabinet goes into the sixties, so I move on to the third.

There, all the way at the bottom, I find what I'm looking for. And so for the second time today I plop myself on the floor in search of vintage goodness. Dust motes kick up as the drawer shuttles forward and a sea of age-spotted cream folders stretch before me, some labeled better than others. There's a cliché that says cops hate paperwork, and you can see the variation in how meticulous the various officers were in record keeping. Some tabs boast simply a surname or keyword; others have names and dates to help. Not that it's too difficult to find *Quinn*. The file is thicker than the rest, almost smack-dab in the middle. I wrangle it out and set it down.

The contents spill at my feet: police reports, interview transcripts, case notes. Faded, though, so to save my eyes, I pull out my phone so I can use the flashlight. A lot of the file is technical, scribbled in longhand by the reporting officer. *Caroline Quinn, body discovered at approximately 9 p.m., signs of strangulation.* Nothing I don't know or couldn't guess. But then I realize there are photos. Black-and-white. The whites are bleached by time, giving everything a washed-out quality, but there she is. Caroline's body. A shudder passes through me.

My grandmother's initial interview is recorded in a tight, juvenile script, the transcriber haphazard with capitalization and punctuation, but I get the gist.

asked miss Ellis if victim had enemies after hesitating she disclosed a name. Joseph Bedecki the school janitor "she flirted with him but we all did. joe's an attractive man. we were flattered by his attention"

I wonder at the accuracy of the officer's transcription. "Joe's an attractive man" doesn't really sound like a teenage girl, even in 1970. But Maura's interview is clear-cut. I thumb through the rest of the file, looking for Grace, but she's not in here. Guess they saw no reason to interview the prime suspect's fifteen-year-old sister. I do, however, find the answer to my other question: Joe wasn't the only suspect.

Paul Rogers, Caroline's ex-boyfriend, has an interview file, and the name jumps right out—Rogers, like Elaine. Then I remember how she said she finally inherited Hotel Seaview when her brothers died, so I'm guessing Paul's no longer with us. He was a sound suspect, though: Overheard getting into a screaming match with Caroline at the dance. Punched her date in the same altercation, a boy named Clark Sawyer. I grab my phone, Google on a hunch. Yep. Caroline's date was the future Mr. Grace Sawyer. This town is far too small for my liking. It's the closest I come to finding Grace in these files.

Beyond Paul, it doesn't seem like the cops looked into anyone else; nailing Joe was too juicy. I skim the evidence log from the search of his office at school. One pair of panties, pink, later identified as Caroline Quinn's. Photos of Caroline and others in various states of undress, apparently taken with a pinhole cam in the girls' locker room. Gross. I note that the photos aren't part of the file. I wonder which pervert absconded with them for his own personal collection.

From the evidence, Joe does look good for it. His interview notes describe him as cagey, quick to anger. Sheriff Vann noted, "Suspect clammed up as soon as we showed him the underwear," with no denial as to where they had come from. Stonewalling. A guilty person would do that.

I take pictures with my phone of the pages I might want to reference later, but for the most part, the file makes the case look cut-and-dried: Caroline was murdered, and Joe did it. Grace may be pissed and taking revenge, but Joe did it.

The door handle jiggles, and whoever's on the other side grunts with surprise. Shit. Amber said no one comes in here! I scramble to put everything back in the file, shove it back into the drawer.

A key scrapes in the lock. The handle starts to turn. At the last second, I dash behind the door, willing myself to disappear into the shadows.

And then the door opens.

CHAPTER TWENTY-FOUR

"Cecelia?" Amber stage-whispers.

The rapid gallop of my heart slows. Of course it's Amber. I emerge from my insufficient hiding place.

"Sorry. I thought it might be your dad, or another deputy," I explain.

"It might have been," Amber admits with a grimace. "Dad finished his interview and is not in a good mood. Come on, you need to get out of here before he sees you."

We sneak back to the lobby, Amber checking first that her dad is out of sight. Then she practically shoos me out the front door. But not before I can get in a final request.

"Hey, one more thing. A favor."

A groan. But she doesn't stop me.

"Maura's personal assistant, Suzanne, was in an accident. I'm sure you heard. Could you look into the accident report for me? Let me know if there's anything hinky?"

Amber looks over her shoulder again. Dad check. Coast clear. "I'll see what I can do. Now *go!*"

It's enough. Finally, I allow myself to be kicked to the curb, where I find Gabriel literally on said curb.

"What are you doing here?" we say at practically the same time.

"They brought you in for questioning?" I ask, piecing it together.

Gabriel gives a solemn nod. "I think they made me come after school hours to fuck with me. Morrow knows I have to work. I had to call in and have someone cover me at the hotel."

That explains Jason, then. "Why you, though?" I ask. "Are you a witness?"

"They're interviewing all of the football players and cheerleaders not present in the locker room during halftime."

"Well, then, where were you?"

"By myself, blowing off some steam." Gabriel coughs. He's a shitty liar.

"You know they don't believe you, either?"

"Yes." He squirms. "But I didn't kill Natalie."

It feels honest, but I can't help thinking about Natalie's blackmail file. She wanted to get revenge on Gabriel for breaking up with her. There's more to their history than he's let on.

"Even though she was spying on your therapy sessions and hoping to blackmail you?"

"She *what*?"

"I found it all on her computer. She has a note that you were doing something shady for money, but she didn't know what."

And he squirms again.

"Gabriel."

"It's complicated, and I'm not exactly going to spill my secret to you on the street, outside of a police station. I barely even know you."

I stay on his heels as he starts walking.

"Fine. You don't have to tell me." *For now,* I don't add. "But I do need your help."

That gets him to stop. I nearly run into his back.

"How can I help you?"

"Town history. You know the stuff that's not necessarily written down, right?"

Gabriel squints against the afternoon sun. "What does town history have to do with Natalie eavesdropping on therapy sessions and blackmailing people?"

"Uh, I'm kind of working multiple angles of inquiry here." I scrunch my face in a way I hope is both adorable and convincing.

Gabriel tilts his head, the full-on skeptic. "Still? I hadn't heard from you about the security footage, so I figured it had come to nothing and you'd dropped it."

"Not exactly. That part did come to nothing, but there's so much more going on."

Gabriel considers me, and I can see his love for history slowly winning over his common sense. "What *exactly* do you want to know?"

"The anecdotal stuff. I read the original police file for the Caroline Quinn murder, and it was pretty basic."

"You *what*? Seriously?"

I shrug. "I'm resourceful. Which is why I'm glad I ran into you. What were the rumors? The conjecture? About other suspects, about how hard the police were really looking at anyone other than Joe Bedecki. Was Mayor Bergen putting pressure on the sheriff to solve the case fast? Also, was that Mayor Bergen this Mayor Bergen's uncle or . . ."

"Father," Gabriel supplies. "He was pretty notorious as a back-to-American-values guy. Fiercely resisted the free-love seventies. Squeaky-clean, on the surface at least."

"So you *do* know all the gossip."

He starts walking again but gestures at me to follow.

"Where are we going?" I jog to catch up.

"We're here," he says, coming to a stop in front of a perfectly pedestrian two-story building with blue-gray siding, rows of shuttered windows, and Colonial-style columns abutting an arched doorway. *Sea glass museum, hotel, or a bar,* my mind goes, until my eyes land on the sign: CITY HALL.

Inside, I discover it *is* a museum, at least in part. SEAVIEW TOWN ARCHIVE reads a plaque affixed to a room to our immediate left. But Gabriel bypasses it, trudging up the stairs to a receiving room with a desk, behind which is Diana Martinez from WestonCon.

"Gabriel, hi! What are you doing here?" And then she lays eyes on me. "With Cecelia Ellis."

"Cecelia is researching town history," he says. Diana's eyes light up, and she only just stops herself from clapping with delight. The way to an archivist's heart, apparently, is through pointed questions about eras in local history.

"Which period are you interested in?" she asks.

Gabriel hangs back, signaling that I have the floor.

"The Caroline Quinn murder?"

Diana's face darkens. "So you're one of those." Her shoulders slump. "Follow me."

The mayor's closed office door pulls at me like a magnet. What might I find inside? But Diana has rounded her desk and bustled past me, beckoning me down the stairs. Destination: town archive.

Well, maybe I can take advantage of my tour guide. Her name was on Natalie's blackmail list, after all. I can't help but wonder why.

The town archive starts to the left of the entrance and circles around the main floor like a horseshoe, Diana explains. Part walkthrough museum, part reference library.

"We offer an audio tour, and you can even explore the full newspaper archive, thanks to Gabriel's mom. It's all in the resource library in the back." Diana's heels clomp over polished hardwood, a stark contrast to the worn speckled-beige carpets upstairs. The archive has seen recent renovation, and there it is—a plaque in the corner bearing my grandmother's name. At least it's not named after her, like the annex at school.

"The first room is early Seaview history, including its founding as a lumber town and its incorporation in 1892, but what you really want is over here. . . ." We follow Diana through several similar dimly lit rooms, made mazelike by cluttered glass display cases with framed old-timey photographs crowding the walls. Soon, we reach the resource library in the middle.

"That's the microfiche," Diana throws over her shoulder. "And you can circle back here to browse." Our destination—the modern era of Seaview—is on the other side.

Caroline's got an entire room of her own. Well, shared with Maura. A display about Caroline's murder starts on one end of the room, and as you walk corner to corner, it morphs into an exhibit on Maura's bestselling book, Seaview becoming a tourist town, and the movie adaptation. Diana stops in the center of the room, throwing up her arms and doing a turn.

"Everything you need is here. But I'm happy to answer any questions."

I'm not so sure that would be true if she knew the scope of my queries.

"Diana?" bellows a voice from afar. The mayor. Speak of the devil.

Always in motion and already halfway to the door, Diana drops a "Holler if you need me," and then she's gone.

"I'll meet you in the resource library?" Gabriel ends on a question, but it seems he intended a statement; he's gone before I can confirm.

It's fine, though. Feels strangely appropriate—reverent, even—to be alone with Caroline and her impact on this town. The teen queen who started it all.

I skip past the photos of Seaview High before, with its sock hops and all-American football players, and instead look for the after.

Ah, there it is: a newspaper glows on a backlit white wall, its headline screaming:

HOMECOMING QUEEN SLAIN

I move on quickly, as the article's details are now familiar.

The maze directs me past a dark corner to a windowless room with three rows of benches before a projection screen that's playing washed-out footage. I'm not alone. A woman sits in the front row, cast in shadowy relief, like a modernist work of art.

Lone woman observes the long dead. 2022, I think, as though she is part of the museum exhibit herself.

But it's what's on the screen that holds our joint interest. Caroline looms over us, her white homecoming dress a shining beacon against the dishwater grays, murky browns, and faded greens of the video. I recognize the field, the concrete stadium steps in the distance—this is the homecoming-court procession. The future queen waves from a raised dais, eyes button-smooth, features blurry, a rosy-cheeked boy with buttery shoulder-length curls on her arm. That's all that remains of the old home-movie film—implications of vibrancy, of detail. You have to close your eyes to imagine she was a real person at a real event. In twenty-four hours, she'll be dead. But for now, she's immortalized in soundless moving picture.

The video changes to a press conference, and a jump in quality. This clip has sound; I startle when an eerily young version of Ben's grandfather speaks into a scratchy mic.

"We are investigating a number of leads at this time." Sheriff Vann's khaki uniform shirt practically blends into the sand-colored curtain behind him, but across the years and despite the grainy quality of the footage, his blue eyes shine. Ben's eyes.

Next to him is unmistakably a Bergen. The family resemblance is strong. High cheekbones and sparkling hazel eyes, only a wisp of salt in his pepper hair, cut short and coiffed just so. The earnest face of an American-values politician. He cuts in, and the camera zooms in close.

"I have complete confidence in the sheriff and his team, and will make it my mission to see that the person responsible for this heinous crime is prosecuted to the fullest extent of the law. Consider it my promise today that before next month's election, we will have our man," Bergen says. I don't miss the grimace from Sheriff Vann beside him.

Is that why they landed on Joe so fast? An election?

And on goes the clip reel, skipping ahead in time to footage of Joe Bedecki being perp-walked at the courthouse. It's my first real look at him. There's a swagger to Joe, a fire in his eyes that lasers right through the camera lens. *You cocky bastard,* I think. *You did it, and we're all still paying for it.*

The woman on the bench turns. I'd nearly forgotten she was there.

"Hello," Reama says, lips now curling into a cat-that-got-the-cream grin.

A shiver streaks through me. "What are you doing here?" The WestonCon ended two days ago.

"Extended vacation. Taking in the sights. A little town lore. You find it interesting as well, I see. Your grandmother's legacy."

I know Reama was at the hotel the night Natalie died, that she can't be the killer, but then *why is she still here?*

"I have to go." I rise on shaky legs, flee Caroline and her toothy white grin, now that the reel's cycled back to her. A dead girl on an endless loop.

And Reama, left behind, still smiling.

✦

I almost sprint to the resource library.

Gabriel's hunched in front of a flickering computer screen, tongue poking between his teeth as he concentrates. The entire place is a tech graveyard, along with an assortment of local guidebooks shoved on metal shelves.

"You're in your element," I say, trying to regain some casual confidence. Trying to *forget* about Reama.

"I'm in *your* element, more like." Gabriel beckons me over, and I find a screen full of search results.

"It's not the full newspaper archives, but Mom had Bron and

me convert the most notable periods from microfiche to digital a few years ago. Everything about the Quinn murder is here."

"May I?"

Gabriel casts off in his rolling chair, and I pull up, flex my fingers over the keys. He's queued up all the search results for "Caroline Quinn," but I have something else in mind. I ignore Gabriel's confused frown as I type "Grace Bedecki" into the search bar.

The archives pull up a wedding announcement from 1975, and a few other random articles. I click on one attached to a photo credit. It's from 1969, a fluff piece about therapy dogs at the local hospital. And there's a young Grace in a smocked candy-striper uniform like from an old movie, hand in the puppy's scruff, grinning for the camera. She's not alone—Maura and Elaine are behind her, caught midlaugh.

"Do I want to know why you're looking up the school admin?"

"Any stories on her, or her husband, Clark?" I barrel past Gabriel's unease.

"He passed away a few years ago. Why?"

"She doesn't think her brother did it."

"So that's why you're searching for her in the newspaper archive." Gabe frowns. "Right."

"Well, fair's fair." I walk my chair closer to his. "You tell me your alibi—your *real* one—and I'll tell you what I'm looking into."

Gabriel scoots his chair away. "That's not a fair exchange. I'm sorry, Cecelia. I can't tell you."

"Did you tell the sheriff?"

His expression is stony. Guess that's a no.

"Then thanks for your help. I appreciate it."

I'm back out in the lobby before I can name the sensation taking residence in my chest: disappointment. Gabriel didn't try to stop me.

Fine. He can have his secrets. But if they include murder . . . I'll find out eventually.

Before I go, there is the matter of Diana, and her name on Natalie's therapy list. Instinct pushes me up the stairs and down the hall to the antechamber where Diana's desk sits. But she's not behind it. A noise catches my attention. It's coming from the mayor's office.

The door is swollen with age. Doesn't quite fit. If you were to sidle close enough, press your ear against it, you could hear the conversation inside.

But the mayor and Diana are having an argument pitched loud enough I don't even have to push my ear to the door. Their voices carry.

"You have one job, Diana!" the mayor explodes.

Diana's reply comes with gritted teeth. "I can't lie to the police."

"This has no bearing on my daughter's murder. Zero."

"Then why did they ask me about it?"

There's challenge in her words. Diana's no pushover.

"And so you told them?" The mayor sounds scared.

Diana doesn't respond right away.

"Not everything. I acknowledged you might be having an affair. But I didn't tell them my suspicions about who. I keep hoping I'm wrong. Am I wrong, Bradley?"

Momentary silence. I'm missing body language and shared glances. But I hear it in her voice. The *I really hope you didn't fuck up* in it.

"We'll discuss this later." The mayor's voice comes out tight, *closer.*

I leap back from the door right in time, perch precariously onto the arm of a chair, play at having been casually waiting.

"Mayor Bergen, hello!"

I receive a grunt of acknowledgment, but beyond that the mayor doesn't bother with pleasantries. He's too keyed up, fists clenched at his sides as he thunders down the hall. An image comes to life in my mind. Those hands, that pent-up anger, unleashed upon a struggling Natalie at the edge of pool. Playing on a loop, like in the room downstairs, this time fully realized, vivid, and real.

CHAPTER TWENTY-FIVE

Ben's blocking the door when I get home.

"We need to talk," he says in a tone that brooks no argument. I follow him to Maura's office like a child about to be scolded. She's nowhere to be seen, and he explains without my needing to ask. "She's at the hospital, visiting Suzanne. And you've been avoiding me all day. Why?"

I have to tell him. No matter if he thinks I've lost it; I go through the whole theory about Grace, revenge, how he might be next on her list. Shell-shocked, he lowers himself carefully onto a chair. I brace myself for the impact, but it doesn't come.

"That makes sense," he says instead. "The thing with Suzanne has been bugging me all day. She's a good driver. Brakes don't easily fail—not that often."

"And I was supposed to be in the car. Grace knew."

Ben pulls out his phone with a frown. "I know this is going to sound bizarre, but have you considered that maybe Grace is the one who killed *Caroline*? She doesn't have a clear motive, but copycatting the murder with Natalie could have been a statement. Maybe she wants to be caught. Take all the glory, finally."

"Grace *does* have a motive. Maybe," I venture, thinking about

Clark Sawyer. "Caroline's date to homecoming was Grace's future husband. Maybe she was jealous. But come on, Ben—do you really think a fifteen-year-old girl would have the strength to strangle a larger, older, stronger person?"

He fiddles with his phone again. "I don't want to show you this, but it may be important." He unlocks his phone, then types and swipes until he thrusts it at me, a picture of an official document on the screen. "This whole thing got me curious, so I did a little digging at my grandpa's. Found this. You'll have to zoom in."

I do, and I gasp. "This is Caroline Quinn's medical examiner report. This wasn't in her police file."

Ben nods. "You can't tell anyone, Cecelia. My grandfather would be in deep shit."

"Why did he save it, though?"

"Keep reading."

It's laborious, zooming in with my fingers and nudging the small screen side to side to read, but when I reach the line he's talking about, my blood runs cold.

```
Water in lungs indicates victim most
likely drowned while being held down
and strangled. Small puncture mark
found on stomach. Elevated levels of
insulin present but inconclusive.
```

"It was ruled death by strangulation and drowning on her death certificate," Ben tells me. "I checked. That's what is in all the news reports, what they said at the trial. But this . . . I don't know why my grandpa hid this, but he did."

"To make their case airtight," I say, answering his rhetorical question, puzzling it together as I go. "Because it's possible . . . probable, even, that whoever killed her injected her with insulin first."

"So they wouldn't have needed great strength to strangle her at all."

"And why would a high school janitor keep insulin around for this kind of thing?" I say, perching on the edge of Maura's desk, deflated. But then I rocket up, lightning-strike thought hitting me. "Grace volunteered at the hospital!"

"What?"

"I saw it in the newspaper archives. Gabriel showed them to me earlier today. I searched her name, and it brought up this cheesy article about candy stripers at Seaview Memorial. She'd have had access to insulin there, no?"

"You were with Gabriel today?" Ben bristles.

"I ran into him at the police station." I don't acknowledge his hurt. There are more important things to discuss. Surely he gets that.

Ben leaves his chair and begins to pace. "If the police had Gabriel in for questioning, you need to be careful around him, Cecelia." Or not. "Natalie was after him. Maybe she was blackmailing him, and he killed her over it."

"I know that," I snap. "The same could be said for Luke, who we know is actively lying. He said he was hooking up with Morgan, but I know she was vandalizing Natalie's dress at the time of the murder."

Ben's eyes go wide. "Seriously?" And then he's silent, anger diffused. "Shit. He's been avoiding me all week. The guy I know, I don't think he's a killer, but stringing along the police, only then to flat-out lie?"

"Doesn't look good."

"No." And then he's back to pacing. Up and down Maura's gleaming hardwoods, his sneakers squeaking as he completes each circuit. "But this whole coroner's report thing, your Grace theory . . . I mean, Luke would have no reason to hurt *Suzanne.*"

"Nor would Gabriel."

That earns me a look of reproach. "Unless you're right that *you* were the intended victim. Anyone who doesn't want you snooping around would have a reason to hurt you."

Luke's helpful ride to school this morning takes on a new meaning. The harping on about Suzanne driving me.

"We have to get serious about all of them," Ben says. "Find out why Luke is lying, how far Grace would go, and why Gabriel was brought in for questioning."

"And Mayor Bergen," I pipe up. Ben doesn't yet know my latest revelation.

"He's having an affair," I assert. "I overheard him arguing with Diana Martinez this afternoon. The police are asking her about it."

"Is he sleeping with her? Secretary cliché?"

"No, not Diana. She said she hoped she was wrong about who it was. It can't be her."

I cross the room to the murder board. Fiddle with the note card labeled MAYOR BRADLEY BERGEN. Trace the red thread to a card about the screaming match before the game. Ben appears with a new note card that says AFFAIR and pins it to the board. There's nothing about the medical examiner's report or the insulin. That'll stay our secret.

"Natalie must have known about her father," he says. I wind a fresh line of red string around the pushpin, trace it back to the mayor's card.

I nod slowly, piecing it together. "The fight wasn't only about a dress."

"Blackmail," Ben says, completing my thought. He completes a lot of things. I follow his jawline and land on his ocean-blue eyes.

"Thanks for doing this with me," I say.

"I should be thanking you," he replies. "If your whole Grace theory is correct, I need to watch my back. And you should be careful, too. If Suzanne was collateral damage, I might have to spend a lot more time with you."

I find I don't mind the idea of that. But his comment also brings me back to the Grace theory. Which conflicts with the Natalie-dad-blackmail theory.

Ben catches my pout. "What?"

"If it *is* Grace, then none of the rest of it matters. The mayor, Luke, Gabriel. Natalie's blackmail scheme. It seems too . . ."

"Coincidental?" Ben finishes for me.

"Complicated," I say. "Convoluted. So many people had a reason to hate Natalie, and so many alibis are up in the air. So many threads. We're no closer than when we started. If anything, we're worse off."

"Then we'll kill several birds with one stone. You said you have the school master key?"

"Yeah, why?"

"We'll check the CCTV footage from outside the stadium. See who went where and when. It'll catch us up with whatever the sheriff knows, since you said Amber's not sharing much anymore."

"You mean *now*?"

Panic streaks through me, picturing us clad all in black, breaking into the school under the cover of night.

"Now you're gun-shy?" Ben sidles close with a lopsided smile. Tips my chin up and captures my mouth in a kiss. "We do have one issue, though. I can get you into the office with the CCTV footage, but I can't promise I can crack the security to access the videos."

A wicked grin spreads across my face.

"Lucky for you, I can. But we have to make a stop first."

✦

Twenty minutes and a wardrobe change later, we're outside Bronte's house, with her in the car.

"No. No *way*," Bronte protests from the back seat. "The worst consequence Amber faces if her dad catches her snooping is some light grounding, but I could be *arrested and charged.* I'd have to report that to colleges I apply to. And my family can't afford a lawyer."

She narrows her eyes at me.

"Why do you even think I can hack into the school's security system?"

"Because you've done it before."

Bronte goes silent. I know I'm right. Even if I feel oily all over, resorting to the Natalie Bergen playbook, exploiting a friend.

"You got Addison Harper the answer key to the AP Chemistry test two years ago. Mr. Diaz is an ecofreak. Paper-free classroom. So the only way to get his answer key would have been digitally."

Ben's eyes go wide. "You've got to be shitt—"

"Shut up, Vann," Bronte snaps back. Her eyes never leave mine. "How do you know about that?"

It's worth the risk. And, besides, I'm asking her to commit a crime. I tell her about Natalie's therapy scheme.

"So are *you* blackmailing me now?" Bronte accuses.

"No, I'm asking you to help me, as my friend. As Natalie's friend."

She snorts. "You just told me my friend was spying on me. Fuck Natalie."

It's so unlike Bronte. Raw and royally pissed.

"You don't mean that. Or maybe you do. But she's dead. We have to find out why. Who did it. Please, will you help us?"

Bronte chews at her bottom lip. Bites down hard until the skin turns an angry purple. Finally, she speaks.

"Give me two minutes to change."

✦

Looking like a team of beat poets in head-to-toe black, we park in the farthest corner of the school parking lot, then steal up to a side door. I turn Morgan's magic key in the lock, and we follow the beam from Bronte's phone flashlight through eerily deserted halls to the front office. There, we find Joe, in a picture on Grace's desk, taken before a Christmas-themed display in a prison meeting room. He's in a plain-blue button-down shirt and khaki pants, face lined with unexpected age, and he smirks from the frame like he's aware we're up to no good.

"It's back here," Bronte instructs, moving past a partition and the principal's office into a cramped corridor.

"How do you know?"

Bronte casts a smug look at me.

"I was an office intern last year."

It must be an Escano family trait, having a dozen and one jobs around town.

We reach the security room, though it's a fancy moniker for a catch-all room, with an industrial printer/scanner, a laminator, a paper cutter, and a desktop computer. Instinctively, Ben and I crouch down beside Bronte as she gets set up at the monitor, poising ready fingers over the keyboard. I'm curious to see her work.

"For the record, I'm not a hacker," she says, reading my mind. The computer is slow to start, and we have to wait for the boot screen. "Mr. Diaz's password was his dog's name plus his dad's birthday. He left Google Docs up. You need to make sure you can get into their phone, in case they use two-factor authentication, and then delete any email notifications. You can get into any app you want that way. Easy stuff. My mom taught me the tricks of the trade."

She can pooh-pooh it as easy, but sounds like hacking to me. I wonder what other phones Bronte has used that trick on. The password-prompt box appears, and quick as can be, Bronte's fingers blur over the keyboard, she hits Enter, and we're in.

"How did you do that?"

"I was here last year when Principal Morris got locked out and had to reset the login. Password's Vikings123."

Sometimes I love boomers.

After a minute of rapid-fire clicking, Bronte gets down to business. "So here's the deal. The system keeps up to one month of records. There are at least thirty cameras around the building, but I'm assuming we want to start with the athletic center. I found the one over the front door, which fortuitously also gives an excellent view of the stadium side exit. There's just one problem."

Bronte's mouse dances across the screen, setting the still image into motion.

"Fuck." I can't help letting out my frustration. "There's no sound."

"There's no sound," Bronte affirms.

Ben nods. "It's not surprising. California is a two-party consent state. Plus, footage with sound would take up more room on the hard drive."

"I don't suppose either of you are any good at reading lips?" I ask, dejected.

"That is not one of my myriad skills related to lips, no," Ben quips.

"Gross," Bronte says. "Nope. There are some things I do not need to know or think about my friends."

"Are we friends again?" Ben says. The question lands between him and Bronte like a grenade. My eyes dart between them, Ben cautiously neutral and Bronte a deer in headlights.

"Of course," Bronte says. Then, after a contrite sigh: "You know I'm sorry about everything. All that matters now is figuring this out together."

"Yes!" I jump in, riding on a rush of belonging. I'm not in this alone. "The no-sound thing is a blow, but we can still see who went where."

"You're right," Ben says. "Maybe we should start with right after the processional, see if there are any clues about where Luke went off to." Ben moves to take control of the mouse, but Bronte swats him off.

I almost forget about that shit-faced little liar. Ben's right. Forge onward. It's also an easier time stamp to find than the fight between Natalie and her dad. We'll work backward.

It's like watching an old black-and-white silent film. Bronte finds us on the screen—her and Amber heading for the locker rooms, me going off in search of a restroom. A bunch of football players, including Gabriel, and cheerleaders, follow after them. Check. Then there's Ben in his goofy Viking costume, bringing up the rear. I steal a glance at him now and find him blushing.

"Don't worry. I think Vikings are cute," I whisper, and give him a kiss on the cheek.

The time stamp reads 8:54. Natalie's about to die.

We skip back, watch Natalie storming off the field. Luke runs after her; they exchange what appear to be heated words; he grabs for her hand, but she bats it away. The resolution is middling, but Luke's stance is clear: he's annoyed. Morgan comes into view, arms flailing—the emphatic gestures of someone screaming. Or pleading. Natalie ignores her. She's got her phone in her hand, and something on it draws a wicked grin to her face. She strides off toward the school and the side path that will take her to the pool.

Morgan, meanwhile, deflates. I imagine her deciding in that moment to go deface the dress. She squares her shoulders and marches into the athletic center. Luke, on the other hand, heads off camera, toward the school.

And then Gabriel exits the athletic center and also heads toward the school. The police must have watched this. That's Luke *and* Gabriel, each without an alibi, heading in the same direction as the victim. I chance a peek to away from the screen to see if Bronte is thinking that, too. If she does, her poker face reveals nothing.

I return to the video. I don't know why Morgan was so scared. The reel proves she was where she said she was.

"Okay, let's back up and find the fight between Natalie and her dad," Ben suggests.

It takes several more minutes to find it; I keep craning my head toward the door, convinced the cops will sense what we are doing, even though Ben assured me the alarm system is off and Bronte's going to delete the last hour of CCTV to cover our tracks. In the glow, there's Natalie and her dad, Natalie already in uniform, dress bag folded over her arm, her dad pacing back and forth. He gestures at the dress, lips moving fast. She puts hands on hips, says something that stops him in his tracks. First, rage ripples over his features; he clenches his fists. Then comes fear.

There it is. The gauntlet thrown down. The identity of his affair partner, I'm sure. Natalie tosses her hair over her shoulder, turns on her heel, and goes inside the building, leaving her father behind. After a moment, Morgan slinks into frame. She must have been listening. But then she does the strangest thing: she raises her hand to Mayor Bergen's shoulder, gives it a reassuring squeeze, then trails her fingers down his arm, leans into his ear, and whispers something before going off to change. And the look on the mayor's face has transformed from fear to a mixture of guilt and excitement.

"May I?" I say.

Bronte moves aside, lets me use the mouse. I skip forward, back to halftime, ahead of where we watched before.

"What are you doing?" Bronte asks.

"Checking on a hunch."

And there it is. A minute or so after Natalie leaves, her father appears. Then Morgan comes out of the athletic center and meets him, and they go off together, away from the stadium.

"What did I just watch?" Ben squints at the screen.

"The mayor cheating with his daughter's best friend. And they either left to hook up or to murder her."

CHAPTER TWENTY-SIX

Déjà vu washes over me as soon as I cross the threshold of To the Sea Funeral Home for Natalie's wake. With a name like that, I half wonder if they offer literal burials at sea. I wouldn't put it past this place.

At first, I attribute the uncanny sensation to fresh grief. The way all funeral homes seem to look, feel, and smell the same. The decaying flowers and overcycled air.

But, no, I've been here before, in this very receiving room. Hiding behind my mother's pencil skirt, peeking through my fingers at the frightening life-sized doll in the coffin to my left. Granddad, cheeks too rosy, expression too slack to be the person he was. I knew, instinctively, that it was wrong.

Now, I think of how much puttylike makeup they had to shellac onto his purpling skin, if they took care to hide the rope burns on his neck. I wonder if it's easier or harder to wrench a young body into a facsimile of their former self.

"They did such a good job. He looks so peaceful," I remember someone saying to my grandmother, who patted them on the arm and replied, "He looks like a schmuck."

All that I remember after that is the yelling: my mom at my

grandmother, my grandmother back. How thankful I was to not have to go up to his body, look too closely at it. I knew it was an *it*, even then. My grandfather was gone. That's why my mom was so upset.

When she got sick, Mom was explicit: no chemicals, no viewing; she wanted to be cremated. I followed her wishes to the letter. There was no wake. I held a small gathering at our apartment, which turned into a packing party by the end. There's a sharp pull in my gut at the memory.

The Bergens are traditionalists. I can't see Natalie in her casket with the black-clad mourners crowded in front of it, their dramatic sobs rising every so often over the din of low, polite chatter. But I know she's there, rendered perfect and serene by some underpaid undertaker.

I wish I weren't here. But I have no choice. Everyone in town has shown up. Everyone. Including all the liars—Luke, Morgan, Gabriel, Mayor Bergen—each displaying varying levels of grief. Morgan's hovering by the door, eyes rimmed red, as if she's still debating whether or not to come inside. Luke sits with his head hung low in the back row of chairs, as far from Natalie's casket as possible— distance due to guilt? Gabriel's in the corner wearing an I-do-not-want-to-be-here dourness. I know it well. I'm sure it's on my face right now, too. I wonder if this is his first wake since his father's death.

And then there's the mayor. My stomach churns with rage at the sight of him standing stoically beside his doting wife as they receive people's condolences. Including Morgan's. Finally, she decides she's in, and the first thing she does is make a beeline for the mayor, grasping his hands with both of hers.

"I am so, so sorry," she says, but her eyes bore into his, begging him to slip away with her.

With no reciprocal signal, reluctantly she relinquishes the mayor's hands and moves over to Dr. Shelby, repeating her condolences. But they're hollow; she can't meet his wife's eyes. Even though I know the affair was entirely cultivated by an adult taking advantage of an underage girl, I can't help but hate Morgan a little for her hypocrisy.

Dr. Shelby is working hard to put Morgan and all the other mourners at ease, the consummate grief professional. Little does she know Morgan has put a knife in her back.

I follow after Morgan. I want the truth.

"Hey, can we talk?" I corral her by the water station, which puts me uncomfortably close to Gabriel, a few feet away. Well, let him listen in, I guess. I have questions for him, too.

"What is it?" Morgan sniffs. She grabs a tissue from her purse and dabs at her nose.

"That night at the game. You left out the part where after you trashed Natalie's dress, you left the locker room."

"What?"

"There's video," I say, leaving out there was no sound. Playing a bluff. "Earlier that night, after Natalie's argument with her dad, I saw the way you touched his arm. Whispered something in his ear. Natalie knew, didn't she?"

Morgan writhes. "I don't know what you're talking about."

"Did the police watch far enough into the video to see you sneaking off with him during halftime? Because I did."

"What the hell is wrong with you?" Morgan shoves my shoulder with her fingers.

"Did you just push me?"

"Hey!" Luke and Gabriel rush to our aid. Luke lines up like a soldier at Morgan's side, while Gabriel thrusts one arm in front of me, as if in protection. And that summons Ben like a beacon. I hadn't even seen him arrive. Amber and Bronte aren't far behind. Gang's all here.

"What's going on?" Bronte's eyes are wide, pleading with me to stop. But I can't.

"I was merely asking Morgan why she's lying. Luke, you may as well answer, since you're here, too. You weren't with Morgan during halftime. She was with someone else."

"What the fuck is it to you?" he says. "Ben, control your girl."

"*Excuse* me?" I explode before Ben or Gabriel have the chance. I can take care of myself. "That's some misogynist bullshit. What? Did you kill Natalie because she refused to be controlled? Because she knew your secret? I saw your texts from that night."

"I *knew* you did something with my phone! What the fuck is wrong with you?"

Adrenaline pumps through me; I teeter on the edge of excitement and panic.

"Why don't you tell the truth about you and Natalie?"

"Me? You think I'm the big liar about Natalie, and you're running around town with Ben playing happy young lovers? Has he told you about *him* and Natalie? Her big secret."

"Luke." It's just one word, just his name, but Ben's tone is deadly cold.

"No, no, if we're picking apart my love life, then it's only fair to talk about Ben and Natalie. You were fucking all last year, even after she officially, publicly hated you."

"Holy shit." That's Amber.

"We shouldn't be doing this," Bronte pleads.

I'm sure at this point people are looking at us. We're causing a scene. But I don't care anymore. I'm thinking about Natalie and Luke's texts. The eggplant emoji plus wolf emoji. One of the princes in *Into the Woods* doubles as the wolf. Natalie was hooking up with Ben. That's what it meant.

"Shut the fuck up, Luke," Ben interjects. "Cecelia, please . . ."

I can't even look at him, though I feel his eyes all over me. Searing betrayal pierces my heart, turning every inch of my skin hot. And wait—

"I wasn't picking apart your love life," I say to Luke. Unless . . . "You really were in a halftime hookup? With who? Why lie that you were with Morgan?"

"This has gone far enough," Gabriel says, finally speaking, as he darts a look of worry my way that sends a fresh wave of rage through me. How dare he *pity me.*

"Are you saying that so I won't ask you about your alibi, *Gabe*? Or were you with Luke and that's why you're defending him?"

"No fucking way," Luke explodes, while the frown on Gabriel's face deepens.

"You're jumping to wild conclusions," Gabriel says. "And we're *at a wake,*" he manages through gritted teeth.

I can't take it anymore. I won't be placated like a stupid child by yet another person who's lying to me. Someone I *trusted.* I drop the final bomb. "Morgan was hooking up with Natalie's dad! They were together during halftime when she was murdered. That's not a wild conclusion. That's *facts.*"

I was right about calling attention to ourselves. Mayor Bergen, Dr. Shelby, and my grandmother appear. The mayor launches into stern-adult mode, someone used to taking charge.

"What the hell is going on here?"

"I don't know, sir," I say. "Maybe you should talk to your

underage girlfriend about it. Was Natalie blackmailing you, like she was all of Dr. Shelby's patients?"

On cue, Morgan starts hysterically crying. Everyone else spits curses, some more heated than others. Anyone who ever had a session with Dr. Shelby is shitting bricks. Some more than others—Amber clearly didn't know, and Bronte can't hide her guilt.

I pause. My adrenaline has faded enough to finally notice the entire room. The whole town, it seems, has exploded into a million side conversations, and I realize it is all my fault. Some truths needed to be called out, but I look from Amber to Bronte to Natalie, the coffin at the side of the room, and I realize I'm adding to their hurt.

And in front of me, poor Dr. Shelby is in shock. "What are you talking about?" she says.

I genuinely don't know which bombshell she means, so I go with the easier one.

"I'm sorry, Dr. Shelby. I found a bunch of video files on Natalie's computer. She recorded your sessions and took notes so she could leverage people. There's a camera hidden at the top of the bookshelves in your office."

I spot Deputy Shields in the crowd and call out to her.

"You should go to the mayor's house now, check Natalie's computer upstairs before they can delete the evidence."

The mayor's eyes blaze with indignant rage. "It was *you*. Sending me nasty texts that night. Trying to *frame me*. You little bitch."

It all happens so fast—he growls and lunges toward me. Gabriel and Ben go to block him, but my grandmother, of all people, beats them to it.

"Bradley Bergen, so help me God, I will kill you where you stand. Back the hell away from my granddaughter!"

Maura pushes him aside, like a linebacker, grabbing my hand and pulling me out of the fray. "Come on, Celia, we're leaving." I hear Morgan sobbing.

We make it as far as the door before Sheriff Morrow blocks the way.

"Those were some tough accusations you were throwing over there, young lady," he says, and I could punch his smug, patronizing face. Or Maura might do it for me.

"My granddaughter is very upset, Kyle. I need to get her home." Maura narrows shrewd eyes at the sheriff and says with a sniff, "And *you* may want to lay off the booze. It appears you have a long night of questioning ahead of you."

With that, she sweeps me out the door, leaving a sputtering sheriff behind us.

CHAPTER TWENTY-SEVEN

The pounding is so loud I can hear it all the way up in my attic room. I jolt out of sleep, groggy enough to think at first I've imagined it. But after a minute, there it is again.

Bam, bam, bam.

I check the time on my phone. Nine-thirty a.m. Fuck.

And now I understand the silence in the house. No squalling grandmother yelling at the fucker who won't stop knocking. Maura must be at the funeral. I'm alone.

Bam, bam, bam.

Whoever it is isn't going away, so I throw on my hoodie over my pajamas and make my way down to the front door. I open it with more force than necessary, prepared to chew out whatever relentless asshole is on the step, but I choke on my curses at the sight of Ben. His dark-blond waves are still wet from the shower, and he's wearing an olive-green slub-knit cardigan I want to sink my face into. But then I remember last night in a full-body nausea flush.

"What are you doing here?" I manage, realizing I'm braless, with bad breath and an unwashed face. I could just *die.*

"Such a friendly welcome."

"I assumed you hate me now, like everyone else." My eyes flick up the stairs, wishing I could disappear.

"Me? It's you who should hate me. I shouldn't have lied about Natalie. I just—" He pauses. Looks over my shoulder. "Sorry, could I come in? Feels weird to pour my heart out on the front porch."

"Meet me in the kitchen. I'll be right back."

Vanity appeased, I make it to the kitchen after ten minutes, mouth minty and undergarments secured. Ben's poured twin bowls of raisin bran, and there's a pot of coffee hissing and spitting on the counter. I spoon wheat flakes into my mouth and wait for Ben to resume his speech.

"I was so terrified you'd lose interest in me. And Natalie had worn me down, convinced me I was nothing but trash that had to be kept secret. I've been licking my wounds since the summer, and you seemed too good to be true. I didn't want to blow it."

"So you were, what? Her secret boyfriend?"

He nods. "For most of last year. At first, it was fun, like a game we got to play, sneaking around. Then it started to suck. And especially when my mom died. At first, I thought we were going to be okay even with the lawsuit. It was between my granddad and her father, not us. But she started acting even worse at school, literally cut me out of our friend group. Spread those rumors about me. But she'd call me on a Friday night and ask me to come by for a hookup. It fucked with me. I'm sorry I didn't tell you. I should have."

"Was it just about us, or were you also messing with Natalie?"

He cranes his neck over to check the coffee, putting off answering the question. But finally he acquiesces. "It did cross my mind. But I swear to you, I didn't hate Natalie. Certainly didn't want her dead. I was mostly just . . . hurt. And then you came along, and I couldn't believe my luck. And then we started a murder investigation together . . . and Natalie was gone, so there seemed no point in saying anything. But last night was weird."

I groan. "Don't remind me. It's been playing on a loop since then. I lost it. I mean, they're all liars. You too, I guess, but I forgive you."

"You do?" He grins.

"I'm the person who exposed a dead girl's dad for hooking up with her underage best friend, in front of not only his wife but the entire town, at a wake. So I don't exactly have a leg to stand on. It's why I'm hiding out here today."

"Wouldn't it be better to get out of here for a few hours, take your mind off everything? I have an idea. A road trip, if you will."

"Go on."

"I looked up Joe. There are visiting hours today. If we leave now, we can make it down to the prison and back before the dance."

"You still want to go with me to the dance?"

"Of course. Do you want to go with me?"

"Yes, but . . . I skipped the funeral today for a reason. I shouldn't go to the dance, either."

"Why? Because a few people are mad at you? Because they'll talk? Fuck 'em. We'll get dressed up, I'll sneak in a flask, we'll dance our asses off, and seriously, fuck 'em."

Ben's enthusiasm is contagious. He grabs me by the hand, twirls me; I spin around and around, giggling. Then I stop. Backtrack.

"Why would we go visit Joe Bedecki in prison?"

"Why not? Could be good closure. I know that on the face

of it, you've wanted to solve Natalie's murder. But we both know this is more than that. Distraction by way of unhealthy obsession. This is taking it to the next level. Going in deep. And, honestly, I've grown up hearing tales about this guy like he's the boogeyman. I wanna meet him. It'll be a wacky adventure we'll tell our kids about someday."

"Aren't you getting a little ahead of yourself? Don't go asking me to marry you."

With one hand, Ben grasps at his shirt, above his heart. The other pats over his pants pocket. "Oh shit, are engagement rings exchangeable? I was going to propose at the dance."

I laugh in spite of myself, hopping off the kitchen barstool to retrieve two travel mugs, now that the coffee has stopped sputtering. "Let's go on a road trip to prison."

✦

Over the next three hours, two-lane highways turn to wine country turn to rolling suburbia, until we pass through a neighborhood of squat ranches, down a palm-tree-lined drive leading to the state prison. The complex is a sprawl of white buildings fenced in, the perimeter dotted with security towers. I expect a big, bad prison like from the movies, but reality is disappointingly municipal. We walk into a beige-on-beige lobby that could be a school district office or a bank.

A bored-looking woman sits behind a plexiglass cubicle cut into the cinder-block walls.

"Are you on the list?" Her eyes narrow, and my heart leaps into my throat. Of course we're not on the list. Shit!

"It's under Ellis and Vann," Ben answers smoothly. "I sent in the questionnaire yesterday."

I stare agog at Ben, seeking an explanation, but everyone else has moved on: we hand over our IDs, sign in, and pass through a bank of metal detectors, and then a security officer buzzes us through a steel door and takes us to a room with half a dozen tables bolted to the floor. I gulp down sudden apprehension: no glass partitions with clunky old phones for talking. Joe and I are going to get up close and personal.

"There was a questionnaire?" I finally get in my burning question once the guard leaves.

Ben browses a vending machine in the corner before plucking a crisp dollar from his wallet, which he exchanges for a bag of Cheetos.

"The prisoner has to put you on the list, too, so I got Maura to make a call."

"Maura?"

"She said she could help," Ben says with a shrug. "Want one?"

I shake my head, too queasy to eat. I pace next to the windows, peer down into a dusty yard with a well-worn basketball court. And right at the point when I'm about to turn to Ben, change my mind, suggest we leave, a door on the far end of the room clicks open and Joe Bedecki shuffles in, in handcuffs and chains. He reminds me of an old stray dog. Lean and wiry, a hard life behind him. But there's a canny alertness behind his brown eyes.

Those eyes narrow at me now, but Joe allows the guard to escort him over to the table where Ben and I are now sitting.

"They said an Ellis wanted to see me. Didn't expect you."

"You know me?"

"You look just like she did at your age."

Of course he means my grandmother. A shiver runs through me.

"Why would she visit you?"

Bedecki leers, revealing a mouth of yellowing, ill-cared-for teeth. A harsh contrast to the Joe from the newsreel, his handsomeness twisted by older age and decades of hard time.

"Why are you here?" he says. "Not that I don't appreciate the company. It's usually just my sister who comes, and she prattles on with stupid, useless Seaview gossip." He zeroes in on me. "Though perhaps that's what you bring me, too. The latest from Seaview."

"A girl was murdered. Just like Caroline," I confirm.

He's messing with me. It's been on the news. He has to know.

"Tragic," he says, without a hint of sorrow in his voice.

"She was strangled. Like you strangled Caroline."

Joe rubs at the handcuffs at his wrists. Twists them around. Taps them to the table.

"And who are you? Her boyfriend?" He's addressing Ben, starving my query of oxygen.

"Yes," Ben says. "I'm Ben Vann." He drops his name like a bomb.

Joe visibly seethes. "Seaview saviors, the next generation. An Ellis and a Vann. All we need is a Bergen, and it would be a party. But . . . she can't come, can she?"

I hide my disgust. I'm starting to wonder if Natalie's coroner missed signs of a shot of insulin. It's the one missing piece to be the perfect copycat of the original murder.

"Did you have a relationship with Caroline?" I probe.

"Define 'relationship.' "

"Did you hook up?"

Joe ticks his head. Guess that slang hasn't made it to prison.

"Go beyond flirting," I clarify.

The corners of Joe's mouth tilt up. "She came to my cubby a few times, yeah. She was a sweet girl." His eyes rake over me, and a sick feeling swirls in my stomach. Then he gives a little grunt. "You're the spitting image of Maura at that age. Maybe even sexier. But don't tell her I said that."

Ben grabs my hand, gives it a squeeze. Whether out of reassurance or to stop me from punching Joe in the face, I can't say.

"You liked my grandmother, then?"

"Maura was . . . fun." There's that Cheshire cat grin. Like he hopes what he said unsettles me. It does.

"She turned you in to the police."

"Everyone makes mistakes," he replies, glib.

"Is that why she visits you? As some kind of . . . penance?"

"Maura and I are good. We made peace a long time ago. Things got a bit out of hand back then, but she did what she had to do. I respect that. And she talks about interesting shit, unlike my sister. And she sends me a copy of every book, before it's published. Makes me very popular with the boys. I'm better than the library."

There's a personal Maura Weston lending library in the prison. Huh.

"Have you read them?" Joe asks. His eyes glitter with mischief.

"I read the one on the boat," I recite, robotically at this point.

"Aww, you haven't read mine?"

"Parts," I say. "And I saw the movie."

Joe smacks his lips, leans back with hands behind his head. "I liked the guy they cast as me. Though you know they made him a teacher for that. Classed it up."

"It was Maura who made him a teacher. For her book."

"I guess 'hooking up' with a teacher is less shameful."

He serves my words back to me like he's throwing knives. I don't appreciate the implication. That he was anything but a huge creep with my grandmother. With Caroline.

"It never bothered you that she wrote a book about what you did?" Ben says, joining the conversation. He leans forward with his elbows on the table. Fearless. I nudge closer to him on the bench, savor the way our thighs touch.

Joe shrugs. "Maura does what she wants." He picks his teeth with a long, yellowing fingernail as he watches me. "So I ask again: Why are you here? I've been locked up a long time, no Rita Hayworth posters hiding holes in my cell wall. I didn't kill the Bergen girl. But you know that."

I offer a nod. "Do you know why someone would copy your murder?"

"No one copied *my* murder. I reckon they paid *homage* to your grandma's book, no?" He emphasizes *homage* like it's real fancy.

"Or maybe someone you know did it to send a statement," Ben throws in.

"That's fucking stupid." Joe slams his fist down on the table.

The guard in the corner goes on red alert, fingers brushing at a taser at his waist. I give him an *All's good* hand signal.

"People are asking questions back in Seaview," I say. "She was killed the exact same way." I pause, raise my eyes to his, make sure he sees me. "You know I found the body."

He laughs, and I wasn't expecting it. Like the stray dog he is, it came out a bark.

"Well, isn't that a coinkidink!" He licks his lips, eyes darting between Ben and me, before landing laser-focused on Ben.

"Have you had a taste yet? You know, Ellis women are tigers in the sack."

Ben tenses beside me, jumps forward just an inch, fists clenched on the table. I stop him, laying my hand on his thigh, giving it a squeeze. No need to defend me.

"Haven't you wondered who did it?" I ask, bringing Joe back to the matter at hand.

"Doesn't concern me." Joe is nonchalant, like we're discussing the weather. "I wish them the best of luck."

A killer offering well-wishes to a killer. Sweet.

"What was it like killing Caroline?" I'm teeing up the question I really came here to ask, if inelegantly.

Joe quirks his head to the side, studies first me, then Ben, as if working out a trick. But he takes the bait. Ish.

"It was great. Made me feel all powerful-like. Takes a lot to strangle a person." He flexes the wan musculature of his sinewy arms, kisses a nonexistent bicep.

"And where did you get insulin back in 1970?" I finish, the non sequitur that is anything but.

Joe's brow furrows, and he practically guffaws. "I don't know. The pharmacy? How would I know? I'm not diabetic."

Exactly. He doesn't know why I'm asking. Ben shifts next to me. He gets it, too.

Joe Bedecki is a lot of things: a lech, a dick, a sad old man. But there's one thing he's not: a killer. Joe Bedecki didn't murder Caroline Quinn.

So why is he lying about it?

CHAPTER TWENTY-EIGHT

On the drive back from the prison, between long stretches of silence, we dissect Joe's accidental admission and pore over our theories of both crimes. Grace is the only true link between the two, but the issue of the insulin remains. The coroner didn't find any marks on Natalie. Could we really be looking at two entirely independent murders, linked by my grandmother's book? Or someone we know who used Seaview's infamous dead queen as cover?

I'm not sure where else to go, who else to talk to. I've royally screwed myself with everyone in this town, and I'm no closer to a real answer.

As much as I don't want to go to the dance tonight, show my face at school, Ben insists. He drops me off at home with less than an hour for both of us to get ready.

Maura nearly tackles me as I come in the front door.

"There you are! I was worried. Were you with Benjamin? Oh, that's adorable. All is forgiven. Come on, I have something for you," Maura offers as preamble. I follow her into the living room, inquire as to how the funeral went.

"It was a mix of somber and uncomfortable, what with the

sheriff and his deputies hovering over the mayor the whole time," she answers breezily. "I left early to visit Suzanne in the hospital."

"How is she?"

"Still in the ICU, I'm afraid, but on the mend." Maura sweeps ahead of me to grab something. "Oh, don't peek!" she shrieks.

Eyes closed, I rehearse what I'm itching to say about my visit to Joe. Questions I have about him and her.

But when she commands me to open my eyes, she awkwardly produces a hanger from behind her back and I forget what I meant to say. On it is a showstopper of a dress. Faded seventies film stock did the soft and sumptuous periwinkle no favors. The cut is sultry fairy tale: a plunging neckline, a belted waist, and a pretty cascade of chiffon for the skirt.

"I had Mama special-order a replica of Liz Taylor's Oscar dress that year. Cost a mint, so you bet I saved it."

"You want me to wear it?"

"Of course! You deserve to look like a million bucks tonight. Have your moment. Unfortunately, I couldn't get your mother into it. She insisted on a midnineties slinky Kate Moss thing in a ghastly sateen green. Terribly unflattering. But in this, you'll look like a princess."

She holds it up against me, preens. "Surely it will fit. Go! Put it on."

This time, I'm happy to serve as Maura's dress-up doll—the dress *is* a dream—so I zip myself in, make myself up as best I can. When I come back downstairs, Ben's standing with Maura in the foyer, looking smart in dark-wash skinny jeans and a black blazer, over one of his signature band tees.

"Wow, I should have worn a tux," he says as I step onto the landing.

"No, you're perfect like that. It's you."

"And if this is you . . . I like it."

"You do?" I pick up the periwinkle skirt and twirl.

"Bunch up, you two. You know I'm going to take photos!" Maura orders, and so we pose on the stairs while Maura fiddles with her iPhone. I can't help but think about poor Suzanne again, who would have been the person in charge of photos if she were here. Odds are good Maura's photos will turn out crooked or blurry, or both.

The jitters start once we're in the car, cruising the short blocks to Seaview High. I bounce my knee nervously, snap down the visor mirror, and needlessly reapply my lip gloss.

Ben pulls into a parking spot, kills the engine. "If you really don't want to go in, we don't have to. We can drive to the beach, dance on the sand."

It's tempting, but as I stare through the windshield to the school, I know I can't run away. There's nowhere to go. I'm an orphan. I spent so much time trying to escape Seaview, but despite the damage I've caused, it has become my home, too. It's Maura and Seaview or bust. I'll have to walk through those doors now or on Monday morning. At least now I look fucking amazing in this dress—and I can walk in with Ben on my arm.

The gym has been transformed: bleachers pushed flush to the wall, round tables dotting the fringes of a dance floor, fairy lights and streamers over every conceivable square inch of the walls, and even a mirrored disco ball hanging from the ceiling, casting fractures of blue light in every direction. No, it's teal, I realize. The lights have been fitted with filters the color of Natalie's last homecoming dress, so the whole gym looks like an underwater grave.

And I'm a dead woman walking. They're here, somewhere.

The friends I've hurt. Yeah, I'm getting a few sideways looks, excited whispers about how they can't believe I showed up. But random kids at school don't matter. Bronte, Amber, Morgan, Gabriel, and even Luke matter.

"Shall we dance?" Ben indicates the writhing mass to our right. "Or drink?" There's a table in the back where a line of chaperones are pouring soft drinks. It feels too soon to dive in on dancing, so I pick drinks. Ben jogs off to grab them and tasks me with finding seats.

I search the folding chairs set out haphazardly along the walls, seeking a spot not already taken by a purse or jacket, when my name stops me cold.

"Cecelia, hey."

The concern in it is pure Bronte. With a bracing breath, I turn to face her. *Them.* They're a pair, as always. Bronte, in the prettiest baby-blue halter dress, and Amber, in a killer navy boned-bustier top with a black jacket and pants.

It's time to clear the air.

"We missed you at the funeral," Bronte says politely, prompting a snort from Amber, who, as always, gifts us with bluntness.

"It was better you weren't there," Amber says. "The funeral was a shit show. Your blackmail bombshell was all anyone could talk about. There was some light jeering when Natalie's parents got up to speak."

"That's awful," I say genuinely. "No matter what she did, or her dad, it's still a funeral. This is all my fault."

"No, it's—"

"Well, yes, but—"

Bronte and Amber trip over each other. Amber defers, and Bronte takes me gently by the elbow.

"Come on. Let's sit down," she says. And they lead me to a table closest to the dance floor, ignoring that it's already laden with other people's belongings. We form a huddle with our chairs. Bronte starts.

"We were worried about you. But you seem better now."

"I am. You can tell your dad there will be no more amateur detecting," I direct at Amber. "I pushed it too far. It was an enticing distraction, trying to figure out the mystery. But real people got hurt."

"You outed the mayor as a sexual predator," Amber says. "Fuck that guy. His leverage is gone, so now my dad can actually look into him properly. No more municipal stonewalling. You're a hero."

"I humiliated Morgan. Is she here?" I search the dance floor. "I want to apologize, but she'll probably punch me."

"She's more of a hair puller," Bronte says, in a rare joke. Amber laughs at her. Their levity helps.

"I really didn't mean to lose my shit at the wake," I explain. "But everyone was lying. And I wanted straight answers."

"Keeping a personal secret isn't always the same as lying." Bronte sounds so small saying it, and I think about her secret. I have to ask. I don't know why I didn't the other night.

"Is Natalie the reason you didn't run for homecoming queen?"

"What? No." Bronte is both emphatic and dodging the truth. Amber catches it, too.

"Come on, Bron. Like the chance of her wrath didn't factor in? We talked about it."

Bronte nibbles on her bottom lip before coming to a decision. "It's not that. She said I was getting everything—valedictorian, a lock for Stanford. Begged me to let her have this one thing. I wanted to be nice. She came to me crying, actually. Really upset."

Amber snorts. "Crocodile tears, I'm sure."

So am I. Natalie was legacy for Stanford, for one. But it's interesting. Natalie didn't go through with blackmailing Bronte. She chose pure emotional manipulation instead. And now I wonder: Is there any proof Natalie actually went after anyone?

"What about Addison?" I ask. "Natalie never used that?"

Exhaling a groan, Bronte rolls her eyes. "No. I didn't even know she knew until you told me about the therapy file. It's humiliating, honestly. I was a sophomore. and Addison was a senior. She begged me, said this one grade would make or break her for keeping her USC admission." Bronte looks down at her nails, picking at a rogue cracked cuticle, and mumbles, "I thought she'd let me be her girlfriend."

Amber cackles but pulls Bronte into a sideways hug, gives her a wet smack on the cheek. "Her loss, my gain."

Bronte focuses in on me again. "Did you think Natalie blackmailed me? That *I* could have done it?"

"No," I answer honestly. "I knew you and Amber couldn't have. You both have alibis. Plus, I hope I have enough good judgment to know you two aren't killers."

"Joke's on you—I've got a knife in this thing." Amber pats the front of her bustier. "And I know you've given up your Harriet the Spy ways, but if you're wondering, my dad finally has everyone's alibis. Except Gabriel's." Amber pointedly looks to her girlfriend, who fidgets.

"Gabriel told your dad where he was."

"Yeah. Conveniently alone, for no particular reason."

"Wasn't he with Luke?"

"No, Luke was with someone else." Amber coughs. "But that's his business. All you need to know is my dad is satisfied enough to eliminate him as a suspect."

So where was Gabriel?

"You really think it could be a student?" Bronte says to me. And to Amber: "Does your dad think that?"

Amber and I give shrugs of vague assent.

"Then why zero in on Gabe and not Ben? Does he have an alibi?"

"Of course he does," I assert. "He was in the locker room. He's on camera going in, in his mascot costume. He doesn't come out during the murder window. Gabriel does."

"I promise you it wasn't my brother."

"I know," I say, because it's what I should say. Because I want it to be true. But even Amber casts a sideways look at Bronte.

"Oh, hey, you found a table!" Ben appears at both the perfect and worst time, hands me a Diet Coke.

"Found friends with a table, more like," I tell him. "But now I'd love to dance."

I wouldn't, really, but the tension at the table is thick, and I don't like the way Bronte is glaring at Ben. So we move to the dance floor, Ben taking care to find a spot with ample room, because he is a stilted, if enthusiastic, dancer. His goofiness is contagious; I can't help giggling and mirroring his painfully un-rhythmic, wild flailing. It's nice to blow off steam after the day we've had. The week. Months, really.

It's strange holding back about the investigation for the first time. Because that has to be over. If the police are satisfied with

Luke's alibi, then I need to leave well enough alone. I've caused enough trouble for one lifetime.

Instead, I take Ben's hands and get lost in the music and in the momentum of the room. After a half hour or so, Ben spins me off the dance floor and dashes off once more to procure drinks. I run up to our table without doing a full sweep, and end up face to face with a double billing of do not want: Morgan *and* Luke.

"Oh, hi." I hover uncomfortably by Morgan's chair, my clutch sitting on the table in front of her, just out of my reach.

"I can't believe you showed your face," Luke says with a drawl. There's no real ire behind it, though.

Morgan peers at me from behind a curtain of bangs, as if she styled them as armor.

"Natalie would hate that dress," she says. "You'd have outshone her."

I note that her dress is pink. Natalie's color. Guess we're both giving the middle finger to a ghost.

"Can we . . . ?" I sit down cautiously, leaving an empty chair between Morgan and me as a buffer. To her credit, she doesn't march away. A boy I recognize as Morgan's escort from the court procession comes up. Caleb. The half-naked Puck. But he's not here for Morgan. There's a flask peeking out from his pocket, and he points at it, then at Luke, grinning.

When he sees me, the joy melts from his expression. "Hey," he says in my direction, guarded. Then he looks over a Luke, widening his eyes meaningfully, a question passing between them, regarding me.

Luke groans, acquiescing to some precursor conversation I'm not privy to.

"Fine," he says. Caleb grabs a seat and hands Luke the flask so he can take a surreptitious sip.

"I don't owe you shit," Luke says after a long draw. "But I'll tell you where I was when Natalie died, because fuck it. Apparently, I'm stuck with you as a friend, because . . . peer pressure. And before you stole my phone, you were actually kind of fun."

I imagine he means pressure from Bronte, Amber, and Ben. Morgan still appears wary. I'm flattered the others would go to bat for me after all I've done.

"And look what happens when you don't get the information you want," Luke says. "Please don't lose your shit again."

"Dramatic." Caleb clucks at Luke, takes the flask back, and drinks.

Suddenly, it clicks together for me: Why Caleb is here. That meaningful look.

"You were together." I point between them. "Halftime hookup."

"Don't go spreading it around," Luke says. "This isn't Los Angeles. Seaview can be backwards as hell, and I'd rather not have the whole town gossiping about it. I'm out to my parents and close friends as bi, but Caleb's not out."

"With no plans to be until I'm the fuck out of this town," Caleb interjects, cheersing the air with his drink.

"That's what Natalie was blackmailing you about?" I can't help asking. "Being bi?"

I don't wish anyone dead, but how fucking low to threaten to out your friend. Never mind Luke threatened her right back. But her hooking up with Ben isn't exactly comparable.

"Blackmail is a bit harsh," Luke says. "I slipped her a few crates of wine and some premium weed. She wouldn't have really done it." A flicker in his eyes says he's not so sure that's true.

"I'm sorry I pushed you," I say. "I wanted the truth so badly I didn't care who stood in my way. That was wrong. And I won't say anything. I've spilled enough secrets, but I'm here if you ever need." I direct the last bit at Luke and Caleb both.

"Keep your hands off my phone, and we're good, Ellis," Luke cracks.

"Shit. Morris spotted Gladys," Caleb says, and I realize Gladys is the flask. "Let's go. You have the key?"

Luke pulls a familiar master key from his jacket pocket, and they run off together to get soused, away from the administration. Now it's just me and Morgan. I look over to the refreshments table and see Ben stuck in a long line.

"I didn't sleep with him," she says, and we both know who she means. How long has she been stewing with that?

"I wanted to. I would have." Her eyes are glued to her hands as she fiddles with her nails. "We made out. During halftime. While Natalie was dying. I'll have to live with that forever."

"I'm sorry, Morgan. I really am."

"Why are you so obsessed with this? None of our friends killed Natalie. None of us. And you barely knew her."

"It's hard to explain," I say. Because it is. And Morgan's the last person I'm interested in confiding in.

Morgan's moved on anyhow, to more troubling thoughts. She bites her lip, ruining her lipstick. "Do you think your grandmother will write a book about this, too? Like a sequel?" Her eyes lock with mine, pleading. "Could you ask her not to put me in it? I will never live it down. It's bad enough people heard at the wake last night. It'll get around town, I know. But a Maura Weston treatment would immortalize my worst mistake. And, oh God—Luke."

"I don't think she'll write another book about the town. And even if she did, Luke's secret is hardly sensational enough for a thriller."

Morgan hums her disagreement. "Your grandmother would. You know I'm a big fan, but the Weston treatment is notorious. You piss off Maura Weston, or if a scandal's juicy enough, a thinly veiled version of it appears in a book."

"I'll talk to my grandmother. I'm sure if I ask, she won't write about you," I say. But it occurs to me my grandmother can hardly write a sequel inspired by this murder if it's not solved.

I feel that familiar itch, to get to the bottom of it, to find the answers, but I immediately tamp it down. No. Tonight is about enjoying myself. No more making a mess of things and earning enemies.

"I'm going to see where Ben is." I rise, grabbing my clutch before I go.

But before I can reach the drinks table, I'm intercepted by the last person I want to see. Grace's eyes are kind, her body broad, making her a human brick wall of concern. No way to go around. The only way out is through.

"Cecelia, dear, how are you?"

A second look at those eyes, and I realize with a start they're Joe's eyes. Like that, I'm back at the prison, pinned under his hungry stare. Grace craves something different, though. If only I knew what.

"I saw what happened last night. And Joe called me from prison. Said you were there today? This isn't . . . It's not normal, dear. This obsession."

And there's her brother in her again, the sour turn to her phrasing as I meet her disapproval.

"I'm fine," I say. "Thanks for your concern. I'm doing research for a project. Like my mom. I wanted to visit your brother to get a primary source. Maybe I'll start a podcast. You never know. It could make a good story for my college applications." It's a ramble, me spitballing excuses. Better she think I'm shamelessly hedging my bets for an elite school than figure out the truth.

"I need some air," I say, meaning it, and careening in the opposite direction, because that is *away*. Even if it's also away from Ben.

A group of students I don't recognize, but who evidently recognize me, are crowding the exit; the pointed glances and sniggers push me from my original plan. The only place left is the dance floor. Where I can disappear in the horde of bodies.

I hover at the edge, gracelessly bopping to the beat of some up-tempo song from a decade ago. The playlist is Natalie's favorites, so guess she loved LMFAO in second grade. And then I see him, our eyes locking across the dance floor. Gabriel. I'd prepared myself mentally to see everyone but him. And, God, he looks good. Hair slicked back, in a crisp white shirt under a sharp velvet-lined red blazer.

But he doesn't exactly seem happy to see me. Still, we close the gap between us, making our way around the fringes of the dance floor in an awkward hello.

"You look amazing," he says. Complimentary, but there's a guardedness there.

"Thank you. So do you."

"You here with Vann?"

I nod. "Trying not to accuse anyone of murder. Normal homecoming-dance stuff." I'm attempting levity, but Gabriel's mouth remains a tight line.

"You know the sheriff kept me at the station until two a.m. last night. And he's had Shields tracking me all day."

So this is the next stop on my apology tour. "I'm sorry," I say, but my heart is only half in it. Gabriel still isn't exactly being honest. "But you're the one who let me believe you were with Luke. Which you weren't. He was with someone else. What are you hiding?"

"That's none of your business."

"But it isn't the sheriff's business either, apparently. You're lying to them, too, about being alone during halftime."

Gabriel confirms my bluff.

"You don't understand this town. How it works."

"So people just get away with murder?"

That earns me a flinch at the tacit accusation, then a scoff. "Yes. All the time. If they're the right kind of people."

"And are you the kind to lie for them?"

We stare at each other, unblinking. An unspoken face-off, where I can't figure out why we aren't on the same side.

"Hey, sorry, that took forever!" I find a Solo cup of Diet Coke thrust into my hand and Ben at my side. "What's going on?"

"Nothing." I take a long sip of my soda. "Let's go outside to get some fresh air," I say. And I grab Ben by the hand and tug him toward the exit, leaving Gabriel behind. The gossipy throng parts for us, and my nerves calm as soon as the cool snap of the night air hits my face and shoulders.

Ben peers at me knowingly. "So it's down to Gabriel," he says. I can see the wheels turning for him.

"Or Grace."

"Or Grace," Ben parrots. "Well, steer clear of both of them. Let's enjoy the rest of the night. If you're really worried, you can go to the sheriff tomorrow."

"With wild theories, not proof."

"You don't know what they have. It could help."

We throw our empties in a nearby trash can, and Ben takes both of my hands in his. Music from the gym reverberates in heavy pop bass, but he twirls me around, leads me in a languid slow dance to a song only he can hear. A kiss is the next step in the choreography. Ben cups my face with a broad hand and tips my chin up just so; our lips touch tentatively, even though it's hardly our first time. But in this dress, at the big dance, this kiss is an event. It's unhurried and perfect.

Right when I'm about to suggest we take off—I've had my fill of dances and drama and anyone who isn't him—he breaks away, moves back toward the school.

"Come on, let's go inside. Get warm."

A coward, I follow. By the gym doors, Ben pauses. "Find us a good spot on the dance floor. I have to ... you know." He indicates the bathroom, then goes beet red. "Pee. I have to pee. Nothing weird."

I send him off with a laugh, head into the gym. My phone buzzes in my clutch. I pull it out, wake the screen, and see I have a text from an unfamiliar number. I tap in, and the dual speech bubbles send a shard of ice through my gut.

That's a pretty dress.

It looked good on Maura, too.

CHAPTER TWENTY-NINE

My eyes dart around the gym. Who sent this? Grace? Gabriel?

Whoever it is, I know Natalie's killer has my number. In more ways than one. The mayor's accusation at the wake comes back to me. *It was you. Sending me nasty texts that night. Trying to* frame me. So this is the killer's game. Spoofing his number and playing with people like a cat with a mouse. It must have been the killer's original plan to use the mayor as a patsy to find the body.

So what is the plan for me?

I head to the gym lobby, eyes darting to the bathroom door. I need Ben, but I can't go in there, so I head back into the dance, scanning for Amber, Bronte, anyone I can trust. But I don't see them.

Buzz.

Another text. I snatch up my phone, with shaking hands, and open it to find a demand blinking in sans serif:

> Meet at the pool during the song. You'll know the one.
> Don't tell anyone. Come alone.

And I turn off the screen, shove the phone into my purse. Someone's fucking with me. I'll find a spot on the dance floor, like Ben asked. I don't even know what song they mean.

Then I hear the warbling horns, building slowly but surely. A baritone, somehow smooth and scratchy at the same time, comes in, singing about seasons. I recognize it immediately. This is the song. The bass vibrates my bones; the DJ has turned it up. He's shouting over the crowd, at everyone: "Come in at the chorus!"

Before I can think, I'm shoving my way through tangled, sweaty bodies, tripping toward the back egress, the one I know leads straight to the pool.

Come alone, the note said, and still I peer around for Ben. This is a terrible idea. But I have to go. *I need to know who it is.*

The chorus hits, the name muffled swiftly as the door shuts behind me. Sweet Caroline. I hesitate at the head of the stairs for a second. Then I rocket down them, something inside me sure I must be at the pool when the next chorus hits. Just like in the book.

I ease off the stairs onto the pool deck, and it's déjà vu. Like last week. Same door, same rippling reflection of water on the faded tiles, same pool.

But no body.

And I'm alone. There's no bogeyman stepping out the shadows to greet me.

My brain catches up with my body. I'm standing here like a fool, Neil Diamond pounding through the ceiling. Surely this wasn't one of Natalie's favorites. Morgan made the playlist, and—

Morgan made the playlist.

"You bitch," I mutter to my presumed audience. Morgan,

pissed at me for the wake, reminding me I don't belong. Putting this goddamn song on, the one from my grandmother's book, the winking reference to her great-aunt.

"It's a shit prank without a fake body!" My voice echoes, almost musical. And because maybe I'm losing my mind, I think, *Fuck it,* and come in on the chorus, shout-sing about that sweet Caroline at the top of my lungs.

My phone vibrates in my hand, and I shriek, nearly drop it. Then again and again, new texts.

> I have a better song for you.

> Oh, Cecelia. I'm down on my knees. Begging you, please.

> Welcome home.

Every fraction of my body sharpens into a single point, insides seized in pure fear. It doesn't sound like Morgan.

I barely feel the next buzz. Still, I lift the screen to my face, scrape over every word.

> You look just like her.

The killer's here.

I spin wildly around, arms in front of my chest as a fruitless shield. Searching the shadows for organic shape, a sign of where they're hiding. So I can flee in the opposite fucking direction.

I'm a sitting duck. In this cavernous room with only two directions to run to get out. The pool glitters to my left, twin locker rooms with ominous dark doorways to my right. I'm frozen in my heels. A new song comes on, a rhythmic four-count of percussion reminding me how far away from everyone I am.

Go, my mind screams. But *which way*? Back the way I came, or through the front door? Which one will push me into the path of a killer?

The sole of a boot squeaks on tile. Behind me. I whip around.

"Cecelia." Gabriel steps into the half-light, phone in his hand.

Gabriel, the history buff. Who'd get his rocks off on how much I look like my grandmother. Mirroring the OG murder with Natalie.

"It's you." My heart spikes into my throat. *Run,* my brain screams. But he's bigger than I am, and could close the distance between us in seconds. I need a plan. Have to time it perfectly. I edge back a foot, then two.

"We need to talk." His voice is a disturbing monotone. Palms out, as if he's trying to calm me down. Like I'm the dangerous one.

"Ben's looking for me," I lie. "He knows where I am."

Anger flashes over Gabriel's features. I take another step backward. Gabriel follows suit. Repeats my name like a platitude. An idea bursts into my mind, and I don't second-guess it. This could be my only chance. I lunge forward, the element of surprise my only advantage as I shove him as hard as I can. Right into the pool.

I'm running like hell toward the stairway to the gym before I hear the resultant splash.

My heels pinch my toes; my calves burn as I sprint up the stairs. Up, up, up, until I hit the door, almost literally. I grab at the handle, jerk it down. But it doesn't budge. I'm fucking locked in.

No, no, no, no, *no.* Denial in full force, I yank the handle down again and again, hoping for a different outcome.

"Help me!" I scream, but the music in the gym is too loud, and who knows if the door is soundproof. It's steel. Heavy.

My adrenaline is pumping too hard, distorting my vision, my hearing. Is that the rush of my own blood, or the whoosh of Gabriel hauling himself from the pool. Is that thumping my heart, or his feet on the slick tiles?

I pound on the door, hurting my fist, but I don't care.

And it opens. I'm so stunned, so fucking relieved, that I don't care that the door whacked me hard in the shoulder. Some floppy-haired, Muppet-faced dude peers at me perplexedly. I push past him and burst into the gym, skirting the dance floor as my eyes strain over the crowd for Ben.

Not there.

I mad-dash toward the lobby, past Bronte, who tries to stop me, but no—I can't trust her. Then there, at the doors, Ben. Relief floods my body. I rush forward, grab him by the arm, and yank him outside.

"Cecelia, what's going on? Where did you go?"

"We need to leave," I demand.

A protest trips on Ben's tongue, but at the last second he holds it, nods, and follows me to his car. I can't breathe, can't think, let alone talk coherently until we're in his Toyota, doors closed.

Ben's hand pauses, keys poised over the ignition. "Where are we going? Do you want to tell me what happened now?"

"Police station" is all I can say, voice shaking. My hands are, too. I bunch them in the fabric of my skirt, take a shuddering breath. My arms and chest ache like I've run a marathon. Panic is exhausting.

Ben doesn't argue; he starts the car and steers us toward downtown.

"It's Gabriel," I say finally, once the school has shrunk enough in the rearview mirror. And I recount the whole chilling affair.

"Shit" is Ben's only reply.

"It's hardly proof, but you're right—I have to tell Sheriff Morrow."

"About that." Ben turns sheepish, and I realize with a start we've coasted right past the turnoff that would take us to the sheriff's office. "They're closed at this time of night. But you can call the emergency line."

Stupid as it is, it knocks the wind out of my sails. It seemed so clear: march into the station, ask to speak to the sheriff, submit to a formal interview.

I pull out my cell and type in the numbers 9-1. My fingers hover over the last button. "I . . . I don't know what to say," I admit to Ben.

"Talk me through it," Ben says calmly. "You saw Escano. He told you he drowned Natalie."

"He didn't, though." My voice is barely audible over the road noise.

"What?"

"He . . . didn't admit to anything. He was there at the pool, and there were the texts. But . . ."

Ben's eye flick between the road and me. "Okay, so he texted you."

"Yes," I answer quickly. But then I remember. "Well, no. Someone texted me. I thought it was Gabriel, but . . . but . . . I don't know for sure. It wasn't a number I recognized."

I must sound mad. I'm beginning to doubt that it happened at all.

"Call the police and tell them you have an emergency, then."

"It's not an emergency, though," I almost whisper. "I escaped. And like I said, it's not really proof. . . ."

Ben's hand reaches across the center console, finding mine.

"Then we'll go in person tomorrow. We'll talk it through tonight, and then we'll go tomorrow, *together*," he reassures me.

Away from the music, from the lights, from Gabriel, the world seems still once more. Peaceful, even. "You're right. I know you're right. We'll go in the morning." I give his hand a squeeze, grateful to have something solid to hold on to. "And where are we going now?" Dense clusters of houses outside the car windows have given way to nothingness, the smell of sea salt increasing with every passing mile.

"Somewhere safe. I was worried about him following us. But he won't find us here."

"Where?"

Ben jitters his knee, taps his fingers on the steering wheel. "We're almost there" is all he says. And so I wait, until the nebulous black coalesces into the gray frame of a house once we finally slow to a stop. There are no lights anywhere—not in the driveway or coming from the house. An uncanny, haunted sensation passes through me.

"Is this your house?"

"Technically, I'm not supposed to be here," he says, giving a nonanswer, then tips his head up to the soulless eyes of dark windows, breathes in the crisp air like a memory. "This is the only place I can still feel her."

Loss streaks through me like a hunger pang. I think of our two-bedroom in Pasadena. How there's another family living there now. Nowhere left to feel anything.

Keys jingle in Ben's hand, and he opens the cranberry-colored front door with a crack.

"Is it safe?" I whisper.

"Ish" is Ben's reply.

And in we step, into the frigid black. And it *is* cold.

"On account of the hole at the back of the house," Ben explains. And then he promptly removes his jacket, places it over my shoulders like a gentleman. I retrieve my cell phone from my clutch and turn on flashlight mode. I ignore the unread texts from Bronte and Amber that wink up from the lock screen. Ben grabs a bulky flashlight from the foyer.

Bright light sweeps over an ordinary-looking foyer, junk mail still cluttered on a side table underneath a row of coat hooks. To our left is a formal living room, to the right, a quaint dining space, both done up in nautical blue and white. I can immediately see Ben's mother in the kitchen, meticulous in keeping the abundance of cream and white spotless but warm, handing Ben a plate of scrambled eggs over the eat-in bar. Past that, though, is a slap back to reality. Heavy plastic sheeting covers a gaping hole in the wall. It must have been the family room.

"Let's go upstairs," Ben says, and I follow carefully, using the light from my phone to guide my steps. His room is toward the front of the house. The door opposite from his is ominously closed. Behind it, there's the faintest whistle. A storm kicking up the ocean air.

Ben grabs a long needle-nosed lighter and lights half a dozen three-wick candles. As they flicker, I can find Ben in the details missing from his room at his grandfather's house: Peeling posters on the wall. Percy Jackson crammed in next to Stieg Larsson on his bookcase.

And his bed. An inviting queen covered in a navy duvet. Ben sits. I sit. And finally, I let the last hour fully wash over me.

He grabs my hand, gives it a squeeze. "It'll be fine. I promise. This is almost over."

I extract my fingers, put them to better use: tease them over his jaw, thread them through his hair. "Kiss me," I demand, because suddenly I need him to. I need something good, something that's mine. The end to my evening, in a gorgeous dress on a date with this boy I like, that should have been, if I weren't a girl chased by ghosts. I'm reclaiming my night.

Ben and I speak the same language, and still I gasp, almost a hiccup, as he eases the zipper of my dress down. His hand snakes over my naked back, tugs me closer, his mouth hungry on mine.

And from there, it's organic: Clothes hastily shed. Diving under the duvet against the chill. Creating our own warmth.

I escape into the feel of our bodies, let my mind cloud and fog with bliss. Because this is something I can control. I breathe it in, let it wash over me.

For the first time in too long, I forget about death.

CHAPTER THIRTY

Cold creeps slowly into my limbs despite the heat of Ben's body beside mine, the duvet too thin for a cavernous, abandoned home. Outside, the wind has kicked up, the beginnings of a rainstorm tapping lightly on the window frame. I'm starting to regret this plan, hiding out on the edge of the world. Maura's house is creaky but cozy. Even if Gabriel could find me there.

Ben groans, extricates himself from the sheets, and modestly shimmies into his boxers. I don't see the point, but it's cute, nonetheless.

"I'm gonna grab some water and snacks. You okay here?"

I pull up on my elbows, nod, hope my hair is adorably mussed rather than disastrous. My phone is across the room, abandoned on the top of Ben's bookshelf when the candles were lit. The one nearest me has a one-inch pool of melted wax all around, and I wonder if you can tell time via wax. I know I need to get up, check my phone, but I'm loath to leave the scant warmth of the sheets. I throw my legs over the end of the bed, donning the duvet like a cape.

My knee catches on the bedside table and pain radiates down my calf. I grab it, hissing, and accidentally dislodge the top drawer. Despite being grown-up enough to use condoms, I fight heat in my cheeks, seeing a box of them sitting right at the front. The temptation to snoop overpowers me. I find a beat-up paperback, a lighter, tissue packs. I squint to read the cover of the book, and find it's a thriller about a small-town detective; it looks good. When I go to put it back, something shiny catches my eye. With two fingers, I extract it from between a mint-flavored ChapStick and a ballpoint pen.

I stare at the key in my hand. *I know this key.*

I have a copy in my backpack at home. The Seaview High School master key.

The same master key Natalie had a copy of, that she would have used to let herself into the school. That the police never found.

But, no, that's ridiculous. This isn't Natalie's key. She made extras. She must have given Ben one, too. For their secret hookups.

The roil in my stomach calms. That's it. A reasonable explanation. I put the key back where I found it. Shut the drawer.

Still, my limbs push me up. I groan into my bustier bra, step into my dress, and flex to get the zipper up as far as I can. I'll need a hand to finish the job. A reminder of how helpless I truly am. Alone, except for Ben.

I grab my phone from the top of the bookshelf while I wait for him to return. Five missed calls. Dozens of texts. All from Bronte and Amber. I ignore the voicemails, stab at the screen to go into my text chain with Bronte. Most recent, right up top, is just my name in all caps.

> CECELIA?

I text back hastily.

I'm fine

Then I catch up, starting at the top of the thread. Bronte sent the first text an hour ago. It leaves me cold in a way that goes beyond the chill of this house.

I hacked into the sheriff's email again and checked Ben's alibi. He wasn't at the game that night. Ben told Amber's dad he was with your grandmother. Says Maura confirmed it.

That doesn't make sense. Ben was with me on the bleachers that night, then ran off to do his thing on the field. He was on the school security footage, in his costume, heading for the locker room. We watched in that dusty, claustrophobic office at school. I fire back a question at Bronte.

But Ben is the school mascot. I saw him there.

A second later, her reply.

They rotate the mascot performers. It was Morris Beckwith that night. I checked with him myself.

The dancing. The mascot at the game was really good. Tonight, with me, Ben struggled with rhythm, uncoordinated. Like the awkward mascot from the assembly weeks ago. Bronte's right.

And the door opens. I hit Send before I can think about it, or finish.

"Why are you dressed?" Ben's brow furrows. I see he has two bottles of water in his hands and a sleeve of Ritz crackers. A late-night feast.

"I was cold," I say. "As nice as the covers were, it's better with layers. Zip me up?"

I turn, sweep aside my tumble of curls, offering my neck. Cold washes across my shoulder blades, then dizzy heat. Ben's body is flush to my back, solid fingers applying firm pressure to zip me all the way. I shiver.

"Thanks," I say, stumbling forward a foot, pulling away a beat too soon and hoping he doesn't notice. My mind is reeling. But I play it cool. Settle one hand on Ben's bare chest, tousle his hair with the other.

"I can't believe I'm dating the school mascot," I tease. "When I saw you in that costume at homecoming, I'll admit I had second thoughts. . . . For like a microsecond."

Ben grabs my arm, spins me around. I tense, but he greets me with a dopey grin, pulls me flush against his chest.

"And now?"

I will my traitorous heart to slow, paste on a smile, and pray to God I'm a half-decent actress. "Vikings are kind of sexy," I say. And I let him kiss me. His tongue in my mouth tastes like ash.

Ben is a liar, and my mind is racing. *Does Ben have Natalie's key? Am I kissing him enthusiastically enough? How close is the nearest neighbor?*

I need to get away.

"Sorry to kill the mood, but I need to use the restroom," I say, breathless.

Ben pulls a face, and my insides clench. "There's only one bathroom I haven't used. Because the electricity is off, you only get one flush on each toilet. It's, uh, the one in my mom's room."

He leads me out into the frigid hallway, flashlight in hand, to the ominously whistling door. Too late, I realize I've left my phone in his room, and I can't go back for it without seeming weird. I don't even have my shoes.

"Is it safe?" I ask, hesitating at the door.

There is no "ish" this time. Only instructions. "Stay close to the wall. The bathroom is on the left." He hands me the flashlight, making it clear he has no plans to open the door, to look inside. Good. His grief gives me a window.

I crack open the door, then sweep the light over the floor before taking tentative steps inside. The main suite is large. *Was* large. The back half of the room is gone, much like that image of the Pacific Coast Highway with a gaping chasm. I struggle to piece together in my mind what it must have been like before, but all I can imagine are the walls and flooring turned to mush. If I dared to move closer to the edge, I could peer down into the former family room. And beyond to the sea.

I follow Ben's directions, sticking close to the wall and making my way into the bathroom. Light sweeps across skin-care bottles, dirty makeup brushes, a teal-and-white toothbrush askew in a ceramic holder. Like their owner could breeze in here at any moment and perform her nightly toilette.

I brace my hands on the counter, stare into the mirror, the harsh light of the flashlight casting me in ghastly relief. Like a dead girl walking.

Would Ben kill me? Do I really think he killed Natalie?

Yes, the voice inside me whispers. I don't know why he did it, but between his lying about being the mascot that night, the school master key in his drawer, trying to convince me over and over that it was Gabriel . . .

God. Did I just sleep with a killer? I glance at the dormant shower, wishing desperately to get clean. I can still feel Ben all over me, like an oily film.

Maybe I could sneak away now, while he thinks I'm using the toilet. Tiptoe into the foyer and steal away into the night. Without my phone, I feel naked. Vulnerable. But these are the variables I'm stuck with. No shoes, no phone, a tiny window. Still, I have to go *now.*

I leave the bathroom, pausing in front of the door to Ben's mom's room. I can do this. With one last deep breath, I pivot to the door and wrest it open.

And find myself face to face with Ben.

CHAPTER THIRTY-ONE

I yelp, stumbling back and back, unable to stop myself, my body falling, because the floor is *slanting downward*. I'm heading for the edge.

Until Ben's strong hands grab mine, pull me forward into his arms. The flashlight lands on the floor with a thump, rolling off to the far wall, casting us in spooky relief.

"You scared me," I say, trying to sound exasperated. Cool. Not terrified.

I extricate myself from his arms, though not too forcefully. I'm still Ben's girlfriend, after all. Or pretending to be until I figure out a new way to save myself.

In the askew dome of light, shadows creep over half of Ben's face, rendering him a new person. One I've never seen. But I'm sure Natalie did, right before she died.

Every atom of my body is electric, panic blowing up every sense I have while also focusing me down to a single point. One feeling. Pure white terror.

"Our friends have been blowing up your phone," he says, tone so sharp it could cut glass.

"Oh, have they?" I try to play it cool, but Ben is past pretending.

"You know about the mascot thing."

I swallow hard. "It wasn't you on the field that night."

"No," he replies matter-of-factly, almost glib.

"But you were at the school."

"Yes."

And there it is. Ben's eyes rake over my face, flickering in the half-light with an emotion I'm not expecting.

Hope.

"This whole thing was you," I say, pushing awe into my tone in place of disgust. If I flatter his ego, get him to let his guard down, will he let me go?

"It got out of hand. Everything after. You were an unexpected surprise."

"I wasn't supposed to find the body, like in my grandmother's book?"

"God, no. I wouldn't do that to you, Cecelia. When you walked in, and then I heard you scream? I felt awful. Putting you through that."

He's painfully sincere. Disarming, even.

"Why did you do it?"

Ben sneers. Gestures around. "Isn't it obvious?" He pauses, sweeps his gaze across the room with a frown. "I haven't been in here since it happened. If I had a therapist, they'd be proud. I think this is a breakthrough."

Ben takes my hands in his. My skin crawls. "Thanks to you. My muse."

I could vomit. Instead, I clasp his hands tighter. So hard I hope it hurts. "How could you do it, though? Such a brutal murder. Especially if Natalie was merely collateral damage. Picked because you wanted to punish her dad. For your mom?"

It's a guess, one that Ben confirms with a nod.

"It wasn't that bad. I injected her with insulin, so she went into shock. Made it easier for us both. She didn't even know what was happening."

"But the coroner didn't find any needle marks."

"Between the toes. Like a drug addict. It's harder to find." He seems so proud of himself. So clever. Like trading murder facts with me is some kind of foreplay.

I can't do this anymore. Can't pretend. I pull my hands away, eyes darting wildly to the door. Sour adrenaline spreads through my limbs, like I'm a trapped animal seconds from slaughter.

Ben's eyes turn to flint. "It bothers you."

"No fucking shit," I bite. "You murdered someone. Like, you planned it. Elaborately. The whole copycat thing, right down to the original police report? That's cold-blooded."

"In my defense, no one knows about that. Except for my grandfather, me, and now you. It was a good tip. A way to get it done more quickly, without arm strain. You know, it actually takes about six minutes to strangle someone. Not three. The copycat thing was just a bit of fun."

"Murder shouldn't be fun."

"And yet you've had a real ball investigating. Don't think I missed how it brought light to your eyes. Purpose to your life."

"It's not the same," I say. *Dear God, I hope it's not the same.*

Ben sneers. "I thought you'd understand, but you don't. *Your* mom wasn't murdered."

"Neither was yours," I can't help shouting, incredulous. "Your mother died in a tragic accident!"

"That could have been prevented if Mayor Bergen had done his job! Instead, he wasted *years* on fucking rock walls. All to keep his numbers up. To get reelected."

"So, what—that gives you the right to murder his daughter in revenge?"

Ben nods, as if pleased that I finally get it. "True poetic justice would have been him going down for it, but I could have never predicted he was off committing statutory rape. Or hoping to. Ignored my texts in favor of his hard-on."

"So what was your backup plan?"

"You helped with that." He grins like a demented jack-o'-lantern. "Grace was a stroke of genius, by the way. But Gabriel became the perfect patsy. A bonus to drive a wedge between you. I can take a little competition."

"Was anything about you real?" My voice breaks on the last word. I was played for a fool, thinking this boy before me was my new hope, an anchor. Instead, he's a sick, twisted parody.

"Of course. I really like you." He says it so convincingly. Earnestly. Ben believes every word out of his mouth. "Everything I did was to keep you safe. Keep you away from the truth, so we could have a future. You're smart, tenacious, hot. You really do look incredible in that dress. And now I know how good you are in bed. . . ."

My stomach churns with disgust, but I swallow past the sick lump rising in my throat. "You're the one who texted me to get me down to the pool, then. Why?"

"To get him down there, too. To get you to believe it, so you would convince the sheriff. I used the planting-some-of-the-victim's-things-in-his-locker trick, a classic. On top of the weed? He'd go down for sure. Still will."

With you dead is left unspoken.

"What weed?" I ask, because I want to know, and also because I need him to keep talking. To give my stupid brain enough time to work. Figure out how the *fuck* I'm going to get out of this.

"Gabriel's dealing. Everyone who cares to know knows. Why do you think he's lying about his alibi?"

"Weed's legal in California," I say. "Why would it matter?"

Ben chuckles to himself. "God, you're new. It's a bit more complicated than that. The Escanos are amateur growers, and the sheriff's always looking for a reason to bust them, take his own cut. Towns like this run on bullshit."

"So you fit right in."

"Ha ha."

I know we've reached the end of the road. Ben's eyes keep flicking behind me. At the flapping plastic sheet that would be easy enough to rip free—and give me to the sea.

Outside, the squawk of a squad car startles us both. Hope streaks through me as panic hardens Ben's resolve. He grabs me by the forearms, flips me around, and shoves me toward the edge.

"Ben, no!" I fight, try to pull myself free, jab my elbows into his torso. Bend my knees and grind my feet into the floor. But he's much stronger than I am, his grip on my arms iron. The floor beneath my feet is springy. Unstable.

Salt air kisses my cheeks. My hair whips around my face.

"I'm sorry, Cecelia," Ben says into my ear.

I use the last weapon I have: psychological warfare.

"Your mother would be ashamed of you."

I seize on Ben's shock, the hot poker of grief and shame and rage I've just thrust into his gut. I stomp a foot onto his, shove a sharp elbow into his ribs. We stumble toward the ocean, but only a few inches. I twist in his grasp, use the momentum to shove him away from me.

And with a strangled cry, Ben falls backward—over the edge of the house.

CHAPTER THIRTY-TWO

I lunge forward, catching Ben by the arms. Searing heat travels up to my shoulders, into the muscles of my back, as I try to wrench him up. I will not let this motherfucker die. He doesn't deserve that.

My toes dig into the cold, wet carpet, but the leverage isn't enough. I can't pull him up. Shit.

"Help!" I scream, praying my rescuers aren't just idling outside, waiting for signs of life. I grunt like a rampaging animal, push and pull with all my strength. I. Will. Not. Let. Go. I will not become a murderer.

"Don't drop me!" Ben cries, cold bravado banished. He's just a boy now, a real person who doesn't want to die. *This* is the person I cared about, who I thought cared about me.

"Hold on!" I cry, fighting to be heard over the crash of the storm.

Ben yanks on my arm, braces himself, then pulls on my opposite forearm. He doesn't make progress, though. Instead, the force, his body weight, scoots me forward, pulls my center of gravity toward the edge.

"You'll pull us both over," I yell through gritted teeth. "Grab on to the floor!"

But Ben doesn't stop. Doesn't try for the splintered flooring inches from his fingers. He keeps on climbing my arms. Excruciating pain radiates up my body; I think he might dislodge my arms from their sockets. My torso is digging into jagged wood, perilously close to a jutting piece of rebar. I'm slipping farther.

He's going to climb me like a ladder, I realize. *A human ladder. If I go down, who cares. Fuck.*

Then, suddenly, there's a weight on my legs. Strong arms, anchoring me. Grabbing me by the hips and starting to pull.

"I've got you!"

Gabriel!

"And I've got *him*," I shriek as Ben wrenches my arm especially hard.

"Bronte, help."

The pressure shifts, Bronte taking her brother's place to secure me while Gabriel gets on his stomach, reaches down to grab Ben's left arm.

"You hang on to the right, and we'll both pull," he says to me. And then to Ben: "Stop for a second. Go when I count to three."

My arms shake as I use both hands to grab Ben's right arm; at least Gabriel's grip is firm. He counts to three, and on cue, we both grunt and pull while Ben uses the last of his strength to hoist himself up.

Ben shrieks, as if in pain, but we don't stop. Sadism, maybe. Or fear of physics. Fear that if we stop, pause for even one second to check, the floor will slip out from under us. It wobbles beneath my stomach even now, Gabriel's added weight beside me creating tiny shocks with every shift of his muscles.

Once we've hauled Ben onto the carpet, then retreated to the far wall and to more solid ground, it's clear why Ben was screaming. The rebar has left a great gash in his thigh. He whines, the big baby. Bronte grabs a bathroom towel to stem the blood, the last nice thing I intend for us to do for him, while Gabriel holds Ben by the arms.

Seconds later, Sheriff Morrow and Deputy Shields burst through the door, guns drawn and Amber on their heels.

"Ho-ly shit," Amber says, taking in the scene.

"Could somebody please fill me in?" the sheriff says, holstering his gun and unsnapping a pair of handcuffs from his belt. Deputy Shields's gun waffles between us. Ben, then me. Me, then Ben.

I point weakly in Ben's direction. "He killed Natalie."

"She's crazy!" Ben's shouting is hoarse, his voice weak, though not his performance. He's a master class in manipulation. "You saw her at the wake. Just went full psycho on me after we had sex. Tried to push me over. Don't believe a word she says," he yells.

But I have something Ben doesn't have: friends.

"He's been lying about his alibi," Bronte says, backing me. "He told her he was at the game as the mascot, but told you he was with Maura Weston."

"And how do you know what he told me, young lady?" the sheriff says.

"Dad, it doesn't matter. He's psycho," Amber cuts in. "We've been worried about Cecelia for days."

Gabriel nods emphatically. "I got these fucked-up texts at the dance, telling me to go down to the pool. That Cecelia was in danger. And then she pushed me into the water. They have to be from him. He wanted her to think it was me."

"Gabriel, I'm so sorry," I say. "For suspecting you. Ruining your jacket." The velvet is a matted mess now.

"That's okay. The wet look is in." He winks at me. It's a tiny moment of levity that almost makes me forget where I am, what's happening. But then Ben starts whining again.

"I didn't text anyone, I swear! And *he* doesn't have an alibi." Ben ratchets up his performance, jerking toward Gabriel. Actual tears prick his eyes, though maybe that's from the pain. A lot of his blood has seeped into the towel now. He needs medical attention.

They'll still have to prove it all, I realize. Everything sounds circumstantial. And Ben is a good liar.

Then I remember the key.

"There's a key in his bedside drawer. It's a master key to the school. Natalie's key. You never found how she got into the building that night. You'll find her DNA on the key, and his. And he injected her with insulin. He told me. You can exhume the body."

"That's not true!" Ben protests. "She's lost her mind!"

But the sheriff considers me. It may be my word against Ben's until further notice, but right now it's enough. Sheriff Morrow snaps the cuffs on him.

And for the first time all night, I can breathe.

CHAPTER THIRTY-THREE

Home. The word is foreign in my mouth. The feeling strange. Numbness mixed with a kick of hope. After the night I've had, I'm happy to take the final step up onto the porch of Maura's towering Victorian. And as I cross the threshold, I think, *Maybe it's my towering Victorian now, too.*

The foyer is dark but for the distant glow of honey yellow cast from the kitchen. Maura left a light on for me. At first comforting, my grandmother's consideration soon turns sour. How am I going to tell her about Ben? She'll be devastated. Especially that he used *her* as his alibi!

At least he'll rot in jail instead of at the bottom of a cliff. The Bergens, this town, will finally see some justice.

But will they? I think of Caroline and my afternoon with Joe.

I don't believe that Joe Bedecki killed Caroline Quinn. He didn't know about the insulin that Ben so lovingly imitated. Whose handiwork did he really copy?

I should have told Sheriff Morrow about Grace, but I was so exhausted, so hyperfocused on Ben. It's nearly five a.m., and all I want to do is sleep. But I don't know if I can.

I remove my heels from my aching feet, pad into the kitchen to make coffee, already dreaming of a lengthy scalding-hot shower. I need to wash Ben off me. The grime of that bedroom. The sweat at the nape of my neck, now sticky and cool, from the exertion of keeping that asshole from dying.

Maura's sitting at the counter, already nursing a cup. She takes in my tangled hair, a grin creeping up her cheeks.

"Good morning, Celia. Or good night for you, I gather. I hope you're strolling in hours past curfew because you got laid. Only excuse I'll accept."

But then she frowns. Takes in the state of my dress. Her dress. A dirt-smeared and ripped mess. "What the hell happened? I swear, if that boy laid a hand on you, I will murder him myself."

"You're right on both accounts. Sort of," I say, grabbing a coffee mug from the cabinet and sliding with a grunt onto the barstool one over from her. "Ben and I hooked up, and then he tried to kill me. All in all, an eventful homecoming."

Being cavalier keeps residual panic from rising in my throat. For good measure, I pour myself a cup of joe and don't even bother with cream or sugar, swallowing down bitter black coffee to echo my mood.

"Excuse me?" Maura says low and slow.

I smack my lips together and elaborate. "Ben murdered Natalie. Once he knew that I knew, he tried to throw me off a cliff. Kind of. We were in his mom's bedroom."

Maura's eyes go wide as she puts together the pieces. "Oh my. Thank God you're safe. And where is Ben now, then?"

"He got cut on some rebar and had to go to the hospital. Then it's off to jail, I hope." I take a long draw of coffee, mouth puckering as I eye the sugar bowl with regret.

"And can you believe he used *you* for his alibi?" I add. "Ass-hole."

I pull my phone from my clutch, find the battery at 4 percent. There's a new text from Bronte.

> Call me in the morning. Hugs, friend.

I smile to myself. At least I have some friends. We'll face the shitstorm sure to come together. And, God, I owe Gabriel a massive apology.

My eyes catch on Bronte's previous message. The one that had stopped my heart.

> Ben told Amber's dad he was with your grandmother.
> Says Maura confirmed it.

That's funny. I turn to my grandmother. "Why did you confirm it with the sheriff? Say Ben was with you if he wasn't?"

"What do you mean?" Maura bats her long lashes in confusion.

There's a pulse of knowing that I feel in my bones: *Fake.*

My grandmother is lying.

I'm not safe. This *isn't* home.

My phone is at 2 percent now, battery icon blinking an angry red. Still in the text chain from Bronte, I swipe my thumb over *H*, then *E*, and am going for the *L* when the screen goes black.

Cold fear invades my body; I peer over at my grandmother, find her quietly sipping her coffee, simply watching me. Waiting.

My mind races. She lied for Ben. Her intern. Or her protégé? Maura was close in Caroline's orbit. Second runner-up. Discovered her body. Flirted with Joe. Did more with Joe? He beyond implied as much to me.

The photo from the newspaper archive. Maura worked at the hospital right alongside Grace. I can see her plucking a vial of insulin from a nurse's cart, slipping it into the pocket of her red-and-white striped apron. Jamming a needle into Caroline's stomach, waiting for her to go limp before finishing her off with both hands around her neck.

My grandmother, the murderer.

CHAPTER THIRTY-FOUR

"Caroline" is all I have to say, scarcely a whisper.

She smiles.

"I'm proud of you, Celia. Whip-smart. Smarter than the rest of these slow fuckers. You figured out not only Benjamin, but me. Fifty-two years, and you're the first one." She goes from beaming to a frown. "I cannot believe that fuckboy blew it for me," she mutters, almost to herself. "But at least it's you. My darling granddaughter."

I cannot tell if that's a threat, or her true, delusional belief. That like Ben, she thinks some tenuous connection between us—attraction and love, or in this case, family—means I'm an ally. That I'll go on with my life, allowing a murderer to walk free. For what? So I won't be alone?

Fuck that.

I need to get out of here. *Now.*

Fifteen feet. The back door is fifteen feet past her shoulder.

But the knife block is closer.

Maura defies her age; catlike, she lunges for the block, brandishing eight inches of shining silver blade seconds later.

On her feet now, she waggles the knife in my direction, her voice a low hiss. "Disappointing. Too much like your mother, then."

I fumble backward off the barstool, ass hitting linoleum seconds later. Scoot-slide away, feet slipping on Maura's fucking dress as I try to get up. I hear a rip as I haul myself to standing, and I derive a sick pleasure at the sneer that pulls at Maura's lips. Good. Fuck her. Fuck this dress. She made me into her doppelganger, living out some sick fantasy she'd failed to accomplish with my mom. But I am my own person. Not a puppet.

And now I'm that much closer to the kitchen stairs, I bolt up them, taking two at a time, ignoring the way my limbs burn after a night of pushing them to their limits.

Maura thunders up behind me. Bitch lied about her bad knees, too. She's tight on my heels, allowing me no time to stop for a breath, or to formulate a new plan. Outrunning her won't work; I'm not at peak strength, and she has more than I anticipated. Plus, there's the knife.

"Agh!"

The blade catches my calf. Searing white-hot pain radiates up my body, and I collapse onto the third-floor landing. I manage to flip onto my back, curl up from my core, then land a two-footed kick into Maura's torso. Screaming, she flies down into the darkened staircase. Did I just kill my grandmother?

"You bitch!"

Guess not. I hear her scrabbling toward me. I crab-walk away as best I can. The gash in my right leg is bleeding profusely, soaking the periwinkle satin of the fucking dress a deep crimson. But no bone peeks through. The wound isn't deep. And I can stand, if I'm careful not to put full weight on my injured limb. I hop-stumble to the end of the hall. Where the fuck can I go? Up was a bad idea. Can I make it to the front door?

"Celia, dear."

I yelp as Maura appears on the landing, hair a wild mess and eyes blazing. The way she ground out her nickname for me deceptively low and calm, turned it into an epithet.

"This is all very unnecessary. All you need do is keep your mouth shut, and you'll get everything you ever wanted." She approaches slowly, like an animal tamer, hands up and palms out, though the butcher knife remains in her right hand. Maura attempts her best pitch as I inch back a step for each one she takes forward.

"I'll send you to the fanciest, most expensive college of your dreams. Hell, I'll donate a goddamn wing to get you in. You'll get everything in my will. Set for life. But this secret, this legacy, it has to stay between us. We're family, baby girl. You're my blood. You're just like me."

"I'm nothing like you," I snarl. "It's like you said. I'm like my mom. Who hated you so much she cut you off."

Maura chuffs. "Your mother was an ungrateful brat who didn't appreciate anything I did for her. For us. Happy to live off the fruits of my labor until her precious daddy died. Always an insufferable daddy's girl."

Mom's scream rockets into my mind. *He's dead!*

Wait.

"Did you kill Granddad?"

"How else was I supposed to know what happens to the human body when hanged by the neck?" she says as if discussing

316

the weather. "Celia, it's all for the sake of my books. Making them better. So I can leave *you* the legacy. The Maura Weston brand."

"You murdered him for . . . research?"

Seaview has a history of murders.

"It's not as simple as that," Maura snaps dismissively. She's close enough for me to see flecks of blood fly off the knife. "If I decide to bump someone off, I like to get creative. And then why not use it? Correlation is not causation, and all that."

Morgan told Amber's dad she thought Seaview had a serial killer.

"How many people have you . . . bumped off?" I've reached the dumbwaiter, but I'm still so far from the front stairwell. Every movement I make hurts like a mofo, but I think if I keep her talking, maybe I'll recover my strength.

Or maybe she'll recover hers.

"Who can say? Maybe just the two. Maybe more. You're suddenly interested."

"You said it was my legacy."

Could I get in the dumbwaiter? Would it take my weight? Or would Maura beat me downstairs first anyway?

"We both know you're not on board. I can read you like one of my books. I've enjoyed this time with you, however. It was nice to bond. Even if it was short-lived."

The contrast is jarring: Sweet-as-pie grandmother. Sharp-as-shit knife. It glistens as Maura steps closer. My hand clenches tight to the dumbwaiter door. This is my best chance.

"So why did you kill Caroline? Because of Joe?"

"Again, so clever." She's a cat, and I am a half-dead mouse she's keen to play with. "You're both a delight and a disappointment. Yes, it was Joe. And how much everyone loved Caroline. She was always nipping at my heels. So I got rid of her. Our pretty home-coming queen."

And then she grimaces. Blink and you'd miss it. But I don't.

I can't help the laugh that bubbles from me. "It drives you crazy that you needed *her* to become *you*. That that's your biggest book. It's still all about Caroline."

"Fuck Caroline," she spits with such ferocity the tiniest bit of foam forms at the corner of her mouth. "I made her so much more interesting in death than she ever would have been in life. *Me. My* name will live on forever as one of the greatest mystery writers of all time. Up there with Christie. And Doyle. And James fucking Patterson. And Caroline will be just another dead girl."

Her ego completely unchecked for the first time, my true grandmother appears before me. The monster who made my mother by way of relief. Maura's cold, unrelenting drive for fame, validation, vindication at any cost, the polar opposite of my mom's selflessness, her empathy, her need to help. I am my mother's daughter. I will carry her with me always, because I am who she made me.

And Maura can go to hell.

But first, I still have unanswered questions.

"How did you get Joe to take the fall? He says he did it."

"Joe's sweet. Dumb but sweet."

Sweet is the last word I would use for Joe Bedecki, but I don't dare interrupt Maura. She's a few feet away now.

"I let Joe know that Grace would serve as my next inspiration if he didn't drop his appeal, play the part of the guilty pervert for the media. A nice, regular payment into his commissary fund twice a year makes it go down a bit easier. Least I can do."

"So generous."

"I don't like your tone."

She flinches. I seize the moment, yanking the dumbwaiter door up. The dark maw belches stale air, a hollow whistle hinting at two stories of free fall.

"It's a dead end, dear," Maura sneers. "You forgot to call the compartment."

"No, I didn't," I say as Maura lunges at me, teeth bared in a snarl. I grab her by the wrists, twist her around with all my strength.

And I push her into the shaft.

CHAPTER THIRTY-FIVE

The house sighs a final agonal breath. Leaving silence.

I hold the air in my lungs. I don't make a noise. I listen. For grunts or groans. Maura hissing and spitting about a broken hip or legs.

Nothing.

A wail, high-pitched and formless, rips from my throat.

I want my mom.

My eyes burn, my cheeks stinging from hot tears, my sinuses seizing to the point of pain. It hurts to cry so hard. I curl into the fetal position on the shining hardwood floors and let go.

Weeks of shoving deep down the wild roar of feelings. Months, if I'm honest. I was numb long before my mom died. Telling myself, *head down, forge forward, the only way out is through.*

I am through, and I am alone.

Utterly and completely alone.

Sorrow is replaced with hollow, horrifying existential terror. The empty, creaking house settles on me like a cement cloak.

I have to get up. I will not bury myself here.

I manage to get my good leg under me, rise to my knees, and stumble to a stand. It's a blur thumping down the stairs, staggering to the front door. But I manage it, flinging the door open . . . to find myself face to face with Reama the superfan. Will this hell never end?

Only she looks different. Corporate, in an ill-fitting blazer-and-pant set.

Then I realize there's a gun in her hands.

"Are you okay?" Her eyes dart behind me, sweeping the foyer and rooms beyond.

"No," I say. The most honest I have been in a long time. I am not okay. I might never be okay again.

"Why do you have a gun?" I croak. "Why are you here?"

Reama softens infinitesimally. "It's my job. I'm an FBI agent. Suzanne woke up and called me. After I heard what happened with the Vann boy, I figured you weren't safe. Where is she?"

I point vaguely in the direction of the hall. "I pushed her into the dumbwaiter shaft," I say. And when Reama's eyebrows arch up, I have to explain. "She tried to kill me."

"I believe you," Reama says. "I believe she killed a lot of people."

"You knew?"

"Suspected. Strongly. Now I know."

"Was pretending to be Maura's biggest fan like some kind of sting?"

"No, I actually am a fan," she says darkly. "How do you think I knew her books well enough to spot the patterns? Wait on the porch."

I am happy to be out in the fresh early-morning air. I stay there, shivering in my tattered vintage ballgown, until police lights flash into the drive. Heavy-footed, droopy-lidded officers stomp into the house. Paramedics arrive, and someone bandages up my leg.

"You'll need to go to the hospital for stitches," they say. A gurney bumps up the porch steps and is wheeled inside. My phone is still dead, a digital brick stuck in what is now a crime scene, so I can't call anyone. But Amber, Bronte, Gabriel, and Mrs. Escano soon arrive, thanks to this tiny town and the power of word of mouth.

✦

"Are you sure about this?" Bronte rebalances the box in her hands, using her knee to get a firmer grip. I mirror the move, flex my aching fingers against the cardboard of my own box, wishing I had Bronte's athleticism. She's not even sweating. A drip of moisture trickles over the puckered scar on my calf. The stitches came out last week, but it's still a mottled pink, hard to miss. And, God, the itching.

"Yeah," I say, nudging the kitchen door open with my hip. We crunch across the gravel to Suzanne's carriage house. "I can't live there right now. Trapped alone with all her things. Unless you want to move in. Keep me company?"

"I don't want to live in a haunted house, either." A joke on the surface, with reality crackling beneath. Some papers have called it a "house of horrors," as if Maura were butchering bodies in the basement. Or maybe it's because of how she died.

"Besides," Bronte adds, "Mom loves our house. And we can finally pay off the mortgage, do some renovations with the book-deal money."

Maura's agent snapped Mrs. Escano up and got her a six-figure deal to write a murder town tell-all. Suzanne joked that publishing is glacially slow except when it's not. Half the town is grumbling they didn't get to the payday first. Plenty of them have appeared on the news, though.

"I may have gotten the shit knocked out of me when that bitch cut my brakes, but I'm well enough to tell them to fuck off," Suzanne has been saying all week. And Maura did cut her brakes. Then she bribed the auto shop to lie about it on the official report.

To my surprise, Suzanne intends to stick around, at least until probate for Maura's estate is settled and until I both turn eighteen and graduate from high school. Maura had too much hubris to think she'd really die, so the throwaway will she made years ago stands. Suzanne is the executor of her estate, and I'm the sole heir. It would have been my grandmother's *Fuck you* to my mom, had she lived—passing over her daughter to manipulate me with her millions.

Well, fuck you, Maura: I have half a mind to tear the whole place down. But for now, finishing out my senior year cohabitating with Suzanne while I decide what to do with the Ellis mansion will do. A part of me knows the house is too spectacular to get rid of. But I still might throw all of Maura's things onto the lawn and light a bonfire. We'll see.

Gabriel's coming out of my new bedroom—the guest room in Suzanne's cozy cottage—as Bronte and I sweep in with the last of my boxes.

"Hey, let me get that." Gabriel jumps in, relieving me of my box, which he adds to the small tower in the corner. It's all my belongings, plus some of my mom's. Mementos and other items that don't deserve to spend a single second more in that house.

"If only I had a girlfriend who liked *me* enough to help me with physical labor," Bronte says with dramatic projection, so that it reaches Amber downstairs. She appears a moment later at the bottom of the steps, a stack of pizza boxes in hand.

"Instead, you have a girlfriend who lovingly feeds you," Amber says, rubbing her back as we all file to the kitchen to eat. "Even if you do like pineapple on your pizza."

"It's a family thing," Gabriel chimes in, loading three slices onto a paper plate.

Amber joins me in raiding the pepperoni box and says in a stage whisper, "What are we going to do with them?" and I feel that familiar and frightening heady rush. That Gabriel is considered mine.

Don't trust it, screams the part of me still reeling from everything with Ben. But the other part of me—the part I'm trying to listen to more these days—thinks maybe I deserve some small slice of happiness right now. And Gabriel makes me happy.

"I'm going to take some boxes to the main house," I say, picking up a cheese and a supreme labeled with Suzanne's name.

"Pizza's here!" I call out, sliding them onto the kitchen island in Maura's house. No—I stop and correct myself—this is *my* house now, too.

The rumble of voices reaches me, and I follow it to Maura's office, where I find Suzanne lying spread-eagled on the floor. "Fuck my fucking back," she groans.

Behind Maura's desk, Reama chuckles, but she doesn't miss a beat as she keeps riffling through a pile of paper.

"Pizza's in the kitchen," I say. "Uncover anything interesting?"

"Some travel itineraries from the nineties that might help," Reama says. She's in town indefinitely on a sabbatical from work. Says the FBI won't officially sanction an investigation on Maura, but she's determined to coerce them into it. I've given her full access to all of Maura's things, in case it helps. "Thank God she was a pack rat."

I'm drawn to the towering shelves, the hundreds of books spanning four decades. The legacy everyone's always droning on about. Turns out it's a legacy of death and destruction. A puzzle I've inherited. But I've got Reama, Suzanne, and all my friends on my team.

Reama appears at my side, yellow legal pad in hand. "I have the master spreadsheet on my home computer, tracking my suspicions and work over the years, but I started a priority list, if you want to look."

My eyes skim over the half a dozen of Maura's titles, publication years beside each and some jotted notes. A Gothic about a family hotel empire and a murder, with the note *Hotel Seaview— Rogers family?* scribbled alongside. A coed slasher next to the name Jessica Swinarski and the question *Adjunct teaching position at Alder University?* A potential trail of my grandmother's exploits and inspirations. A shiver passes through me.

Suzanne hauls herself up from the floor with a protracted groan, joins Reama and me as we sweep our eyes over book after book.

"We have our work cut out for us, eh? She was prolific," Suzanne says with a cough, then a curse. I catch her reaching for her pocket, for the vape that's no longer there. Her brush with death put the fear of God into her, and the ICU detox from nicotine made it easier to quit. Doesn't stop her from being grumpy about it, though.

"Where do we even start?" I can't help the tinge of hopelessness in my tone.

"*We* don't start anywhere," Suzanne scolds. "Your only job is to graduate from high school and get a fuckton of therapy."

"I should probably get a new therapist," I joke.

"I can get you a summer internship or something," Reama says. "When you graduate, we'll talk. You're clearly nosy enough to make a great FBI agent."

"You think?"

"UC Irvine has a stellar program," Reama replies keenly. "Something to consider."

Indeed.

What neither of them knows won't kill them. Because my plan is that alongside a fuckton of therapy, I have no intention of stopping. Perhaps this house can serve a purpose, with all the clues it may contain. And all that blood money can be put to good use.

I gaze up at the kaleidoscope of colorful spines, each one a window to a real-life mystery. My grandmother the serial killer?

Death has always followed me. Time for me to do the chasing.

ACKNOWLEDGMENTS

This is my grief book. Written as the world grieved a new reality and far too many lost, and as I continued to grieve my mother, it has been the most difficult, stressful book I have yet undertaken, though sure not to be the last. I have to thank everyone who was with me on the journey, witnessing my chaos-process and providing support as my anxiety cycled to new dizzying heights. The only way out is through, and somehow this became a book in the end.

Elizabeth Stranahan—I am so grateful every day to have you as my editor. You've helped me become a stronger writer over the past two years, and made a stressful process much, much easier with your flexibility, encouragement, and great ideas. I could weep with happiness for getting to be on your team.

My agent, Elana Roth Parker, for, as ever, supporting my wild ideas and career pivots and barrage of text messages. You are my calm port in the tumultuous sea of publishing.

The entire team at Crown and Random House, especially Phoebe Yeh, who still shocks me by reading my books and saying nice things about them. To amazing copy editors who continue to save me time and time again from my own carelessness: thank you, Melinda Ackell and Elizabeth Johnson. Casey Moses, cover designer extraordinaire, thank you so much for responding to my Instagram DMs and being literally the best cover designer a girl could ask for. When I saw the first cover concept I legit screamed. You're brilliant. Thank you to cover photographer Maggie Holmgren and stylist Derek Svitko. Kimberly Small, Sarah Lawrenson, Kathy Dunn, Natali Cavanagh, Erica Stone, Michael Caiati, the entire Get Underlined team, and everyone I'm surely missing at Random House sales, publicity, and digital marketing for all your support of *The Ivies* and *Pretty Dead Queens*.

Natalie Simpson, Jessica Van Allen, and Britney Brouwer for critical reads (and rereads) as I was drafting. Jessica, especially, for checking me on The Youth as needed and listening to every bonkers idea I had for this book along the way. To so many who read versions at various points: MK Pagano, J. Elle, Laura Kadner, Kara Kennedy, Devon Harry, Leighton Williams, Katherine DiGilio, and FT Zahra. Lexie Krauss for offering your invaluable local knowledge and letting Deputy Shields live on as your name twin. Jennieke Cohen for video-call check-ins and for reading with a keen and thoughtful eye. To Aziza Aba Butain for the swanky LA hangouts and for lending me your sister's beautiful name for Reama. Victoria Van Fleet for a marathon coffee-shop session that helped me finish!

I couldn't have made it through the pandemic (even though we're still sort of in it!) and particularly the highs and lows of this book (and *The Ivies* release) without the support in DMs and on video chat from so many friends (some already accounted for), including Lainey Kress, Deeba Zargarpur, Gretchen Schreiber, Mary E. Roach, Sophie Gonzales, Kara Thomas, Emmy Neal, Alex Brown, Alyssa Colman, Miranda Johnson, Mara/bookslikewhoa, Bethany Pullen, Amy Tintera, Liselle Sambury, Laura Fussell, Kevin Savoie, Lindsay Puckett, Diana Urban, Kevin van Whye, Emily Wibberley, Rebecca Schaeffer, Adrienne Kisner, Nisha Sharma, Liz Parker, Mary Elizabeth Summer, Emma Theriault, Emily Lloyd-Jones, Dana Mele, Amerie, Heather Kaczynski, Elly Takaki, and more I'm sure I am missing. Good friends are hard to find and you are all gems.

Thank you to Jason Mitchell for answering all my questions about local sheriffs and law enforcement—any inaccuracies remaining are 100% on me, taken in the name of creative liberties.

Thank you to Laurie Elizabeth Flynn, Jessica Goodman, and Jennifer Lynn Alvarez for early blurbs that put a blush on my cheeks. I am truly humbled by your reading and saying such nice things. To my wonderful amazing *Pretty Dead Queens* street team—thank you for coming along with me for this ride, and all your beautiful, creative bookstagrams, booktoks, and beyond.

To Marize Alphonso, longtime friend and an amazing kitten mommy who fostered the best cats ever. Might as well thank the cats, too, right? So to the newest members of my fur family, Bronte and Leo; my old man cat Teddy; and my dearly departed Marshmallow Fluff cat Peeta.

Thank you to Peacock for launching just in time for me to mainline nine seasons of *Murder, She Wrote* and then power through every available episode of *Dateline* for good measure. Dame Angela Lansbury: you are a BAMF. And thank you, internet, for a Jessica Fletcher meta joke that got my brain humming.

To found family and bio family alike—thank you to Patty, Sylvia, and Holly in California, and all my aunts, uncles, and cousins who continue to offer their unwavering support (and make me itch with embarrassment that you read my books). And though she is gone, I think of her every day and would not be where I am now without a lifetime of her belief in me and my writing: thank you to my mother, Dorothy.

ABOUT THE AUTHOR

Alexa Donne is the acclaimed author of *The Ivies,* which *Kirkus Reviews* praised as "a thrilling boarding school story with a satirical edge," and *Brightly Burning* and *The Stars We Steal,* sci-fi romance retellings of classics set in space. A graduate of Boston University, she works in TV marketing and in her "free time" mentors with WriteGirl, organizes the Author Mentor Match program, and runs one of the most popular writing advice channels on YouTube. *Pretty Dead Queens* is her love letter to *Murder, She Wrote,* though it came out much, much darker. She lives in Los Angeles with two mischievous cats. Discover more about Alexa on her website alexadonne.com.